WHEN RAIN CLOUDS GATHER
&
MARU

Bessie Head

Introduced by Helen Oyeyemi

virago

VIRAGO

This edition first published in 2010 by Virago Press

11 13 15 17 19 20 18 16 14 12

When Rain Clouds Gather first published by Victor Gollancz 1969
Maru first published by Victor Gollancz 1971
Published by Pearson Educational Limited 2008

A CIP catalogue record for this book
is available from the British Library.

ISBN 978-1-84408-622-1

Typeset in Goudy by M Rules
Printed and bound in Great Britain by
Clays Ltd, Elcograf S.p.A.

Papers used by Virago are from well-managed forests
and other responsible sources.

Virago Press
An imprint of
Little, Brown Book Group
Carmelite House
50 Victoria Embankment
London EC4Y 0DZ

An Hachette UK Company
www.hachette.co.uk

www.virago.co.uk

VIRAGO
MODERN CLASSICS
544

Bessie Head

ead (1937–1986) was born in South Africa and is one
's best-known writers. She trained as a teacher then
s a journalist for *Golden City Post*, a Drum publication,
left for Botswana. She remained there, with the pre-
tatus of refugee, for fifteen years before she gained
ip in 1979. *When Rain Clouds Gather* was her first pub-
vel in 1968, followed by *Maru* (1971) and her intense
erful autobiographical work, *A Question of Power*
he wrote short stories, and *A Woman Alone* (1990), a
of autobiographical writings, and *Tales of Tenderness*
(1990). A selection of famous and previously unpub-
ks have been released posthumously.

Also by Bessie Head

When Rain Clouds Gather
Maru
A Question of Power
The Collector of Treasures
Serowe: Village of the Rain Wind
A Bewitched Crossroad
A Woman Alone
Tales of Tenderness and Power

INTRODUCTION

Bessie Head was a witness to the early years of apartheid and its spirit-breaking classifications and restrictions. South Africa's Immorality Act of 1950, which outlawed interracial relation-ships, acted as a negation of her very existence. Yet Head was adamant that love affairs are more important than socio-political revolutions. She wrote, 'I have no logical argument as to why these things are more important, except that I believe in the contents of the human heart . . . a silent and secret con-spiracy against all the insanity and hatred in mankind.'

In these, her first two novels, Bessie Head makes it under-stood that love between equals is the only true power in the world. She offers us men and women who are fully alive to each other. They dream the same dreams. Her men, Makhaya in *When Rain Clouds Gather* and the eponymous hero of *Maru*, are intensely perceptive, imbued with a 'feminine sensitivity' that raises them above the level of 'grovelling sex organs' that Head complained African men were traditionally reduced to within their communities. Her women give themselves over to passion that barely stops short at terrible vulnerability. Paulina, Makhaya's lover, strains boldly towards joy, with her colourful skirts and her equally vivid declarations, 'You mustn't think I'm a cheap woman, but I love you.' *Maru*'s Margaret Cadmore, outwardly impassive apart from the occasional tear, has a tumultuous inner life that she finally anchors in her art and the complex ways in which she loves the two men in her life. But the cognitive dissonance involved in falling in love is sometimes almost beyond endurance, even for people as strong as these. In Bessie Head's world, people are 'frightened into' showing each other compassion, and only give way to love 'under extreme pressure and pain'. Head's love stories highlight the great risk of making a gesture of faith in mankind, whose wickedness can be extraordinary. As I read the scene in *Maru* where Margaret Cadmore stands before a classroom full of jibing students, my hands curled up into fists for the harrowing moments that follow as the woman's nerves fray. Her humiliation and the sensation of hatred – her own and that of the children's – is scarred onto the page with an authenticity that feels hard won.

Born in a mental asylum in Johannesburg to a white South African mother, disowned by her mother's family and raised in a Coloured family in Natal, Head never knew her black father and confessed to the 'desperate guesswork' of trying to write as what she called 'an African of Africa'. At twenty-seven, she obtained permission to leave South Africa (on the condition that she never return) and spent the next twenty-two years in Botswana; fifteen of those as a refugee while the authorities refused her Botswana nationality. She wrote to friends in England, Norway and America, feverishly making plans to leave for Nigeria, for India, for Kenya – anywhere but this country that didn't want her. Still . . . 'The best and most enduring love is that of rejection,' Head wrote to Randolph Vigne. In another letter she told him, 'You know perhaps nothing about a little village . . . in an African village it's goddam deep and dangerous.' Village children threw stones at Head's young son and called him 'Bushman'. Her neighbours accused her of infanticide and only left her out of their talk once she'd had a breakdown.

Makhaya, the protagonist of *When Rain Clouds Gather*, is a disillusioned South African activist, newly released from prison for plotting an explosion; he has just escaped across Botswana's border fence 'and on into whatever illusion of freedom lay ahead'. Golema Mmidi, his adoptive home, is a village at a crossroads in its history; its inhabitants submit to the authority of a chieftain, but the villagers are also receptive to the prospect of agricultural reform brought by Gilbert, a white British volunteer. The horror of village life that Head darkly hinted at in her letters ducks uneasily out of sight on the periphery, only showing its naked face when Makhaya and Paulina drive out towards the village's cattle post in the drought-parched desert. Then, at last we see the vultures in the trees, sitting 'full and gorged'. It is then we see a newborn calf preyed on as it lies beside its dead mother, and it is then that we see what has happened to Paulina's son, a cheerful little artist who made the best of his solitary existence herding the family's cattle by making wood carvings with his pocket knife. We are forced to stand with Makhaya looking in at the door of the hut, bearing the sight for Paulina, who might run mad if she saw. Reading this passage brought to mind another meditation on the death of a child written five years earlier, Ingrid Jonker's *The Child who was Shot Dead by Soldiers at Nyanga*: 'The child is not dead . . . /the child grown to a man treks through all Africa/the child grown into a giant journeys through the whole world.' Here, however, Head as a narrator makes no attempt to mitigate the desolation of the scene. It's as if the story is questioning the technology by which a child becomes a giant, or even a man, in such a place as Golema Mmidi. And because Makhaya loves Paulina he takes the loss into himself, 'confused and angry that there was only this dead, unanswering silence in his heart . . .' Nini Etlinger, a pen-friend who had loaned Head the money for a typewriter, advised her, 'You really must not write with your heart on fire. It's not literature. I really mean it.' Head broke off all contact with her and never renewed it, despite wholehearted repentance on Etlinger's part. By the time she was thirteen Head was already developing an awareness of what a story is able to do; how it can teach, entertain and propose a wholly new future all at once. In a short story published in the magazine of the Anglican orphanage where she received her education, truth features as a means of crossing a river, a way of moving forward. But the bridge is built of stones that cannot be walked upon without great pain.

Maru begins so peacefully. The hero comes home to his wife at the end of a blue-skied day and says to her simply, 'My sweetheart.' And once you've come to the last page of the novel it is the grace of that moment that may compel you to reread the first few pages in a new and triumphant light. The beginning and the end of this love story slide into each other with ferocious ease, like a snake eating its own tail. Margaret Cadmore, a San orphan, is adopted by a forthright English missionary, who has her educated and sends her away to a Botswana village to take up her first teaching position. Margaret, made virtually silent and expressionless by a lifetime of abuse from her peers, is a powerfully disruptive presence in the life of the village, where other San are kept as slaves. Margaret is not beautiful, but her gaze is eloquent and when she speaks, something about her voice is enchanting. She wins the love of Maru and Moleka, bosom friends who become bitter opponents. Moleka is unable to overcome a dread of breaking convention to openly proclaim love for a San woman. Maru is a future chieftain of the village, a man whose eyes are lit with the conversation of gods. He tests Margaret's dignity and creativity, taking her bed away from her and giving her art paper, paint and charcoals instead. And he doesn't claim Margaret for himself until her heart is completely broken. This is the book that Bessie Head wrote as a response to Hodder and Stoughton's request that she follow *When Rain Clouds Gather* with something like an African version of *The Catcher in the Rye*.

At that period in her life, Head wrote her tales at night in her hut with a candle balanced on her knee. What might she have been if she had been free of Botswana and South Africa? From across an ocean there is a faint answer of sorts. In 1939, two years after Head was born, Billie Holiday wrote that bitter hymn to loneliness, 'God Bless The Child'. Holiday, another extraordinary artist, never knew her father and would have been taken for a Coloured woman in South Africa too. Holiday got forty-eight years out of a life of chequered romance, sorrow, drugs and religious schooling – one year less than Head's forty-nine. Like Holiday, Head brings her grief to her work – and perhaps this is part of what sends a thrill through us readers, who may think that all we have to do is close the book when we no longer want to see into these wounded worlds, these spirited trials at hope.

After reading *Maru*, Megan Biesele, an American anthropologist, went to live in the Botswana desert with people of the San tribe (called Marsarwa in the novel), who taught her their language until she was able to read *Maru* aloud to them, chapter by chapter. The San made Head a necklace of shells, seeds and grass and sent it to her, along with their thanks for what she had written. *When Rain Clouds Gather* and *Maru* are fairytales about the transformations that love can wreak. And they transform love into a force to be feared and a force to be thankful for.

Helen Oyeyemi, 2010

ix

When Rain Clouds Gather

For
Pat and Wendy Cullinan,
Pat and Liz Van Rensburg,
'HOORAY!' and U-Shaka,
and for Naomi Mitchison, who loves Botswana.

CHAPTER ONE

The little Barolong village swept right up to the border fence. One of the huts was built so close that a part of its circular wall touched the barbed-wire fencing. In this hut a man had been sitting since the early hours of dawn. He was waiting until dark when he would try to spring across the half-mile gap of no-man's land to the Botswana border fence and then on to whatever illusion of freedom lay ahead. It was June and winter and bitterly cold, and his legs were too long to allow for pacing in the cramped space of the hut. Every half hour the patrol van of the South African border police sped past with sirens wailing, and this caused an unpleasant sensation in his stomach.

I'll soon have a stomach-ache if I go on like this, he thought.

His nerves weren't so good, too easily jangled by the irritations of living. In fact, the inner part of him was a jumble of chaotic discord, very much belied by his outer air of calm, lonely self-containment. The only way you could sense this inner discord was through a trick he had of slightly averting his face as though no man was his brother or worthy of his trust. Otherwise, his face was rather pleasing to the eye. It was often wryly amused. Its general expression was one of absorbed, attentive listening. His long thin falling-away cheekbones marked him as a member of either the Xhosa or Zulu tribe.

Towards noon, when there was a lull in the wailing sirens, the old man who owned the hut pushed open the door, letting in a shaft of sunlight. He held in his hands a steaming bowl of thick porridge. The man by now had a dreadful stomach-ache, and the sight of the food did not immediately please him.

'Well, how are you, son?' the old man asked.

'I'm all right,' the man lied. It did not seem quite dignified to admit that he had stomach trouble.

'I've brought you a little food,' the old man said.

'Thank you,' the man said. 'But could I go out for a while and stretch my legs?' He had to ease the painful knots in his stomach.

'It's not safe,' the old man said. 'I can't guarantee who may or may not be a spy. Once you are caught here it will make it unsafe for those who come on behind. I would no doubt go to jail too.'

The young man was bent over the hand-carved stool on which he sat, and the old man thought he might be cold.

'Why not take a little brandy?' he asked sympathetically. 'I know a place nearby, and I can send for some if you want it.'

The man looked up, relieved, and nodded his head. He took out a pound note and handed it to the old man. The old man smiled widely. He had not known of one fugitive yet who did not need it. Besides, with a little brandy inside they soon became talkative, and he liked all the stories. He stored them up against the day when he would be free to surprise his village with his vast fund of information on fugitives. He closed the door and shuffled away. A dog barked nearby. There was the chatter of women's voices, and music and singing. A child began to cry loudly. Men laughed, and the man in the hut was briefly surprised that a whole village could live in the wail of those sirens that had tied his stomach in such tight knots. Soon the old man shuffled back again. Because relief was near at hand he noticed how the dust of the mud floor rose up and shimmered and danced in the sunlight as the old man pushed open the door. The old man had not only the brandy but a bowl of food for himself, as well. It pleased the young man in the shadows that he did not close the door because as soon as he had taken a few careful sips from the bottle, he could clearly discern the gentle, interweaving dance pattern of the sunlit dust. The slow, almost breathless rhythm eased away the knots of stomach trouble, and he unconsciously smiled to himself in this sudden warm glow of expansive relief that was now his abdomen.

Noting this the old man said, 'I say, son, what's your name?'

'Makhaya,' the young man replied.

The old man screwed up his eyes, perplexed. The sound and meaning of the name were unfamiliar to him. Tswana-speaking tribes dominated the northern Transvaal.

'I don't know it,' the old man said, shaking his head.

'It's Zulu,' the young man said. 'I'm a Zulu.' And he laughed sarcastically at the thought of calling himself a Zulu.

'But you speak Tswana fluently,' the old man persisted.

Quite drunk by now the young man said rather crazily, 'Yes, we Zulus are like that. Since the days of Shaka we've assumed that the whole world belongs to us; that's why we trouble to learn any man's language. But look here, old man, I'm no tribalist. My parents are – that's why they saddled me with this foolish name. Why not call me Samuel or Johnson, because I'm no tribalist.'

'Jo!' said the old man, using a Tswana expression of surprise. 'And what's wrong with the tribe?'

'I have a list of grievances against it. I haven't got time to go

3

into them now . . .' He paused, trying to collect his thoughts in the haze of brandy that was clouding his brain. 'Makhaya,' he said. 'That tribal name is the wrong one for me. It is for one who stays home, yet they gave it to me and I have not known a day's peace and contentment in my life.'

'It's because of education,' the old man said, nodding his head wisely. 'They should not have given you the education. Take away the little bit of education and you will be only too happy to say, "Mama, please find me a tribal girl and let us plough." It's only the education that turns a man away from his tribe.'

The conversation threatened to become a vast, meaningless, rambling digression. Good storyteller that he was, the old man brought it back to the main points at hand. Why was the young man here? What was he fleeing from? A jail sentence, perhaps?

The young man looked at him suspiciously. 'I'm just out of jail,' he said. He closed the brandy bottle and picked up the bowl of porridge. And then some anxiety seemed to jolt him for he put the bowl down again, searched the inside pocket of his coat, and took out a little scrap of paper. He struck a match and burned the paper. Then he picked up the bowl of porridge and would not utter another word. The old man was left to put two and two together. Perhaps scraps of paper and jail sentences were the same thing in the young man's mind. Why did he jump so at the thought of one tiny scrap? And what was this about tribalism? What about the white man who was the only recognized enemy of everyone?

'Oh, so you have no complaints about the white man?' the old man said, struggling to pry some information out of the tightly shut mouth.

The young man only turned his face slightly, yet the light of laughter danced in his eyes.

'Ha, I see now,' the old man said, pretending disappointment.

'You are running away from tribalism. But just ahead of you is the worst tribal country in the world. We Barolong are neighbours of the Batswana, but we cannot get along with them. They are a thickheaded lot who think no further than this door. Tribalism is meat and drink to them.'

The young man burst out laughing. 'Oh, Papa,' he said. 'I just want to step on free ground. I don't care about people. I don't care about anything, not even the white man. I want to feel what it is like to live in a free country and then maybe some of the evils in my life will correct themselves.'

The wail of the approaching sirens sounded again. After they had swept past, the old man left the hut, closing the door behind him. Makhaya was left alone with his thoughts, and since these threatened to trouble him, he kept on numbing them with a little brandy sipped straight from the bottle.

The sun set early in winter and by seven o'clock it was pitch dark. Makhaya made ready to cross the patch of no-man's-land. The two border fences were seven-foot-high barriers of close, tautly drawn barbed wire. He waited in the hut until he heard the patrol van pass. Then he removed his heavy overcoat and stuffed it into a large leather bag. He stepped out of the hut and pitched the leather bag over the fence, grasped hold of the barbed wire, and heaved himself up and over. Picking up his bag, he ran as fast as he could across the patch of ground to the other fence, where he repeated the performance. Then he was in Botswana.

In his anxiety to get as far away from the border as fast as possible, he hardly felt the intense, penetrating cold of the frosty night. For almost half an hour he sped, blind and deaf and numbed to anything but this major fear. The wail of the siren brought him to an abrupt halt. It sounded shockingly near and he feared that his crashing pace would draw attention to

5

himself. But the lights of the patrol van swept past and he knew, from timing the patrols throughout the long torturous day, that he had another half hour of safety ahead of him. As he relaxed a little, his mind grasped the fact that he had been sucking in huge gulps of frozen air and that his lungs were flaming with pain. He removed the heavy coat from the bag and put it on. He also took a few careful sips from the brandy bottle and then continued on his way at a more leisurely pace.

He had not walked more than a few paces when he again came to an abrupt halt. The air was full of the sound of bells, thousands and thousands of bells, tinkling and tinkling with a purposeful, monotonous rhythm. Yet there was not a living thing in sight to explain where the sound was coming from. He was quite sure that around him and in front of him were trees and more trees, thorn trees that each time he approached too near ripped at his clothes. But how to explain the bells, unearthly sounding bells in an apparently unlived-in wasteland?

Oh, God, I'm going crazy, he thought.

He looked up at the stars. They winked back at him, silently, blandly. He could even make out some of the star patterns of the southern constellations. Surely, if his mind was suddenly disordered through the tensions of the day, the stars would appear disordered too? Surely everything became mixed up to a person who had just lost his mind? He shook his head, but the bells continued their monotonous, rhythmic tinkling. He knew some pretty horrifying stories about tribal societies and their witch doctors who performed their ghoulish rites by night. But witch doctors were human, and nothing, however odd and perverse, need be feared if it was human. Taking this as a possible explanation of the bells restored his balance, and he continued on his way, keeping an alert eye open for the fires or huts of the witch doctors.

Soon he saw a fire in the bush, a small bit of self-contained light in the overwhelming darkness. He headed straight for it, and as he approached, the flickering, crackling light outlined the shape of two mud huts and the forms of a woman and a child. It was the woman who looked up as she became aware of approaching footsteps. He stood still, not wishing to alarm her. She appeared to be very old. Her small eyes were completely sunk in the wrinkles of her face. The child was a girl of about ten, who kept her head bent, idly drawing a pattern with a stick on the ground. He greeted the old woman in Tswana, politely calling her 'mother' in a quiet, reassuring voice.

She did not return the greeting. Instead she demanded, 'Yes, what do you want?' She had a loud, shrill, uncontrolled voice, and he disliked her immediately.

'I was looking for shelter for the night,' he said.

She kept quiet, yet stared fixedly at the direction from which his voice came. Then she burst out in that loud, jarring voice, 'I say you are one of the spies from over the border.'

Since he did not respond she became quite excited, raising her voice even louder. 'Why else do people wander about at night, unless they are spies? All the spies in the world are coming into our country. I tell you, you are a spy! You are a spy!'

It was the shouting that unnerved him. The border was still very near, and at any moment now the patrol van would pass.

'How can you embarrass me like this?' he said in a quiet, desperate voice. 'Are women of your country taught to shout at men?'

'I'm not shouting,' she shrilled, but in a slightly lower voice. His words and consistently quiet speech were beginning to impress her.

'Well, my ears must be deceiving me, mother,' he said,

amused. 'Tell me whether you can offer me shelter or not. I'm no spy. I've just lost my way in the darkness.'

The fixed stare never wavered. She said, curtly, 'I have a spare hut. You may use it but only for tonight. You must also pay. I want ten shillings.'

She held out a shrivelled old hand, cold and hard with years and years of labour. He stepped towards the fire and handed her a ten-shilling note. She reached behind her for a small carved stool and said, 'Sit here. The child will sweep the hut and put down some blankets.'

The child stood up obediently and disappeared into one of the huts. He sat down opposite the crude, rude phenomenon who continued staring at him. The wail of the patrol siren again sounded quite near, almost behind his back. He held her glance calmly.

'I know you are a spy,' she said. 'You are running away from them.'

He smiled. 'Perhaps you just want to annoy me. But as you can see, I'm not easily annoyed.'

'Where do you come from?' she asked.

'From over the border,' he said. 'I have an appointment to start work in this country tomorrow.'

'Why didn't you come by train?' she asked suspiciously.

'But my home is so near, in the Barolong village,' he lied.

She turned her head and spat on the ground as an eloquent summing up of what she thought of him. Then she sat with her head averted as though she had abruptly dismissed him from her thoughts. The bells were still tinkling away.

'What are all those bells for?' he asked.

'They are tied around the necks of the cattle because they are grazing freely in the bush,' she said.

He felt ashamed at the thought of how they had terrified him and they were only cow bells. He also wanted to laugh out loud, and to suppress this he said conversationally, 'I'm not an owner of cattle. I suppose the bells are there to locate them if they get lost?'

'Of course,' she said scornfully. 'Cattle wander a great distance while grazing.'

Meanwhile the child had crept quietly back to the fireside. Half-consciously his gaze wandered in her direction, and he was startled to find the child looking at him with a full bold stare. There was something very unchildlike about it and it displeased him. His glance flickered back to the old woman. She was staring again and he even imagined that he saw a gleam in the sunken old eyes.

My God, he thought, what a pair of vultures they are.

Aloud he said, 'Is the room ready now, mother?'

She merely turned and pointed to one of the huts. He stood up immediately, relieved to be rid of their unpleasant company. He struck a match as he entered the dark hut. It seemed to be a storage shed. A large grain basket stood in one corner, and there were a number of earthenware pots encircling the room. A space had been cleared on the floor on which were placed wide square covers made of animal skins. He struck another match to take a better look at what he was to sleep on. The feel of it was like thick soft velvet, squares upon squares of the sewn-together skins of hundreds of wild animals. He only removed his shoes and overcoat. The overcoat he flung over the top cover for extra warmth. The bed seemed well worth ten shillings to him because it was very warm.

He lay on his back staring up at the dark, too tense to sleep. A good gulp of brandy would have knocked him out cold but he dared not touch it. He distrusted the suspicious old hag. She seemed to know too much about the border. What would prevent her from stepping down there and informing the police? There was good money in it, if she knew about that too. A cold sweat broke out on him as he imagined her at the fence, shouting at the patrol van. And what about the child and her awful, unchildlike stare? He listened alertly to their every movement. For a time there was a low murmured conversation, and then he heard the fire being scraped out. Then the door of the next hut was pushed open. The old hag coughed a bit. There was more murmured conversation and a brief silence. Then the door was opened again and he could tell that it was the child who had gone out because the old hag was coughing inside.

He lay quite still as the door of his hut was carefully and quietly pushed open by the child and equally quietly and carefully closed behind her. She dropped lightly down on her knees and moved her hands over the covers until they reached his face.

'What do you want?' he asked.

The hands darted back and there was a brief silence; then she said, 'You know.'

'I don't,' he said.

She kept quiet as though puzzling this out. At last she said, 'My grandmother won't mind as long as you pay me.'

'Go away,' he said, abashed, humiliated. 'You're just a child.'

But she just sat there and would not move. He really could not stand it. He raised himself and struck a match and took out a ten-shilling note and handed it to her.

'Here's the money,' he said fiercely. 'Now go away.'

Her eyes were wide and uncomprehending in the brief flare of the match, but she grasped the note and fled. From the hut next door he heard the brief plaintive explanation of the child and the loud surprised chatter of the old woman.

'You mean he gave you the money for nothing?' she said, beside herself with excitement. 'This is a miracle! I have not yet known a man who did not regard a woman as a gift from God! He must be mad! I knew it all along in my heart that he was mad! Let us lock the door to protect ourselves from the madman!'

What a loathsome woman, he thought, and yet how naïve she was in her evil. He had known many such evils in his lifetime. He thought they were created by poverty and oppression, and he had spent the last two years in jail in the belief that, in some way, a protest would help to set the world right. It was the mentality of the old hag that ruined a whole continent – some sort of clinging, ancestral, tribal belief that a man was nothing more than a grovelling sex organ, that there was no such thing as privacy of soul and body, and that no ordinary man would hesitate to jump on a mere child.

He had sisters at home, one almost the same age as the child and some a few years older. But he was the eldest in the family, and according to custom he had to be addressed as 'Buti', which means 'Elder Brother', and treated with exaggerated respect. As soon as his father died he made many changes in the home, foremost of which was that his sisters should address him by his first name and associate with him as equals and friends. When his mother had protested he had merely said, 'Why should men be brought up with a false sense of superiority over women? People can respect me if they wish, but only if I earn it.'

For all his strange new ideas, the family had not wanted to part with him. In fact he had left his mother in a state of complete collapse, and though at the time he had pretended to be unmoved by all the tears and sighs, it was all this that had made him drink brandy throughout the afternoon.

His reasons for leaving were simple: he could not marry and have children in a country where black men were called 'boy' and 'dog' and 'kaffir'. The continent of Africa was vast without end and he simply felt like moving out of a part of it that was mentally and spiritually dead through the constant perpetuation of false beliefs.

I might like it here, was his last thought before falling into a deep, exhausted sleep.

It was not yet dawn when he arose and left. In the faint early light he saw a little footpath leading away from the huts, and because it wound its way northward and away from the border, he decided to follow it in the hope that it would lead him somewhere.

At first not a thing stirred around him. It was just his own self, his footsteps and the winding footpath. Even the sunrise took him by surprise. Somehow he had always imagined the sun above hills, shining down into valleys and waking them up. But here the land was quite flat, and the sunshine crept along the ground in long shafts of gold light. It kept on pushing back the darkness that clung around the trees, and always the huge splash of gold was split into shafts by the trees. Suddenly, the sun sprang clear of all entanglements, a single white pulsating ball, dashing out with one blow the last traces of the night. So sudden and abrupt was the sunrise that the birds had to pretend they had been awake all the time. They set up a shrill piercing clamour all at once, thousands and thousands of them. For all their clamour they turned out to be small dun-coloured creatures with speckled dun-coloured breasts, and their flight into the deep blue sky was just like so many tiny insects. More secretive types of birds lived in the depth of the bush, and these were very beautiful, ranging in colour from a shimmering midnight blue to bright scarlet and molten gold. Unlike the chattering little dun-coloured fellows, they called to each other in soft low tones and, being curious about his footsteps, frequently flashed briefly onto the footpath ahead of him.

I wonder what the birds live on, he thought. The land on

either side of the footpath was loose windblown sand and thorn-bush. Often the thornbush emerged as tall, straight-trunked trees, topped by an umbrella of black, exquisitely shaped branches, but more often it grew in short low tufts like rough wild grass. Long white thorns grew on the branches, at the base of which were tightly packed clusters of pale olive-green leaves. And that was all. As far as the eye could see it was only a vast expanse of sand and scrub but somehow bewitchingly beautiful. Perhaps he confused it with his own loneliness. Perhaps it was those crazy little birds. Perhaps it was the way the earth had adorned herself for a transient moment in a brief splurge of gold. Or perhaps he simply wanted a country to love and chose the first thing at hand. But whatever it was, he simply and silently decided that all this dryness and bleakness amounted to home and that somehow he had come to the end of a journey.

The little footpath spilled out suddenly onto a wide dirt road, and he had not walked far before a truck came lumbering up behind him. Like the gaudy-hued birds, the truck driver was curious about such an early traveller. He stopped the truck and called out, 'Are you going to the station?'

'Yes,' Makhaya said.

'It's always best to start early in the morning because the journey is long,' the man said. 'But you are lucky this time, I can give you a lift.'

Later, he blessed the man silently. By truck it was a two-hour journey with not a hut or a living being in sight. On foot it might well have taken the whole day. The only discomfort about the journey was that he had to invent lie after lie. The truck driver was talkative and kept on prying into his personal affairs.

'You've been to see relatives at the *moraka?*' the truck driver asked.

The word *moraka* was unknown to Makhaya, and it was only

13

later that he was to learn that it was a cattle post. But he said, 'Yes.'

'And are they well?'

'No,' he lied. 'My mother is ill.'

'Jo! And why doesn't she go to hospital?'

'She's a very stubborn old woman.'

This seemed to be a huge joke to the truck driver. He laughed loudly. Then he said, 'I see. You look like a teacher to me.'

'I am,' Makhaya lied again.

'In what village do you teach?'

'I'm not teaching at present. I've resigned to start a business.'

The truck driver looked at him with interest. Makhaya half-averted his head, ill at ease. Should he tell the man he was a refugee? His experiences of the previous night had made him distrustful.

'I say,' his questioner went on, 'what's your tribe?'

He hesitated, trying to think of the nearest relationship to Zulus in the northern tribes. 'Ndebele,' he said.

'Don't be ashamed to mention it,' the truck driver said sympathetically. 'Foreigners are always welcome in our country.'

And so it went on and on until Makyaha was exhausted from having to invent so many lies. He almost cried with relief when the truck driver dropped him off at a railway crossing and continued on his journey to some unknown destination. Makhaya stood for a moment at the crossing to get his bearings. A sprawling village of mud huts was on one side of him and the railway station on the other. Clustered near the station were whatever brick buildings there were. It was a dismal-looking place and the brown dust of the dirt roads and footpaths was on everything. He was very hungry and stopped a passer-by and asked where he might buy some food. The man pointed to a filthy-looking restaurant which sold porridge and a plate of boiled meat for a shilling. A sign painted outside the dreadful eating house amused him. It said: HOTELA.

Because he had entered the country illegally he had to report to the police, register himself as a refugee, and apply for political asylum. Again, a passer-by pointed out the police station among the cluster of brick buildings. A British flag still flew above the small whitewashed building. The country was going through a year of self-government prior to complete independence. He stepped into a small office above which was written: STATION COMMANDER.

A British colonial police officer sat behind a desk on which was piled a jumble of papers. A notice on the wall above his head proclaimed: WORK FASCINATES ME. I CAN SIT AND WATCH IT FOR HOURS. He had quite a pleasant, good-looking face with arched eyebrows and green eyes. As commander of the station with no superior to jump to attention for, he exuded a great air of self-importance. He stared impassively at Makhaya for some time, then he said, 'So you have come?'

Makhaya could make nothing of this remark and kept quiet.

'It's past eleven o'clock and I've delayed my tea waiting for you,' he said. 'In fact, I was just about to come and pick you up. Sit down, Mr Makhaya Maseko.'

'How do you know my name?' Makhaya asked, startled.

'I know everything,' he said coolly. 'I also want to impress you, so that you don't start any of your funny tricks around here. You may think this country is a backwater, but we have the most efficient intelligence service in southern Africa. We also read the newspapers.'

He bent down and picked up a newspaper that had been carelessly flung on the floor. Makhaya's picture was on the front page under a headline: DANGEROUS SABOTEUR FLEES BANNING ORDER.

'I'm not dangerous and I'm not a saboteur,' he said, annoyed.

'I know,' the officer said. 'You just dream about it. You just walk about with little pieces of paper describing how you're going to blow everything up.'

He assumed a businesslike air searching among the jumble on his desk for a paper and pencil.

'You will have to answer a few routine questions,' he said. He paused, then said, 'Do you like Kwame Nkrumah?'

The complete unexpectedness of the question took Makhaya off guard and an automatic 'No' slipped out before he had collected his wits. The officer grinned and relaxed into his casual manner.

'That's all,' he said. 'Fill in this form and you can go.'

Makhaya sauntered out, uncertain of what to do next. Quite near the railway station was a post office. Around the post office was a fence, and an old man sat outside the fence, squatting very low on his haunches. He sat quite still, staring ahead with calm, empty eyes, and he looked so lordly for all his tattered coat and rough cowhide shoes that Makhaya smiled and walked up to him and greeted him. The old man withdrew his abstracted gaze and turned a pair of keen friendly eyes on Makhaya.

'You are a sociable man,' he said, smiling. 'Are you a stranger here?'

'Yes,' Makhaya said and hesitated, not knowing what to say next.

The old man nodded his head as though he understood everything.

'Perhaps you are stranded?' he queried.

'Yes,' Makhaya said again.

'But you look and sound like a well-educated man,' he said in surprise.

Makhaya laughed. 'Well-educated men often come to the

crossroads of life,' he said. 'One road might lead to fame and importance, and another might lead to peace of mind. It's the road of peace of mind that I'm seeking.'

The old man kept silent but he was thinking rapidly. The young man was very attractive, and he had a difficult daughter whom he wanted married before he died. The man's speech and ideas also appealed to him.

He said very carefully, 'Most of the time we Batswana live in the wilderness and loneliness. We are used to it but I don't think you can stand it. Where do you come from?'

'South Africa,' Makhaya said.

The old man shook his head. 'That terrible place,' he said. 'The good God don't like it. This is God's country.'

'God's country,' Makhaya echoed, surprised.

'Didn't you know?' the old man said with a twinkle in his eye. 'God is everywhere about here, and it's no secret. People can't steal a thing from you, not even a sixpence. People can't fight, not even to kill an enemy.'

Makhaya kept quiet, absorbing this strange philosophy. Everything about the old man pleased him, and noting this the old man said slyly, 'Why not come and stay with me for a while, son?'

'But I am almost penniless,' Makhaya said.

'A poor person like me can still be hospitable,' the old man said. 'Besides, a lot is happening in my village and a well-educated man like you can bring a little light.'

CHAPTER TWO

The old man was not exaggerating when he said that a lot was happening in his village. Many factors had combined to make the village of Golema Mmidi a unique place. It was not a village in the usual meaning of being composed of large tribal or family groupings. Golema Mmidi consisted of individuals who had fled there to escape the tragedies of life. Its name too marked it out from the other villages, which were named after important chiefs or important events. Golema Mmidi acquired its name from the occupation the villagers followed, which was crop growing. It was one of the very few areas in the country where people were permanently settled on the land.

Normally, in other parts of the country, whole families would migrate in November to their lands on the outskirts of the villages to help with the ploughing and planting, returning to their villages in late January and leaving the June harvest to the women and children. Although people on the whole had to live off crops, they paid little attention to the land. The pivot of their lives was the villages. Not so with the people of Golema Mmidi. Necessity, even, in some cases, rejection and dispossession in previous circumstances, had forced them to make the land the central part of their existence. Unlike the migratory villagers, who set up crude, ramshackle buildings on the edge of their lands, they built the large, wide, neatly thatched huts of permanent residence. They also had the best cultivated land and kept a constant watch on the thornbushes which sprang up in every conceivable place like weeds. True enough, the villagers did not differ so greatly from everyone else in their way of life. The men attended to the cattle business and helped with the ploughing, while the women were the agriculturists or tillers of the earth. Like everyone else, they fenced their land with the thornbushes and supplemented their incomes with wood carving and basket-making. A few like Makhaya's new-found companion, the old man, Dinorego, were skilled in the *diphate* trade – that is, the making of mats and blankets from the skins of wild animals.

Over a period of fourteen years Golema Mmidi had acquired a population of four hundred people, and their permanent settlement there gave rise to small administrative problems. Due to this, a paramount chief named Sekoto had recognized it as a ward of his territory and for administrator had appointed his troublesome and unpopular younger brother, Matenge, as subchief of the village. The appointment took place in the sixth year of settlement, and although the residents politely addressed their subchief as 'Chief', what had made Matenge unpopular in his brother's household – an overwhelming avariciousness and unpleasant personality – soon made him intensely disliked by the villagers, who were, after all, a wayward lot of misfits. Thus, appeal cases from Golema Mmidi were forever appearing on the court roll of the paramount chief – appeals against banishment, appeals against sentences for using threatening and insulting language to a subchief, and appeals against appropriation of property by the subchief. Knowing his brother well enough, the least the paramount chief could do was always to side with the appellants; and after a threat or two, the devil that drove Matenge would quickly subside, only to awaken its clamouring and howling a few months later.

One day, a strange, massively built, blue-eyed young man walked into the paramount chief's office. He introduced himself as Gilbert Balfour and explained that he was but recently from England and had visited the country three years previously on a student's travel grant, and that to this visit he owed his choice of career – to assist in agricultural development and improved techniques of food production. The country presented overwhelming challenges, he said, not only because the rainfall was poor but because the majority of the people engaged in subsistence farming were using primitive techniques that ruined the land. All this had excited his interest. He had returned to England, taken a diploma in agriculture, and now had returned to Botswana to place his knowledge at the service of the country.

Then, for almost an hour he eagerly outlined a number of grand schemes, foremost of which was the role co-operatives could play in improving production and raising the standard of living. The paramount chief listened to it all with concealed alarm, though throughout the interview a smile of pleasant interest was on his face. Of course, he was widely known as a good chief, which is the way people usually refer to paramount chiefs. He attended all the funerals of the poor in the village, even accepted responsibility to bury those who were too poor to bury themselves, and had built a school here and a reservoir there. But because he was a chief he lived off the slave labour of the poor. His lands were ploughed free of charge by the poor, and he was washed, bathed, and fed by the poor, in return for which he handed out old clothes and maize rations. And to a man like this Gilbert Balfour came along and spent an hour out-lining plans to uplift the poor! Most alarming of all, the Englishman had behind him the backing of a number of voluntary organizations who were prepared to finance his schemes at no cost to the country.

At first the young man's ideas caused the chief acute discomfort, especially his habit of referring to the poor as though they were his blood brothers, and the chief was a shrewd enough judge of human nature to see that the young man was in deadly earnest. But halfway through the interview, a beaming smile lit up the chief's face. He would put this disturbing young man in Golema Mmidi, and if he could survive a year or more in the bedlam his brother Matenge would raise, that would be more than proof of his sincerity. One thing he was sure of – either the young man would be completely destroyed, or he could completely destroy his brother, and he wanted his brother destroyed for all the family feuds and intrigues he had instigated. Towards the end of the interview, he allocated a 250-acre plot for an experimental farm and a 7,000-acre plot for a cattle ranch.

It was about all this that the old man talked to Makhaya on their hour and a half walk to the village of Golema Mmidi. The village had no post office, and Dinorego had come to the railway village to take out some of his savings and purchase provisions that he could not buy in his village. When he had bought everything he needed, he put the provisions into a flour bag and slung it over his shoulder. The road they took ran parallel with the railway line, and once again it was just the thornbush on either side and the blue sky. Makhaya noticed that the old man had an odd way of walking. It was a quick shuffle, a propelled shuffle as though a small private windstorm was pushing him from behind, and his speech too had the odd propelled quality of his walk.

'It's not right,' said Dinorego. 'A well-educated man should not be stranded in our country. But you will find that things happen slowly here. They say this is a country where people ought not to live and it is true. Batswana people often go without food and water and so do their cattle. Cattle are grazed where a bit of grass grows, but water may only be found ten miles away. Life is like this: you graze cattle here one day; the next, you take them on a long search for water. It is such a hard life that I myself long ago gave up the cattle business. In all my years I have known of only one man who thinks he can change it. His name is Gilbert. He came to our village three years ago and started the cattle co-operative. Also a farm to try out better ways of crop growing, and it is from this I mostly benefit as I only grow crops.'

Dinorego stopped abruptly, put down his bundle and spread his hands out to explain himself more clearly. Makhaya listened in his absorbed, attentive way, a faint smile on his face.

'A Motswana man thinks like this: "If there is a way to improve my life, I shall do it." He may start by digging a well with a spade. He digs and digs, slowly moving the earth to one side with a spade. When it has become too deep, he sets up two poles in the earth with a pole on top and a handle. To this he attaches a rope and a bucket. Then he sends his son down into the well. The son digs and digs, each time sending up the earth in the bucket. At last water is found. Now, along comes someone and tells the man about rainwater dams that are made with scrapers. So the man inspans the oxen and makes a dam for watering his cattle by removing the earth with a scraper. That is how he progresses. Each time he feels he has improved himself a little, he is ready to a try a new idea.

'In my village, people have long been ready to try out new ideas, but everything is delayed because of the fight that is going

22

on between our chief and Gilbert. First of all the fight was about who is the good man and who is the evil man, though everyone well knows who the evil man is. In spite of this, many secret things were done to damage and delay the starting of the farm and cattle co-operative. Last year the secrets all came out into the open in the battle over Pelotona, the permit man. It is the rule that a permit must be written out for every beast that is sold. Before Gilbert came, Pelotona used to work for the chief because he was the big cattle speculator of the village. A cattle speculator works like this: a man brings his beast to him which he looks over and then says, "Oh, I shall pay you six pounds for that beast." But in his heart he knows he will get sixteen or twenty pounds for the same beast at the abattoir. This is the only way that a poor man may sell cattle because he cannot order railway trucks to transport his cattle. On this business our chief became very rich, then along came Gilbert with a new idea: the cattle co-operative belongs to the people and each member is to get a fair price. To get this fair price each beast is weighed on a scale and the owner is paid the same live weight as would be given by the abattoir. Seeing this good fortune, the whole village joined the cattle co-operative, putting our chief out of business.

'Now, Pelotona is a free man. He had a change of mind and walked over to work for Gilbert. The next thing our chief placed a banishment order on Pelotona, which made Pelotona straightaway run to our chief's brother Sekoto, who is also our chief's superior. The chief's brother came over and said, "You need not think because you are my relative that you can do what you like." People were also much surprised to see a white woman come over from England and say in a very loud voice: "Pelotona stays right here. We are paying his salary." All this commotion over a poor and humble man like Pelotona.'

There was a short silence. Makhaya was very moved by the vividly told little story, and there was a kind of defiance in the man Gilbert that found an echo in his own heart.

'Tell me more about Gilbert,' he said quietly. 'He interests me.'

'I have no words to describe Gilbert, son,' Dinorego said. 'Just as I take you as my own son, so do I take Gilbert as my own son, which fact surprises me, since he is a white man and we Batswana do not know any white people, though some have lived here for many years. Many things caused me to have a change of mind. He can eat goat meat and sour-milk porridge, which I have not known a white man to eat before. Also, whenever there is trouble he comes to me and says, "Dinorego, should I stay here?" which fills my heart with fire since I am just an old man with no power. I reasoned: If Gilbert goes, who will pour out knowledge like rain? Everybody is selfish and wants to keep what he has to himself. There was my friend, Mma-Millipede, who had fifty-two fowls. They were wandering free, being eaten by the eagles. I took her myself to Gilbert. He says, "If you have fifty-two fowls you must build a coop, fifteen feet by twenty-five feet. Make it six feet high. Keep one cockerel for every fifteen hens. Never keep more than two or three broody hens in the coop at one time. Buy egg-laying mash . . ." and so on. Mma-Millipede now always has eggs for sale.'

The old man was silent awhile, then continued, 'In this world are both evil and good men. Both have to do justice to their cause. In this country there is a great tolerance of evil. It is because of death that we tolerate evil. All meet death in the end, and because of death we make allowance for evil though we do not like it.'

'I might like it here,' Makhaya said, wistfully.

'This country appeals to few people,' said Dinorego. 'There is too much loneliness. I stay alone with my youngest child. Her name is Maria. She likes all things modern. Because of this she is also taking lessons from Gilbert in English. One day she was looking at pictures in a book which Gilbert gave her. There was a kitchen with shelves. So she carved the shelves in the mud wall. Then, too, she cooks goat meat with curry powder and this improves its taste. Now all the women round about have shelves in their kitchens and cook the meat with curry powder.'

There was an abrupt change in the scenery. The low wild thornbush suddenly gave way to acres and acres of cleared land, cultivated for ploughing. Perching on the outer borders of each plot were small groups of mud huts. At a railway siding, they crossed over the line and walked along a wide path that had been scraped by a bulldozer. The pathway wound and curved into the distance, and in the distance two low blue hills met and swept down to each other. At a fork in the road, a few tall, slender trees lined the pathway. Dinorego took the turning to the left.

'If you follow the other road,' Dinorego said, 'you will soon come to the farm and cattle co-operative. This is our village. It is called Golema Mmidi, which means "to grow crops".'

A narrow footpath led through the trees which were planted by the old man on a slope that led down to his home. The short walk through the trees made Makhaya feel that the sudden clearing ahead of ploughed land was immense. Three huts stood nearby in a wide yard hedged with thornbush.

A young woman bent over, sweeping the yard with a grass broom.

'Maria,' the old man called. 'I have a guest.'

Those were familiar words to the young woman. Her father never seemed able to step out of his own village without bringing back a stranger. She straightened her back, glanced briefly at the tall stranger, and noticed immediately that he had the tired look of one who had travelled a long distance.

Perhaps he will want some water to wash, she thought. It's a good thing I kept the big water pot near the fire.

She dropped the broom and walked quickly to one of the central huts and came out with two hand-carved stools which she placed on the ground for the men to sit on. Dinorego introduced her to Makhaya. She bent her knees in a slight curtsy and clasped two small hands together in the Tswana form of greeting.

'Tea will soon be ready,' she said. 'Would the guest like water to wash?'

It was the crisp clear voice of a busy, preoccupied, self-absorbed woman, and there was an almighty air of neatness and orderliness about her. She was very thin with a long pretty neck on which was poised a serious, quiet face, and her small black eyes never seemed to gaze outward, but inward. In fact, she was often in the habit of staring meditatively at the ground. Makhaya was instantly attracted to her.

Thunderous footsteps made Makhaya swing sharply around. This made the old man laugh.

'It's Gilbert,' he said. 'He always surprises people because no one expects such a big man.'

He was not big, he was a giant, and his massive frame made him topple forward slightly and sway as he walked. He never wore much except short khaki pants and great hobnailed boots, and because of this, the sun had burned him a dark brown hue, and this in turn accentuated the light-blue colouring of his eyes so that they glittered. Life never seemed to offer enough work for his abundant energy, and his gaze forever restlessly swept the horizon seeking some new challenge, while at the same time his mind and hands could busy themselves with the most immediate and insignificant details in a continuous flow of activity like a wave. Thus, having already included Makhaya and Dinorego in his horizon, he walked straight into the central hut, said something that made Maria laugh, and came out almost immediately with a stool and the tea tray.

'Dinorego,' he said, pleasantly. 'Why didn't you tell me you were going into town? I could have given you a lift, as I wanted to go in too to buy a new mantle for my lamp.'

'It's a good thing I did not ask for a lift, Gilbert,' the old man said. 'Today I was meant to acquire a new son. His name is Makhaya.'

Gilbert held out his hand and smiled widely, easily. 'Hullo, Mack . . .' he stumbled as he had not really grasped the sound of it.

'It's just a tribal name,' Makhaya said, smiling at his embarrassment. 'You can call me Mack if you like.'

The words, 'It's just a tribal name,' caused an instant pause in the activity of the wave. To Gilbert, it was the first real hand-clasp he had experienced in the loneliness in which he found himself in tribal Africa. He stared at Makhaya, taking in the quiet, wryly amused expression and the air of lonely self-containment.

'Are you a stranger in this country?' he asked.

'Yes,' Makhaya said, then added, 'I also ought to be passing through because I'm a refugee.'

'To where?' Gilbert asked.

'I don't know yet,' Makhaya said.

Gilbert said nothing, yet the expression on his face went blank the way it always did when someone aroused sympathy in him.

Maria came up and said very formally to Makhaya, 'Sir, the water for your wash is ready.'

Makhaya picked up his bag and followed her to one of the huts. Gilbert turned to Dinorego and said, 'He's quite a strange fellow.'

'Not only that, Gilbert,' the old man said quickly. 'He has some wonderful ideas. When I first met him he said, "A man comes to the crossroads. The one road leads to fame and the other to peace of mind. Is there peace of mind for a man like me?" And I straight away thought: "This is the very man my son Gilbert has been looking for to help him in his work. Since he is a well-educated man perhaps they can have some understanding." What do you think?'

He blinked innocently at Gilbert.

Gilbert kept quiet for a moment, then said, decisively, 'I'll invite him to have supper with me.'

Gilbert gazed thoughtfully into the distance. The quietly amused words, 'It's just a tribal name,' kept on recurring to him. He needed, more than anything, someone with the necessary mental and emotional alienation from tribalism to help him accomplish what he had in mind. Three years of uphill battling had already made clear to him his own limitations in putting his ideas across to people, and he had also learned that change, if it was to take place at all, would in some way have to follow the natural course of people's lives rather than impose itself in a sudden and dramatic way from on top. He hadn't the kind of personality that could handle people, because everything in him was submerged in the work he was doing. He lacked sympathy, patience and understanding, and there were all those weird conflicts he had had with Matenge that had kept him lying awake at night. There seemed to be no escape from the man, but what had contributed more than anything else to those sleepless nights was his own inability to understand the workings of an extremely cunning and evil mind, a mind so profoundly clever as to make the innocent believe they are responsible for the evil.

As soon as Makhaya emerged from the hut, Gilbert stood up and said abruptly, 'Would you care to have supper with me? I'd like to talk to you.'

Gilbert led the way out of the yard, up the slope and through the trees. A flock of goats suddenly appeared, herded home by a small boy. The sun had already set, and as though they knew this, the goats flicked their tails briskly and rolled anxious yellow eyes at the two men watching them as much to say: 'We are late, but one day we will stop and talk.' The small boy waved, walking in the same manner as the briskly trotting goats.

As though he understood goat-talk, Gilbert laughed happily. He said to Makhaya, 'Botswana goats amaze me. They just walk about eating all this dry paper and bits of rubble and then turn it into meat and milk.'

They walked on and soon came to the wide pathway which forked with a turning to the left and one to the right: Gilbert took the turn to the right and they arrived at a big gate, roughly made of tautly strung barbed wire. Gilbert lifted the wire latch and swung the gate open, and then closed it again once Makhaya was inside. He raised one hand and said gaily:

'This is Utopia, Mack. I've the greatest dreams about it.'

And all that Makhaya could see of Utopia in the dimming light was the outline of several mud huts. Near one of these was parked a Land Rover and to this hut Gilbert walked. He pushed open the door and struck a match to light a lamp. The interior was simply furnished with a bed in one corner, a table, two chairs and some boxes on which were strewn, in haphazard order, books and magazines. Makhaya sat down on one of the chairs while Gilbert pumped a paraffin stove which stood on the floor in a corner of the hut. Supper was to be a few tins of canned food emptied into a pot and heated briefly over the stove and then poured out roughly onto two plates. But while he busied himself, Gilbert chatted about this and that.

'I like it here,' he said. 'I'm running away from England. You know what England's like? It's full of nice, orderly queues, and everybody lines up in these queues for a place and position in the world. I let all that go hang and hopped out.'

He paused and looked at Makhaya with a friendly glance. 'What exactly are you running away from?'

'It's not so much what I'm running away from,' Makhaya said. 'It's what I'm trying to run into. I want a wife and children.'

Gilbert looked half-surprised and half-amused at this unexpected reply.

Makhaya laughed. 'I want some part of myself to go on when I die,' he said. 'And since I found myself so near death over the past two years, I thought it best to find a wife before I found anything else.'

'Are you that simple?' Gilbert asked, and laughed too.

'Yes,' Makhaya said.

'I don't know if the same applies to me,' Gilbert said, suddenly thoughtful. 'Ninety per cent of the time I don't want a woman. Then also there's that ten per cent when I'm lonely, but I don't know of any woman who'd go for the ten per cent.'

'She would,' Makhaya said. 'But provided she had a life of her own too.'

Gilbert looked at him with an almost childlike innocence. 'You seem to be quite an expert.'

Makhaya averted his face in discomfort. He could not explain that experiences went hand in hand with a depth of bitterness and resentment because he did not fully understand the root cause of an attraction that had made women pursue him; that if love was basically a warm fire in you, you attracted all the cold people, who consumed your fire with savage greed, leaving you deprived and desolate. The robbery he recognized but not the cause.

'I have sisters,' Makhaya said at last. 'Also, there have been women and women in my life, I suppose because I searched for them.'

They were silent for a while, eating. Then Gilbert said quietly:

'Would you say, from what you've seen of her today, that Dinorego's daughter was one of those women who had a life of her own?'

Makhaya did not reply immediately. He thought of the small black inward-gazing eyes and the pretty air of preoccupied self-absorption. He'd have liked a woman like that. She might have so easily become a part of his inner harmony and the peace he was striving for. But an instinct warned him to push the dream away from him. Three years was a long time and he was a stranger to it all.

'Yes,' he said, slowly. 'I'd say she's that kind of woman.'

Gilbert's eyes lit up with laughter. 'She's hard to get,' he said. 'She makes all these little rules and you can't budge her from them. When I first came here I asked her to marry me and she said, "I can't marry you, Gilbert, because I'm not an educated woman. You won't be happy with an uneducated woman." So I said, "All right, get educated then." Now I'm sorry I ever said it because I've been teaching her English in exchange for lessons in Tswana. All I've got out of it is an inferiority complex over my inability to grasp Tswana.'

This odd little confession warmed Makhaya's heart to the man. There might have been so many things that could have stood up as a barrier between a possible friendship, like Makhaya's background and his distrust and dislike of white

31

people. Instead, he found himself confronted by a big man who allowed himself to be bullied by a small woman. They sat in companionable silence for a while, then Gilbert stood up and cleared away the plates and crouched down on one knee, pretending to fuss about putting them in a basin. He half-turned and looked at Makhaya.

'I could do with a friend around here,' he said, slightly embarrassed. 'Are you looking for a job?'

'Yes,' Makhaya said.

'Tell me a bit about yourself. What work were you doing in South Africa?'

'There's not much to tell,' Makhaya said. 'I worked for a newspaper in Johannesburg. It was the only sort of thing where black people could see their faces on the front page and read about their neighbours, but it was lurid. And since I went out on the stories I could see that it was not so far from the truth because people who are down in the hovels are lurid. The only thing is, it's a law of life that they rise up but there are man-made laws to keep them down there. After a time it begins to drive you crazy. You either drink too much, or you join underground sabotage movements which are riddled with spies. You keep a piece of paper in your pocket with a plan to blow something up, and you get thrown into jail for two years before you've blown anything up.'

'Do you still feel committed to all this?' Gilbert asked.

'Wouldn't I have stayed there if I had?' Makhaya said, half-questioning himself. 'I don't know. Nothing is quite clear to me.'

Gilbert stood up and swung around decisively. 'Can you drive a car?' he asked.

'Yes,' Makhaya said.

'Driving a tractor is much easier,' he said. 'Part of your job would be to learn tractor-ploughing and the use of planters, harrows, and cultivators. The other half would be to teach women agriculture.'

Makhaya stared at him in amazement. 'But I know nothing about agriculture,' he protested.

'I have the lectures,' Gilbert said, almost impatiently. 'I know what's needed but I can't teach. I can't put my ideas over somehow, and not only because my grasp of Tswana is poor.'

He sat down on a chair and for almost an hour talked eagerly, the way he had with the paramount chief, only this time to a keenly attentive listener.

He felt that he had stumbled onto one of the major blockages to agricultural progress in the country. The women were the traditional tillers of the earth, not the men. The women were the backbone of agriculture while the men on the whole were cattle drovers. But when it came to programmes for improved techniques in agriculture, soil conservation, the use of pesticides and fertilizers, and the production of cash crops, the lecture rooms were open to men only. Why give training to a section of the population who may never use it but continue to leave it to their wives to erode the soil by unsound agricultural practices? Why start talking about development and food production without taking into account who is really producing the food?

At each turn he had been struck by the complexity of the structure. Golema Mmidi was, for most of the year, a village of women with all the men away at the cattle posts. Dinorego was the only full-time male crop producer in the village. All the rest were women. What Gilbert had in mind was to bring the two, cattle production and crop production, together. The system of uncontrolled grazing far out in the bush, apart from ruining the land, was only producing low-grade beef. If cattle were brought to the crop-producing areas, they could be fed on the crop residues and grain surpluses, and this would raise the grade of the beef. There was a serious reason for finding urgent solutions: the country was in the grip of a severe drought, which had already lasted five years and was becoming worse with each succeeding year.

'Well, Mack, what do you think?' he said at last.

Makhaya spread out his hands, helplessly. It was a whole new, astonishing world.

'I think I'll accept the job,' he said.

'You can move in tonight,' Gilbert said.

He picked up the lamp and led the way to a nearby hut which was furnished on the same lines as his own. Then they walked to the home of Dinorego to fetch Makhaya's baggage. The old man's heart was full of joy. He thought he had indeed acquired a son in Makhaya. Once the two young men's footsteps had retreated out of earshot, he turned to his daughter and said, 'Well, what do you think of the stranger, my child?'

'He's all right,' Maria replied, with profound indifference.

She stood up from her place at the fire and went to bed. The old man sat for a long while contemplating the flames. Would he see no grandchildren? Would Maria never love a man?

CHAPTER THREE

Not anything in his life had prepared Makhaya for his first week in his new employment. There was so much that excited the interest of Gilbert about the country, and he was anxious to impart three years of observation all at once to Makhaya to give him a base on which to work.

Golema Mmidi was in the eastern part of the country, in a watershed area that received an average annual rainfall of eighteen inches, while vast stretches of the western regions were almost desert and received an average annual rainfall of nine inches. Thus, the eastern watershed was also the most heavily overstocked and overgrazed and overpopulated part of the country. Because of this, much of the softer, sweeter types of grass had long since disappeared from the area, and great stretches of land were covered by a species known as the carrot-seed grass. This was a tough, quick-growing little annual. Its short impoverished leaves grew close to the ground in a spread-out, star-shaped pattern from the centre of which arose a thin stalk, profusely covered by close-packed little burrs. These burr grass seeds clung to the mouth parts and legs of the animals and were so transported from place to place.

The carrot-seed grass grew in profusion all over Golema Mmidi. When Gilbert first arrived and fenced in the 250-acre plot for cultivation, he had left a wide strip of land between the fence and the cultivated area. At first, on this border strip, the carrot-seed grass grew.

Over a period of two rainy seasons, a number of interesting changes took place on this border strip. Springing up between the carrot-seed during the first season were the long frail, feathery stalks of the wind-blown eragrostis, a lush sweet grass. Within two years, this type of grass had gained dominion over the border strip area, crowding out the carrot-seed grass, which by then had ceased to grow. This amazing development caused Gilbert to place the carrot-seed under closer observation in a rough, home-made laboratory. He noted that carrot-seed showed a preference for impoverished soil, but once the burr casing had liberated the tiny seed, it rotted, forming a humus layer in the soil. Thus, while not liking rich soil, it had the ability to build up the humus layer in impoverished soil and was the tough pioneer which paved the way for a more fragile species of grass to gain its hold on the soil again.

Other miracles too had taken place in the border strip. The minute star faces of wild flowers peeked up amidst the now dense grass: white stars and purple stars and the lacy curving sprays of delicate blends of pale-pink blossoms with, here and there, the jaunty yellow-gold of strange freakish daisies with stems that were one inch wide and flat as rulers, topped by flowers with the odd shape of inverted whorls. A strange gourd too crept along the fence, the hard outer husk of the fruit enclosing enormous seeds which were covered by a thin film of syrup that tasted like honey.

Had all this strange new growth lain dormant for years and years in the soil? He questioned the villagers, but only Dinorego, one of the earliest settlers, retained a wistful memory of when the whole area had been clothed by waist-high grass and clear little streams had flowed all the year round. The pathways of the streams were still there but dry and empty now.

Gilbert travelled all over the eastern watershed area and in dismay often came upon abandoned villages that had been turned into sandy wastelands through the grazing of the cattle and the goats. In some of these wastelands even the carrot-seed grass had completely died out, and the only type of vegetation that held the soil together was the thornbush. These observations convinced him that only large-scale fencing of the land and controlled grazing would save the parts that had not yet become completely eroded and uninhabitable to both man and animals. But it was his enthusiasm for fencing and his criticism of the tribal land tenure system that first brought him to a head-on clash with the fuming Chief Matenge.

Not fully understanding the complexity of the land tenure system, Gilbert had announced that it was a hindrance to agricultural progress. Matenge's brother, the paramount chief, had broken precedent when he allowed Gilbert to fence the land. Fencing of tribal land was not allowed, as ownership of the land was vested in the tribe as a whole. No man could claim that he had purchased a plot of tribal land and anyone who asked was merely allocated a portion free of charge by a chief. This system was designed to protect the interests of the poor and to prevent the land from falling into the hands of a few rich people. Intent on his own schemes for reclaiming eroded soil, Gilbert was shocked to discover that he was the centre of a violent storm. Chief Matenge, aware that he was about to lose his lucrative cattle-dealing business with the villagers, grabbed onto the fencing of the farm and cattle ranch to convince the villagers of Gilbert's evil intentions towards them. In alarm, the villagers called a meeting and sent a deputation of old men to Gilbert.

Was it true, they wanted to know, that Gilbert had in reality secretly purchased land from the paramount chief and was using the name of co-operative to enslave the people? That was what Chief Matenge had told them. At first Gilbert was dumbstruck by the accusation. Then he realized that he had endangered his work by criticizing the land system and creating the impression that he favoured freehold tenure.

No, Gilbert had replied, he was not proposing an alternative to the tribal land tenure system. He believed that co-operative organization was similar to communal ownership of land, and he felt that progress could be achieved if enclosed grazing land, farm machinery, boreholes, and marketing societies were the responsibility of the members.

Dinorego, who had acted as interpreter of the deputation, pointed to the fences. Why had barbed-wire fencing been set up around the land? It was something that was not allowed. They did not doubt the word of the young man, he said kindly, but all the commotion was over the fences.

Gilbert took them to the border strip area to show them how good grass regained its hold on the land once the earth was protected by a fence. All the old men could not but agree that they had not seen such grass in Golema Mmidi for a long time. He also took them to the cattle ranch where the same miracle had occurred. The cattle ranch had been divided into four camps. Two were to remain empty for some time. In one of the empty camps, he wished to observe the speed with which the natural grasses of the area recovered. In the other he had had the land de-stumped and ploughed and a drought-resistant type of grass seed sown. From this he would be able to judge whether indigenous grasses or imported drought-resistant grasses would be best suited for cattle grazing.

In the two occupied camps he had retained one hundred

cattle which he had purchased from the co-operative members. The best of these were to be used in a stock-breeding experiment, and these would then be resold to members wishing to restock their herds. The last camp was also an experiment to raise the grade of the meat. The cattle of camp number four were fed on a special type of corn that produced only stems and leaves and was grown on the farm as part of the year's crop. Water, bonemeal, and salt licks were also provided within the fenced-off area of this camp.

Gilbert explained that without fencing he could not gather all this valuable information. Also, it was his hope that all the cattle of Golema Mmidi would one day graze on co-operatively owned feeding grounds, and the fencing of these feeding grounds was most essential for a number of reasons. There could be no overstocking once a fence was erected. The plan was to keep no more than two hundred cattle at a time on a ranch of seven thousand acres. If fewer beasts were kept, they could be better fed, and this would bring an increase in their cash value. Fencing also reduced the hardship and labour of cattle-rearing. No longer would cattle stray and get lost in the bush, and it prevented the spread of infectious diseases like foot-and-mouth.

The old men were deeply impressed. They all were or had been cattlemen and immediately grasped the significance of what they saw and heard. The young man's entry into their village had not gone unnoticed, nor had his deeds or his ability, though educated, to live under the same conditions as the poor. But the deputation was concerned about the young man's truthfulness and sincerity, for everyone from the chiefs down to the colonial authorities had lived off the poor in one form or another and in the name of one thing or another, like cow tax, hut tax, manhood tax, and tax on not paying manhood tax. Gilbert gained two advantages out of this meeting with the old

men of the village: the establishment of the co-operative movement in Golema Mmidi and the friendship of Dinorego.

Out of the two, it was difficult to say which he valued more.
Without the villagers' enthusiasm for co-operatives, his dreams
would have remained at a standstill. Yet without the friendship
of Dinorego he might not have survived the frustrations of three
years and the continual enmity of Chief Matenge.

Progress was slow. The main purpose of the 250-acre plot was
to try and prove whether, if run with modern machinery, it
could win crops under all but the most severe drought conditions. Yet he was under pressure to make the farm economically
viable; he had established it on grants and donations which
would not continue indefinitely. The distractions were
immense. The drought became worse with each succeeding
year, and the rainfall pattern became exceedingly unpredictable.
At times a whole year's rain might fall in one month or one day
or one hour. For the past two years, few of the villagers had
reaped an adequate amount of crops.

When he first arrived in Golema Mmidi, all the ploughing was
done by oxen, and these were always in a weak condition by the
time the first rains fell. Almost six weeks of the rainy season had
to pass by before the oxen, fed on the fresh green growth, were
strong enough to plough. In the meanwhile, all the good rain
needed by the crops might fall in those six weeks. This created
anxiety, and often a man would harness his plough team too soon,
only to have them topple over from weakness created by the
long walks in search of the scant grazing during the dry season.

Gilbert's solution to this predicament was a thrift and loan
club which enabled the villagers to hire machinery from the
farm so that they could take immediate advantage of any rainfall. Most of the men of the village had taken their first lessons
in tractor-ploughing at the farm.

All this covered the range of his achievements so far, yet these achievements seemed to him very unsatisfactory. Apart from growing crops for food, crops that brought in cash had to be grown too. This called for trying out new ways of making the land produce all the crops a man might need to support his life. His views reached out to no one but Dinorego. Gilbert was to find that strange prejudices surrounded people's eating habits and the types of crops they were prepared to grow.

He had approached the authorities to inquire as to the amount of research that was being done in the country on breeding drought-resistant strains of seed. He found out that the most intensive research had been done on millet. Millet was really a stranger to southern Africa, where sorghum and maize are eaten as a daily staple. Yet fifteen thousand varieties of millet had been tested in the country, and the authorities had finally bred a type that could produce a crop in only three inches of rain, with a few most-needed advantages. Witchweed, which is a parasite that is germinated by and lives on the roots of maize and sorghum plants, stunting their growth, was germinated by this type of millet as well, yet the plant remained unaffected by it. Also, the red-billed weaver bird that lives off sorghum seed and caused heavy damage to crops each year bypassed the millet because the ear produced a lot of spiky hairs that irritated the throat of the bird.

'So everybody is growing millet?' Gilbert queried the authorities.

'No,' they said. 'Everybody is still growing sorghum and maize.'

He looked at them dumbfounded. Were they deliberately sitting on research information? And they merely laughed at his look of baffled surprise.

They also shrugged. They had done their best to publicize the millet discovery, and what had happened? Countries at the ends of the earth had grabbed it, but the discovery had made no impact on Botswana because certain minority tribes, traditionally considered inferior, had long had a liking for millet and had always grown it as part of the season's crop. Therefore, other tribes who considered themselves superior would not grow it nor eat it. These 'inferior' tribes lived in the wastes of the Kalahari Desert, where the rainfall barely averaged nine inches a year, and it was their success in growing millet under such conditions that had first aroused interest in millet breeding. But the agricultural authorities decided it wasn't the policy of their department to interfere with the traditional prejudices of the Batswana people.

'But why don't you tell people that millet is a cash crop?' Gilbert said, hotly. 'Why don't you say, "If you don't want to eat it, grow it and market it. Grow it and make this the greatest millet-producing country in the world because it's the one kind of crop that's certain to do well here."'

They shrugged again. 'Can't people reason things out for themselves?' they said.

He looked at them appalled. So that's what colonial authority amounted to? Do your bit and the job was done. He bought the millet seed and walked out. One day, these colonial authorities were so unfortunate as to pick up a rumour that all was not well with Gilbert in the village of Golema Mmidi. They wrote him a pally letter: 'Why not come and join us, old boy?' He sent them an unprintable reply.

It was Dinorego who confirmed the story of the authorities. It was true, he said. Millet was only grown and eaten by 'inferior' tribes. But once Gilbert grew it on the farm as a cash crop, Dinorego quickly followed suit and grew it on his own land.

Drought-resistant breeds of maize and sorghum, which more

people in Botswana were prepared to eat, were hard to find. There was a certain species of slightly drought-resistant sorghum, but this species produced a layer of black substance just under the outer husk, and when pounded and cooked, it made the porridge look black in colour. For this reason it was unpopular and never grown.

Year in and year out people had grown the exact same crops. Somewhere along the line they had become mixed up with tribal traditions. They had become fixed. They were: sorghum, maize, watermelon, and sweet reed. There was even a feeling of safety about them. Never mind if the hot sun of the drought years burned whole fields of sorghum and maize. Never mind if the rain was no longer what it used to be in the good old days when the rivers ran the whole year round and the dams were always full. You just could not see beyond tradition and its safety to the amazing truth you were starving – and that tough little plants existed that were easy to grow and well able to stand up to rigorous conditions and could provide you with food.

How could a start be made? How could people and knowledge be brought together? Could the women of the village be given some instruction? And why not? Women were on the land 365 days of the year while the men shuttled to and fro with the cattle. Perhaps all change in the long run would depend on the women of the country and perhaps they too could provide a number of solutions to problems he had not yet thought of. Things could start in a small way with crops like millet, with talks, with simple lectures, and with some practical work done on the land.

Gilbert had drawn up a broad rough outline of his plans for instructing women, and this he handed to Makhaya to study.

Makhaya in turn had a mind like a sponge. It soaked up knowledge. By the end of one week he had fully grasped the background against which he was to work. Strange as agriculture might have been to him a week previously, he settled down quite happily with books on soil conservation and tractor-ploughing, and catalogues of wild veld grasses. He was quite unaware that while he sat up reading at night, Chief Matenge was losing a considerable amount of sleep over his presence in the village and his employment at the farm.

Chief Matenge lived in the central part of the village in a big cream-painted mansion. He had once been married and divorced, his wife retaining the two children of the marriage. For many years he had lived alone in the cream mansion until quite recently he had acquired a guest and friend in a certain politician named Joas Tsepe. The central part of the village was about two miles from the farm and it contained, apart from Matenge's mansion, one very poor general dealer's shop, which supplied the villagers with only the bare necessities like sugar, tea, flour and vegetable fats, and cheap materials and shoes; one three-roomed shack, which was the village primary school; and a square brick building that was the depot for collecting and distributing mail from the post office of the railway village, twenty miles away. Mail was received and distributed once a week at this depot. A group of mud huts clustered about the cream-painted mansion, and in these mud huts the servants of Matenge lived, not servants in the ordinary sense, because they were paid no wage, but slaves he had received as part of his heritage.

The mansion, the slaves, and a huge cream Chevrolet, which he parked under a tree in the yard, were the only things that gave Matenge a feeling of security in the village. At least this part of it was in order. The chiefs had always lived in the mansions while the people had lived in the huts. His world had always known two strict classes: royalty and commoner. Golema Mmidi was a village of commoners. No one could claim even distant relationship to royalty and dispute his authority, and the old men whom he had elected as advisers on village affairs were not so much advisers as messenger-boys who had to transmit his deeply resented orders to the villagers. True enough, there was Mma-Millipede, a commoner, who had once been married to the son of a chief. But she was also a rejected woman and, in his eyes, a degraded woman. He was aware of her popularity in the village and that people often consulted her, but after investigations he found out that this was only because of respect for her religious views, and she no longer troubled him. The villages were full of such cranky old women with a bit of missionary education and the Tswana version of the Bible.

Still, he felt insecure. He should have reigned supreme over the commoners, and yet his eight-year administration of the village had dealt one shattering blow after another to his self-esteem. It was he who displayed the arrogance and pride that were part and parcel of the bearing of a great chief, and yet life had placed an amiable, pleasant nitwit of a brother in the supreme position, who was not above shaking hands with the commoners and talking to them as equals. It was he, Matenge, who really commanded the largest following of diehard traditionalists, the ones who from generation to generation saw to it that things remained as they were and whose company and advice were anathema to his carefree, pleasure-loving elder brother, the paramount chief. It was he, Matenge, who understood tribalism, that it was essentially the rule of the illiterate man who, when he was in the majority, feared and despised anything that was not a part of the abysmal darkness in which he lived. (Matenge was the epitome of this darkness with his long, gloomy, melancholy, suspicious face and his ceaseless intrigues, bitter jealousy and hatred.) All this was tribalism and a way of life to the meek sheep who submitted to it. And all this had been highly praised by the colonialists as the only system that would keep the fearful, unwieldly, incomprehensible population of 'natives' in its place.

And yet, things were changing rapidly. The colonialists were withdrawing, and the change was not so much a part of the fashionable political ideologies of the new Africa as the outcome of the natural growth of a people. Matenge could not see this. His brother the paramount chief could, and swam with the outgoing tide, enjoying himself the meanwhile. Matenge could not see this because it had always been his policy to transfer hate from one object to another, and if at last he found himself involved in the political ideologies of Africa and the cauldron of hatred, it was because it was the last camp that reflected his traditional views.

At first Matenge had hated his brother because he felt the chieftaincy should be his, and this hatred drove him to overreach himself until he was discovered in a plot to assassinate his brother. For this his brother smilingly and politely banished him to Golema Mmidi under the guise that he was being given an administrative post. The shock of it kept him quiet for some time, but soon he transferred his hate to the villagers, most notably Dinorego, who had refused to sit on his advisory council. For this he tried to get Dinorego banished from the area, but the banishment order was immediately rescinded by his brother. And so it had gone on. The villagers were aware of the tug of war, but they feared Matenge too much to take open advantage of it. They merely avoided him as much as possible. Then, along had come Gilbert Balfour, who, with his brother's backing, destroyed Matenge's lucrative cattle-speculating business overnight. The hatred, which had by now become a mountain, was once more transferred to Gilbert. And if the times had not really changed he might have won this last battle and got Gilbert removed from the village by the colonial authorities.

Co-operatives were not a popular cause. The cattle-speculating monopolies were in the hands of a few white traders, but once the people had voted a government into power that gave its support to co-operatives, the traders had reacted in panic and started paying inflated prices for cattle. It all depended on how long they could hold out in competition against the co-operatives. Some people welcomed this development. The traders had become rich at the expense of the people, and now they were paying these same people fantastic sums of money for cattle. Surely that's the best way a greedy man may dig his own grave? In the meantime, a fierce battle raged and co-operatives was the dirtiest word you could use to the monopolists.

The agricultural authorities also believed they had a monopoly over the future development of the country, and they were not inclined to favour independent initiative, nor outsiders. Development was an 'in' business, for locals only. They were prepared to welcome Gilbert 'in', as he was a white man, but to their extreme chagrin, they found that he had independent ideas about that too.

It seemed impossible to Matenge that one man could stir up so much trouble among the important people and still remain in the country. And he kept the pot boiling all the time, in the hope that one side or the other would step in and rid him of his arch enemy.

Almost a week passed before Matenge became aware of Makhaya's presence in the village and he got to know of it through the only friend he had, Joas Tsepe.

Joas Tsepe was the under-secretary-general of the Botswana

National Liberation Party. There were four or five such liberation parties with little or no membership among the people but many undersecretaries general. All these parties opposed the new government. At first, this opposition had set as its goal the liberation of the Botswana people from colonialism. But after the self-government elections, it forgot about the colonialists and set itself to liberate the Botswana people from a government they had elected into power. The opposition maintained that the people did not know what they were doing. They claimed that the colonialists had rigged the elections, although prior to the voting the opposition had anticipated this colonial treachery and had specially asked to be represented at the ballot counting table. Strangely enough, in front of their very eyes, power had passed into the hands of the ruling party. Strangely enough too, Joas and quite a few others of his clan served six-month sentences for rigging election papers. They also spent some time blowing hot air about the stupid Botswana people who had voted for chiefs and then, to their amazement, found that they had a government of the sons of chiefs with an anti-chief policy. Joas's party and the other opposition groups quickly reorganized themselves into pro-chief supporters, as the chiefs had by now become the only disgruntled section of the country.

The opposition political parties had long been aligned to the Pan-African movement. They also called themselves the vanguard of African nationalism in southern Africa. To many, Pan-Africanism is an almost sacred dream, but like all dreams it also has its nightmare side, and the little men like Joas Tsepe and their strange doings are the nightmare. If they have any power at all it is the power to plunge the African continent into an era of chaos and bloody murder.

Joas Tsepe, although born in Botswana, spent a number of years working in South Africa. There he also acquired a number of grievances, which even the whole world acknowledges as being justifiable. Having made a little reputation for himself as a speaker at political meetings, he was one day, from some mysterious source, given the order to go back to his country to fight for the liberation of his people. This mysterious source also supplied him with money which enabled him to remain unemployed and devote himself full-time to the liberatory struggle, and also to purchase a car. Every six months, he left the country 'on a mission', for which mission he was supplied with an air ticket to travel to various parts of the earth.

All this VIP treatment gave Joas a swollen head. He was already the minister of finance in the shadow government, and this caused one to pause and puzzle out the motives of the financier of his mysterious source of money, since Joas was ill-equipped educationally to handle the complicated business of government, and a course in economics would have been far better than the VIP trips. Was it perhaps the intention of the secret financier to re-establish the rule of the illiterate and semi-literate man in Africa? Or was Joas his tool? Was it easier for a man like Joas to take his orders? Because Joas was a parrot. Not only that, he was a belly-crawler and it was his agility at belly-crawling that had won him the friendship of Matenge. Since he had come out of jail after the self-government elections, Joas lived as the permanent guest of Matenge. He had a co-operative to organize which would help Matenge to re-establish himself as the cattle-speculator of Golema Mmidi, and he had to educate the African masses in African socialism.

It was on a Friday afternoon that Joas passed by the farm and noticed the presence of a stranger. Devoured by curiosity, he swung into the farm gates on the plea that he needed water for a long journey. He took one close look at Makhaya and almost choked with excitement. The newspaper with Makhaya's picture on the front page was in his car, and his car could not seem to drive fast enough back to Matenge.

He burst in on Matenge, waving the paper. 'We've got him this time, Chief,' he said, dramatically.

Matenge looked bored. That was the way a superior had to behave to an inferior. Getting no response, Joas opened the paper and held it before Matenge.

'Gilbert is keeping a refugee at the farm,' he said.

The whole weekend Matenge stewed and simmered. Gilbert had overshot himself. If there was anything the new government disliked, it was a refugee, and because of this, no man in his right senses would harbour or employ one. Early Monday morning, Matenge climbed into his cream Chevrolet and drove to the village of his brother, Paramount Chief Sekoto.

CHAPTER FOUR

Even those who did not like chiefs had to concede that Paramount Chief Sekoto was a very charming man. His charm lay not so much in his outer appearance as in his very cheerful outlook on life. In fact, so fond was he of the sunny side of life that he was inclined to regard any gloomy, pessimistic person as insane and make every effort to avoid his company. It was his belief that a witty answer turneth away wrath and that the oil of reason should always be poured on troubled waters.

Chief Sekoto had three great loves: fast cars, good food, and pretty girls. All the good food had made him very fat, so that he gave the impression of waddling like a duck when he walked. And one of the pretty girls had caused a major disruption in his otherwise serene and happy life. It happened like this. About two miles from his official residence, he had built a palatial mansion. He had sternly forbidden his wife to set foot in this mansion on the grounds that it was here that he entertained important guests with whom he discussed top-secret affairs. But it wasn't long before the wife and the whole village knew that this was the house where Chief Sekoto kept his concubines. Still, not a murmur of protest was raised against him, it being taken for granted that a chief was entitled to privileges above those of ordinary men. For many years Chief Sekoto carefully divided his attention between his two homes until one day he chanced upon an exceedingly beautiful woman, lost his head, and for three months took up permanent residence in the mansion of the concubines. The villagers took it lightly. The scandal was huge entertainment in the humdrum round of their daily life. Not so for the chief's family.

Towards the end of the third month, Chief Sekoto was forced to take a long business trip. His absence from the village gave his family the opportunity to make short work of the troublesome concubine. The chief's eldest son drove up to the mansion, bundled the concubine roughly into a car, and sped with her out of the village to some unknown destination. Not only that, the foolhardy young man had an intense, upright character and quarrelled violently with his amiable father and walked out of the house, forever. This experience was a great shock to Chief Sekoto. He knew in his heart that he would never give up the pretty girls, but after that he kept his hunting grounds well away from home.

Every weekday morning, Chief Sekoto listened to cases brought before his court, while the afternoons were spent at leisure unless there were people who had made appointments to interview him. This particular Monday morning a lively and rowdy case was in session when, out of the corner of his eye, Chief Sekoto saw his brother Matenge drive up and park his car opposite the open clearing where court was held. Nothing upset Chief Sekoto more than a visit from his brother, whom he had long classified as belonging to the insane part of mankind. He determined to dally over the proceedings for as long as possible in the hope that his brother would become bored and leave. Therefore he turned his full attention on the case at hand.

The case had been brought in from one of the outlying villages, called Bodibeng, and the cause of its rowdiness was that the whole village of Bodibeng had turned up to witness the trial. A certain old woman of the village, named Mma-Baloi, was charged with allegedly practising witchcraft, and so certain were the villagers of her guilt that they frequently forgot themselves and burst out into loud chatter and had to be brought to order by the president of the court with threats of fines.

Evidence was that Mma-Baloi had always lived a secret and mysterious life apart from the other villagers. She was also in the habit of receiving strangers from far-off places into her home who would not state what dealings they had with Mma-Baloi.

Now, over a certain period, a number of the children of the village had died sudden deaths, and each time a mother stood up to describe these sudden deaths, the crowd roared in fury because the deaths of the children and the evil practices of Mma-Baloi were one and the same thing in their minds. The accused, Mma-Baloi, sat a little apart from the villagers in a quaking, ashen, crumpled heap; and each time the villagers roared, she seemed about to sink into the earth. Noting this, Chief Sekoto's kindly heart was struck with pity.

Further evidence was that about a week ago a strange young woman had turned up in the village of Bodibeng and made straight for the hut of Mma-Baloi, where she had died a sudden death. This had made Mma-Baloi run screaming from her hut, and it was only the intervention of the police that had saved Mma-Baloi from being torn to pieces by the villagers.

Chief Sekoto was silent for some time. The insanity of mankind never ceased to amaze him. At last he turned to the accused and said gently, 'Well, mother, what do you have to say in defence of yourself?'

'Sir, I am no witch,' said the quavering old voice. 'Even

53

though I am called the mother of the witches, I am no witch. Long ago I was taught by the people who live in the bush how to cure ailments with herbs and that is my business.'

She pointed a shaking finger at a bag placed near her.

'I would like to see the contents of the bag,' Chief Sekoto said with a great show of interest. The bag was brought to him and its contents tipped out on the ground. They were a various assortment of dried leaves, roots, and berries. He examined them leisurely, picking up a few items for closer inspection. This very deliberate gesture was meant to puncture a hole in the confidence of the crowd, who annoyed him. While he fiddled about he was aware of how silent and intent they had become, following his every movement with their eyes. Thus holding the stage, he turned to the old woman and said:

'Proceed with your defence, mother.'

'About the deaths of the children of which I am accused, I know nothing, sir,' she said. 'About the young woman who died in my home last Saturday, I am also innocent. This young woman came to me on recommendation, being grievously ill. We were discussing the ailment when she fell dead at my feet. Never has such a thing occurred before, and this caused me to lose my mind and run out of the house.'

'This is quite understandable, mother,' Chief Sekoto said sympathetically. 'Even I should have been grieved if some stranger was struck with death in my home.'

He swept the crowd with a stern glance. 'Who issues the certificates of death in Bodibeng?' he asked.

There was a short, bewildered silence. Then a car and a messenger had to be found to fetch the doctor of the Bodibeng hospital. There was a delay of two hours as the doctor was engaged in an operation. Throughout this long wait the court remained in session. At one stage Chief Sekoto received an impatient note: 'Dear Brother,' it said. 'Please spare a few moments to discuss an urgent matter.'

Chief Sekoto replied: 'Is it life or death? I am at the moment faced with the life or death of an old woman. I cannot move.'

There was no reply. Chief Sekoto watched his brother's expression out of the corner of his eye. Foremost in the Chief's mind was the necessity to plan an escape route from the glowering thunderstorm. He called the president of the court and whispered, 'Ring up George Appleby-Smith and tell him I'm coming to lunch.'

It was near noon when the doctor arrived. His evidence was brief and to the point. Yes, it was true, he said. There had been a surprising number of child deaths in the village of Bodibeng, and death in each case had been due to pneumonia; and yes, he said, he had performed a postmortem on the body of a young woman last Saturday afternoon. The young woman had died of a septic womb due to having procured an abortion with a hooked and unsterilized instrument. He would say that the septic condition of the womb had been of three months' duration.

All that was left now was for Chief Sekoto to pass judgment on the case. This he did sternly, drawing himself up to his full height.

'People of Bodibeng,' he said. 'It seems to me you are all suffering from derangement of the brain.'

He paused long enough to allow the villagers to look at each other uneasily.

'Your children die of pneumonia,' he thundered, 'and to shield yourselves from blame you accuse a poor old woman of having bewitched them into death. Not only that. You falsely accuse her of a most serious crime which carries the death sentence. How long have you planned the death of a poor old woman, deranged people of Bodibeng? How long have you caused her to live in utter misery, suspicion, and fear? I say: Can dogs bark forever? Oh no, people of Bodibeng, today you will make payment for the legs of the old mother who has fled before your barking. I say: The fault is all with you, and because of this I fine each household of Bodibeng one beast. From the money that arises out of the sale of these beasts, each household is to purchase warm clothing for the children so that they may no longer die of pneumonia.'

He turned and looked at the old woman, changing his expression to one of kindness.

'As for you, mother,' he said, 'I cannot allow you to go and live once more among the people of Bodibeng. It is only hatred that the people of Bodibeng feel for you, and this has driven them out of their minds. As hatred never dies, who knows what evil they will not plot against you? I have a large house, and you are welcome to the protection it offers. Besides, I suffer from an ailment for which I am always given penicillin injections at the hospital. Now I am tired of the penicillin injections and perhaps your good herbs may serve to cure me of my troubles.'

He stood up, signifying the end of the case. The people of Bodibeng fled in confusion from the courtyard, but the old woman sat for a long time on the ground, silent tears of gratitude dripping down into her lap.

Chief Sekoto walked over briskly to his brother's car, opened a door, and heaved himself inside.

'We must make haste, brother,' he said. 'I have an important appointment to keep.'

The first words his brother uttered really surprised Chief Sekoto.

'I wish to be relieved of the administration of Golema Mmidi,' said Matenge.

56

Chief Sekoto furrowed his brow. This was most unexpected. He dreaded what was coming next.

'Have you had another clash with the young man, Gilbert?' he asked lightly.

Matenge turned his deep doom-ridden eyes on his brother. 'He is now harbouring refugees at the farm.'

'Oh, is that all, brother?' Chief Sekoto asked, relieved. 'I see no harm in that. The world is always full of refugees. How many has Gilbert taken in?'

For an answer, Matenge held out the paper with Makhaya's picture on the front page. Chief Sekoto studied the face carefully and felt a sharp stab of jealousy. The man was too attractive, he could steal all the women in the country. Chief Sekoto did not enjoy the thought of a competitor so near his own hunting grounds.

'You mean there is only one refugee, brother?' he asked, anxiously.

Matenge nodded.

'Well, what's the trouble then? Why do you want to resign?'

'I see,' Matenge said with heavy sarcasm. 'You haven't read the story.'

'But I haven't the time, brother. I'm already late for the important appointment.'

Matenge swung around furiously on his brother. 'Either I go or the refugee goes,' he said. 'How can people feel safe with a criminal and murderer in their midst? That is what the story says; he is a criminal and murderer who walks around with bombs in his pocket. Why should Gilbert take in such a man unless it is his intention to murder me? There is no other reason why Gilbert should associate with a murderer. He is doing nothing at the farm.'

Chief Sekoto edged towards the door. 'Brother,' he said, 'such criminology is outside my jurisdiction. You must report this matter to the police. You must report this to George Appleby-Smith as he patrols your area. In the meantime, please avail yourself of my hospitality and have lunch at the house. Tell the wife I am called away by an important appointment.'

Chief Sekoto swung his short dumpy legs out of the car, closed the door and, without looking back, waddled over briskly to a small white sports car. He was literally suffocating. Inside the fat, overstuffed body was a spirit that fiercely resented intense, demanding, vicious people. It was as though they had the power to trap him inside a dark airless tunnel when all he wanted was the casualness of the free air and the silly chatter of a pretty, painted-up woman.

The small white car roared into life. Chief Sekoto pressed the accelerator down to the floor and then, at a speed of over a hundred miles an hour, streaked out of the village like a continuous blur of white light. Within barely fifteen minutes he had covered twenty-eight miles and approached the railroad crossing where Makhaya had been dropped off by the truck driver on his first day in Botswana. The chief slowed down, drove past the railway station and into a yard which contained a small white-washed house. It was the home of his friend, Inspector George Appleby-Smith, the green-eyed police officer who had interviewed Makhaya and granted him political asylum.

George Appleby-Smith was twenty years younger than Chief Sekoto, and yet a strong bond of friendship existed between the two men. They had known each other for five years and often went hunting for game in the bush together. Game-hunting was George's chief passion, but he was abnormally afraid of snakes, so Chief Sekoto's gun was always reserved for shooting at snakes. Jokes were a favourite topic of conversation on these excursions.

For example, George would inquire, 'Tell me, Chief, what's the difference between a barber and a sculptor?'

A long interval of silence would ensue during which Chief Sekoto furrowed his brows vigorously. At last he'd say, 'I must say I don't really know, George.'

'Well, it's like this, Chief. The sculptor makes faces and busts and the barber curls up and dyes.'

The collection of these droll jokes was George's leisure-time hobby. He had a way of holding all the laughter of the world in his eyes, yet he rarely smiled and rarely twitched a muscle on his face. He liked his work and was very dedicated. Yet he summed up law and order and all pompous phrases in one expressive word: Bullshit. What he liked in all the bullshit was people. They were like a complicated crossword puzzle to him. They exercised his agile, inventive mind which had a peculiar ability to streamline the complex into a single and clear detail. Nothing alarmed a prisoner more than to be told by George that he was not speaking the truth, and it was the blunt and authoritative manner in which he said this that always unnerved them.

Chief Sekoto never summed up for himself why it was George's company so delighted him, but both were casual, freedom-loving men, and they only parted company on their ideas on women and food. George, being a bachelor, ate terrible food. It was always soup with a little bit of cheese on the plate, while Chief Sekoto usually ate roast leg of mutton for dinner. But somehow George managed to serve roast leg of mutton when Chief Sekoto came to dine.

George was already seated at table when Chief Sekoto walked into the dining room and said:

'I'm a little upset today, George. Have you got any beer to calm my nerves?'

George stood up, went to the kitchen and returned with a glass and a small bottle of beer. Chief Sekoto looked anxiously at his friend. When George was silent and kept his face expressionless, it was a sure sign that he had something on his mind.

'Don't tell me I've run away from troubles, only to find you have troubles too, George,' he said in despair.

George looked down at his plate to hide the laughter in his eyes. 'I saw your brother heading past this way, Chief,' he said, quietly. 'Did he by any chance visit you?'

Chief Sekoto was silent for some time. 'I don't really understand my brother,' he said, glumly. 'I gave him a position that was meant to protect him from the wrath of his enemies. At the time he was plotting my death many people said: "You should have this brother of yours killed." I said: "No, leave the man to his Maker." And what payment have I received from this generosity? Nothing but trouble. Golema Mmidi is now famous for trouble, and if that is not enough, my brother comes to me today and tells me that Gilbert is plotting his death and has especially employed a dangerous refugee to help him.'

George stared reflectively at the wall, and after some time said softly, 'Chief, would you mind if I put your brother in jail?'

Chief Sekoto leaned forward, interested. 'For how long?' he asked.

'I don't know,' George replied. 'It's just a feeling. Some people are on tenterhooks about his association with Joas Tsepe. Tsepe is under the illusion that he will be able to establish a secret military camp in the bush. He has no idea that his every movement is known. The day he smuggles those guns over the border, he's in for the high jump. If you like, we can delay matters until he brings your brother into the deal and we rope him in as well.'

Chief Sekoto nodded his head vigorously. 'I've no objection to my brother going to jail, George,' he said. 'Only it must be for a long time. But what about the refugee? My brother wants him removed.'

'It's not what he wants,' George said, calmly. 'But what I want. What I want is for Gilbert to carry on with his work because everyone else is bullshitting around.'

Chief Sekoto laughed heartily. 'I made a promise to Gilbert that I would come and work on his farm if it succeeds,' he said. 'Now I see that with your help, my friend, I shall be spending my old age in hard labour. But you must promise me something. You must spy on the refugee and tell me if he is eating up all the women.'

George looked affectionately at the old man, marvelling at his ability to take everything in life so lightly. Some other man might be ranting and raving by now, after all that had happened. The chief's eldest son, with whom he had quarrelled, had brought the anti-chief policy into government. It wasn't a ruthless policy. In fact, there was an overall recognition of the hold custom and tradition had on the lives of the people, and in deference to this, all chiefs' salaries had been increased. A chief was still a father figure but somehow thrust to one side, the accent being on nation rather than tribe. Nonentities had been raised up from the dust by the people's vote, and it was they who now reigned supreme on the local government councils. If George Appleby-Smith felt a pang of regret at the death of the old order, it was because life had been simpler with the decisions and power in the hands of one man. If it was complex now it was because chiefs had had a long reign and deeply resented relegation to the status of rubber stamp. Whereas in former times a chief was the upholder of law and order, in these days he consorted with strange fellows who were hell-bent on blowing everything up, and who glibly promised to restore to him his lost political influence. Few chiefs appreciated the salary increase. Many voiced complaints about the younger generation, who no longer bowed the knee but merely politely raised their hats. The chiefs were unable to see that people could not go on being children forever and their humble servants. True enough, the change itself was not dramatic. Even Chief Sekoto still kept his unpaid slaves. But George, with one foot in the past and his youthfulness in the present, was very emotionally involved in upholding the aims of the new, conservative government which wanted everything to happen bit by bit. He was prepared to deal deathblows to any forces that planned its premature overthrow.

'I can promise you I'll spy on the refugee, Chief,' he said, with mock grimness. 'Even though it will delay my own promotion by five years. "So George has now gone soft on refugees?" they'll say. "We knew we couldn't trust the bugger."'

He looked at his watch and regretfully parted company with his amiable friend. The lunch-hour break for him was over. Chief Sekoto remained, eating and drinking at a leisurely pace. The cunning old man was waiting for his brother to pass and return to his own village, and only then would he get into his car and streak back home.

A short while later he heard the approach of a car. He stood up and peered out of a window and saw his brother draw up outside the police station, get out of the car and walk to the office of George Appleby-Smith. After five minutes, his brother emerged and without looking around walked straight to his car, climbed in, and drove in the direction of Golema Mmidi. Not believing his good luck, Chief Sekoto waited until the cream Chevrolet had disappeared in the dust, and breathing a sigh of relief, he walked out to his own car. But just then he saw George Appleby-Smith walk out of his office towards a grey police Land Rover. The chief watched George drive off after his brother in

62

the direction of Golema Mmidi. Chief Sekoto closed his eyes. What would happen now? Since he could not bear to think about it, he heaved himself into the car and drove back home at an ungodly speed.

George too was a fast driver. He soon passed Matenge and within twenty minutes arrived in Golema Mmidi and drove up to the farm gates. No one was in sight. Out on the farm fields, the five specially hired and government-trained tractor drivers were doing the winter ploughing. He parked the Land Rover outside the farm gate, lifted the wire latch, and walked in the direction of a small brick building which was the farm office. There he found Gilbert and Makhaya, standing at a table, absorbed in the study of a map. The map was a plan of the farm's fields, and Gilbert was filling in the crops he intended planting during the coming season.

The two men looked up at his entry. George Appleby-Smith was apologetic. He profoundly respected Gilbert.

'I won't take up much time,' he said. 'Please fill in this form, Mr Maseko. It's an application for residence. I have to take it back with me.'

Makhaya took the form but he was a little surprised. It had not occurred to him to apply for residence in Botswana. George walked up to the table and studied the map. To one plot Gilbert had allocated Turkish tobacco.

'Don't tell me you're going to grow tobacco in this desert,' he said, amazed.

'Why not?' Gilbert said. 'Golema Mmidi has the exact amount of rainfall of a certain area in southern Africa where Turkish tobacco is grown very successfully. It's a very good cash crop too, and if everyone in Golema Mmidi grows a bit and we market it co-operatively – why, we'll all be rich in no time. The only problem we're faced with is the flatness of the land. It

63

needs a slight slope and well-drained soil. We'll either have to create this artificially or lay down pipes.'

George Appleby-Smith was very impressed, and after this made a great show of minding his own business by staring at a wall. Gilbert glanced at him slyly, smiled to himself and continued his work.

Makhaya completed the form and handed it to the police officer, who looked at him in an odd quizzical way.

'Step outside with me for a moment, Mr Maseko,' he said.

They walked for a moment in silence towards the gate, then George stopped abruptly.

'Chief Matenge, who administers this village, wants you removed from it on the grounds that you're a refugee,' he said. 'What he wants has never really mattered to me. We don't see eye to eye. But this time he has a point. The government doesn't encourage refugees. It would like you all to push off somewhere.'

Makhaya kept silent, not knowing what to say.

'In fact,' George Appleby-Smith continued, 'things are so bad that if anyone sticks his neck out for a refugee, he's not likely to get promoted for five years.'

'You mean you'll stick your neck out for me?' Makhaya asked, amused.

'That's what I'm saying, but only on the guarantee that you don't let me down and mess around in the politics of southern Africa.'

'You don't have to bother,' Makhaya said, sharply annoyed. 'I'm not begging anyone in this country to shove me around.'

The green eyes blazed with anger. 'Don't give me that bullshit,' George shot out. 'And if you've got any bullshitting chip on your shoulder, keep it to yourself.'

They stared at each other in this brief flare of anger. Makhaya was the first to regain his humour.

'Tie a man's hands behind his back and then ask him if he's going to chop down a tree,' he said, smiling. 'I wish the whole of southern Africa would go to hell. Only I don't know what to do about getting it there.'

'Smart guy,' George drawled, also smiling. 'It's not your philosophy of life I'm after, but a straight, practical "yes" or "no". Are you going to leave politics alone?'

Makhaya looked at him with a pained expression. 'No, I won't,' he said. 'I may have run myself into a dead end. I may be sick of everything, but the day I fix myself up, I'll do whatever I think is the right thing to do.'

George Appleby-Smith looked at him for some time. 'I'll still stick my neck out for you,' he said, quietly.

He half-turned to go, then remembered something. 'Report your presence in this village to Chief Matenge tomorrow morning at eight. He's responsible for the comings and goings of people and has to know, for the record, whether you intend staying here.'

He walked to his Land Rover, climbed in, and drove off. Makhaya remained where he was some minutes longer. If there was anything he liked on earth, it was human generosity. It made life seem whole and sane to him. It kept the world from shattering into tiny fragments. Only a few, quietly spoken words: 'I'll stick my neck out for you.'

As he entered the office, Gilbert looked up and smiled. 'What did that funny cop have to say?' he asked.

'Nothing much,' Makhaya said. 'Except that I should report my presence in the village to Chief Matenge tomorrow morning.'

CHAPTER FIVE

Chief Matenge really believed he was 'royalty'. So deeply ingrained was this belief in him that he had acquired a number of personal possessions to bolster the image. One was a high-backed kingly chair and the other was a deep purple, tasselled and expensive dressing gown. In this royal purple gown, he paced up and down the porch of his mansion every morning, lost in a Napoleon-like reverie. Of late, this pacing had been often done to the accompaniment of loud chatter from Joas Tsepe. Loud is perhaps an understatement of Joas's speech. He was a platform speaker who never got down from the platform. He was hoarse-voiced. He was always in a sweat. He gesticulated. He had attended so many conferences that his ordinary speech was forever an underlined address: 'Mr Chairman, and fellow delegates . . .'

Usually, Matenge paid little attention. Joas came from a certain tribe of the Kalahari Desert who were still regarded as slaves. The chief also despised the literature of Joas's political party. In this respect he reflected the attitude of his country. The tide of African nationalism had swept down the continent and then faltered at the northern borders of Botswana. During the pre-election campaign, the politicians had had to chase after the people, who kept on moving back and forth to their cattle posts and lands, seemingly unaware that destiny was about to catch up with them. But they couldn't get away from the blaring megaphones, and after a time they paused awhile, to listen. One crowd of politicians shouted that the people should take up arms, and embark upon the 'Unbroken Line' with 'freedom' as their grand aim. You have nothing to lose but your chains, they were told. People listened with mounting anxiety. They could see well enough that they were important to these men.

But what did it all mean? What was this 'Unbroken Line' and where were the chains? The politicians could not perceive that the conference table terms meant little to a people who never read a newspaper and who were completely out of touch with the latest trends, but they pushed ahead all the same, glibly spouting the meaningless phrases. They invaded people's homes on hut-to-hut campaigns, blindly gesticulating and shouting that they were 'in the grip of the force and direction of the law of change', as they were wont to call this new phenomenon, African nationalism.

The other political party – the sons and relatives of chiefs – was more cunning. It kept its distance. It played catchy little folk songs everyone knew. It talked about cattle and crops and all the familiar Botswana problems. People were soothed, perhaps even a little disappointed. The latter crowd was too well known; all their faults and failings and private evils were openly discussed in the villages.

Then the pamphlets started circulating, each party stating its views. The sons of chiefs collected the data from the experts and issued neat little manifestos outlining the problems of the country – water, agriculture, cattle development. The sons of slaves attacked the 'imperialists and neo-colonialists' who were still skilfully manipulating the affairs of an oppressed people. But they put over their ideas very badly, with many spelling errors:

'You will get a psudo-independence if you do not vote for us,' the pamphlets stated. 'Do not stamble. We are people in the clear who know the line. We will eleminate ignorant disease.'

It was one of the most pathetic of elections. The sons of chiefs, who had had all the advantages of education, pounced on the spelling errors of the sons of slaves, who had little or no education.

'Can such men run a country?' they asked, gleefully.

Thus, driven with their backs to the wall, the sons of slaves resorted to low-down mud-slinging. The chiefs all had syphilis, they said. For such defamatory statements, many served jail sentences. Others, like Joas, were imprisoned for getting voters to sign papers on the pretext that his party and the party of chiefs were one and the same thing. For all this, the sons of slaves found themselves more despised than they had ever been before.

Matenge, being educated, soon cast aside the literature of Pan-Africanism. But Joas as a person made sense to him. His own crooked mind and Joas's crooked mind tallied. Besides, Joas had a remarkable amount of inside information on Matenge's arch enemy, Gilbert.

'I'll tell you what the Imperialists are up to now, Chief,' he said one day. 'First they sent the missionaries. Now they send volunteers like Gilbert. What is a volunteer? Volunteer, my eye. I have top-secret information about these training camps in England. Gilbert has been sent here to pave the way for the second scramble for Africa.'

This particular morning, Joas was hopping mad. He stood in one corner of the porch, gesticulating, fuming, his eyes almost darting out of his head in self-righteous indignation. On the previous day he had approached a registrar of co-operatives in an attempt to get his cattle co-operatively registered.

'And do you know what Smedley said to me, Chief? He said, "I'm afraid I can't register your co-operative, Mr Tsepe." I said, "And why not?" And he said, "I'm not going to allow co-operatives to be used for political propaganda." So I said, "But everyone is a politician these days, Mr Smedley. Why discriminate against me? A certain other person I know got his co-operative registered in one day. Aren't you practising racialism, Mr Smedley? This matter won't rest between you and me. I am going to report . . ."'

Matenge held up his hand with a sudden, imperious gesture. In his pacing he had noticed the approach of Makhaya, accompanied by the old man, Dinorego. Matenge stared intently at Makhaya and made several errors in his summing up. The flinching, averted face and slightly hunched-forward shoulders he interpreted as the sign of a weak and cowardly character. And the very marked air of calmness in the long strides he associated with the type of man who would never put up a battle.

Matenge slowly descended the steps. The descent was regal, kingly, spectacular. Makhaya jerked up his head in surprise. The sham of it all appealed to his sense of humour, but one look at the face of Matenge instantly aroused his sympathy. It was the face of a tortured man, slowly being devoured by the intensity of his inner life, and the tormented hell of that inner life had scarred deep ridges across his brow and down his cheeks, and the icy peaks of loneliness on which the man lived had only experienced the storms and winters of life, never the warm dissolving sun of love. Being himself a lonely man, Makhaya instinctively sensed this. But they differed. Makhaya's was a self-protective loneliness, and he had the sun inside him all the time.

Dinorego politely bowed his head and greeted Matenge. His greeting was dismissed with a slight gesture of the head, which contained in it an inheritance of centuries of contempt for the ordinary man. Matenge never once took his eyes off Makhaya, as though by this concentrated stare he intended to pulverize Makhaya into non-existence.

'Who are you?' he asked.

'Makhaya Maseko.'

Matenge bent his head slightly and a mocking smile played around his mouth. 'I hear you have begun to work with Gilbert at the farm,' he said.

'Yes,' Makhaya said.

'It worries me. Gilbert just makes arrangements with people but the authorities do not approve of his actions, nor the people he chooses to associate with. Having a refugee at the farm is going to give it a bad name, including the whole area in which it is placed.'

'What's wrong with a refugee?' Makhaya asked.

'Oh, we hear things about them,' he said. 'They get up at night and batter people to death.'

He glanced briefly at Dinorego, then continued. 'I'll tell you something about Gilbert. He knows nothing about Botswana agriculture. He ought to be in England, where he received his training in agriculture. The only man who knows how to do things here is a Motswana man. Most of the trouble here is caused by people from outside and we don't want you. We want you to get out. When are you going?'

Makhaya looked at the man in amazement and disbelief, almost overwhelmed by the viciousness in his voice.

'But I'm not going away,' Makhaya said, as calmly as he could, though a sudden rush of anger made his voice quiver.

'If you don't go away I'll make things difficult for you here,' Matenge said.

'What else can I say, except go ahead?' Makhaya said.

Matenge smiled. 'You know what a South African swine is?' he said. 'He is a man like you. He always needs to run after his master, the white man.'

Matenge turned and ascended the steps, unaware that a murderously angry man stood staring up at him. There was a wild element in Makhaya. He had seen and faced death too often to be afraid of it, and taking another man's life meant little to him. Several times Dinorego said, 'Let's go, my son.' But Makhaya just looked at the old man with a pained, dazed expression and his eyes glistened with tears. Dinorego misinterpreted this, and tears also rushed into his eyes.

Joas Tsepe ran lightly down the steps. 'I'd like a word with you, Maseko,' he said.

Makhaya laughed harshly, sarcastically. 'I don't know who you are,' he said. 'But Maseko is my father's name and I haven't given you permission to use it.'

He turned abruptly and walked away. Dinorego shuffled anxiously beside him. He kept glancing at Makhaya's face but could not understand his mood. It was tight and withdrawn.

'I am struck with pity for what has happened, my son,' he said. 'But you must keep calm. Some people say the chief has high blood pressure and will surely die of this ailment one day.'

Makhaya looked at the old man with a queer expression. 'The chief is not going to die of high blood pressure,' he said. 'I am going to kill him.'

And he said this with all the calm assurance of a fortune-teller making a prediction. Dinorego went ashen with shock.

'No,' he said sharply. 'You must never, never do that, my son.'

'But he is concentrating on killing someone,' Makhaya said. 'And he is doing this, not with guns or blows, but through the cruelty and cunning of his mind.'

Dinorego absorbed this rapidly. It had a strange ring of truth. The series of crises and upheavals in Golema Mmidi fully justified Makhaya's theory.

'Can't you concentrate too, son?' the old man said quickly. 'Can't you concentrate and be as clever as the next man?'

This quaint reply and the anxiety of the old man completely dashed away Makhaya's anger. He laughed but he also felt a twinge of remorse. Makhaya felt that anger had made him utter unduly harsh words to that other grinning, uncomfortable fellow who had run down the steps. Perhaps he was just another of those twopenny-ha'penny politicians who sprang up everywhere like mushrooms in Africa these days.

'Who is the other man?' he asked.

'His name is Joas Tsepe,' Dinorego said. 'He and the chief are acting like spies against the new government.'

'Is the new government popular?'

'Oh yes,' said Dinorego. 'It is very popular. People can vote for it for twenty years. Men like Joas do not speak the language of the people. Who can understand cheating and murder when such things are not the custom here? Some say the new government cannot improve people's lives because the leaders come from the chiefs. But we can wait and see, and if they are no good, one day we will chuck them out.'

They turned out of the circular clearing in the central part of the village and took the road that led back to the farm.

'What is the time, son?' Dinorego asked. 'I want to introduce you to my friend Mma-Millipede. She is anxious to meet you and cannot wait any longer.'

Makhaya looked at his watch. It was eight-fifteen. And there was a twenty-minute walk back to the farm. The old man shook his head.

'I cannot trust my friend Mma-Millipede,' he said. 'She will delay us.'

But Makhaya waved this aside. On the way to Chief Matenge, the old man had told him a very moving story about Mma-Millipede and the great tragedy in her life.

Mma-Millipede, he had said, had grown up side by side with him in a village in the northern part of Botswana. The mother of Mma-Millipede and his mother were such great friends that they privately arranged a marriage for their two children at some future date.

It so happened that while growing up Mma-Millipede became very interested in the Christian religion. On the surface this was not unusual. Women lived idly in the villages during the dry season while the men were busy the year round with the cattle. To fill in the dull round of the day, many women drifted to the church, where they were also able to obtain a bit of mission education. But in spite of the advantage they had over men educationally, few of the women developed a new personality. They remained their same old tribal selves, docile and inferior. Perhaps Mma-Millipede was one of those rare individuals with a distinct personality at birth. In any event, she was able to grasp the religion of the missionaries and use its message to adorn and enrich her own originality of thought and expand the natural kindness of her heart.

The family of Mma-Millipede was one of the poorest in the village. But the recognition Mma-Millipede had gained for her religious views soon brought her to the attention of the chiefs, in particular one named Ramogodi, a drunkard and dissipated boaster and the son of the reigning chief. It was Ramogodi's pride that he was sexually attractive to women. This was true. There

73

were few women in the village who had not been his bedmate at some time or other. But whenever he waylaid Mma-Millipede, she just stared at him, seriously. Thus, Mma-Millipede unconsciously challenged the pride of a vain man, and he became determined to have her as his wife.

His haughty mother approached Mma-Millipede's family. They refused to offer their daughter in marriage to a chief's son, fearing that she would be treated as a slave in the household. The haughty woman interpreted this refusal as an insult to the royal house and proceeded with plans to force the marriage.

She found out about the proposed marriage of Mma-Millipede to Dinorego and forced Dinorego's parents to arrange another bride for him with all speed. Thus, terrorized into submission, the family of Mma-Millipede had no choice but to allow their daughter to marry Ramogodi. There was only one child from the marriage, because Mma-Millipede and her religious ways soon bored Ramogodi. He was often away from home, making hay with his former sweethearts. Still, Mma-Millipede continued to live in his house as his wife and bring up their son.

After many years came trouble. The youngest brother of Ramogodi acquired a very beautiful wife, and Ramogodi took it into his head that he also desired the same woman. Things came to such a pass that Ramogodi's brother committed suicide by hanging himself. He left a note saying: 'I cannot stand the way my brother is carrying on with my wife.'

This made Ramogodi the most hated man in the village, but in spite of that, he divorced Mma-Millipede and within three months married his brother's wife. The son of Mma-Millipede had to be exiled to a far-off village because he could not be restrained from the urge to kill his father. The shock of it all almost deranged the mind of Mma-Millipede, and in an

74

effort to help her forget the past, Dinorego and his wife persuaded her to come and live with them in Golema Mmidi, where they had settled. A few years later Dinorego's wife died of heart trouble, but the long and close friendship between Dinorego and Mma-Millipede continued. Mma-Millipede had become a trader of all kinds, and she also purchased the skins of wild animals, which Dinorego made into mats and blankets.

As Dinorego and Makhaya approached the home of Mma-Millipede, which was not very far from the home of Dinorego, they turned off onto a small footpath that wound and curved its way into the bush. The sudden clearing revealed the identical pattern of mud huts perched on the edge of the land. The yard was crowded with children. There were a lot of goats, and Makhaya got the impression of goats and children rolling in the dust.

'The children belong to the families of Golema Mmidi,' Dinorego said, smiling. 'They are supposed to be out in the bush grazing the goats, but here they all are playing at the home of Mma-Millipede. I told her she will one day become bankrupt through having to feed all these children and goats, but she pays no attention.'

An old woman walked slowly across the yard in a forward-bending manner as though her back troubled her. She wore a very long dress and had a scarf tied round her head. The children set up a clamour when they saw Dinorego, and she swerved round in her walk.

'Batho!' she said, addressing Dinorego. 'But I say, you are about early today, my friend.'

'I have brought my son about whom we spoke the whole week,' he replied.

'Batho!' she said again.

She turned and looked at Makhaya, closely. There was something so lovely in the expression of habitual good humour and kindness in her face that it evoked a spontaneous smile in him. Once he got to know her well, he was to find that she often prefaced sentences with the word 'Batho,' which means, 'Oh, People,' and may be used to express either sympathy, joy, or surprise.

Whatever conclusions the old woman had come to through her inspection of Makhaya's face, she determined to keep them to herself and discuss them with the old man once Makhaya had left. To indicate this, she glanced meaningfully at Dinorego from under her eyes.

In reply Dinorego said, 'My son cannot stay long. He is just on his way to work.'

'Indeed! I am ashamed of you, my friend. What about the tea? There is always time for tea. Besides, I must gather some eggs to send to Gilbert. I was just about to feed the fowls.'

She pointed to a basket in her hand which was full of corn seed. This made Makhaya look towards the chicken house and recall the vivid words of the old man on their first day of meeting: 'If you have fifty-two fowls, you must build a coop fifteen feet by twenty-five feet ...' And indeed, the chicken house stretched the entire length of the yard. Three of its walls were built of a mixture of smoothed mud and bricks, while the front part was enclosed with chicken wire and had a small gate. Poles were spaced at neat intervals round the walls, over which was suspended a thatched roof. There were troughs for food and water and boxes for broody hens. Fat sleek fowls pecked in the dust.

A child emerged from one of the huts with a tea tray, and once they had seated themselves, Mma-Millipede wanted to know all sorts of little things about Makhaya. 'Do you eat well, my son?' she asked. 'Do you often get ill? If you get ill, please inform me so that I may accompany you to hospital as you are now far away from your home and relatives.' About all these small things she chattered in her kindly motherly way, and they seemed like mountains of affection to the lonely Makhaya. He noted how the old man nodded his head contentedly in this sun of kindness and how the goats kept frisking their short tails and raising their forelegs high in the air, pretending to crack each other's skulls in mock battles, while the children tumbled in the dust. He was a little repelled at first by the generosity of the strange old woman. It was too extreme. It meant that if you loved people you had to allow a complete invasion by them of your life, and he wasn't built to face invasions of any kind. And yet, this isolation he so treasured had often been painful, because he too felt this eternal human need to share the best and worst of life with another. Thus he looked at the old woman questioningly. He wanted a few simple answers on how to live well and sanely. He wanted to undo the complexity of hatred and humiliation that had dominated his life for so long. Perhaps, he thought, her life might provide him with a few clues.

Makhaya would have been amused at the chatter of the old people once he had left.

'I say, my friend,' Mma-Millipede burst out excitedly. 'The young man is too handsome. Can you imagine all the trouble if he is not of good character? I am even afraid to think of it.'

She was thinking of all the men who were away at the cattle posts and the mines and how Golema Mmidi was just a village of women for the greater part of the year.

'I was thinking that the young man would make a good husband for my daughter,' Dinorego said. 'What do you think, my friend?'

Mma-Millipede looked at her friend for some time. She had a lot of reservations about Maria. Even her shrewd eye had not succeeded in penetrating the barrier of aloofness and hostility that were a natural part of the young girl's personality. But she had long suspected that there was more than met the eye in the friendship between Maria and Gilbert. It had been of such a long duration that almost everyone had come to take it for granted, in particular her good friend. The only thing that prevented Mma-Millipede from voicing her suspicions to her friend was the fact that, to her, Gilbert was a foreign man, and foreign men were a fearful unpredictable quantity in an otherwise predictable world.

'I shall have a talk with the child, my friend,' she said at last. 'I shall try to find out for you what is on her mind.'

Back at the mansion, Matenge was reviewing the short interview he had had with Makhaya. He was reviewing it intensely, in a one-track way.

'So the refugee says he's not leaving,' and he said this over and over, staring sightlessly at the grinning Joas Tsepe. Tsepe, too, was still smarting under the rough snub given him by Makhaya. Joas was not the kind of man who could stop and examine himself. He could not see how unpleasant his too familiar manner was to other people, and he would never know that the inferiority complex, which was the driving force of his life, was also a dangerous little bully.

'I can sum up a man like that from a mile, Chief,' he said. 'He's a traitor to the African cause.'

Eventually, Matenge's one-track sentence drove him to his car and to the office of Inspector George Appleby-Smith.

'The refugee says he's not going,' he said, looking down into the expressionless face of the police officer. 'I have made an ultimatum. I want him removed because he is a dangerous criminal who is using the farm as his hideaway. No one is safe in my village. I don't see how the authorities can allow him to remain there.'

'I quite get your point, Chief Matenge,' the officer said. 'The only thing is that the matter is no longer in my hands. It is now the responsibility of the chief immigration officer, Major Ross. He has promised me he will make a decision concerning Mr Maseko in one week's time.'

After Matenge had walked out, George Appleby-Smith remained staring at the wall ahead of him for a long time. He had not so very long ago been on the phone with Major Ross, had 'stuck his neck out', as he said he would, and been assured that Makhaya would be granted a residence permit in one week. His assistant-in-command of the station entered and had to click his heels several times before he gained the attention of his superior. George Appleby-Smith looked at him with laughter-filled eyes.

'Sergeant Molefe,' he said. 'Tell me why I hate people?'

The sergeant remained stiffly at attention. He was used to the oddities of George Appleby-Smith. 'I think you only hate people when you have a headache, sir,' he said.

Once the week was up, Matenge took it upon himself to drive the three hundred miles down to immigration headquarters, perhaps hoping to influence the decision concerning Makhaya's removal. He knew everything was on his side. Political refugees were never allowed permanent residence in Botswana, and it did not take too many complaints to engineer their removal.

But the major hemmed and hawed a bit and made a show of looking through a file, then dropped a bombshell.

'Makhaya Maseko,' he said. 'Ah . . . let me see. Here it is. We

79

found out that he qualified for residence and granted him a residence permit yesterday. It is already on its way to him.'

That inner howling devil once more retreated. Matenge walked out crumpled, and each time he faced a defeat his eyes would get a peculiar hollow look in them and he would quicken his pace in walking. Particularly someone in a superior position to him could make him crumple this way. On this occasion, the shock was accompanied by fear. He felt his position threatened, and he felt that the threat to his position was his association with Joas Tsepe. He felt that the granting of the residence permit to a refugee was to spite him for his association with Joas. He determined to rid himself of the company of Joas Tsepe. Fortunately for Joas Tsepe, his political party just at this time sent him away for six months on an important 'mission'.

In the meanwhile, shortly after his failure to banish Makhaya, Matenge was struck down with a severe attack of high blood pressure. He was in hospital for one month, and during this one month a number of rapid changes took place in Golema Mmidi and at the farm.

CHAPTER SIX

One might go so far as to say that it is strong, dominating personalities who play a decisive role when things are changing. Somehow they always manage to speak with the voice of authority, and their innate strength of character drives them to take the lead in almost any situation. Allied to all this is their boundless optimism and faith in their fellow men. One such personality in the village of Golema Mmidi was Dinorego, and it was his support of and belief in Gilbert that swayed the villagers over to a support of the cattle co-operative. Another such personality was Paulina Sebeso, who was to bring the women of the village to the farm and help open up the way for new agricultural developments in Golema Mmidi.

Paulina Sebeso was quite a newcomer to the village, having lived there for not more than a year and a half by the time Makhaya arrived. She came from the northern part of Botswana, which fact immediately ensured her the friendship of Dinorego and Mma-Millipede. Northerners really pride themselves on being inexplicable to the rest of the country. They speak Tswana at a faster, almost unintelligible pace and have added so much variety to the Tswana language as to seem to an outsider to be speaking a completely foreign tongue. Thus, when northerners greet each other they say: Good-day, branch-of-my-tree; while everyone else simply says: Good-day, friend.

The implication in the greeting, branch-of-my-tree, was a rather true one for northerners. At one time they had been the most closely knit of all the tribal groupings, each one claiming at least a distant relationship to even the most insignificant member of the clan. But, once the family structure began breaking down under the migratory labour system, it was they who most readily practised intermarriage with foreigners.

Unfortunately for Paulina Sebeso, she married, at the age of eighteen, a foreign man from Rhodesia whose tribal tradition it was to commit suicide when his honour was at stake. It wasn't a remarkable marriage and her husband wasn't a remarkable man, being rather of a mild, passive, stay-at-home temperament. He worked as a bookkeeper for a certain large company, for which he received a wage of thirty pounds a month. By careful saving he managed to build a two-room brick house for his family, and also every year added a heifer or two to their stock of cattle. He had worked for the company for sixteen years when a new manager was appointed. Before long the new manager claimed that two thousand pounds had been embezzled. He also produced evidence that a number of receipt books were missing. The only people who handled both the money and the books were Paulina's husband and the manager. There was a doubt. On the one hand, the company believed the claim of Paulina's husband that he was innocent of the crime. He had worked for them for a long time, was known to be of sober habits and the sum stolen was too large an amount to have been stolen by an African man. Petty pilfering had occurred here and there but never vast sums. On the other hand, the receipt books had been removed in such a skilful manner as to suggest that the embezzling had taken place over a number of years.

In the end the company charged both Paulina's husband and the new manager with the theft. On the day he was notified of this, Paulina's husband awoke in the night and hanged himself from a tree in the yard. He left a note, once again claiming innocence. The company, being anxious to regain its money, dropped the court case and immediately seized the property of the dead man, claiming that the suicide was in fact an admission of guilt. Thus, being dispossessed of a home almost overnight, Paulina moved, with a son aged ten and a daughter aged eight, to the village of Golema Mmidi. The son, named Isaac, lived at a cattle post twenty-five miles away, herding his mother's cattle, while Paulina and the small girl remained in the village to grow crops. The eight-year-old girl, named Lorato, was thus able for most of the year to attend the village primary school, while the boy, Isaac, was tied to the cattle post and received no education at all.

Perhaps Paulina was not a very beautiful woman. She was tall, thin and angular, with a thin, angular face. She was also flat-chested and like all flat-chested women, this was a sore point with her. It was hard to find a suitable stuffed-up breast bodice in a country like Botswana, especially if you have to live in the bush, so she was in the habit of stuffing hers with carefully crumpled bits of paper. But she had lovely big black eyes that stared at everything in a bold way, and her long straight black legs were the most beautiful legs in the village. She had a decisive way of walking as though she always knew where she was going and what she wanted. She was fond of gaudy-hued skirts with strong colours like orange and yellow and red, and the bigger and brighter the splashes of colour, the more she liked them.

Since she was not by temperament given to brooding on the past, she soon recovered from the tragedy in her life and set out to build up a new life in Golema Mmidi. Part of her plans also included a man, as she was a passionate and impetuous woman with a warm heart. It never really mattered what kind of man he was or the magnitude of his faults and failings. It was just enough that her feelings be aroused and everything would be swallowed up in a blinding sun of devotion and loyalty. Of course, if she were to find a man who accidentally managed to gain the respect of the whole world at the same time, then this loved one could magically become ten thousand blazing suns.

She had her land and home not far from the farm gates. There, directly in the path of the setting sun, Makhaya was in the habit of coming to watch the sunset. Just as at dawn, the sun crept along the ground in gold shafts; so at sundown it retreated quietly as though it were folding into itself the long brilliant fingers of light. As he watched it all in fascination, the pitch black shadows of night seemed to sweep across the land like an engulfing wave. One minute the sun was there, and the next minute it had dropped down behind the flat horizon, plunging everything into darkness. On intensely cold nights, it threw up a translucent yellow afterglow, full of sparkling crystals, but otherwise it puffed itself out into a thin strip of red light on the horizon. As his eyes became more and more accustomed to the peculiar beauty of Botswana sunsets, he also noticed that the dull green thornbush and the dull brown earth were transformed into autumn shades of warm brown, red, and yellow hues by the setting sun.

One evening, Makhaya walked right into a great drama. The thornbush was seeding and it did this in a vigorous way. One spray of seed struck him on the cheek, and on a closer inspection, he noticed that all the branches were profusely covered with beanlike pods. These pods twined tightly inward until they were coiled springs. Once the pod burst, the spring ejected the seeds high into the air. He stretched out his hand, broke off a pod and pressed it open. A few minute kidney-bean-shaped seeds slithered onto his palm. He stared at them in amazement. Could this rough, tough little thornbush be a relative of the garden bean? He decided to take the seeds back to the farm and question Gilbert.

Paulina, meanwhile, had watched these comings and goings at sundown with avid curiosity and at last, being unable to contain it, had sent the little girl to Makhaya with a message. This particular evening Makhaya stood just a stone's throw away from her yard, and being absorbed as he was in the popping, spraying drama around him, he did not at first notice the child standing near him. And even when he did, he looked down rather absent-mindedly into a pair of small beady black eyes.

'Sir,' the child said. 'My mother says she sends you her greetings.'

'Who is your mother?' he asked.

The child pointed in the direction of the huts. Makhaya glanced up briefly, was struck in the eye by a vivid sunset skirt of bright orange and yellow flowers and momentarily captivated by a pair of large bold black eyes. He looked down at the child and sent back a cruel message.

'Go and tell your mother I don't know her,' he said.

He turned and, without looking either left or right, walked back to the farm. Paulina, on receiving his message, flamed with confusion and humiliation. So distressed was she that she rushed over to her friend Mma-Millipede.

'Mama,' she said. 'I've made a terrible blunder.'

And, half-hiding her face in her hands, she explained her blunder.

'You've done nothing wrong, my child,' Mma-Millipede said, calmly. 'It's just that Makhaya is a foreign man and not accustomed to our ways. The women of his country might have an entirely different approach when they wish to arouse the interest of a man.'

Paulina sat in thoughtful silence for a while. As far as she was concerned, there was only one woman equal to her in the whole village.

'Perhaps he is attracted to Maria,' she said, and it nearly killed her to utter these words.

Mma-Millipede hesitated. The old man, Dinorego, had remarked that very day that Maria no longer attended her English lessons. These used to take place at just about sunset and last for an hour each evening. But now, for the last three days, Maria had sat at home by the fire instead of going to the farm as she usually did. Mma-Millipede was hesitant to impart this information to Paulina, as already she looked the picture of despair.

'Look here, my child,' she said, firmly. 'The man is a newcomer and you can't go jumping to conclusions. Besides, I suspect that Maria has long been in love with Gilbert, only you are not to spread this about.'

These words prevented Paulina from giving way completely to despair. She even gossiped quite gaily with Mma-Millipede about trifling matters, then a short while later arose and left for her own home. But Paulina's revelations of her interest in Makhaya caused Mma-Millipede a few hours of anxious thought. Mma-Millipede was of the old school, among whom, to a certain extent, foreigners were still taboo. Also, her experience of men had been a very limited and disastrous one. Most of all she feared that another tragedy would be too much for her impetuous young friend.

'I hope Makhaya is a good man,' she said over and over to herself.

Just at this time, Makhaya was trying to avoid a situation at the farm that both exasperated and amused him. To Gilbert, agriculture was a vast, rambling, intricate subject. The slope of the land and even the stones that lay on that land would spark off a thousand speculations in his mind, and there were so few good listeners in the world that Makhaya found himself trapped and almost forced to listen to long discussions on the marvels and wonders of the earth. Not that Makhaya minded. It was a welcome change to be hearing about these things. There was much more than South Africa that he was running away from, and it included everything that he felt was keeping the continent of Africa at a standstill. On the one hand, you felt yourself the persecuted man, and on the other, you so easily fell prey to all the hate-making political ideologies, which seemed to him to be the order of the day. Yet these hate-making ideologies in turn gave rise to a whole new set of retrogressive ideas and retrogressive pride, and it was almost a mania to think that the whole world was against you. And how many pompous, bombastic fools had not jumped on this bandwagon? Yet the very real misery was still there. No matter what kind of fool you made of yourself, people in southern Africa were still oppressed.

At some stage, and in an effort to solve his own dilemma, he decided to strike out on his own. He saw this mass of suffering mankind of which he was a part, but he also saw himself as a separate particle, too, and as time went on he began to stress his own separateness, taking this as a guide that would lead him to clarity of thought in all the confusion. It was rare. It was an uphill task in a part of the world where everyone tended to cling to his or her precious prejudice and tradition, and the act of letting go of it all greatly increased a man's foes. You find yourself throwing blows but weeping at the same time, because of all the people who sit and wail in the darkness, and because of all the fat smug persecutors to whom this wailing is like sweet music, and some inner voice keeps on telling you that your way is right for you, that the process of rising up from the darkness is an intensely personal and private one, and that if you can find a society that leaves the individual to develop freely you ought to choose that society as your home. Makhaya had made the first move along this road but at the same time he was often stricken with guilt. If Joas Tsepe had called him to his face, 'a traitor to the African cause', he would have agreed in his heart because he threw most of his blows at Africa and had done so for a long time. Thus when Makhaya met Gilbert, he was almost a drowning man, and this world of facts and scientific speculation seemed so much easier to handle. Therefore Makhaya turned to agriculture for his salvation, and also to Gilbert. And he did this in guilt and fear of his intuitions because they seemed to him to lack any practical solutions as to why so many people could be persecuted by so few and why so many starved while a few had more than they could eat.

Gilbert was a complete contrast to this wavering, ambiguous world in which Makhaya lived. He was first and foremost a practical, down-to-earth kind of man, intent only on being of useful service to his fellow men. There was nothing fanciful in him, yet the workings of his mind often confused and fascinated Makhaya. It was like one gigantic storage house of facts and figures and plans and intuitive judgments and impressions. The wheels kept on turning at such a fast pace that Makhaya never ceased to be amazed at the way Gilbert always spoke in a calm, almost soft tone, while the loud humming of these wheels was almost audible. Gilbert's mind was also like a stop watch. He could abruptly break off a conversation and, ten hours later, pick it up at the exact same point where he had left off. Gilbert prided himself on being an unusually well-informed man. No doubt the sun did too. No doubt the sun knew why the clouds formed and why the wind blew and why the lizards basked in its warmth, and all this immense knowledge made the sun gay and bright, full of trust and affection for mankind. But there were shut-away worlds where the sunlight never penetrated, haunted worlds, full of mistrust and hate, and it was about this side of life that Makhaya was particularly well informed. This sharp contrast in outlook called for a compromise, and Makhaya debated awhile and then gave way. Although manly and independent-minded enough, he found it necessary to say 'yes' or merely listen on far too many occasions, and he consoled himself with the thought that he had a lot to learn. In any case, Gilbert's company and friendship disturbed him far less than most people's did, although Gilbert's views on African and world politics were extremely naïve and childlike.

Since poverty was so much a part of his work, Gilbert was fond of expounding on what the British socialists and the trade union movement had done to alleviate the atrocious living and working conditions of the poor. He several times mentioned his uneasy suspicions of the new Botswana government with its debates on democracy and a tax system that too eagerly encouraged private enterprise.

'Where is all this talk of democracy going to get us, Mack?' he said one day, glumly. 'Only a reasonably developed country can afford the time to debate these pros and cons. What we need here is a dictatorship that will feed, clothe and educate a people. I could work well with a dictatorship which says, "Look here, Gilbert, fill in this poverty programme."'

He looked at Makhaya, half laughing, half in deep earnest. Makhaya returned an almost hostile look. Not any politics in the world meant anything to him as a stateless person, and every political discussion was a mockery, he felt, of his own helplessness. Since he kept so silent, it forced Gilbert to add, apologetically:

'I'm not saying that the dictator should stay there, forever, Mack. He must eventually give way to the democracy. But in my opinion a dictatorship is the best method for governing a country like this. What do you think?'

Makhaya nearly laughed out loud. Gilbert's statements were an explanation of his own personality. He was a man only impressed by results, and he had been unable to produce these in Botswana the way agricultural experts had produced them in Russia and China. Makhaya wanted to put forward the idea that certain types of socialism might not be suited to African development. Africa had a small population, and it might well be that socialism of every kind was an expedient to solve unwieldy population problems. But his mind swerved away from even this. If a man talked about governments and political systems, he'd soon want to be a part of the whole rotten crew. He preferred to live in the bush.

'Why not leave this country, even Africa, to trial and error?' he said slowly, uncomfortably. 'This is only my opinion. I don't think I approve of dictatorships in any form, whether for the good of mankind or not. Even if it is painstakingly slow, I prefer a democracy for Africa, come what may.'

Whether this was a satisfactory remark or not, Gilbert never referred to politics again. Makhaya did not care because, more than anything, he hated politics. Perhaps people could be fed after all, and once it came to the time when a man had to die, he might be more proud to count up the number of his fellow men he had helped to live, rather than the number he had bombed into oblivion.

It was this private anxiety to put his life to a useful purpose that made Makhaya an amenable listener to the long agricultural discussions, and since Gilbert had at last found a potential convert to his faith, he often pressed Makhaya into having supper with him. The food was quite often cooked by Maria, who had always been Gilbert's companion at this hour because of the Tswana and English lessons. On the two occasions Makhaya had been present, he had not failed to notice, with his sensitivity to atmosphere, that his presence was deeply resented by Maria, worse still since Gilbert absent-mindedly talked agriculture, overlooking her, whereas at this time the hour was usually spent in loud chatter, arguments and laughter. Makhaya could quite clearly hear these friendly exchanges as his hut was very near Gilbert's. They pleased and surprised him, and he came to the conclusion that the aloof Maria had put a great deal of effort into the friendship. To no one else did she condescend to laugh and talk in such a gay, free manner. He understood her temperament, it being very much like his own, and he immediately interpreted the hostility as an inability to admit a stranger into a close relationship. It was this that made Makhaya take walks out into the sunset. But there was also a wide streak of unselfishness in Maria, and she in turn made an elaborate gesture of staying away. It only confused matters and exasperated Makhaya because, for almost three nights after that, Gilbert kept breaking off in the middle of a conversation to say:

'I wonder why Maria isn't coming around anymore?'

And then he'd stare at Makhaya as though Makhaya had something to do with it.

On the evening that Makhaya brought back the thornbush seeds, everything came to a head. Makhaya found Gilbert and Pelotona, the permit man, seated around a log fire near Gilbert's hut. He joined them, and for a time the discussion was about salt licks, bonemeal, and fodder which were needed at the cattle ranch. Pelotona lived in a hut on the ranch, and for a year had managed both the ranch and cattle co-operative, being assisted by Gilbert only on cattle-trucking days. After a while, Pelotona stood up and left for his home on the ranch.

Noting that Gilbert's mood was silent, reserved and aloof, Makhaya referred to the seeds which he still held in his hand. Gilbert took them and immediately brightened.

'You know,' he said, 'I noticed the very same thing. I looked it up and found out that the thornbush is an acacia, a branch of the legumes, which includes peas and beans . . .'

And he had that expression on his face when he was about to launch out into the miracles and wonders of nature, but suddenly he broke off and slipped back into a mood of intense, reserved silence. He stared at Makhaya for a while and then said:

'I hope you don't love Maria, too.'

So that's what it all came to, Makhaya thought, and smiled. And he just sat there in the shadowy light of the fire and maintained a deliberate silence. It was all none of his business, and he was experienced enough to know that people who reach a deadlock in their emotional relationships often blame this on others. Gilbert simply misinterpreted this silence and stood up abruptly and walked into his hut. Makhaya did the same, with the only exception that Makhaya was at peace in his mind and hugely enjoying himself. He lit a lamp and picked up a book and then lay full length down on the bed to read. Gilbert paced about in his hut for a bit. He was disturbed and unaccountably angry with someone, but his mind refused to acknowledge who it was. After a time he put on a thick blue jersey and walked down to the home of Dinorego.

He found the old man and Maria seated near an outdoor fire. They both looked up at his approach and then maintained an alarmed silence, as they could both see that something was wrong. It wasn't the same Gilbert with that rushing expression of joy on his face, and he walked slowly with his arms folded across his chest. He deliberately ignored Maria and greeted the old man in a quiet voice.

Maria stood up and said in a slightly trembling voice, 'Would you like some tea, Gilbert?'

He did not reply but she rushed away into one of the huts merely to get away from this nervous atmosphere and then stood there, trembling from head to foot, unable to reach out for a cup and saucer.

The old man looked at Gilbert solicitously. Whatever was wrong, he was not prepared to go into a panic until he had heard the worst. Dinorego had great faith in his own reasoning ability. It was always there, at the forefront, like a cool waterfall on his thoughts. Gilbert sat down and continued his intense staring into the fire. Eventually the old man said, 'What's the trouble, son?'

Gilbert raised his head and looked at the old man. 'I'm going to marry your daughter,' he said, quietly.

For once, Dinorego was completely deprived of his speech. Not only that, his ready wit and sound moralizing on every event also deserted him.

'Do you have any objections?' Gilbert persisted, since the old man just stared at him.

'I am trying to put my thoughts together, son,' Dinorego said at last. He had expected to hear a forecast about the drought, or that all the farm machinery had broken down, and just right now all that familiar side of Gilbert had been replaced by a man he hardly knew. He looked for a crutch and called out to his daughter. She appeared like a swift shadow and stood just outside the circle of light.

'Do you hear what Gilbert says?' he said. 'Gilbert says he is going to marry you. Are you agreeable?'

'Yes, Papa,' she said.

The world righted itself a bit.

'And when do you intend this marriage to take place, my son?' the old man asked, kindly.

'Tomorrow,' Gilbert said.

Dinorego raised his hands in the air, as though saying that the whole business was a bit too much for him.

'As you can see, I am very pleased, my son,' he said. 'Only . . .' and he turned to Maria. 'My child, you must go to Mma-Millipede at once. She will know what to do about the marriage which is to take place tomorrow.'

Gilbert stood up and accompanied Maria for a short while along the dark footpath. From where he sat, the old man heard shouts of laughter and arguments, and he sat there smiling to himself, contemplating the mystery of youth. He had never seen any other man survive so much frustration, difficulties and trouble as Gilbert had, and here he was preparing to rush into more. And Gilbert, once Maria had left him, stood at the crossroads near the farm and looked up at the stars and laughed. If the old man really knew, Gilbert's life was simple and uncomplicated. Life to him meant love and work. It meant getting out of the rut and the habitual way of doing things. It was like all the rivers and sunsets and the fish in the rivers and the trees and pathways and sun and wind. But most of all it was work. Because lack of work meant death. And while he thought of all these things, Gilbert's mind was once more recalled to the workaday world. Those trees – he had forgotten to enlighten Makhaya on the full meaning of the life of the thorn scrub. He turned and swung his way back to the farm.

The lamp still burned in Makhaya's hut and Gilbert knocked

and, without waiting for a reply, pushed the door open and walked in. Makhaya balanced the book on his chest, glanced up briefly and noticed the excitement that shone in his friend's eyes. This friend grabbed a chair, sat down and took up the conversation at the point where it had been abruptly broken off.

'The thornbush is most definitely an acacia, Mack,' he said. 'Now, the twining around of the seed-pod is a device for ejecting the seeds when they are ripe, so that they will be flung away from the parent plant. This also explains why the thornbush is able to encroach so rapidly on cultivated land. It's the toughest little plant I know, but the goats are browsing it to death. Did you know that goats are natural browsers?'

'No,' said Makhaya, smiling inwardly.

'Goats prefer shrubs to grass, however lush and sweet,' he said. 'But they will eat grass when it is in seed. Much of northern Africa is desert today because the goats destroyed the thornbush. I've nothing against the goats, you know. Without their meat and milk we'd all starve in Golema Mmidi, but we'll have to do something about controlling their eating habits, one of these days.'

Gilbert sat for a moment in deep thought, no doubt trying to invent new eating habits for the goats, but there was too much he had to keep a tab on tonight. His own emotional life kept intruding into his scientific speculations, and he suspected himself of having committed some grievous crime. It was unthinkable that he had precipitated himself into marriage through jealousy of Makhaya, and he was trying to work around this thought before springing the surprise.

'You know,' he said, in a burst of generosity, 'I'd meant to tell you this some time ago, Mack. You're Kipling's "Thousandth Man". Do you know the poem?'

'No,' Makhaya said again, and it was an effort for him to control his laughter. He felt he knew what was coming next.

'Somehow I knew this the day you stepped into Golema Mmidi,' Gilbert said. 'And it's just today that everything's clear to me . . .'

He quoted a few lines from the poem:

'One man in a thousand, Solomon says,
Will stick more close than a brother.
And it's worth while seeking him half your days
If you find him before the other.'

But Makhaya had a few reservations about Mr Kipling's sweeping statements. It was just chance that had brought him to Golema Mmidi, and it was only chance and luck that operated in his destiny.

'I suppose you mean by that that you're no longer mad at me,' he observed, dryly. 'You nearly bit my head off not so long ago.'

'It's not you I was mad at, Mack,' Gilbert said. 'It was Maria. You've no idea how she's made me run in circles for three years. Now it's all ended so easily, I can't believe it myself. I don't know why I never thought of going to Dinorego in the first place. You know what he said: "Do you hear, Maria? Gilbert says he's going to marry you. Do you agree?" And all she said was, "Yes, Papa." Just that, after saying a thousand different things to me. So, I thought she'd change her mind and I said we'd get married tomorrow.'

By this time, Maria had already reached the home of Mma-Millipede. She found her alone, reading the Tswana version of the Bible.

She was a little apprehensive as the door was pushed open and Maria stepped in, especially as a visit from Maria was rare, and then the child just stood there, a little breathless, flustered and tongue-tied.

'Batho! What's the matter, my child?' she asked anxiously.

'Papa sent me to tell you I am to marry Gilbert tomorrow.'

'But why the haste?' said Mma-Millipede, quite taken aback.

Maria sat down. 'There's no haste, Mama,' she said, in her earnest way. 'It's I who have delayed matters. Gilbert has asked me to marry him for three years.'

'Does Papa agree?' the old woman asked.

Maria nodded and Mma-Millipede smiled inwardly, pleased that all her conjectures were at last confirmed. But curiosity overcame her and she said, 'Three years is a long time to delay a marriage, my child. Gilbert might have become impatient and run away to England; then not only would you have lost him, but we too.'

Maria stared at the old woman with small withdrawn eyes and shook her head a little helplessly. How could Mma-Millipede expect to understand all the complications of life? She placed one small straight hand on the table, a way she had of showing that sentiment should always be separated from facts.

'Gilbert is a man with many strange ways,' she said crisply. 'A person has to get used to these strange ways. For some time now he has kept a lizard in the house whom he treats as a person and which is now accustomed to being spoken to like a person. Its name is Skin. Each night it is put down beside the lamp to have a meal off the insects that gather there. Also, I have often seen it asleep on the pillow, like a child, with its legs spread out. Gilbert does not live in this world but in some world about which I know nothing.'

Mma-Millipede nodded her head slowly, with an expression on her face which clearly said: Oh, People, is that what foreign men are like?

'Are you sure you want to marry, my child?' she asked, kindly.

The young girl shrugged, helplessly. 'I don't know my own mind, Mama,' she said, in despair. 'I don't know what I want. You must help me.'

'But you help yourself with your understanding, my child,' the old woman said. 'As you know, we all live in a world that is full of danger. If a person cannot see this, he must be protected from the danger.'

Maria stared meditatively at the table. 'I thought so too, Mama,' she said slowly. 'I don't care about myself, but nothing must harm Gilbert.'

These words suddenly relieved Mma-Millipede of the burden of sentiment that was clouding her practical mind.

'There is so much to do,' she said. 'And so little time. We have to give a party. How often is there a wedding? Once in a blue moon. More likely it is death or ailments that bring people together. Two or three goats will have to be slaughtered and some chickens for high diet. I am out of rice. Has Papa any rice?'

'We have plenty, Mama,' the young girl said.

'And what about a pretty dress in which to get married?' Mma-Millipede said. 'Never mind, we shall buy it tomorrow.'

She sat for a moment, ticking off the items in her mind. The goats would have to be slaughtered early in the morning and then hung up to drain. No doubt she would have to accompany her old friend to the wedding ceremony, and there was only one other woman in the village capable of managing the party arrangements while she was away – Paulina Sebeso. She stood up, searched for an old jacket, and, accompanied by Maria, walked to the home of her friend, Paulina.

They passed the farm and the lamp still burned in Makhaya's hut, and the two men still chatted like ancient blood brothers. They passed another home, where the old man sat, staring pensively into the fire, contemplating the twists and turns of a long life which might end any day now, he thought, since his last and youngest child was about to marry. But if Dinorego thought about death near his softly glowing fire, Paulina Sebeso thought about life and how to have it more abundantly. And the bright crackling flames of her fire danced upward into the black sky. She sprang to her feet as the old woman and the young woman approached.

'I have a surprise,' Mma-Millipede said.

And once she heard what it was, Paulina Sebeso turned round and too vigorously pushed a log into the fire. She did this to cover up her confusion, and the disturbed fire sent sparks in all directions. Paulina was unashamedly joyful that a stroke of luck had removed her deadliest competitor.

CHAPTER SEVEN

Early the next morning, at the home of Mma-Millipede, bedlam reigned. The women of the village were there, and two goats, slaughtered and skinned, hung up by the feet from a tree to drain off the excess blood. Until the blood flowed down to a trickle, there was nothing much for the women to do except stand as close to each other as possible and create the most ear-splitting din. This whole process is sometimes known as talking, but it has been said that it is only Basotho women who out-match Batswana women at this art; that is, you stand about a foot away from your companion, heave up your chest, puff up the side veins of the neck and then let all you have inside you come out, full blast. Somehow you laugh at the same time, and unusual this sound is too, as though all the glass in the world were being hurled into a deep pit and shrieking in agony. This noise attracted all the goats in the village to the home of Mma-Millipede, for they knew from long experience that it was the signal for a thousand potato peels to fall on the ground. They added to the din by fighting, pushing and bleating for the best positions. And, of course, Botswana is one of the greatest tea-drinking countries in the world, so that the clatter of over a hundred teacups added the final touch to the shattering symphony.

Everyone had brought along a little something to put into the pot. Mostly it was potatoes, and these little gifts were tied up in gay blue, red and yellow checkered cloths and hung from the waists of the women, and these checkered splashes of colour swayed about as they talked. At a sign from Paulina, an abrupt and deathly silence fell on the gathering. A few women moved forward and sliced out the hard fat that had surrounded the intestines of the animals and which, when heated, melted down into oil. This fat was divided into equal portions and placed in two large iron pots which stood near the fire. On top of this fat they poured small packets of curry powder. Another group of women advanced on the slaughtered goats and, within a short space of time, sliced away all the meat, leaving behind the bony skeleton. The meat, fat, and curry powder then boiled away in big pots. Everyone moved over to small wooden tables, on the top of each of which was placed a basin containing water; and then, with strained, absorbed faces, the women peeled the potatoes, tossing them one by one into the basins. Even the goats quietened down, absorbed in munching the peels with their small dainty mouths.

A shrill high-pitched voice, the owner of which was carefully submerged in the group, broke the silence. 'I am wondering about the foreigner who has recently come to the farm,' it said.

Since everyone had been wondering too, everyone kept quiet.

'Who knows if he is married?' the shrill voice persisted.

'Why don't you direct your questions to Paulina Sebeso?' a voice at the farthest end of the crowd shouted, and then, with a hint of sarcasm, added, 'After all, she's the big brains around here.'

Everyone turned and stared at Paulina. She had caught the slight edge of sarcasm and was angry. Yet she remained calm.

'I know nothing,' she said, in a deliberately flat voice.

'But you have eyes, Paulina Sebeso,' the sarcastic one continued. 'You must have noticed that the foreigner is very handsome.'

Paulina turned and stared at her tormentor. The owner of the sarcastic voice was Grace Sebina, a rough, wild, promiscuous woman. They had been at loggerheads for some time.

'If your eyes chase all the men, Grace Sebina,' she said crisply, 'please don't put them on me.'

All the women stared at each other in shock. It wasn't polite to call a prostitute a prostitute in black and white terms.

'You don't have to be so rude, Paulina Sebeso,' one of the older women said, reprovingly. 'Grace Sebina is portraying our own thoughts. We all think the foreigner is handsome. We only want to know if you think the same.'

Paulina stood there and bit on her tongue, too late, while they all stared at her innocently. It was bait-talk. It had been planned. They all had permanent lovers or husbands while Paulina Sebeso had none, and even a tradition was forming about her. A few men had said she was too bossy. Then they all said it, overlooking the fact that they were wilting, effeminate shadows of men who really feared women. Things went along smoothly as long as all the women pretended to be inferior to this spineless species. The women had been lying to themselves for so long in their sexual frustration that they would not admit the real reason why Paulina dominated them all was because she was the kind of woman who could not lie to men. They followed the leadership of Paulina because she was so daring and different. It would have upset their world to have Paulina find a man she could get along with. They were determined to keep her trapped in a frustration far greater than their own. In fact, on several occasions, this powerful little clique had stepped in and with a few poisonous, cunning words destroyed tentative friendships. The innocent glances were therefore a challenge. Would she make a bid for the foreigner? And if so, was she prepared to face the consequences?

Paulina turned and stirred one of the pots with a big wooden stick. It wasn't the women and their intrigues she feared but the untrustworthiness of men with no strength or moral values. It was as though a whole society had connived at producing a race of degenerate men by stressing their superiority in the law and overlooking how it affected them as individuals. These things Paulina felt intuitively, but had not thought out in a coherent form. Strangely enough, she now began to look with hope upon the event of the previous evening, when Makhaya had spurned her gesture of friendship. If he had walked straight into her yard on her invitation, she reasoned, might he not too have walked into every other woman's yard?

So when the older, reproving woman said, 'We see, Paulina Sebeso, you have no words to defend yourself?' she turned round and smiled.

'What can I say, Mama,' she said. 'I have seen the foreigner about in the village. It seems to me he has big ears, and I don't see how a man with such big ears can be handsome.'

The women turned and looked at each other with meaningful glances as much as to say: We are not so easily fooled by you, Paulina Sebeso.

Paulina was not like the women of Golema Mmidi, although she had been born into their kind of world and fed on the same diet of thin maize porridge by a meek, repressed, dull-eyed mother. But even as a small child she kept on putting her nose into everything. 'What's this, Mama?' she'd say, with a face screwed up with fun and mischief. She was so lively and med-dlesome that her mother constantly kept a little switch nearby, and it was quite a common sight in her village to see Paulina racing through the thornbush with her mother hard on her heels, waving the switch. Because of this early practice, once she attended school she became one of the fastest runners on sports competition days. Her athletic ability had ensured her more education than most of the women in the village, and it was only the prospect of a secure and stable marriage that had made her discontinue attending school. But throughout her life she had retained her fresh, lively curiosity and ability to enter an adventure, head first. It was all this that really distinguished her from the rest of the women, even though her circumstances and upbringing were no different from theirs.

She had travelled a longer way, too, on the road of life, as unexpected suffering always makes a human being do, and yet her thoughts were as uncertain and intangible as the blue smoke of the fires which unfurled into the still winter air and disappeared like vapour. Caught up in this pensive mood, she hardly saw basin after basin of potatoes being pitched into the huge pots, yet she continued to stir the food with quick vigor-ous thrusts of the wooden spoon, and she hardly heard the women chattering about the marriage ceremony, which was taking place at that moment in the untidy office of George Appleby-Smith. (George, like the women, felt it to be an ordi-nary and natural outcome of events, because everything the unusual Gilbert did seemed to be harmonious and acceptable like the sunrise and sunsets. George had only added a little drama and humour of his own. His office had not been swept out for some days, and he had kept the wedding party waiting while, with a straight expressionless face, he swept the room out.)

'I say, Paulina Sebeso,' one of the women said, 'you're letting the chickens burn.'

Paulina started and poured a little water into a smaller pot in which two chickens were roasting in their own fat, and for a time, the chatter of the women imposed itself on the tangled wisps of her thoughts . . .

'But I must say the daughter of Dinorego is a lucky devil,' someone said enviously. 'From now on she will live in comfort, as white men know how to make money, not like our men, who don't like work.'

'Do you suppose she had this comfort foremost in mind?' someone else asked.

'You can't tell with Maria,' the other replied. 'She's too clever.'

Since Paulina also shared this envy of Maria's strange, unfathomable personality and was guilty about it, she turned on the speakers, wrathfully, 'I don't like people to discuss a person who is not present.'

'Goodness! Paulina Sebeso,' one of the speakers said with an injured air. 'You are in a cross mood today. Are you perhaps pregnant?'

But Paulina's reply was drowned in shrieks of laughter, and even Paulina stood there laughing in confusion at herself. Many strange moods possessed her this day, as though, through some premonition, she was being warned that her whole way of life was about to change.

The change itself was to be a devious, subtle one, the threads of which were woven by three people who were to walk into the yard a few hours later: Gilbert, Mma-Millipede, and Makhaya. Of the three it was only Makhaya who was vitally necessary to her existence. Mma-Millipede's spur-of-the-moment wedding party for everyone drew together the first few strands, which in turn were to draw in hundreds of other strands, affecting the whole future pattern of life in Golema Mmidi. But it was all in the air that day and was in part responsible for Paulina's changeable moods, her pensiveness and unfamiliar uncertainty. She was relieved, therefore, when at noon she stepped back from the cooking pots and seated herself on a stool in the shadow of a hut. A group of women, who had been idle, stepped up to the pots, getting ready to supervise the dishing up of the food when the wedding party returned.

Shortly after this, the five farm workers and Pelotona, the permit man, walked into the yard, followed a little later by Mma-Millipede, Dinorego, and Maria. Maria looked much put out by being the centre of attention for the day, because she was essentially a quiet and humble personality. It all made her pretty, serious face more serious than usual, and she was at pains to conceal herself behind the ample figure of Mma-Millipede. Not even her new frock of pale blue cotton, sprigged with small pale pink roses, could boost Maria's morale. The women of the village also put on constrained masks as they walked about serving the food in silence. They only let themselves go when they were a group together with no men present.

After a slight delay, Gilbert and Makhaya also walked into the yard, absorbed in a conversation. At least, Gilbert was doing the talking and Makhaya the listening. Since she had only waited for the appearance of Makhaya, Paulina looked up and stared at him in a still, intent, almost dispassionate way. She noted how he never once looked at the face of the speaker but kept wrapped up in himself and walked as though he was a single, separate and aloof entity. And yet at the same time he concentrated so intensely on what was being said to him that he seemed to have established an invisible bond between himself and the speaker. Then Gilbert seemed to say something that indicated the end of the conversation and, picking up a hand-carved stool, walked over and sat down on the right side of Mma-Millipede, who had Maria sitting on her left. Makhaya, in turn, looked around the gathering with a slight expression of surprise on his face, as if his absorption in Gilbert's conversation had made him unaware of his surroundings. Paulina's heart turned over at this, and she bent her head and smiled to herself.

The old man, Dinorego, touched Makhaya on the arm and indicated a vacant seat next to him. Makhaya sat down.

'You know, son,' Dinorego said confidingly, 'I thought the day I met you: "Well, here is a most suitable man to marry my daughter." Today, I cannot recover from my surprise, although I am very pleased that she is married to Gilbert. It means he will make his home here and we shall progress.'

Makhaya merely laughed in reply, especially at the latter part of the old man's speech. Moralizing seemed to be Dinorego's speciality.

'And what about you, son?' the old man continued. 'Might you not like to marry here too?'

Makhaya turned his head and looked at the old man, directly, half-amused, half-serious.

'Most men want to achieve great victories,' he said. 'But I am only looking for a woman.'

The old man nodded his head profoundly, but at the same time he sensed snags in that simple statement. Makhaya appeared to him too complicated a man to have such straight-forward desires.

'Might she be very educated or might she not be educated, son?' he asked.

'I know what I want, Papa,' Makhaya said quietly. 'Because I've had so much of what I did not want.'

The old man said nothing but stared thoughtfully into the

distance. There were things in Makhaya he would never understand because his own environment was one full of innocence. The terrors of rape, murder and bloodshed in a city slum, which was Makhaya's background, were quite unknown to Dinorego, but he felt in Makhaya's attitude and utterances a horror of life, and it was as though he was trying to flee this horror and replace it with innocence, trust, and respect. In many ways, Gilbert's background was much closer to that of Dinorego than was Makhaya's, because it contained this same innocence and a lack of understanding of evil. Still, Dinorego was an old man, governed by his own strange rules, and in the short space of time he had known him, he felt a closer bond with Makhaya, the way God usually feels towards the outcast beggar rolling in the dust.

'You must approach my friend Mma-Millipede,' Dinorego said at last. 'She will enjoy your conversation. She may also help you to find the woman you seek, as she knows the heart of everyone.'

Two women came up and handed the men plates of roast chicken, with rice and potatoes, which they carried on a tray. Then they moved over to Mma-Millipede, Gilbert and Maria and also served them. Gilbert took his plate and set it down on the ground before him. Just at that moment he had an urgent matter to discuss with Mma-Millipede, and the food could wait. He looked at Mma-Millipede anxiously. Would she be able to help him? he asked.

Mma-Millipede turned her face towards Gilbert and smiled. She adored him, as she identified him with her own love of mankind.

'You know there is nothing I would not do for you, my son,' she said.

But at the same time she calmly started eating and pointed at his plate, indicating that he should do the same. 'If you don't eat,' she explained, 'the ants will soon invade your plate.'

Thus Gilbert was forced to delay his urgent proposal. Mma-Millipede in the meantime noticed the predicament of her friend, Paulina Sebeso, who seemed to have her big, dark eyes glued on the face of Makhaya, and so intent was she on staring that she seemed to have forgotten herself completely. Mma-Millipede felt acute distress.

My friend is going to make a fool of herself over the man, she thought.

Over the years, Mma-Millipede had traced two distinct relationships women had with men in her country. The one was a purely physical relationship. It caused no mental breakdown and was free and casual, each woman having six or seven lovers, including a husband as well. The other was more serious and more rare. It could lead to mental breakdown and suicide on the part of the woman, because, on the one hand, it assumed that the man was worthy of adoration, while in reality he was full of shocks and disappointments; and on the other, this adoration assumed the proportions of a daily diet of a most dangerous nature. Since Mma-Millipede had to sew the funeral garments, she had come to dread this latter type of relationship and gave preference, against her conscience, to the former. Surely, she reasoned, it was far better to have a country of promiscuous women than a country of dead women? Mma-Millipede looked over at Makhaya. No matter how hard she tried, she could not form a judgment on his character because of her inhibition about foreign men. She sighed deeply.

She put her plate down, momentarily debating ways in which she could question Gilbert about Makhaya's character. These questions would have to be very subtle and not reveal her real interest, which was to protect and advise her friend, Paulina

Sebeso. At the same time Gilbert also put down his plate and turned towards Mma-Millipede.

The problem was this, Gilbert explained. He wanted the women of the village, first and foremost, to start producing cash crops which would be marketed co-operatively through the farm. The idea was to get capital in hand which would open up the way for purchasing fertilizers, seed and the equipment necessary to increase food production in Golema Mmidi. Once people had enough to eat, other problems like better housing, water supplies and good education for the children could be tackled. Now, said Gilbert, one of the easiest and most profitable cash crops to grow was Turkish tobacco. If each woman cultivated a small plot of Turkish tobacco, harvested and cured it herself, and if it were all marketed co-operatively, the profits could then be spread out to good purpose. Could Mma-Millipede persuade the women to attend lessons at the farm on how to cultivate Turkish tobacco and how to build a curing and drying shed?

Mma-Millipede nodded her head vigorously. Like Gilbert, she had vision and she clearly saw the wondrous benefits that would accrue to the people of Golema Mmidi.

'Are you going to give the women instruction, my son?' she asked.

'No, not me, but Makhaya,' he said. 'I've specially asked him to accept responsibility for this side of the work. The farm itself takes up all my time, Mma-Millipede, but I'm anxious that it should not progress beyond the living conditions of the people of Golema Mmidi. Both have to grow together. I chose Makhaya for this side of the work because I think he will enjoy imparting knowledge to people.'

Mma-Millipede sat rigidly silent on receiving this news, yet her mind began to work at a rapid and alert pace. The only woman who would have the courage to persuade the other women to attend lessons at the farm was Paulina Sebeso, and having to approach Makhaya at a closer level, in the company of other women, might help her friend to put this sudden adoration on a sounder basis. But Mma-Millipede still needed a little information in order to be able to advise her friend on how she should conduct herself without coming to grief.

'Is Makhaya a man of good character?' she asked innocently.

Gilbert stared at her in surprise. Why, all his future plans depended on Makhaya. Not only that, he had had no way of starting the plan of this new venture until Makhaya had arrived. He had no way of explaining to Mma-Millipede the real subtleties of his relationship with Makhaya, that he was someone he now leaned on heavily for courage to push ahead with his ideas. Gilbert had long known that his survival in Golema Mmidi depended on many complicated factors, one of these being Chief Sekoto. It did not take him long to find out that Chief Sekoto did not care deeply about development projects and that he, Gilbert, was the medium through which Chief Sekoto inflicted revenge on his brother Matenge. Gilbert had been fearful of being critical about the African way of life, which seemed to him a deadly, chilling society which kept out anything new and strange. It was as though people looked at each other all the time, questioning themselves: Am I exactly the same as my neighbour? The fear was to differ from the next man, and he could see it in so many little ways, even in Golema Mmidi – the way a great scientific discovery like the drought-resistant millet meant nothing against traditional prejudice. Would the superior Motswana turn overnight into a Kalahari Bushman if he ate millet? He seemed to think so, irrespective of the fact that millet was just an innocent food which an 'inferior' tribe had developed a liking for. This damned millet, even though fields and fields of it could be grown in this country. Of course, he had had Dinorego, who copied him in everything, but once Makhaya had come to the village a lot of his silent tortures had blown away in the wind. It mattered very much to Gilbert to have as a friend a man who looked as black as everyone else and yet was not at all a part of these chilling group attitudes. And there was more to Makhaya's personality than that – a gentleness that communicated itself as strength and gave peace to others, a complete lack of fear, and a background of persecution which made it so easy for him to identify himself with the rags and tatters of the poor. But there was more still, there was more, and he bent his head searching around for some coherent explanation of his liking for Makhaya. He grasped the first thought that flashed across his mind:

'Makhaya is one of the most truthful men on earth,' he said. 'You can depend on him. Besides, he is a real friend to me.'

Mma-Millipede was very moved by this declaration. 'Gilbert,' she said, seriously. 'I think I accept your word. Tomorrow I'll send a friend to the farm who will discuss the matter with you. I think she will also bring along her friends. Excuse me, I shall approach her right away.'

Mma-Millipede arose and walked slowly in the direction of Paulina Sebeso. It was most urgent to her future schemes that she prevent Paulina from staring any longer at Makhaya like a felled ox. But Mma-Millipede's sudden rising had left Maria without her shelter, and all at once she looked like a fragile wild flower, about to be blown away in the wind. Gilbert turned his head and looked at her, feeling strangely uncertain that he was really married to this changeable, unpredictable woman. There were two women in her – one was soft and meditative and the other was full of ruthless common sense, and these two uncongenial personalities clashed and contradicted each other all the time. He wasn't ever sure if Maria was in need of his constant protection or whether everyone was really superfluous to this still, midnight world of quiet self-absorption in which she lived. She was in one of her self-absorbed moods right now. He moved over to Mma-Millipede's vacant seat, took one of her hands in his, and bent his head teasingly near her face.

'What are you thinking about, Pal?' he asked.

She raised her head and stared at him steadily, and that steady stare always meant fireworks. 'Are you going back to England one day?' she asked abruptly.

The edges of his eyes crinkled up in amusement. 'We might have to,' he said.

Maria placed her free hand straight out on her knee, indicating she had made a rule from which she was not going to budge. 'You will have to go back to England by yourself,' she said, flatly. 'I shall not live in England with you.'

'You mean you don't love me, Pal?' he asked, pretending despair.

'It's not that, Gilbert,' she said crisply. 'I won't feel free in England.'

And a lot of funny things occurred to Gilbert all at once. Of late, the Joas Tsepe crowd had been issuing blood-curdling pamphlets about the volunteers in Botswana, calling them the unemployed of Britain who had come here to cheat the Batswana out of jobs. If the Joas Tsepes overthrew the government by force, as they were always threatening to do, he would be frozen out of the country. He had not felt free in England either, at least not in the upper-middle-class background into which he had been born, where the women all wore pearls, and everyone was nice and polite to everyone, and you could not tell friend from foe behind the polite brittle smiles; and if your mother's brother bought his wife a mansion, your mother had to have a mansion too or threaten to commit suicide, and then your mother almost did commit suicide a few years after you were born because all the polite women kept on remarking on how you were such a big-boned lad with an ungainly walk and didn't somehow quite fit.

'You really *ought* to send the child to dancing school, Elizabeth,' they all said. 'It's sure to correct his walk.'

And his stupid, neurotic mother had sent him to dancing school, and the dancing teacher had sent him home in tears because he had given her a belly punch when she had tried to force him to dance, and since the belly punch had worked on the dancing teacher, he also tried out a few on his mother; and the way it is with neurotic women, she soon invented a number of excuses as to why it was he lived almost the year round in a tent among the trees. The birds had trailed tiny footpaths through the dense-white, dew-wet grass on summer mornings, and the leaden winter skies had looked like great swathes of eternity which were there to stay, forever and forever. But he found out that there was no eternity: only the ever-changing pattern of life. And it was from his tent among the trees that he had learned his humility and tenderness, and that this humility was not compatible with the great causes of the world but only with some work done, preferably in a quiet backwater like Golema Mmidi.

Still, from some unknown quarter, Gilbert had acquired a number of conservative ideas about married life – like it was the man who was the boss and who laid down rules.

'You're not Dinorego's daughter anymore,' he said to Maria, in a quiet threatening voice. 'You're my wife now and you have to do as I say. If I go back to England, you go there too.'

The woman of common sense retreated rapidly before the threat, and the other woman softly contradicted her, 'I did not say I won't obey you, Gilbert. I only wanted to find out what was on your mind.'

But thoughts of home, of England, had struck Gilbert with a sudden, deep loneliness. The feel of the still, blue, Botswana winter day had the same feel of the February days in England when the snowdrops came out. He stood up and pulled Maria by the hand, and together they walked away far into the bush, where the scarlet and gold birds talked to each other in low, soft tones.

CHAPTER EIGHT

Paulina Sebeso awoke early the next morning. She was in a slightly unbalanced mood, and the clear, sparkling light of the heady winter morning added to her intoxication. On the previous day at the wedding party Mma-Millipede had told her certain things that had made her heart drunk with joy. She had had to struggle to concentrate on the details of the tobacco-growing project, and Mma-Millipede, noticing this, had added a number of stern warnings: You must above all control yourself, my friend. You must pretend you are interested in the tobacco and give yourself time to study the man. Foreign men need studying, even though I accept Gilbert's word that he is a good man.

Not long after Paulina had lit her small outdoor fire to make tea and heat washing water, ten other women walked briskly into the yard. Twenty more had been willing to join the tobacco-growing project, but they first had to get the permission of their husbands. The ten women who joined Paulina were agog with excitement. They seated themselves around the jutting mud foundation of one of Paulina's huts and ragged her about not having washed yet, nor made tea.

'Goodness! The tobacco won't run away,' Paulina said gaily, and she splashed some water into a basin.

It was always like this. Any little thing was an adventure. They were capable of pitching themselves into the hardest, most sustained labour with perhaps the same joy that society women in other parts of the world experience when they organize fêtes or tea parties. No men ever worked harder than Batswana women, for the whole burden of providing food for big families rested with them. It was their sticks that thrashed the corn at harvesting time and their winnowing baskets that filled the air for miles and miles around with the dust of husks, and they often, in addition to broadcasting the seed when the early rains fell, took over the tasks of the men and also ploughed the land with oxen.

As always, when women left their own homes for the day, they took with them their food supplies in the bright checkered cloths, and these they undid now. One of the women stood up and collected small helpings of tea-leaves and powdered milk from each bundle, and then both the powdered milk and tea-leaves were poured at the same time into the boiling water. By the time Paulina emerged, dressed and washed, with her small daughter, tea was ready and poured. Also a plate of flat, hard sorghum cakes was handed around. Paulina took a few of the cakes off the plate and wrapped them in a cloth and handed this to the child, instructing her, as it was school holidays, to go and spend the day at the home of Mma-Millipede. Then they all drank the tea with clouds of vapour rising up from the mugs into the cold air. Each woman then carefully rinsed her mug and tied it up once again in the checkered cloth. They arose and walked in a brisk, determined group to the farm, Paulina taking the lead as she always and automatically did.

They found the farmyard deserted, but tractors whirred out in the fields as the winter ploughing was still in progress. Maria, however, emerged from one of the huts and waved and smiled. They hardly recognized her. She seemed quite changed, and not one of the women could ever recall when Maria had ever looked anything but pensive. They all fell on her, teasing her mercilessly and talking all at once.

'Hmm, married life changes a person,' they said. 'Tell us! How does he kiss? Come on, tell us!'

Maria waited until the uproar had died down, smiling in her secret way all the while. Then she raised one hand.

'You must all wait until Makhaya comes off the land,' she said. 'He is taking lessons in tractor-ploughing, as this is new to him. He will be here quite soon.'

'Where is the husband?' they asked.

'He's working in the office,' she said.

The women again settled themselves around the jutting mud foundation of the hut, and the tea-drinking ritual was once more repeated, amidst much laughter and jokes about married life to discomfort Maria.

They had just tucked away their mugs when Makhaya appeared. He walked to his own hut to remove a blue overall and then approached the women. They all stood up and said, 'Good-day, sir,' together. Makhaya paused, looked at them, smiled and said, 'Good-morning' in a friendly, natural voice as though he was long accustomed to receiving people as his guests. Then he said, 'Follow me,' and led the way to a part of the yard where a small plot of tobacco had been cultivated.

The experimental plot was forty-eight square yards. It had been scaled down to this size by Gilbert as being the most manageable area for each individual woman to cultivate in her own yard. But one hundred such plots were needed to produce the quantity of tobacco that would be profitable to market, and this also meant that a hundred or more women had to become involved in the project.

The small group of women, including Paulina, at first felt a little inhibited. They were unaccustomed to a man speaking to them as an equal. They stood back awhile, with uneasy expressions, but once it struck them that he paid no attention to them as women, they also forgot he was a man and became absorbed in following his explanations. And this was really part of the magic of Makhaya's personality. He could make people feel at ease. He could change a whole attitude of mind merely in the way he raised his hand or smiled. But he never exerted himself, seeming to leave it to the other party with whom he was communicating to do all the exerting and changing.

He stood and pointed to the plot on which foot-high tobacco was already growing. It was growing on a gently sloping mound, and this had been created by building up the soil in a heap, the same as when one constantly pitches ash in one place. The need for this mound was to assist in draining the soil, as well-drained soil was needed for the tobacco. He also broke off a tobacco leaf and explained that the very dark blue-green colouring meant that it was an unripe leaf, but once the leaf had matured it changed to a pale, light olive green.

He stopped talking awhile and turned and looked at the women to ask them a few direct questions. The experimental plot would be ready for harvesting in about three months' time. If the women harvested, cured and dried this first batch together, they would gain the necessary experience and be able that much sooner to cultivate, harvest and process their own tobacco. Therefore, it had been decided by him and Gilbert that the first tobacco curing shed be built in the yard of someone who lived nearest the farm.

'Who lives near the farm?' he asked.

The women all turned and looked at Paulina Sebeso. Makhaya also followed the direction of their glance, and a faint, quizzical expression flitted across his face, as though he knew the woman but could not remember under what circumstances he had met her. Certainly, the gaudy-hued skirt was familiar. Certainly, he remembered the big, bold eyes. Paulina bent her head in alarm and embarrassment.

'I live near the farm,' she muttered.

It was only when they had collected the equipment and walked in the direction of the sunset house that Makhaya recalled the brief incident of two nights ago when a small girl had approached him and touched his hand. He was very fond of children, and as they walked into the yard he turned to Paulina and said, 'Where's the child?'

'She's at the home of Mma-Millipede,' Paulina replied, but she averted her head, as the unexpected question made her feel strangely vulnerable and exposed.

They set down the equipment for building the shed – pick-axes, spades, tar matting, and pitch – and Makhaya walked about the yard looking for a suitable site. In a secluded corner of the yard he stumbled upon a gigantic operation. It was the work of the little girl. She was in the process of building a model village, all carved out of mud. There were mud goats, mud cattle, mud huts and mud people, and grooved little footpaths for them all to walk on. He stood staring at it for some time, a look of pure delight on his face. Then he turned and chose a site as far removed as possible from this sanctuary of genius, and with lengths of string marked out the shallow foundation for the tobacco curing and drying shed.

The women, with pickaxes and spades, scraped out the foundation. The plan of the shed itself in no way resembled the instructions sent to Gilbert by the tobacco-research station, as the curing sheds too had been scaled down to a measurement of ten feet by ten feet and were to be built with materials that were easily available in Golema Mmidi – like lots of mud. Makhaya divided a twenty-foot square into two chambers. One was to be a closed shed, with no draughts, which would provide the warmth and humidity needed for the colouring stage of the tobacco leaf. In this shed the leaves would be placed on the floor in single layers, on sacks. The other shed was to contain the curing racks for drying the leaf and was to have a removable roof to control the amount of sunlight received by the leaf. To prevent the white ants from rising up the mud wall, a layer of pitch and tar matting was placed in the foundation. This would also serve as a flooring for the closed shed.

Maria also appeared and assisted in the building of the thick mud walls. It was her intention to cultivate a patch of tobacco for her father, whom she also wanted included in the scheme. For some time little could be heard except the soft padding of women's feet as they walked to and fro with piles of mud and the tap, tap of Makhaya's hammer as he worked on preparing the curing racks. Paulina had deliberately chosen the job of mud-mixing. It called for more vigorous exertion and was also a lookout post during the brief pauses when no mud was needed. But she never saw much, in spite of her elation, because the object of her brief devouring looks kept his head bent at his own task, and so quiet was he that after a time even the women forgot his presence and began to chatter and gossip loudly.

Towards noon Maria washed her hands in a pail of water and approached Paulina.

'I'm going home to prepare some food,' she said, quietly. 'You must tell Makhaya that I shall put aside some lunch for him.'

Paulina rested one bare foot on her spade. 'Why can't

Makhaya eat with us?' she said haughtily. 'After all, he's working with us.'

'But he doesn't like goat meat and sour-milk porridge,' Maria explained mildly.

'Did he say so?' Paulina demanded.

'No, he hasn't complained,' Maria said. 'Gilbert doesn't like it either, although he has said nothing. I can just see by their expressions that they dislike it.'

'Goodness!' Paulina said in a fierce whisper. 'So you encourage foreigners to stick up their noses at our diet? Haven't you heard the saying: When you are in Rome, you must do as the Romans do? If people don't like our diet, they must starve. There's nothing else.'

Maria looked at her steadily. 'Don't get mad now,' she said. 'I was just explaining a fact.'

She shrugged and walked away quickly, as she disliked a word battle with Paulina, who always managed to get in the last punch. Paulina waited until she had left the yard, then she dropped her spade to the ground as a signal to the other women to stop work. The walls were five feet high and complete; only the rough surface had to be smoothed, and this would be done more easily after the mud had had time to dry a bit. One of the women immediately walked over to the fireplace to start a fire to warm up the goat meat while the rest filed to the water bucket. Paulina walked determinedly over to Makhaya. He was still crouched down on one knee, on a sack, and had almost completed the curing rack.

'Will you eat food with us, sir?' she asked.

'Yes, thank you,' he said, without looking up. 'My name is Makhaya. What's yours?'

'I'm Paulina Sebeso,' she said, making it sound an important fact.

But she did not move away and Makhaya looked up, slightly amused, slightly inquiring. She looked down at him with a haughty expression.

'Perhaps you don't like goat meat and sour-milk porridge?' she queried, in a somewhat penetrating voice, mostly for the benefit of her friends, who had stopped abruptly and were staring.

'I like goat meat,' Makhaya said quickly and untruthfully.

But privately he loathed it. The meat was tough and had a weird taste, like thick squeezed-out grass juice or wild herbs. Paulina instantly sensed the lie and decided to rub it in.

'I just wanted to know,' she said, still using that penetrating voice. 'Goat meat is all we eat. Sour-milk porridge is a daily diet. We Batswana even sometimes eat rotten meat through which the worms crawl. We just wash away the worms.'

Makhaya turned his head and found himself faced with the riveted glances of ten pairs of keen, thrilled eyes. And there was this loud-mouthed woman whose long, straight black legs dominated him in his crouched position. He rose quickly, relieved to see that he was a whole foot taller than she was. He stared at her with a look that said, So, you want something from me, do you?

Aloud he said, 'Well, don't wash off the worms for me. I won't notice them.'

The 'don't wash off the worms for me' brought a shriek of laughter from the gallery and also from Paulina, who rushed away in confusion to one of the huts. But it served to permanently break the ice between Makhaya and the women. Once they had washed their hands, they crowded near him, asking him all sorts of questions, which he answered in a carefree, casual way.

'Tell us about your country,' they said.

'But it's just like yours,' he said, amused. 'There are people there and the same kind of stars.'

'But our country isn't the same as yours,' a voice piped up, boldly contradicting him. 'You have electricity and water and we don't.'

'I don't know anything about the water and electricity,' he said.

'Why?' they all asked at once.

'It belongs to the white man at present,' he said. 'He'll tell you so, if you go there. I think the country even belongs to him.'

The women all stared at each other with wide eyes. Hmmm, so he was a politician, as the rumour had it in the village? These politicians were supposed to be feared in Botswana. But he was nice. They smiled at him, to reassure him, which amused Makhaya very much.

And this 'Tell us' went on for the whole length of the lunch hour, and no doubt that quiet, brotherly attitude of sympathy was very sincere, because Makhaya had an infinite capacity to attend to the details of life, and it often pleased him to turn careless or insignificant ideas into something quite their opposite. But only one woman sat a little apart, with a thoughtful look on her face. She was curious about the man behind the brother because, when she had come right up close and looked him straight in the eye, she had found almost nothing there, just a blank, calm wall; and since she was so acutely aware of him, she was also aware of the significance of that wall. You see, it said, I'm quite safe. No one can invade my life.

Yet it was not so much the privacy of his inner life and the wall he had built around it that troubled Paulina. She was first and foremost a physically alive woman, and she was also physically frustrated, and what she needed most of all was someone who would end this physical frustration. So intense was this need that it had made her very sensitive to men, especially the type of man most likely to fulfil it. It was only an equally blind and intense desire to own and possess a man to herself that prevented her from having any lovers, and this latter need always asserted itself over her physical desires. But in a society like this, which man cared to be owned and possessed when there were so many women freely available? And even all the excessive love-making was purposeless, aimless, just like tipping everything into an awful cess-pit where no one really cared to take a second look. And Paulina was too proud a woman to be treated like a cess-pit. But she wasn't sure either of anything morally definite. In fact, the word 'moral' was really meaningless to her. She simply wanted a man who wasn't a free-for-all. No doubt, the other women longed for this too because intense bloody battles often raged between women and women over men, and yet, perversely, they always set themselves up for sale to the first bidder who already had so many different materials in his shop that he was simply bored to death by the display.

And she liked this reserved man and the quiet about him, as though he could pick and choose a bit and use his discrimination, but what troubled her, when standing quite close to him, was that this calm, blank wall applied not only to the expression of his face but to the feel of his body as well, as though it did not exist, as though it was not there at all. Yet he seemed a man who was very conscious of his appearance. No doubt, in his own country, he had spent a great deal of his money on clothes, for the different changes of black sweaters that he wore about the farm were expensive ones. There was a gay life that had gone hand in hand with those expensive clothes, she thought. Perhaps pretty, perfumed women too, those who wore red high-heeled shoes and stockings and painted their lips. She stared at Makhaya intently, trying to see all those women and how they had laughed and talked to him, because in Golema Mmidi there was no perfume, red shoes, and lipstick. But Makhaya sat there talking to the barefoot, illiterate women of Golema Mmidi as though he had done this all his life, just as throughout that morning he had worked side by side with them, like a brother.

He makes us feel at ease, she thought, because he has no feeling. He takes away the feeling in us that he is a man. But my heart tells me it's not true. Mma-Millipede was right when she said the man needs studying.

Once Paulina became thoughtful, she also experienced her most sane moments and placed a curb on the rash, impulsive gestures she continuously made. Also, a little humility entered her life, making her less sure that everything in the world ought to belong to her. It was in this subdued mood that she picked up her spade to work again. There was not much mud to mix, only a little for the smoothing of the walls. Two women delegated themselves for this job, while the rest sat along the jutting mud foundations of the huts and, in pairs, began weaving the long smooth, dried river reeds into roofs and doors for the sheds. Maria also returned and teamed up with Paulina, who had just put down her spade. Makhaya, who had by this time fitted the curing racks in one of the sheds, seated himself alongside Maria. He had a few short sticks in his hand and took out a pocket knife and began slicing away at the wood.

'What are you doing?' Paulina asked, after a time.

'The village has no trees,' he said, and held up one of the pieces of wood which he had shaped into a tall, slender palm tree. 'Do you think the child will mind if I interfere?'

Paulina kept her head bent, and when she replied it was barely above a whisper and very polite: 'She will appreciate it, sir.'

Makhaya took one of the reeds off Maria's lap and split it up into the shape of palm fronds. These he dipped into the pitch bucket nearby and then carefully clustered the ends onto the top of the trees. He also placed the foot of each tree into the pitch bucket to prevent its future damage by the white ants; then he curled a finger around each tree and walked over to the village. Gilbert walked into the yard a short while later and stood gazing at the almost complete tobacco sheds with the same delight in his eyes as Makhaya looked on the minute village of mud people and animals. To Gilbert this shed meant the difference between having no money and the capital to set up a network of boreholes and reservoirs in Golema Mmidi. It meant water for every household, for vegetable gardens, for irrigation schemes, for cattle-grazing grounds in the village, and for improved methods of crop production. He walked over to where Makhaya was crouched down on one knee beside the miniature village and removed the last tree from his hand. Then he stood back and surveyed the layout of the village. Once he had decided on the most suitable spot for the tree, he crouched down beside Makhaya.

'Each household will have to have a tap with water running out of it all the year round,' he said. 'And not only palm trees, but fruit trees too and flower gardens. It won't take so many years to turn Golema Mmidi into a paradise. Look, Mack, do you think we could get a hundred of these sheds done before the rainy season? If so, we'd be able to get the tobacco growing off the ground this year.'

'There's only one person here who can supply the answer to your question,' Makhaya said. 'She's wearing an orange and red skirt and she's sitting next to your wife. But I'd advise you to just hand her those one hundred membership cards and let her work out the details for herself. She seems to run this whole village by sheer will-power and even tried to get me to eat worms for lunch.'

Gilbert laughed and looked round in the direction of where Maria was seated. He saw the bold coloured skirt and the equally bold-looking eyes as Paulina turned her head in his direction. It was held at a very proud angle, but unconsciously proud. He turned and looked at Makhaya. He'd noticed Mma-Millipede approach this very woman on the previous day and also, like Mma-Millipede, had noted the way in which she had stared at Makhaya.

'What makes the world turn round, Mack?' he asked, smiling.

'I don't know,' Makhaya said, as he was absorbed in studying the future needs of the tiny village, and Gilbert wanted to say something, but had an abrupt change of mind.

'It's polythene pit dams,' he said. 'We'll need water right away to help the tobacco along, and I've figured out a way in which we can trap the storm waters in a deep pit lined with polythene.'

He stood up as he had noticed that one of the roofs was complete and that Paulina and Maria held it together and were approaching the pitch bucket. He picked up the tar brush and walked over to them, as he wanted to get to know the woman in the bright skirt. He was also in a mood of quiet elation, gathering in a number of scattered details all at once. The village to him these three long years had really only meant Dinorego, so much so that he knew every corner of the old man's mind, and Dinorego was like a patch of cloth that had grown on Gilbert. Everything had its start there, but once the start had been made so many others, like Maria, Mma-Millipede, Pelotona and the silent, reserved men who sold cattle to the co-operative, had grown on him too until his whole outlook was entirely Tswana, until the day would never arrive when he would be able to extricate himself. Since there was no way out, the only other alternative was to get to grips with a whole life in a narrow, confined space. Because it was a harsh and terrible country to live in. The great stretches of arid land completely stunned the mind, and every little green shoot that you put down into the barren earth just stood there, single, frail, shuddering, and not even a knowledge of soils or the germinating ability of seeds or modern machinery could help you to defeat this expansive ocean of desert. And people, mentally, fled before this desert ocean, content to scrape off bits of living from its outskirts, where a few roads had been built or where a lonely railway line hugged its way along the eastern border area. This fleeing away from the overwhelming expressed itself in all sorts of ways, particularly in the narrow, cramped huts into which people crept at the end of each day, and those two bags of corn which were painstakingly reaped off a small plot.

It was his understanding of this mental flight that gave him a different outlook on subsistence farming. If a man thought small, through fear of overwhelming odds, no amount of modern machinery would help him to think big. You had to work on those small plots and make them pay. Once they began to pay you could then begin extending the production. But you had to start small, and because of this small start, co-operative marketing was the only workable answer, and its principle of sharing the gains and hardships would so much lessen the blows they had to encounter along the way. Maybe they could start with tobacco growing, scaled down to small plots, and cotton and millet and groundnuts and . . .

He looked up at Paulina from his crouched position near the mat and smiled. It wasn't really her he saw but that look in her eyes, not really boldness after all but the natural expression of a powerful and alert personality, and beyond that, all such a personality could accomplish. Why, one day there'd be some real family life and all the men would be back in the village again and the cattle would be right nearby behind enclosed, communally owned grazing grounds, and in summer the cattle would feed on grass that was three feet high and dripped with dew, and some of the men might like to engage themselves entirely in the business of producing high-grade beef and others might like to turn Golema Mmidi into one of the greatest tobacco-producing areas in the country, and by that time some of the women would have become so expert in the tobacco business they might like to help along, or they might be a little rich and swanky by then and worry about the ladder in their new stockings or discuss their children's ailments over dainty cups of tea.

'Are you the friend of Mma-Millipede?' he asked.

'Yes,' she said.

'She said I'd meet you today,' he said. 'But she omitted to give me your name.'

Paulina told him her name and he bent his head for a while concentrating on putting a coat of pitch on the lightweight roof to make it waterproof.

'How many women would like to grow tobacco?' he asked.

'Every woman in the village,' she said.

'Are you sure?' he asked, looking up.

She looked down at him, and smiled. 'We who are here are the bravest,' she said. 'We are the only women who have smoked cigarettes and drunk beer. That is why whatever we do is also done by the other women, though they are afraid to smoke and drink because they will be beaten by their husbands.'

Gilbert looked down but he smiled in huge enjoyment. 'Has Maria smoked cigarettes too?' he asked.

Paulina looked across at Maria, who stood opposite her, and Maria stared back. The girl had never been a part of them. She had just always lived her own life in which no one shared and she was full of quiet shocks. It wouldn't surprise anyone, except perhaps Gilbert, if she declared herself unmarried within a few days, as she had been known to say grass was green on one day and then flatly announce that it was yellow on the next. She must not only have smoked, Paulina suspected, but also reeled with beer. If so, she kept this experience to herself, as though everything she did was special and exceptional. You either had to say very bad things about Maria or leave her alone. Therefore, Paulina kept quiet. Maria looked at Gilbert's bent head and she only straightened one small foot to emphasize her point.

'I haven't smoked cigarettes, Gilbert,' she said in that flat, dry voice of statement. 'And women who do so aren't brave. They are only boasters.'

She looked across at Paulina with hostility. She really feared her as a woman. Like all the other women, she suspected that men secretly liked Paulina, and she did not care for the thought that Gilbert might find her gay and carefree generosity appealing. Gilbert looked up and caught this exchange of hostile looks between the two women.

He turned to Makhaya, who was approaching, and said, 'Mack, you'd better take my wife home. See you get something other than worms to eat. I'm going to stay here a bit and wind up the work.'

Makhaya stood looking at Paulina for a brief moment, a faint smile on his face. She was entirely unaware that her skirt was the same flaming colour as the sun, which was about to go down on the horizon, and that both were beautiful to him. But being Makhaya, he kept this to himself and started walking away. Then the group of women also filed out and stopped to chat with their new casual friend awhile and walk on. Then the small girl with bright, black beady eyes stepped into the yard, her tiny skirt swishing about like a gust of wind with the rhythm of her walk. Makhaya stared at her in surprise and delight and then bent his head attentively to what Maria was saying, and they walked away together. Paulina noticed all this with a strange, black, helpless rage in her heart. Why did everyone she ever wanted have to go away? And always in the company of women who did not particularly want them. She was a little startled that the child had been tugging at her hand for some time.

'Mama,' she said. 'Mama, who put the trees in my village?'

'It's Gilbert's friend. You must run and thank him.'

The child sped out of the yard and Paulina looked at Gilbert, who was still intent on finishing the roofs.

'Will you have some tea before you go, Gilbert?' she asked, suddenly remembering polite Tswana customs.

'Yes, make some tea,' he said without looking up, but once she had turned her back he rested on one knee and looked at her with a strange expression. She was invaluable to him, and without her energy and initiative nothing would start, and more than anything else in the world he wanted one hundred women, at least, to start growing tobacco. But perhaps she cared only about Makhaya and not the tobacco, at least so it seemed to Gilbert, and if something went wrong with her intentions towards Makhaya and he took up with someone else, she might collapse, everything might collapse. Far too many of his calculations depended on the unpredictable human factor, and it wasn't like machines and experiments which you could control. He couldn't judge what Makhaya would do once he became aware of the woman's interest. Like Mma-Millipede, Gilbert suddenly found himself plunged into anxiety. He stood up and walked over to where Paulina was busy near the fire.

'You know, Paul,' he said, 'to get one hundred women organized into a tobacco-growing co-operative will be a lot of hard work. I'd like you to be put down officially as part of the staff and on a salary. Would you agree?'

Paulina swung round with her quick, generous smile. 'The job has to be a success first,' she said. 'You mustn't worry about the tobacco, Gilbert. The women will grow it as they have never worked for money before, and we Batswana like money.'

The child stepped back into the yard and Gilbert suddenly felt light-hearted. He liked optimism too; in fact, he knew he could build a world on nothing. He swung the little girl onto his lap.

'How many children do you think I ought to have, Paul?' he asked.

'Goodness, I don't know,' she said.

'I think I'll just close my eyes and make as many as I want,' he said gaily.

He took the cup of tea she held out to him and drank it quickly because it was nearly pitch dark. Then he set the child down and swung his way homeward. No sooner had he left than Paulina turned to the child eagerly.

'What did the friend of Gilbert say?'

'He said I have no grass for my cattle and goats to graze on, Mama.'

'Is that so?' Paulina said, half-talking to herself and smiling. 'Did he say he'd make some?'

'Yes,' the child said.

Paulina gazed thoughtfully into the fire. It had surprised her when Makhaya had inquired about the child. Batswana men no longer cared. In fact, a love affair resulting in pregnancy was one sure way of driving a man away, and it was a country of fatherless children now. Perhaps, she thought, this man still had tribal customs which forced him to care about children. Every protection for women was breaking down and being replaced by nothing.

And there was something so deeply wrong in the way a

woman had to live, holding herself together with her backbone, because, no matter to which side a woman might turn, there was this trap of loneliness. Most women had come to take it for granted, entertaining themselves with casual lovers. Most women with fatherless children thought nothing of sending a small boy out to a lonely cattle post to herd cattle to add to the family income. But then, such women expected life to give them nothing. And if you felt the strain of such a life, all the way down your spine, surely it meant that you were just holding on until such time as a miracle occurred? And how many miracles an ordinary woman needed these days. Paulina sighed bitterly and deeply, exhausted by the tensions and excitement of the day. Who was she after all to imagine that such a strange and complex man like Makhaya would love her? She turned on the small girl and spoke to her with a sharp note of exasperation in her voice.

'Now, why are you just sitting there?' she said. 'Fetch the plates and I'll dish up the porridge.'

The small girl looked at her, startled. That tone of voice was most unlike her gay mother, but she sprang quickly and obediently to her feet, dropping a small ball of wool and some knitting she had been busy on. Paulina picked up the piece of knitting and could make nothing of the untidy jumble of stitches. She smiled to herself, and yet perversely spoke in the same sharp tone to the child when she returned with the plates.

'What's this?' she asked.

'I am making a cap, Mama,' the little girl whispered.

'You silly thing,' Paulina said, half-wanting to laugh. 'Why didn't you ask me to help you? Are you keeping secrets? Is this cap for a boyfriend at school?'

'No, Mama,' the child said, a look of frightened guilt on her face. 'The cap isn't for my boyfriend. It's for Isaac.'

'So you keep boyfriends at school and tell me you're making this cap for your brother at the cattle post,' Paulina persisted, oddly enjoying torturing the child.

The small girl squirmed. She and her brother Isaac had always had secrets between them that they did not care to share with adults. But how could she let her mother accuse her of having a boyfriend at school?

'When we were at the cattle post the other day, Isaac asked me to make him a cap,' she whispered faintly. 'He said he had a bad cold and was coughing every day.'

As she feared, this bit of whispered information seemed to make her mother more cross than before because she fell into this sudden, brooding silence and did not eat her porridge. Then she picked up the knitting and bent towards the firelight and unravelled it. Then she picked up the needles and, with quick rapid movements of her hands, began knitting the cap. The small girl kept her eyes glued on this handiwork, in fascination, watching a cap grow before her very eyes under the click, click of the needles. After half an hour, Paulina paused abruptly, broke off the thread of wool and spread the garment out on her knee. She looked considerately at her daughter.

'I'm sending this cap to Isaac tomorrow,' she said. 'Also a bottle of cough mixture. Now, you must keep this a secret. I'm going to send a message that you made the cap for him.'

She peered closely at her daughter's face, and the child looked down in embarrassment.

'But if he is ill, he needs the cap quickly,' the mother said, guilty of having spoiled the pleasure of her child.

To her surprise, the small girl burst into a flood of tears. It wasn't that Paulina did not feel like crying too. They were afflicted by the same ailment – loneliness. But if a grown woman cried, all those hot tears might melt the iron rod that was her backbone. Then how would she arise on the morrow to face another day? The note of exasperation crept back into her voice.

'Go to bed,' she said, crossly. 'And I want no more noise.'

Far away, at the cattle post, the small boy Isaac was already asleep in his hut. The nights were bitterly cold, in these winter days, but for some time now he had fallen asleep in a hot, flushed daze, with a high fever. It wasn't a bad cold that troubled him. He had tuberculosis.

CHAPTER NINE

The busy brown birds shrilled the day long in the bush, long contented shrills, punctuated by the rasping flutter of their wings as they hopped from thorn tree to thorn tree. In fact, the whole earth had this contented feeling because it was July. No one liked June and its icy blasts, nor the sandstorms and high winds of August and September. And no one liked the summer months, when it might or might not rain and when it was always too hot to live and breathe. But July was like living at the bottom of a deep, blue ocean because it was really as though winter had settled a sheet of glassy blue light over the earth. You were never without the cloudless desert sky in Botswana, but in July the sunlight had to filter through a dense, blue cloth, and this filtered light covered everything with a glossy, soft sheen. Mysterious blue mists clung like low, still clouds, all day long, on the horizon, and at evening they trailed in cold draughts along the winding footpaths.

Makhaya found his own kind of transformation in this enchanting world. It wasn't a new freedom that he silently worked towards but a putting together of the scattered fragments of his life into a coherent and disciplined whole. Partly life in the bush was like this. In order to make life endurable you had to quieten down everything inside you, and what you had in the end was a prison and you called this your life. It was almost too easy for Makhaya to slip into this new life. For one thing he wanted it, and for another he had started on this road, two years previously in a South African prison, the end aim in mind being a disciplined life. But the Botswana prison was so beautiful that Makhaya was inclined to make a religion out of everything he found in Golema Mmidi. It did not amount to much. It even seemed as though the population of goats exceeded that of people. They certainly produced more babies than the women of Golema Mmidi, who were chronically short of male companionship, and as though the mother goats sensed this they paraded their babies up and down the village, the little ones trailing obediently behind them, nodding their small, tired heads. All the planning and projects Gilbert discussed with him, night after night, were on a very small scale and the smallness of it all was to ensure its success. Gilbert felt that you could not plunge a community that had lived off subsistence farming for generations into large-scale production overnight.

It was as though the concept of working with acres and acres of land was incomprehensible to the majority of poverty-stricken people, who were content to scrape a living off a thin ribbon of earth. There wasn't much bother and fuss about subsistence living either. Large chunks of the year went by just watching the sunrise and sunset, and who knew too if the subsistence man did not prefer it this way? It was easy, almost comparable to the life of the idle rich, except that the poor man starved the year round. Not in Africa had the outcry been raised, but in the well-fed countries. Something had to be done about the man who lived on subsistence agriculture, because without his co-operation the world could not be properly fed.

Gilbert took this a little further. Voices had to be raised in Africa too, and they had to come from men like Makhaya who deeply craved a better life, not only for themselves but for all these thousands and thousands of people who walked around with no shoes.

Maybe, some people would have been surprised and amused at Makhaya's many private speculations on Gilbert and also the exaggerated importance he attached to the personality of Gilbert. Maybe they were accustomed to accepting and treating white people as ordinary human beings, but for Makhaya this was a completely new experience. At first Makhaya thought it was the agriculture that made him feel so at ease and at peace in Gilbert's company, but then the agriculture was something he grasped at to save his own life and there was still the man, Gilbert, who sat there talking and for whom Makhaya could not account. He had been accustomed to reacting in only one way to a white man and that was with a feeling of great unease. Most southern Africans reacted in this way, and few black men in their sane mind envied or cared to penetrate the barrier of icy no-man's-land which was the white man and his world. The black man preferred to retreat to his own world among all the garbage and filth and noise, where a lot of people would be real and familiar and to whom your reactions would be such as to fill you with a sudden flood of relaxed warmth. It just surprised Makhaya that he had this feeling in the company of Gilbert all the time, and he would often sit and look at Gilbert with a slightly puzzled expression on his face. In the end Makhaya reduced it all to his one criterion for judging all of mankind – generosity, of soul and of mind. Many experiences had led him to the belief that the peace of the world rested with that one word. Because of this, it had become a policy with him to give immediately whatever was asked of him, and he really only felt a hatred towards people who consistently displayed selfish attitudes.

Makhaya's other griefs were more difficult to resolve, as these turned inward to his own life and his own need to attach a meaning to it. It was because his inner life had been a battleground of strife and conflict that made him attach such importance to its meaning. There was something in this inner friction that had propelled him, all by himself, along a lonely road, and he could not help noticing its loneliness because everything he desired and needed seemed to be needed by no one else in his own environment, among his own people or clan. This was aggravated by the fact that he had been born into one of the most custom-bound and conservative of tribes on the whole African continent, where half the men and women still walked around in skins and beads, and even those who moved to the cities moved with their traditions too. There seemed to be ancient, ancestral lines drawn around the African man which defined his loyalties, responsibilities, and even the duration of his smile. There was some woman he had to buy at some stage, the way you bought a table you were going to keep in some back room and not care very much about. It was only once his father had died that he was able to come forward with his own strange Makhaya smiles and originality of mind. It was a new young man who stood there, quiet and dignified, gentle and relaxed, but there was nothing in his own environment to account for all the secret development that had taken place in him.

Things wouldn't have been so bad if black men as a whole had not accepted their oppression, and added to it with their own taboos and traditions. Once he had pulled away from these taboos, he found the definition of a black man unacceptable to him. There were things like *Baas* and *Master* he would never

140

call a white man, not even if they shot him dead. But all black men did it. They did it. But why? Why not be shot dead? Why not be shot dead rather than live the living death of humiliation? And this agony piled up on all sides in a torrential fury because it was not just that one thing that was wrong, it was a thousand others as well.

He had seen it in the slums of all the cities of South Africa where black men had to live and how a man walked out of his home to buy a packet of cigarettes and never returned and how his seemingly senseless murder gave a brief feeling of manhood to a man who had none. Thousands of men died this way to boost up the manhood of a manless man. But there were many other reasons why a man became a murderer, and at one stage Makhaya had acquired enough hatred to become a mass murderer. He lived on this touch-and-go line with his sanity, finding nothing to stabilize him. Of course, there was the gorgeous, exotic, exuberant round of the black man's life – his prostitutes, his drink, his music, his warm happy laughter. Eventually he slipped into this gay, happy round of living, but not before he had had a look at the type of woman he was supposed to marry and have children with.

Prostitutes, he was to decide, were the best type of women you'd find among all black women, unless a man wanted to be trapped for life by a dead thing. A prostitute laughed. She established her own kind of equality with men. She picked up a wide, vicarious experience that made her chatter in a lively way, and she was so used to the sex organs of men that she was inclined to regard him as a bit more than a sex organ. Not so the dead thing most men married. Someone told that dead thing that a man was only his sex organs and functioned as such. Someone told her that she was inferior in every way to a man, and she had been inferior for so long that even if a door opened somewhere, she could not wear this freedom gracefully. There was no balance between herself and a man. There was nothing but this quiet, contemptuous, know-all silence between herself, the man and his functioning organs. And everyone called this married life, even the filthy unwashed children, the filthy unwashed floors, and piles of unwashed dishes. Before all this Makhaya retreated, repelled. Yet his other life was horrible too, and he would not have been able to maintain it indefinitely without becoming a complete wreck. Perhaps he had even subconsciously engineered his arrest at this time by carelessly keeping the plans to blow up a power station in his pocket.

It was to amaze Makhaya after all this that an old woman in the village of Golema Mmidi, named Mma-Millipede, was to relieve his heart of much of its ashes, frustration, and grief.

Mma-Millipede made the first move towards establishing a friendship with Makhaya, partly motivated by her liking for the quiet, reserved young man and partly through her involvement in the emotional life of her friend Paulina. One evening, as Makhaya sat at supper with Maria, Gilbert, and the old man Dinorego, he was handed a little note by Dinorego. It said: 'I would be very pleased if you could pay me a visit, my son. Everyone ignores an old woman like me, therefore I am ever lonely. Your friend, Mma-Millipede.'

It was a bit of an exaggeration on the part of Mma-Millipede, but Makhaya put the note in his pocket; and as soon as supper was over, he stood up, leaving Gilbert and the old man in the middle of a discussion about whether, in the end, subsistence farming would evolve into co-operative farming. He liked this one theme of Gilbert's, but he also liked the tone of the little note.

Mma-Millipede was a little surprised at the promptness with which Makhaya responded to her note, and quite a space elapsed before she could collect her thoughts. She had, as usual, been indulging in her favourite pastime – reading the Tswana version of the Bible, and on this particular evening the wandering tribes of Israel were being settled by Joseph in the land of the Pharaoh.

'. . . lo, here is seed for you,' Joseph was saying. 'And ye shall sow the land. And it shall come to pass in the increase, that ye shall give the fifth part unto Pharaoh, and four parts shall be your own, for seed of the field, and for your food, and for them of your households, and for food for your little ones . . .'

These words deeply touched the heart of Mma-Millipede. It was her own world. It was Botswana. In her childhood a custom had prevailed where one-fifth part of the harvest of the corn had been given to the chief, and he had taken his one-fifth part of all the gifts and it had been brewed into a beer from which all had sipped as a thanksgiving for the harvest. But what had Pharaoh done with the gifts of the tribes of Israel? For they were lonely in Pharaoh's land and Jacob, the ancient father of Joseph, called his son and said:

'I pray thee, my son. Bury me not in Pharaoh's land. Carry me out and bury me in the burying place of my fathers . . .'

Mma-Millipede was about to weep at the loneliness and unease of the ancient Jacob. She saw and felt it all vividly but at this moment Makhaya knocked at the door, and his tall, thin shadow stepped ahead of him into the candlelit hut. His sensitive eye took in at one glance the little black Bible and the loneliness and grief of the old woman.

'Hullo, Mama,' he said with his quiet smile.

The old woman stared up at him, confusing him with the image of Joseph which was still in her mind.

'I am surprised you visit an ugly old woman,' she said at last, smiling too.

'But you called me, sweetheart,' he teased back. 'Besides, I've visited many types of women but none have looked as lovely as you.'

'Oh, this pleases my heart,' the old woman said, with quaint dignity. 'Who has ever called me sweetheart before? Will you have some tea, my own sweetheart?'

She fussed about unnecessarily, and looked a little flustered as her heart was suddenly overcome with a sentimental liking for Makhaya, and sentiment was not really a part of Mma-Millipede's temperament, at least it was buried deep down under all the harsh realities she had faced in her long life. Makhaya sat down opposite her and pulled the Tswana version of the Bible towards him as she poured the tea. He scarcely glanced at the words.

'Are you religious, Mama?' he asked lightly.

Mma-Millipede looked at him with an alert glance. 'If you mean, am I good, I can right away say no, no, no,' she said. 'Goodness is impossible to achieve. I am searching for a faith, without which I cannot live.'

Makhaya kept quiet because he did not immediately grasp the meaning of this.

'What is faith, Mama?' he asked curiously.

'It is an understanding of life,' she said gently.

He looked at her for a moment and then placed one long black arm on the table and pulled up the sweater sleeve which was the same pitch black colouring as the skin on his arm.

'Do you mean this too?' he asked, quietly. 'Do you know who I am? I am Makhaya, the Black Dog, and as such I am tossed about by life. Life is only torture and torment to me and not something I care to understand.'

He might have said it was much more than torture and torment, that it was an abysmal betrayal, a howling inferno where every gesture of love and respect was repaid with the vicious, snapping jaws of the inmates of this inferno until you were forced to build a thick wall of silence between yourself and the snapping jaws. But he would throttle himself to death behind this wall because love was really a warm outflowing stream which could not be dammed up. The familiar pained expression crept over his face as he looked at the old woman. And the old woman knew this.

'What is a Black Dog?' she asked abruptly.

Makhaya laughed his bitter, sarcastic laugh. 'He is a sensation,' he said. 'He awakens only thrills in the rest of mankind. He is a child they scold in a shrill voice because they think he will never grow up. They don't want him to, either, because they've grown too used to his circus and his antics, and they liked the way he sat on the chair and shivered in fear while they lashed out with the whip. If Black Dog becomes human they won't have anyone to entertain them anymore. Yet all the while they shrieked with laughter over his head, he slowly became a mad dog. Instead of becoming human, he has only become a mad dog, and this makes them laugh louder than ever.'

Mma-Millipede looked down. The quietly spoken words carried in them a violent torrent of hatred, and she was swept out of her depth, uncertain if there was anything in her own life with which to counter this hatred. The pitch black arm still lay across the table, like a question mark, and she was pitch black too, but she had lived all her life inside this black skin with a quiet and unruffled dignity.

'You are not a Black Dog, my own sweetheart,' she said in despair. 'I have never seen such a handsome man as you in my life before. You must not be fooled by those who think they are laughing. I don't know these people but my search for a faith has taught me that life is a fire in which each burns until it is time to close the shop.'

She looked up at Makhaya and he stared back at her aloofly. With that aloof stare he was trying to force something out of the old woman as he began to feel the real hard depth at the centre of her life. Mma-Millipede wavered. She had wanted to chat with him about little things; how he liked his work and whether he wanted a woman. But now all her feelers had to concentrate themselves on this frightening depth of hatred he had revealed in himself. He smiled suddenly, quite clearly observing the uncertainty on her face.

'Maybe you are right, Mama,' he said. 'Maybe I blame the whole world for my own private troubles. Maybe it's just a hollow feeling inside that's driving me mad.'

He pointed in the direction of his heart. 'There is a hollow feeling here,' he continued. 'Some time ago I used to pour all the drink in the world into it to try and fill it up. I was dissatisfied with myself. That's what hollow inside means.'

'My own sweetheart,' she said, tenderly. 'The hollow feeling inside is a search for a faith because that is what a person cannot live without.'

'Can you look on life again with trust once it has become soiled and tainted?' he asked.

The old woman looked at his face. Perhaps he did not know it but the unconscious expression of his face was one of innocence and trust. How was it possible for him to have looked on evil and yet to have retained that expression?

'You are a good man, my son,' she said with firm assertiveness.

'What makes you see good in everything?' he asked, amused.

'It is because of the great burden of life,' she said quietly. 'You must learn only one thing. You must never, never put anyone away from you as not being your brother. Because of this great burden, no one can be put away from you.'

It was the first, of all that she had said, that immediately touched the depth of his own life. Makhaya understood anything that appealed to his generosity because, in the depths of him, he was a lover of his fellow men. Yet the savagery and greed of these fellow men had set him to flight. At the same time the experiences of all forms of twisted, perverted viciousness had knocked out of him most of these evils. The problem was to control this desire for flight for, in turn, it became an act of hatred against all mankind.

'Who is my brother, Mama?' he asked.

'It is each person who is alive on the earth,' she said.

He smiled, having half-expected that reply from the old woman, and he had a perverse desire to push the Tswana version of the Bible off the table. The woman had a fire inside her that radiated outward and he could feel it and it warmed him. He didn't like that little black book because it really meant damn-all to a black man like him. Too many mincing, squeamish little missionaries had danced around it, and if God was to mean anything to a Black Dog he just had to have the humility to put on the skin of the Black Dog. He just had to go around being black in Africa if, from now on, he wanted anyone to care about him. But Makhaya cared not two hells about an old man in the sky. He liked this direct people-caring and this warm fire in an old woman. He sat up a little because he wanted to jolt her a bit. He wanted to find out what the base was, if it was real or only an illusion.

'I don't think I understand you,' he said. 'I don't think I accept the other man as my brother. You know what's going on in Golema Mmidi? Well, the same thing is going on wherever there are poor people. Chief Matenge is one lout, cheat, dog, swine. But Matenges everywhere get themselves into a position over the poor. I hate the swine. Sometimes I don't know what I feel about the poor, except that I, being poor too, say I've had enough of swines. I say I've had enough of those tin gods called white men, too. I want to see them blow up but I've run away, not because they are my brothers, but because a crowd is going to do the blowing up. I don't like crowds. I'd like to kill if I had to but I'm not sure what I'm killing when I'm in a crowd. I'm not sure of anything anymore, least of all who my brother is.'

Mma-Millipede searched her mind in vain. There was a judgment day when the sheep would be separated from the goats, without Makhaya's help, and she was searching around in her mind for a way to inform him of this without having to refer to the Bible. It was something people liked or did not like and she knew this wild-hearted man did not like it. She knew missionaries too and they had tainted the Bible by not making the words they preached out of it match their deeds.

'Maybe I don't see life in a big way,' she said apologetically. 'But people who err against human life like our chief and the white man do so only because they are more blind than others to the mystery of life. Sometime life will catch up with them and put them away for good or change them. It's not the white man who makes life but a deeper mystery over which he has no control. Whether good or bad, each man is helpless before life. This struck my heart with pity. Since I see all this with my own eyes, I could not add to the burden by causing sorrow to others. I could only help. That is why I cannot put anyone away from me as not being my brother.'

Makhaya smiled wryly. He had not heard anything like this before, and he hadn't expected to hear it from an old woman in the Botswana bush. He hadn't expected anyone to tell him that generosity of mind and soul was real, and Mma-Millipede sustained this precious quality at a pitch too intense for him to endure. He could give up almost anything, and hatred might fall away from him like old scabs, but he would never stop putting people away from him. He would never let them rampage through his soul because, unlike Mma-Millipede, he had no God to clear up the rubble. He had only his own self, Makhaya, Black Dog, and that was all he trusted not to let him down.

He stood up soon after that, with all Mma-Millipede's treasures in his pocket. He was never to know how to thank her for confirming his view that everything in life depended on generosity. The relationship between them from then on was to be one of continuous give and take, and who took and who gave and when and how was never counted up.

Still Mma-Millipede was strangely disturbed that evening. It had been one of the most exacting conversations of her life, especially as her thoughts on life, on understanding, were always hesitant, tentative. Yet on this evening she had spoken with calm authority on truths she was unaware of having thought deeply about. Partly it was the strangeness of the person she had spoken to which had so shaken her. She had been unprepared for the violent intensity of hatred and turmoil behind the quiet, still, carved face, and partly too it was the abrupt way in which she had been brought too close to another human life for the first time in her life. He had sat there, seemingly aloof and alone, yet at the same time, he had caught hold of an invisible thread of her life and attached it to his own. This togetherness dissolved all the loneliness in the world, and it had given Mma-Millipede the confidence to utter words she would never have dreamt of in the ordinary way. Mma-Millipede was left with the feeling that a rich treasure had entered her life. She sat there for a long while with her hand on her cheek, pondering these things.

Why did he call himself Black Dog and then give her such a terrifying picture of what a Black Dog was, she puzzled. How could a young man who had awakened such a quiet affection in her heart be himself so tormented and broken? But how could Mma-Millipede understand all things? Apart from one or two missionaries and Gilbert, she had never known white people. She had never had to live with a twisted perverted mentality which pinned up little notices over a whole town that said: This town is for white people only. Black Dogs may only enter through the back door because they are our servants and we are God, permanently, perpetually. We are this way because we have white skins, like peaches and cream. We don't smell like Black Dogs do and we are also very clever. We invented machinery. We, we, we.

It was hard to be charitable towards a civilization like this. It was hard to sit back and contemplate the real wonder of the white man's world which was this civilization. As Makhaya walked back to the farm in the pitch-dark night he was even sorry that he had once more aroused his own deep and bitter hatred. For he hated the white man in a strange way. It was not anything subtle or sly or mean, but a powerful accumulation of years and years and centuries and centuries of silence. It was as though, in all this silence, black men had not lived nor allowed themselves an expression of feeling. But they had watched their lives overrun and everything taken away. They were like Frankenstein monsters, only animated by the white man for his own needs. Otherwise they had no life apart from being servants and slaves. The strain was too much to bear any longer, not when a man was under pressure to assert his own manhood. He wanted them to give way on the continent of Africa, for they understood everything except the life inside a man. If this were not so they would have accepted the fact that black men were

human too and not some strange animal they tarred and feath-
ered and hung up from a tree to die. He wanted them to give
way on a continent where nearly everyone wore no shoes and
where poverty was not a shameful sin to be hidden under the
bushes. More than that he wanted them to remove their guns
which at this present time in southern Africa were pointed at
millions and millions of unarmed people. They must know what
would happen one day in southern Africa. They must know,
somewhere deep down, that one day all those millions of
unarmed people would pitch themselves bodily on the bullets, if
that was the only way of ridding themselves of an oppressor.

The whole world knew this. There was this curious philosophy. 'Violence breeds hatred and hatred breeds violence. Hatred
can only be defeated by love and peace.'

But had Hitler been defeated by love and peace? Six million
Jews had quietly died before Jewish people earned the right to
live on this earth. Had six million Africans to die in southern
Africa before black men earned a dignity too? The philosophy
of love and peace strangely overlooked who was in possession of
the guns. There had been love and peace for some time on the
continent of Africa because for all this time black men had been
captivated by the doctrines of Christianity. It took them centuries to realize its contradictions, and Mma-Millipede's
generation was the last of the captivated generations. The contradictions were apparent to Makhaya, and perhaps there was
no greater crime as yet than all the lies Western civilization had
told in the name of Jesus Christ. It seemed to Makhaya far
preferable for Africa if it did without Christianity and Christian
double-talk, fat priests, golden images, and looked around at all
the thin naked old men who sat under trees weaving baskets
with shaking hands. People could do without religions and
Gods who died for the sins of the world and thereby left men

without any feeling of self-responsibility for the crimes they committed. This seemed to Makhaya the greatest irony of Christianity. It meant that a white man could forever go on slaughtering black men simply because Jesus Christ would save him from his sins. Africa could do without a religion like that.

This was the sum total of Makhaya's revolt, and if he regretted having aroused all the tortures which were slowly falling away from him in Golema Mmidi, it was because they disrupted his feeling of friendship and respect towards Gilbert and all the new mental outlooks he was assuming. It was only through Gilbert that he discovered in himself a compassion for the whole great drama of human history. Only Gilbert admitted the mutual interdependence of all men. The raw materials of all the underdogs had gone into the making of those aeroplanes and motor cars, and Gilbert had been surprised to find the underdogs living in such abysmal conditions while his own country had prospered to an almost unbelievable state of wealth. There was no way for him to grasp such poverty, except to live under the same conditions as the poor. Makhaya formed his own conclusions from this. He saw Gilbert's culture as one that had catalogued every single detail on earth with curiosity, and it revealed to him great gaping holes in his own culture and how impossible it would be for Africans to stand alone. His own culture lacked, almost entirely, this love and care for the earth and had all its interest directed towards people. He had grown up in an atmosphere where the most important thing in the world was the stranger whose shadow darkened the doorstep. People were the central part of the universe of Africa, and the world stood still because of this. Makhaya deviated slightly from this pattern as he was born with a natural inclination for his own company. Thus, Gilbert's scientific outlook was a welcome alternative to him.

He felt, too, that all the tensions, jealousies, frustrations, and endless petty bickering which make up the sum total of all human relationships were in reality unnecessary. This belief was necessary to his own survival, as the desire to retaliate in a violent way against all human selfishness and greed was a powerful urge in him. He found himself, over this period, beginning to combine the two – the good in Gilbert with the good in his own society. Perhaps he did so because he needed to save himself. Some part of him was even fearful that he was being mocked by the gods, and that one day he would find himself pitched back into the nightmare over which he had had no control, just as he had had no control over the living processes which had created him, Makhaya, a man with a black skin, which in turn made men with differently coloured skins jar the quiet and peace of his being and allow him no peace, night or day, to live with a natural part of his body. He suspected that Botswana society had its own merry-go-round, as he had seen from the behaviour and attitudes of Matenge and Joas Tsepe, but he did not have a stake in Botswana society. He did not want a stake in any man's society, and that's why Gilbert and his ideas appealed to him so deeply.

What else could a man do, except seek a manageable life? What else could he, Makhaya, do, except wait here a bit until he lost his hate? It was he, Makhaya, the individual, who was seeking his own living life because he was fearful of the living death a man could be born into. In the meanwhile it seemed to him, for his own private needs, that he should free himself of hatred and concentrate his mind on the details of life in Golema Mmidi.

This life was indeed a full one and, for a beginning, a very pleasant and manageable one. Two weeks after the first tobacco curing and drying shed had been built, one hundred and fifty women joined the tobacco-growing project. This meant that a number of sheds could be built, simultaneously, on one day, as the women were now organized by Paulina Sebeso into small work groups. They were able to copy the pattern of the first shed with ease, and if Makhaya's blue overalled person was all about the village, it was to help with the construction of the drying racks, which were a complicated affair worked on a collapsible pulley system. The old man Dinorego joined Makhaya in his work. After a few days, Makhaya left this job completely to the old man and started work on small dams which were to be a source of extra water supply. It was too risky to depend on rainfall alone to give the tobacco project a good start, Gilbert reasoned. Who knew when the drought would break, and already the one farm borehole was heavily strained with having to supply the whole village with good drinking water, plus sustaining the cattle at the ranch.

The dams were to be built on each homestead and they were for the purpose of trapping whatever storm water might rush along the ground during the brief rainy season. They were to be pits, blasted out with dynamite, to a depth of seven feet and a width of fifteen feet by fifteen feet. Their capacity would be eight thousand gallons of storm water. The bottom of these pits had to be lined with three layers of mud and polythene and the sides to be supported with sandy, concrete-filled plastic bags. In each case a deep furrow was to be dug to catch the runoff storm water and lead it into the dam. Again, the materials were simple and the costs kept low. The polythene was to be on the farm account until expenses could be deducted from the co-operative sale of the tobacco. Dynamite was commonly used to blast out pit toilets, as water-flush cisterns were almost unknown in this waterless country.

So, almost the day long, Golema Mmidi rocked to the blast

of dynamite charges, and huge quantities of earth and rock were hurled high in the air. Makhaya, who buried and set off the charges, was often near enough to be splattered by rock and earth. He liked the drama and the irony, for not so very long ago he had come out of jail for wanting to use this very dynamite against the enemies of human dignity. It was like a self-mockery, this splattering rock and earth, to realize that he was indeed powerless to change an evil and that there were millions and millions of men built differently from him who enjoyed inflicting misery and degradation on a helpless and enslaved people. By contrast, Golema Mmidi seemed a dream he had evoked out of his own consciousness to help him live, to help make life tolerable. But if it was a dream, it was a merciful one, where women walked around all day with their bare feet and there were no notices up saying black men could not listen to the twitter and chatter of birds. The small brown speckled-breasted birds who lived in such huge colonies in Botswana were fat, gorged things. Dinorego solved the mystery, for him, of their eating habits. He took Makhaya a little way into the bush and broke open the surface of the earth. It crawled, just under the surface, with the soft juicy bodies of white ants, and thousands of birds lived on these juicy morsels the day long.

So many of the barefoot women, too, competed to do him a little favour. He never had to worry about where a cup of tea, which smelled like wood smoke, would come from, or what he would eat for the next meal. It was always there, brought by a rush of eager hands. Paulina Sebeso had to stand back and watch this jealously, but no other woman felt jealous as he shared out his attention among them all equally and then stood up at the end of the day and went his own way. Dinorego was very impressed by Makhaya's relationship with the women. It seemed to him that Makhaya was well versed in ancient African customs, where the man maintained his dignity and self-control in front of women, except that in former times this man had maintained it over a harem of concubines, while Makhaya had none.

Mma-Millipede, of course, shared every secret with her friend Dinorego, and since Paulina Sebeso was like their own flesh and blood, being also a northerner, they were both anxious that she obtain for herself this young man whom they both loved. Nor could Dinorego fail to notice how Paulina trailed silently behind them each evening on their homeward journey and that every recognition of her existence by Makhaya filled her big black eyes with the shining look of rain falling on wet leaves. Not that Makhaya failed to notice it either, after some time. His first reaction was one of helpless surprise, because, in spite of his good looks, he was quite unaccustomed to being adored by a woman in a single-minded way. That is, adoration was patient and waiting while love or, if you liked, plain sexual passion banged everything about. It either shouted or thought it knew too much, and it had always left him cold and had not involved his heart. Therefore, if he wanted to get involved now it would be on his own terms and at his own pace. He ignored Paulina Sebeso as carefully as he ignored all the women, but he also sat in her yard and drank wood smoke tea until the stars came out. Then he would stand up and say, abruptly, 'Well, I'll be going now.'

But Paulina Sebeso had a very pretty little girl who walked like a wind-blown leaf, and Makhaya was in a mood just then to like a little girl like that. He turned up one Saturday afternoon with a box in which he had thin strips of rubber, packing straw, glue, and green paint, and together he and the child set out to make grass for her miniature village. They worked the whole afternoon on this in absorbed silence, like two children of the same age who took life very seriously. Paulina worked nearby in silence too. Like all the other women who were now working daily on the sheds and dams, she had to stamp large quantities of sorghum for a week's supply of porridge. Now, all over the village the sound could be heard of wooden pestles being pounded into wooden stamping blocks. Every three minutes or so Paulina paused and poured a minute quantity of water into the stamping block to soften the hard orange and pink corn seeds. This in turn made the crushed, powdery corn quite damp, and once she had winnowed away the husks, she had to spread out the corn meal on sacks to dry. She was so preoccupied that it was some time before she noticed Makhaya standing nearby, observing her. It upset the accuracy with which she hurled the pestle into the stamping block, and she looked up at him in exasperation, wanting him to go away.

'I want some tea,' he said by way of explanation. 'But I'll light the fire and make it.'

'Goodness!' she said in alarm, holding onto the thick wooden stick. 'Don't touch the fire. It's a woman's work.'

Makhaya narrowed his eyes, that amused magical smile on his face. 'Goodness!' he said, imitating her speech. 'It's time you learned that men live on this earth too. If I want to make tea, I'll make it, and if I want to sweep the floor, I'll sweep it.'

Paulina shook her head and continued stamping. Makhaya turned the world upside down every day. He issued orders no one could counter, and he issued them with a smile that begged for an excuse for being the sole controller of everyone's life and the stars and the moon too.

'Quiet men are dangerous,' she said to herself with a smile.

But they filled the world with peace, these quiet men. Everything ran on smooth wheels with a mathematical order and precision. The child sat near her village, carefully painting the grass green while the man, with equal care, scraped out the old ash with a flat stick and set a fresh, crumpled paper on the outdoor fireplace. Paulina watched the fire-making with a critical eye, and it occurred to her for the first time why the ancestors had set certain jobs aside for women and certain jobs for men. Men and women were unalike mentally. Look at how this man built a fire! He treated each stick as a separate living entity, and because of his respect for each stick, he moved his hands slowly, with many pauses, placing the firewood down at carefully calculated angles. This fire was set for a limited purpose. It was meant to boil water for tea and burn beautifully, without smoke, in a straight blue flame. A woman worked differently. She grasped a bunch of sticks in her hand, but it wasn't the tea only but a thousand other purposes that fire would serve. At one moment it had to burn brightly but the next the flames had to be pulled apart and simmer the pot of meat. A fire was only a rag bag to a woman, and because of this she threw the firewood on the flames in haphazard confusion. In protest, the fire smoked like mad and food and tea and wood smoke all got mixed up together. But would people ever eat and stay alive if housework was so precise and calculated like this bright, smokeless, quick-burning fire?

From habit, she dropped the wooden pestle and rushed towards one of the huts. She would catch the last of the flames and mess them up with a clutter of wood and set the porridge pot over this smoke haze for the evening meal. Jarred by this sudden, frantic activity, the mathematical fire-maker and tea-maker retreated with a profound look of annoyance on his face. He could not even bear to look at the way Paulina sloshed the tea into the teacups. He walked towards the thornbush hedge and stood with his hands in his pockets, looking towards the horizon.

But the look of annoyance was soon banished because the sun was about to drop behind the flat horizon. It was just a big yellow ball and the air danced with sparkling crystals. The faint blue mists shivered like homeless dogs and slyly crept into the hedged yard for a bit of warmth.

'Here's your tea, my friend,' the woman said, approaching him.

'Thank you,' Makhaya said, politely, ever careful to keep himself the homeless foreign alien.

'You must not say "thank you" once you are used to a person,' the woman said.

'It depends on whether the person is used to me,' he said. 'Are you?'

She looked at him, half-laughing, half-puzzled. He always confused her with the speed with which he replied to careless, thoughtless remarks and the way he had of taking conversations up and down hills and valleys and mountains.

'I should be afraid to say I am used to a person like you,' she said.

The answer pleased him, and he turned again to the sunset. He wanted no one to be as rash as to say they understood his soul, especially when he had put up so many 'no trespass' signs. He wanted everyone as the background to his thoughts, not through arrogance, but because this emotional detachment was essential to real love and respect. The distances also revealed to him his true relationship to both friend and foe, and in the end both friends and foes might be acceptable if they always lived on the other side of the hill. But within all this, as Mma-Millipede had discovered, he employed a number of undercover tricks to bring him close enough to those whose warmth and love he craved. Ah, but happiness, anyway, was dirt cheap in Botswana. It was standing still, almost in the middle of nowhere, and having your face coloured up gold by the setting sun. He heard the small girl approach behind him and sit down next to her mother to sip tea. He had found out from her that she also had a brother, a few years older than she was.

Without turning around he asked, 'Where's the boy?'

'He's at the cattle post, looking after the cattle,' Paulina said.

'You ought to employ someone older who does not need an education,' he said.

She kept quiet. Wages were a problem. An employed person had to be paid a monthly salary, and she barely earned thirty pounds a year from the sale of her cattle. Cattle were all that stood between her children and herself and outright starvation, and she had to keep the costs down. Makhaya turned round and looked at her. He was only thinking about the small boy. If an old man like Dinorego had found the cattle business such a harsh life, how much more terrible must it be for a young boy? Paulina looked down.

'I know the child must attend school,' she said. 'But I cannot afford to employ somebody.'

'How many cattle do you have?' he asked.

'Eighty,' she said.

He was silent for a moment, making a swift mental calculation. 'You must sell the damn beasts,' he said.

She looked up, shocked. A Motswana without any cattle at all might as well be dead. 'I cannot do that,' she said.

'But you will have nine hundred pounds in the bank,' he said. 'It's enough money to live on for four or five years, and the boy will be free to attend school.'

The idea of selling all the cattle was totally unacceptable to her. She could not see beyond cattle to anything else which would offer her a haven of security. If her husband had been alive, the boy would most certainly be at school. She compressed her lips and looked at Makhaya with hard, realistic eyes.

'Why do you care?' she said roughly. 'You are no relative of mine.'

He laughed because he was unsure if her remark meant he was someone out to swindle her.

'We'll talk about relatives some other day,' he said. 'I'm now talking about those damn beasts, which are more of a burden than a help to you. I've said, after you've sold the burden, you will know what you are eating for four or five years. That's time enough to look around and find another way of earning a living. I'll help you because I'm interested in the same thing.'

She was unconvinced. 'Why do you want to help me?' she asked. 'Why don't you go and get rich by yourself? Each man helps himself in this world.'

He looked at her, exasperated. 'I'm not really necessary to anyone, least of all to Gilbert,' he said. 'I can feel myself leaving this country, perhaps even tomorrow. But if you think you need my help, I'll stay and help you.'

'Perhaps you had better go away,' she said in a shaken voice. She could not follow the strange twists and turns of his mind, and this filled her with a bitter, furious despair. No one could accept anything they could not understand. Besides, when had anyone helped another, free of charge? It wasn't a custom. She looked up at him apprehensively. If he really believed her and went away, she would die. He returned her look with a look of speculative calculation. There were other ways of saying what he had to say, but he was forcing friendship and understanding on her because he needed this in a woman more than he needed anything else. He walked across the short space that separated them and sat near her on the jutting mud foundation of the hut.

'You don't understand, Paulie,' he said. 'Poor people are poor because they don't know how to get rich. I also live in this small dark room and I have counted the change over and over. Now,

I'm tired of counting the change. I'm going to be a millionaire. But poverty is like glue. All poor people stick on me and they have to become millionaires with me. By this I mean that there will be no poverty left in Africa by the time I die.'

He sat there in silence. There was much more he wanted to say. There was space enough in her country for the poor to become rich, and the evil that men do to each other was not to be found in such major proportions here. He could feel it and this was at the base of his new feeling of hope and peace. She sat in silence too, while her mind worked in that one-track feminine way. There was a point at which love reached the over-limit stage and then levelled itself out onto a still plateau. It was like a nightmare and it was lonely. Yet he kept on adding and adding to the nightmare with his gentle, persuasive speeches.

'Tell me how you will help me to get rich,' she said at last.

Makhaya looked at her in surprise. Millionaire-hood was not a practical reality to him but a strange subconscious process. There would be a day when he would hold out his hand and all the money in the world would fall into it. This he was sure of because his whole life was strained to that point, and he simply left it to his subconscious to do the building, brick by brick. One day, the whole superstructure would be there, glittering with gold walls. Why, he had spent a lifetime absorbing all the tenderness, sorrow, and fear of the world, and there was a web and design in it. He smiled at her.

'I don't know,' he said. 'Except that sometimes I think I am God. I don't see why God, who owns the whole earth and heaven, should starve. He'll use his brains, won't he?'

Paulina hid her face in her hands and laughed. But the next moment she sat up with a jolt. The fire was slowly dying away with no one to attend to it. She jumped up and rushed over with outstretched hands to catch the last, flickering flames and thrust them back vigorously into life again. The thick porridge was done. There was only the goat meat to boil in the weak curry-powder gravy.

She looked over her shoulder at Makhaya mischievously and said, 'Will you eat food in my house, God?'

CHAPTER TEN

Matenge came back to Golema Mmidi in mid-August and found himself faced with the progress of mankind. Commoners were up and about everywhere, busy like ants, building dams for themselves. They were also laughing and had some new language up their sleeve, like 'cash crops'. This sent Matenge into a fuming rage. Barely ten years ago the commoner had always to approach a chief or sub-chief and ask him for permission to progress. This desire for progress had usually taken the form of wanting to build a small brick house with a tin roof. But brick houses were for chiefs alone, and how could an ordinary commoner want to bring himself up to the level of a chief? Or again, he might desire to set up a borehole for watering his cattle. The chief could say yes or no. If in some demented mood he said yes and then the commoner prospered, it would not be for long. This unfortunate man would one day be notified by the chief that a road was to be built in the pathway of his borehole. Would the commoner please quit? And not so many months after that the chief acquired a new watering place for his cattle.

Although he did not know it, Matenge was a thoroughly cornered rat, partly because his brother was playing football with him, and partly because he was faced with an entirely new situation in Golema Mmidi. There were too many independent-minded people there, and tragedies of life had liberated them from the environmental control of the tribe. Never before had people been allowed to settle permanently on the land as they were doing in Golema Mmidi. In the not so very far back bad old days, those who desired to be permanent farmers had had their huts burned down and been driven back to the villages. So the cheerful Paramount Chief Sekoto, who casually broke the rules and needed to possess no man's soul, was perhaps an unconscious assistant of the progress of mankind. But all things are unpredictable under the social structure of African tribalism. It seems to hold within itself terrible and secret currents which are geared toward eternal enmity of the individuals who stand alone; and who knew if one day Chief Sekoto might not turn demented too and unleash a bombshell of destruction on Golema Mmidi?

Matenge's crises were always silently prepared. No one ever knew what was going on in that lonely mountain-top which was his soul. The village was just presented with his thunderstorms, and their fierceness and savage intensity were the outcome of months of brooding. But he was ailing these days and it took him longer than usual to find his new victim. His dizzy spells alarmed him and he spent many hours quietly relaxing on his porch in his royal purple dressing gown, while he kept his servants dancing up and down in attendance on his needs. Being only servants and anxious to please him, they also kept him informed of all the developments in the village. The name of Paulina Sebeso was frequently mentioned by the servants.

Yet, at this time, a far greater crisis than any Matenge could ever produce was to strike down on the village of Golema Mmidi and the country as a whole. It all began so quietly. The weather was the usual for this time of the year; that is, from mid-August to mid-September the country was suddenly and abruptly plunged into the most intense and stifling heat. Scorching winds, too, blew in from the west, bringing with them huge swirling columns of red desert dust. All this misery was welcomed. The intense heat precipitated the first summer downpour. The old people and cattlemen knew this, and they remained contented in the swirling dust and heat. They never had any calendars but when they looked towards the sky, they knew it was September, the month when the rain clouds gathered. No matter that this was a country of two years of good rain and seven years of drought, the rain clouds always gathered in September.

But September came around and no rain clouds gathered in the sky. At the cattle posts, far out in the bush, the spade-dug wells were drying up, but still the cattlemen were not unduly worried. The huge, hulking, cavernous-bodied, russet brown Tswana cow was a strange beast. No one seemed to know of its origin, but everyone knew of its adaptation to the hazards of local climatic conditions and of its ability to go for long periods without food or water. Man and beast had always lived this way. If there was no food or water for a man, then there was nothing for his cattle either. Both were as close to each other as breathing, and it had never been regarded as strange that a man and his cattle lived the same life. No doubt the cattlemen who lived in the lonely, isolated cattle posts at first stared in disbelief when their cattle began dropping dead before their very eyes. There were always droughts. There had been many in each man's lifetime, but never in the memory of man had the cattle dropped dead. By the time the men panicked, hundreds and thousands of cattle had died.

The truth was no one knew what to do, and the authorities,

who by this time were becoming aware of the extent of the tragedy that was taking place in the bush, had no way of establishing communication with the thousands of men at the isolated, unmapped cattle stations. Eventually, all the cattlemen were to be driven out of the bush, overcome by thirst, each trailing behind a few emaciated beasts. But they were a reasoning, steady crowd, these cattlemen. They moved slowly and thought slowly, often with a quiet humour. It was reasonable to them that the vultures should gather above a man's cattle post, for who could bury all these cattle which were dying daily? They watched in calm apprehension as one beast after another toppled dead to the ground. This was reasonable too. When had the dry season ever spanned ten long months? The rain of the previous year had all fallen in November. There had been a day in November when the sky had emptied itself in one long angry downpour. Then all the rain had fled away. But the lack of rain had not troubled the cattlemen. They had their wells along silted-up river beds where the water flowed underground all year round. True enough, the grazing had been burned bone-dry by the hot January sun, but they had an ancient belief that bone-dry grazing was better for their cattle than fresh, green grass, wet with dew. Now, nodding their heads, they slowly absorbed a new truth: if cattle ate bone-dry grass for ten months, a day would arrive when all cattle would drop down dead.

Once they reached this point in their reasoning, all the cattlemen picked up their long sticks and began driving what was left of their herds back to the villages, to arrive there with ghastly tales of how the bush was one big graveyard. But the vultures are feasting, they added humorously.

The first wave of cattlemen who had exhausted their reasoning powers arrived in the village of Golema Mmidi in the late afternoon. They hastily erected kraals for their cattle with thornbush and instructed their wives to water the cattle sparingly. Then they retired to the yard of one of their fellows, and all sat in a circle on wooden stools, silently drinking bowls of sour-milk porridge. Disaster had indeed struck down swiftly on their small world, and each man sat in a mountain of aloof reserve to prevent his fellow from starting the sorrowful tale:

'My friend, I had two hundred cattle just yesterday. Out of this, one hundred and twenty have died. I have just counted the beasts. I now have eighty.'

They had seen the bush strewn with dead cattle on their way home. No one had stopped to look behind at the weak cows who had lain down to calve and die in the process of giving birth. The one thought in each man's mind had been to hasten home, even if he only had one beast left. Cattlemen could talk about this with humour and resignation to any other person but one of their fellows. It was not long before this group of silent men was joined by that super-reasoner, Dinorego. He came into the yard with his cheerful shuffle, holding onto the remnants of his tattered coat. The men moved aside immediately. They respected and trusted no one more deeply than Dinorego. Once the old man had seated himself, the owner of the yard, a tall, taciturn man named Rankoane, threw the stiff, dried-up carcass of a small wild buck into the circle of men.

'Look what I found, my friend,' Rankoane said. 'It's not only the cattle which are dying.'

The big dark eyes of the little animal were wide open, and he lay on his side with his four delicate legs stretched out stiffly, just the way the cattle lay when they dropped down dead. The men stared at it in fascination, really seeing death for the first time – they could not bear to look on their cattle in this posture of death. Rankoane enjoyed this effect. He enjoyed the contemplation of death and was one of the few men who could stare at it boldly. He bent down and removed the carcass and threw it to one side. Dinorego nodded his head several times, profoundly.

'We have received this news some days ago,' he said. 'The news came by phone to my son, Gilbert. It was the police officer, George Appleby-Smith, who phoned. He said, "Gilbert, do you know of the way cattle and wild beasts are dying in the bush?" And Gilbert said, "I am not surprised. Look at how it rained last year, all on one day in November." I was present when this phone call came, and my son Gilbert put down the phone, struck with pity. My heart too was struck with pity. I said, "The Good Lord has prevented me from keeping something which dies."'

The men looked at Dinorego with deep interest. The mention of the name of Gilbert had suddenly filled their hearts with hope, where before had been a passive resignation. No one had any clear idea of why he had headed home except that it seemed the most reasonable thing to do. But they were all members of the cattle co-operative and greatly prided themselves on having joined this new and strange association. Perhaps Gilbert, who had new ideas each day, would tell them what to do with all the cattle they could no longer feed.

'What has Gilbert to say about the deaths?' one of the men prompted tentatively.

Dinorego looked at the men triumphantly. 'The rain has not come,' he said. 'But still we will plough. Come, let us go and see Gilbert.'

With one abrupt gesture, the men put down their porridge bowls and stood up. Rankoane's wife, who was watering the cattle nearby, looked at them in amazement. They looked like men about to go into battle, so stern and concentrated were their expressions. Just as they were about to leave the yard,

Paulina Sebeso approached them. She clasped her hands politely together in greeting but she was wild with anxiety. She fixed her eyes on Rankoane.

'Please spare a moment, Rra Rankoane,' she said. 'I want to ask you something.'

Rankoane detached himself from the group and walked towards her with his angry-looking expression. Rankoane was always rude and offhand to women.

'What is it?' he asked impatiently.

'Your cattle post is near mine,' Paulina said. 'Why didn't you persuade my son to come home with you? What's the good of him staying in the bush when there is no water and the cattle are dying?'

A queer, guarded look crept into Rankoane's eyes. 'So, your son has not come home, Paulina Sebeso?' he asked quietly.

'I don't understand you, Rankoane,' she said, wildly. 'What are you saying?'

The man shrugged. He had more than enough troubles to bear. His whole livelihood had almost vanished before his very eyes.

'I told your son to go home two weeks ago,' he said. 'I expected him to be here, that's why I did not stop at your cattle post today.'

He walked away to join the group of men, but then he turned round once and looked back at Paulina with a twisted expression of pain on his face. At the same time he was trying to escape responsibility by not telling the woman why he had ordered her son home two weeks previously. It must have been just about this time too, after he had brought the cattle back to the kraal for the night, that Paulina's son had come to him.

'I don't know what's wrong with me, Uncle,' the boy had said. 'I am coughing up blood every day.'

But Rankoane knew at one glance what was wrong. Tuberculosis was the one major killer in the country, and the small boy with his red feverish eyes was seriously ill with it. Also, the diet they were eating now, plain porridge with salt and water and no milk, must have brought the boy's ailment to a serious stage. Rankoane merely smiled because he did not want to alarm the boy who looked like a thin, bony scarecrow in his father's oversized jacket.

'We are all coughing,' he said. 'The reason why? There is too much dust and no rain to settle it. Dust in the lungs causes one to cough up blood. The one way to cure it is by drinking beer, but since you are young and cannot drink the beer you must go home tomorrow with the cattle and your mother will take you to hospital.'

The small boy grinned at him cheerfully, with big, white teeth. He was amused at Rankoane's reference to beer and the man-to-man tone of his voice. Still, he was worried. He could not take the cattle back to the village and burden his mother with them.

'Can't I leave the cattle in your care until I come back from the hospital, Uncle?' he asked.

Rankoane had shifted uncomfortably. He was now drawing up a half bucket of water from his well and he could not add to his own worries. Besides, Paulina Sebeso was a resourceful woman and she would know what to do. He explained this to the boy, who nodded. The last thing he would get from his mother was a scolding. She made a joke of life and he already knew what she would say when he unexpectedly arrived home: 'Goodness, Isaac, don't tell me you have eaten up all your rations.' And he would say: 'No, Mama, I have come home because I am coughing up blood every day.' This would most surely strike his mother as unusual, as she would not know of

Rankoane's story about the dust in the lungs. The thought of his mother and her surprise and concern filled the small boy's heart with warm comfort. He stood up and walked back happily to his own roughly built hut, and it was the memory of this last conversation he had had with the boy that made Rankoane look back at Paulina Sebeso with a pained expression. He ought not to have done so, for his look froze Paulina to the ground and she could not move, so lifeless and numb was the feeling in her arms and legs. Several times Rankoane's wife called to her, after the men had walked away. Eventually, she put the bucket down and walked over to Paulina.

'I say, my friend, what's the matter?' asked Rankoane's wife.

Paulina looked at Rankoane's wife almost bitterly. Women who had husbands made the deep well of her own loneliness more acute to her.

'I'm thinking of going to the cattle post tomorrow to fetch my son,' she said.

'My, but you are brave, Paulina Sebeso,' the other woman said. 'I hear that the bush is now full of dangerous beasts that are feasting off the dead cattle.'

Paulina Sebeso stared at Rankoane's wife. People in comfort and safety said things like this to people who always faced the storms and winters of life.

'You're a silly fool, Segametse,' she said and walked away with her head held up proudly. But halfway to her own home she almost dropped it to the ground in despair, and so hangdog and depressed was she that she nearly collided into Makhaya, who stood at the entrance of her yard, looking out towards the smeared, murky red glow which was the sunset.

'Oh Makhaya,' she said, looking up at him with a taut, strained face. 'My whole life is turned upside down.'

'It's nothing,' he said, smiling down at her. 'The boy is young.

It wouldn't occur to him to come home with the cattle. We'll go together to the cattle post tomorrow and bring him and the cattle back to the village.'

And that was all he said before walking away, back to the farm. There was nothing else he offered her except his kindness and help. On other days she questioned this relentlessly because he kept it unrelated to any human feeling. He seemed to ignore the fact that he awakened a fire in someone else's life with his generosity. But on this day it lifted the weight off her arms and legs. He had not even asked her, as Rankoane had done, if her son had come home but had simply produced immediate solutions to her trouble. This filled her eyes with a quiet, wondering look. Yet Makhaya could have ended this odd game with a gesture or a few words or even a look. He knew how much Paulina Sebeso loved him, but still he hesitated. He would not have liked it if Paulina gave up and stopped loving him because it was like a warm sun on all the shadows of his life. It was just that there were things he could not put in words, that a woman's life was a clutter of small everyday things – of babies, gossip, pots, food, fires, cups, and plates – and that all these things had crashed into his consciousness during the month he had worked on the dams and tobacco sheds with the women.

Makhaya walked into the farm yard just as the cattlemen were rising from their discussion with Gilbert. They looked at Makhaya curiously with his strange, strongly marked facial bone structure. They had yet to learn from their wives about the tobacco project and the dams that were being built to trap some of the storm water, but on this evening there was no time for introduction to the stranger. The sight and sound of their cattle crashing dead on the ground were still full in the men's eyes, and they walked away with the heavy tread of people who were grieved beyond consolation. Makhaya turned and looked at his friend Gilbert and started in surprise. He knew Gilbert so well by now that he could judge his every mood, and on this evening he was in a mood of high elation, even though he kept his face quite serious and listened attentively to Dinorego, who was summing up the situation for him.

Dinorego was saying, 'We can progress too, even though we are uneducated men. The mind of an uneducated man works like this: he is a listener and a believer. Most of all he is a believer. The uneducated man has been condemned for many years by the authorities. They came to us and said, "We have found new grazing land in the west. Move the cattle over because the eastern side has no more grazing left." Yet no one moved. The west is lion country. Some time ago people were eaten by lions and that is enough. This is a belief in our minds that we will be eaten by lions therefore we cannot go west. Today, once all the cattle have died, the authorities will say, "You see, we told you." But it is strange to me that they did not create the belief that the uneducated man could shoot the lions.'

He paused and looked at the two men with his shrewd, twinkling eyes and both men burst out laughing. It was only a pity that Dinorego was not the prime minister of Botswana, as no one could defeat his reasoning power or his faith in progress. He also liked an audience and spread out his hands appreciatively and continued:

'Nearly every agriculture man knows about the progress of the uneducated man. They are always coming to us saying, "Look, I can show you how to plough eighty morgen of sorghum." Once he has produced a field of eighty morgen, the uneducated man will be consumed by jealousy and try to do the same. What he sees, he believes. But he never questions a matter like an educated man. The miracle must be placed before his eyes, then he will try to perform a miracle too.'

Gilbert looked at the old man intently, the blue flame of elation dancing brightly in his eyes. 'What would you say if I said that the deaths of all these cattle, in Golema Mmidi, are a miracle? What would you say if I said I was hoping it would happen?' he asked.

The old man kept deadly silent as he suspected a trap in these unexpected words of Gilbert, and Makhaya leaned forward with interest as he was now about to hear the reason for the suppressed excitement of his friend. Gilbert raised his hands like a gambler who foresees only the gains that will come without any losses. He had three years of research and experiments behind him, but the cattle population of Golema Mmidi had been too huge and unwieldy for his plans. For planned and scientific production of high-grade beef, he needed a drastically reduced herd. He also needed the men near the food-growing areas where beef production and food production could be combined. He had everything on hand too, the latest developments in fodder crops for cattle feed and silage-making and his own experiments with the natural grasses of Botswana and imported grass seed.

To the cattlemen he had merely presented the government's emergency plans for dealing with the situation, and these were that there was to be an accelerated slaughter of emaciated beasts at the abattoir. These emaciated beasts would be boiled down into corned beef. This slaughter of cattle would bring in about ten pounds per cow for each man, which was better than nothing at all, and it was designed to relieve the situation until free emergency rations would arrive in about one month's time. Thus each man would contribute so many head of cattle from his herd, and those that were left would be kept alive for one month on the fodder in the farm's silage pits. The men had agreed to this arrangement. They had also agreed to retain within the co-operative a certain sum of the money they received for the wholesale slaughter of cattle. This would act as an incentive to the cattlemen to recoup from their losses and restock their herds. He also told the men that since they had an organized cattle co-operative in the village the government had already agreed to drill a free borehole, whose equipment and management would in future be taken over by the co-operative.

This was all he had told them, but to Makhaya and Dinorego, on whom he depended for the fulfilment of his dreams, he allowed his mind to leap ahead to three years from that date when all the thick forests of thornbush that surrounded Golema Mmidi had given way to acres and acres of cultivated fields on which crops grew, under irrigation, the year round. Golema Mmidi would have about ten to twelve boreholes and reservoirs by that time and as many more big dams to hold back every drop of storm water. And he willed his two companions to see it, how Golema Mmidi would supply the whole country with the fresh fruit and vegetables it lacked, and apart from bringing in the highest profits for the best-grade beef, it would also create the first industries in the country. Why, he had already picked up a cigarette manufacturer and made him sign a contract to buy tobacco grown by the Golema Mmidi tobacco-growing co-operative, and this manufacturer was already building a factory in northern Botswana.

'People have said to me, "Oh, forget farming in this dry country,"' he said intensely. 'I've kept my mouth shut all these years, but my eyes have taught me that Botswana is a farmer's heaven. It's better than countries with a high rainfall. Farming under irrigation is controlled and predictable farming. Also, the long dry season is more suited to crops like potatoes and tobacco, which need well-drained soil. We've a minimum of crop-destroying pests to deal with too, and the soil is rich and fertile.'

He looked at Makhaya with his eyes full of dreams, because Makhaya had proved himself the magician who could make tobacco co-operatives appear overnight. He wanted Golema Mmidi to be co-operative in everything as that was the only way of defeating the land tenure system in the tribal reserves and the only way of defeating subsistence agriculture which was geared to keeping the poor man poor until eternity. Makhaya smiled back quietly and affectionately at his friend. He liked this kind of talk. He liked the idea that the whole of Golema Mmidi would be full of future millionaires. It blended in with his own dreams about Africa because he could not see it other than as a continent of future millionaires, which would compensate for all the centuries of browbeating, hatred, humiliation, and worldwide derision that had been directed to the person of the African man. And communal systems of development which imposed co-operation and sharing of wealth were much better than the dog-eat-dog policies, takeover bids, and grab-what-you-can of big finance. Therefore, in Makhaya's mind, the poverty and tribalism of Africa were a blessing if people could develop sharing everything with each other.

'I like everything you say, Gilbert,' he said with deep feeling. They looked at the old man, who always had the last word on everything. But Dinorego kept silent. He was regretting that the world had decided to improve itself only when he had become such an old man with a few years left to live. Now, each time he decided he would rest in peace, he kept on learning more about life, and he was not feeling so contented about dying.

'I'm going to the cattle post tomorrow,' Makhaya said, breaking the silence.

Gilbert and the old man looked at him in surprise. These were the familiar words of a Motswana man, but they sounded strange on Makhaya's lips.

Makhaya wanted to laugh out loud at their surprise. He felt no desire whatsoever to own these huge beasts. They would be an intolerable encumbrance to him. Hesitantly, he explained that he had promised Paulina he would accompany her to her cattle post to see if everything was all right with her son.

'The boy may be ill,' he said. 'She expected him to come home with someone named Rankoane whose cattle post is near hers, but he says the boy should have arrived home two weeks ago. Rankoane says the wells have dried up.'

It chilled Gilbert to hear this and he felt a sharp stab of pain at the way he had light-heartedly talked of scientific beef production amidst all this tragedy.

'Mack, you know it's a whole day's walk to the cattle posts,' he said. 'The three of us will leave first thing in the morning with the Land Rover. I also want to see for myself what is happening in the bush.'

He looked across at Makhaya with all the elation gone out of his eyes. His mind had jumped too far ahead into the future, but the present was painful and terrible.

'I hope the boy is only ill,' he said. 'He may be dead.'

Makhaya said nothing, yet once Maria came out of the hut and called the three men to eat, his stomach was just tight, painful knots and he excused himself and walked away to his hut. He lay down for some time in his hut, in the darkness, with a strange sensation of having no thoughts in his head, only to discover, with an explosive shock, that he had been talking to himself all the time. He had no idea of what he had been saying to himself because it was an incoherent expression of the concentration of pain inside him. What sort of man was he who only gave way to love under extreme pressure and pain? Perhaps, he had read somewhere, men and women just loved each other without reason or purpose, but he did not belong to this world, not when everything inside him was in revolt. If he loved Paulina now and admitted it to himself, it was because he sensed that she might be facing tragedy, and that she could not face it alone. He swung his legs off the bed, stood up, and walked out of the farm to the home of Paulina Sebeso. There was complete darkness in her yard as she was already in bed. He knocked on the door of the hut she used as a bedroom.

'Who is it?' she asked, as she was not yet asleep.

'Makhaya,' he said, quietly.

She was silent awhile, then jumped out of bed and unlocked the door. He could not even see her face in this pitch-dark night, and there was still this struggle within his aloof self, so uncertain was he of life.

'Gilbert will also be coming to the cattle post tomorrow,' he said, oddly, excusing himself because he was about to invade her life through his fear of tomorrow.

She still kept silent, half-wanting to laugh and half-wanting to cry. Then she closed her eyes to add to the darkness, because nothing that you said seemed quite so bad when everything was dark.

'Makhaya,' she said softly. 'You mustn't think I'm a cheap woman, but I love you.'

'Why cheap?' he said, amused. 'There are no cheap women. Even those you buy love you, while we men rarely do. Perhaps I'll find out what love is like as we go along together.'

Makhaya was thankful, too, for the dark as he entered her hut. For so long there was this grey graveyard in which he had lived. And who could tell what ghosts really do when they come alive in the dark night?

CHAPTER ELEVEN

It was just as though everything was about to die. The small brown birds had deserted the bush, and the bush itself no longer supplied the coverage and protection for the secret activities of the scarlet and golden birds. Here and there, faint patches of green clung to the topmost branches of tall thorn trees, but not a green thing survived near the sun-baked earth. The sky had lost that dense blue look of the winter days and spread itself out into a whitish film, through which the sun poured out molten heat in pulsating waves from dawn to dusk. In this desolation the vultures reigned supreme. They gathered on the ground in huge flocks of sixty to a hundred and held important discussions in hoarse, rough voices and flapped their long, sloppy brown feathers in imperious indignation. They could afford to be imperious, indignant and important, for they were to be a burial society for over six hundred thousand cattle. They were amazed and wondering if they would manage it all or if they should send messages to fellow brethren in Africa and India. But whatever their deliberations, they were fearless and proud, for these mean, fierce birds knew that they were always the last visitors on a stricken part of the earth.

Barely three miles away from the village of Golema Mmidi the impact of all this struck the small party that had left for the cattle post early in the morning. During the night, a cow that had belonged to one of the cattlemen had lain down to calve and died in the process. A jackal had hovered near her the whole night and at dawn set himself to devour the newborn calf. The approach of the Land Rover disturbed him and he arose and slunk away into the bush. Gilbert slowed down the vehicle near the cow and his exclamation – 'Oh, this is terrible!' – hardly conveyed the deep sense of shock Makhaya felt. From that day Makhaya was to become peculiarly Motswana in his outlook. Coming from a country of green hills and fresh bubbling streams, he was from that day to treasure every green shoot that sprang up in this dry place, and he would fear to waste even a drop of water. Paulina was the only one who was not deeply perturbed by what she saw. She had lived through times like this before, when the bush was bare and the ploughing season delayed indefinitely. To her, it even seemed like an unreal and lovely spring morning when life was just beginning anew again instead of dying, and her feelings relived over and over again a whole night's dream.

He just sat there beside her looking as cool and aloof and unchanged as yesterday, while nothing of her own life was left to her, as though she had become an appendage of his body like an arm or a leg. It wasn't a pleasant feeling, as no secure promises had been made. On the one hand, a woman distrusted extravagant promises and, on the other, lived in fear of the silence of a reserved man who only expressed himself in deeds. Maybe women invented marriage, as their imaginations had invented most other things in man's social life. They can't help saying, 'Are you my property? I must own you.' And now Paulina busied her mind with these things while the sky and the bush exploded into a hot, white glare of heat.

Gilbert turned round and half-smiled at all the dreams in the woman's eyes.

'Am I still going in the right direction, Paul?' he asked. 'The bush is so changed, I can't make out a thing.'

That is, if he ever had. Like the Tswana language, the bush belonged to all the Batswana people, who had created its footpaths and mapped out its length and breadth in their minds. It had often amazed him to discover that cattlemen drove their cattle home, through the bush, in pitch darkness, with an unerring sense of direction, while he, Gilbert, had several times lost his direction within the fenced farm lands, and his legs and arms bore lots of scars from his having pitched himself into a barbed-wire fence at night. But Paulina had footed it this way every three or four months to take her son his food rations and see if all was well with him at the cattle post, and not so long ago, the call of birds had filled these empty spaces. They were always after something, these lovely birds, and she had always kept corn seed in the pocket of her skirt to scatter along the pathway. Now, the vultures, full and gorged, adorned the bare trees, and beneath their resting places lay the white, picked bones of the dead cattle. Those in the trees stared arrogantly at the passing vehicle, and those on the ground merely waddled out of the way. They were the kings of the bush and would remain so throughout this long year of no rain and no crops.

They passed a few empty drinking pools in the bush, and around these were scattered the carcasses of the tiny wild buck. Hundreds had gathered at their favourite drinking places, because about this time every year storm clouds brooded on the horizon and the rain fell down in blinding sheets of water and the scene changed overnight into carpets of fine green grass and splashes of purple and yellow flowers and the drinking pools filled up with sky-blue water. The memory of all this drove them

182

to their drinking pools, where they died. The cattlemen had a similar memory. Towards the end of the long dry season they too left their watering places along the river beds, and moved with their cattle into the bush where the grass grew in tangled confusion under the trees, and watered their cattle in the drinking pools of the wild buck. A few of the cattlemen, expecting rain at any time, had deviated towards these water pools on the journey homeward, only to have their huge herds fall down there and die. It happened over and over in Botswana that year.

Long before they reached Paulina's cattle post they saw the vultures circling above it in the sky. This marked it out right away as one of the death points. Once they drew close, they could see that not a living thing moved on the ground. All those eighty cattle lay scattered about, quite still, quite dead. It was like the final statement of all the terrible story of the bush. But there was still hope in the heart of the mother. She somehow expected her son to creep out of the lone and solitary hut, and she knew already how she would comfort him and dismiss all this as being of no account. So no one moved once Gilbert had stopped the car some twenty yards from the hut, and each person sat silently absorbing the desolate scene until the vultures began swooping down in a straight column on the already decomposing carcasses. This jerked the woman into action and she scrambled out of the car and raced towards the hut. But Makhaya reached the door before her and pulled her back and looked at her briefly with an angry expression. What was inside there was only for him to see. He pushed open the door and looked in. There was only a heap of clean, white bones lying on the floor. They lay in a curled, cramped position with the bones of the hands curved inward. The white ants and maggots had vied with each other to clear all the flesh off the little boy. And Makhaya stood there so silent and still, absorbing this terrible sight, confused and angry that there was only this dead, unanswering silence in his heart, as though he had only expected to see such sights. Paulina touched him on the back, and he swung around sharply with an expression of hurt surprise on his face.

'The boy is dead,' he said sharply. 'Why do you want to go in?'

'I must see the body,' she said, but with dry, taut lips. 'I must see the body because it is our custom.'

'You see,' he said, in a deliberately harsh voice. 'All these rotten customs are killing us. Can't you see I'm here to bear all your burdens? Come on.'

And he walked towards the car, knowing she would meekly follow him. He stood nearby and waited until she had climbed in, then he turned, almost with relief, to Gilbert, who sat at the wheel of the car with an ashen face.

'Is the boy dead, too?' Gilbert asked.

'Yes,' Makhaya said shortly, and he had no idea that the hurt expression was still on his face. It was like having a smudge there and not knowing you had it. As though, Gilbert thought, he wanted to feel for everyone and get the matter over with. A small light of friendship and understanding stirred in Gilbert's eyes, and sensing this Makhaya spoke so trustingly to him:

'We don't know what has caused the death of the child, my friend,' he said. 'So, we will have to call the police. Could you please take my wife home and notify the police at the same time? I'll remain behind.'

These few simple words put new life into Gilbert. He nodded briefly and turned the car round, and he and Paulina drove back in the direction of Golema Mmidi. Makhaya was left alone with the vultures. Surrounded by tragedy and seated in the shade of a ramshackle mud hut in the Botswana bush, he began to see himself. In retrospect he seemed a small-minded man. All his life he had wanted some kind of Utopia, and he had rejected in his mind and heart a world full of ailment and faults. He had run and run away from it all, but now the time had come when he could run and hide no longer and would have to turn round and face all that he had run away from. Loving one woman had brought him to this realization: that it was only people who could bring the real rewards of living, that it was only people who give love and happiness.

As though to confirm his new trend of thought, he stirred a foot and found it brushed against a bundle of something, carefully tied up. He opened the bundle and in it was a collection of wood carvings, done by the small boy to occupy himself during the lonely hours of cattle herding. Among the assortment he picked up a thick porridge spoon, one and a half feet in length. A great deal of effort had been put into the production of this spoon. The small boy had probably intended it to be a gift to his mother. He had decorated the long handle with the twisting pattern of a snake's scaly body, and almost every detail, right up to the venomous eyes, had been reproduced. The design was bold and vivid and he had burned it into the wood with a red-hot piece of iron. Makhaya looked at it for some time, struggling to capture a living image of a child he did not know. He hoped he and Paulina would never create a child who would be expected to carry burdens beyond his age.

All the other carvings concerned themselves with the animals the small boy had observed in his surroundings, wild bucks, tortoises, monkeys, and birds. The birds were carved into a majestic, charcoal boat, and half a dozen of them sat tail to tail with their heads in the air, like kings. One carving in particular aroused Makhaya's curiosity. The piece of wood was not more than six inches in length, and half of the grain was a livid flesh colour and the other was snow-white. Out of this the boy had carved a minute crocodile with the same attention to detail as the snake design. Where had the boy seen a crocodile? There were none along the eastern border area where the cattle grazed. And the surrounding area was thornbush forest, and the tiny piece of wood was a foreigner to the area.

Makhaya bent to tie up the bundle and the slight clatter of wood against wood made him look up at a comical drama that was played out barely six paces away from him. A wild jackal had been swiftly approaching the graveyard of cattle, and thinking himself alone with the vultures, he had concentrated his whole mind on his forthcoming meal. The unexpected noise brought him to a dead halt, and his first reaction was one of abject fear.

Looking neither left nor right, he almost slunk into the ground and then, a moment later, lifted one right paw in pathetic, pitiful apology, at the same time baring his sharp, jagged teeth in a savage snarl. Since the snarl went unchallenged, the poor thing quickly recovered himself and swivelled his foxy face in Makhaya's direction. The sun was behind the jackal, but as he turned to Makhaya, the sun's reflection shone in his beautiful amber eyes in honey-gold flashes. The jackal had a soft, thick, honey-gold coat too, with a contrasting streak of silver and black fur down his back. He stood for a few seconds, eyeing Makhaya fearfully, and then turned and bounded away into the bush. It occurred to Makhaya that a wild animal was more afraid of man than a man need be of it, and its one thought was to retreat as far from man as possible. It seemed to him that in essence most of his reactions had been like those of the jackal, from the day he had been born. For some time his mouth quivered with amusement at the strange antics of the wild animal. Maybe that panic-stricken beast had a jackal society where he felt sane and secure, but no human society was sane and normal. Yet Makhaya needed to come to terms with his society because he needed a woman and children.

He could not go on thinking of the heap of bones that lay inside the hut, because death was like trying to clutch the air, and you had to let it be and slowly let it pass aside, without fuss and indignity. Instead, you had to concentrate the mind on all that was still alive and treat it as the most precious treasure you had ever been given. Besides, he had felt all the pain he was capable of feeling the night before, and it had directed his actions along this new path. So, he sat there thinking about his new life with Paulina. Even ordinary things like cups, brooms, pots, and houses were a pleasure to him to contemplate, once he had become aware of their existence, as though all these things would anchor him firmly to the earth. They also strengthened his resolve to be a future millionaire, for many a future millionaire must have had a dead child in his life who had died from lack of proper food, and he must have had a one-room hut in which he could hardly move and breathe. He must have lain awake at night, craving a four-room house with a kitchen, bathroom and taps, and mentally clothed this house with ornaments, chairs and beds, and he must have said he would always spend five pounds but get ten pounds back as change. If a man didn't have dreams like this, in Africa, he would end up food for the vultures too.

These horrible creatures guzzled and guzzled, seeming to have bottomless appetites. The wind swept huge columns of sand up into the sky, which carried the odour of death with them and brought more vultures, in thick, black patrols. They swooped down with their big wings outstretched like supersonic jets. Some of the fully gorged birds made way for the newcomers, flying up into the thorn trees and adorning the bare branches in monstrous, silent, carved postures. Even the wind blew according to its own mad pattern. For hours tiny gusts flew in harassed circles around the thornbush until they all converged into a roaring turmoil of air and red dust which would race madly for a mile or so along the earth and then sweep up and disperse itself in the sky.

Makhaya stood up at last, sickened by the ceaseless clack, clack of the vultures' beaks. Away from the little hut and the vultures was the endless, dead vista of scorched earth and twisted dry thornbush. He leaned against a dead tree and closed his eyes, all his capacity for thought slowly seeping out of him. This bush on all sides was the most awful life imaginable, and it occurred to Makhaya that it must have been this unrelieved, heavy isolation which had driven the lively-minded Dinorego out of the cattle business. Yet thousands of people lived like this, like trees, in all the lonely wastes of Africa, cut off even from communication with their own selves. Was it any wonder that life stood still if a man became a tree? Therefore, he, Makhaya, could run so far in search of peace, but it was contact with other living beings that a man needed most. Maybe even Utopias were just trees. Maybe. Maybe he walked around in hopeless circles, but at least he was attempting to reach up to a life beyond the morass in which all black men lived. Most men were waiting for the politicians to sort out their private agonies.

At this point he ceased thinking altogether, and the sun passed its topmost peak in the sky and began sinking towards the horizon. At about three o'clock Gilbert returned with the police officer George Appleby-Smith and a doctor. Makhaya sat in the car drinking a little water and eating food which Gilbert had brought along, while the policeman and doctor made their reports. Gilbert also sat in the car but he kept silent, too. Eventually the doctor came out of the hut and walked towards the car.

'I'd say the poor little fellow died of malnutrition,' he said.

He kept quiet a moment, screwed up his eyes, and looked away. The hospitals were full of children who died in the posture of the little boy in the hut, their knees cramped up to their chins, their bony fingers curled into their palms like steel claws. Most of those who survived would be mental defectives or cripples – while this little boy had mercifully died.

'The policeman wants to know if it's all right to bury the boy here,' he added quietly.

Only Makhaya moved. 'I'll accept responsibility for that,' he said. He turned round and picked up a small can of petrol, jumped out of the car, and walked to the hut. George Appleby-Smith stood in the dark hut, staring at the little heap of bones, with an expressionless face. All these sights were supposed to be all in a day's work to him. But he stored these experiences away to give him the courage to run his area the way he thought it ought to be run, even befriending 'security risks' like Makhaya. All those authorities had kicked up such a dust about his allowing a 'security risk' to settle in Golema Mmidi, but they never had occasion to come out into the bush to see how children died, while he, George, saw everything, every day. He turned towards Makhaya with one of those very rare smiles.

'Hullo, Makhaya,' he said. 'You settling down?'

'You still sticking your neck out for me?' Makhaya countered, also smiling.

Makhaya bent and poured a little petrol over the heap of bones, struck a match, and within a few seconds converted the pathetic sight into ashes. Then he scooped up the ashes into a small container which was lying in a corner of the hut. There was not a trace of the agony and fright in which the little boy must have died. Apart from the tin container, the small boy's bedding, half a bag of ant-riddled sorghum meal, and a badly-burned porridge pot, there was nothing else in the hut. They took with them only the tin container and the tied-up bundle outside the hut. It was long past sundown when they arrived in the village of Golema Mmidi. Even George Appleby-Smith had nothing to say. Droughts and dead children made him lose his sense of humour, and he got into his own car with the doctor and drove away. Maria walked quickly into the yard in her aloof, serious way. The whole village knew by now that Paulina's child had died and they were all in her yard, not talking but just sitting in heavy silent groups, like the trees. Makhaya suddenly could not bear this most exacting of all African customs, not just then, not with his emotional involvement with Paulina. He handed the tin container to Maria.

'Please take this to Paulie,' he said. 'Tell her I thought it best to burn what was left of the child.'

Gilbert walked with his wife to the home of Paulina but Makhaya walked to his own hut, still clutching the tied-up bundle of wood carvings, and dropped on the bed in a deep and dreamless sleep. An hour later Maria knocked on the door. She had a tray with food and a cup of tea. There was silence inside the hut so she pushed the door open and walked in, setting the tray down on the table. She stood looking down with a slight smile at the sleeping man. Being an African man he ought to have known that nothing happened on the continent of Africa without all Africans getting to know of it. In some mysterious way, the news had travelled around the village of Golema Mmidi that Makhaya had spent the previous night at Paulina's home, even though Paulina had made no mention of it to anyone. God knows what they expected of the poor man, but it had added a twist of drama to an everyday event of mourning a death, which event everyone had to participate in. People were genuinely sorry for the bereaved Paulina, but they soon forgot it when only Maria and Gilbert turned up for the show with the remains of the dead child in a tin container. A lively titter of whispering started and Maria heard it all, silly things that would keep women twittering for days. If you can't face a crowd you must be a person who hates people, irrespective of a lifetime of individual deeds of kindness to individual people. That's why deviationists and independent-minded people were so few in Africa. But it wasn't because of the crowd that she awoke Makhaya. They had dispersed and gone their way by now. It was because of Paulina and the way she blamed herself for the death of her child in a quiet, final and despairing way without the usual tears or hysterics. She kept on looking at everyone with that haughty stare as much as to say, 'Why don't you all go away?' Only Mma-Millipede suspected that this quiet attitude meant that Paulina might try to kill herself, and she had confided this aside to Maria and said that she would remain behind, even for the whole night if necessary.

Maria bent and shook the sleeping man awake. 'Have some food,' she said in a kind and gentle voice because she was sorry, in her personal and private way, for everyone's suffering.

Since she hesitated, he turned to this twin soul of privacy and isolation and asked, 'Do you know what I saw today, Maria?'

'No,' she said curiously.

'Even the trees were dying, from the roots upward,' he said. 'Does everything die like this?'

'No,' she said. 'You may see no rivers on the ground but we keep the rivers inside us. That is why all good things and all good people are called rain. Sometimes we see the rain clouds gather even though not a cloud appears in the sky. It is all in our heart.'

He nodded his head, fully grasping this in its deepest meaning. There was always something on this earth man was forced to love and worship by reason of its absence. People in cloudy, misty climates worshipped the sun, and people in semi-desert countries worshipped the rain.

'Paulina is blaming herself for the death of the child,' she added softly, frightened at involving herself in the feelings of this sensitive man.

'I knew she would,' he said, and paused in his eating and looked up at her. 'I couldn't say anything about it with everyone there. Have they gone away?'

'Yes, but Mma-Millipede is still there.'

He put the unfinished plate of food on the tray and stood up, waiting for her to pick up the tray and leave the hut. Then he blew out the candle and picked up the bundle of wood carvings.

'What a way for you to come home, little boy,' he whispered, and stepped out into the dark night. The wind had died down and the stars shone down in the low, black sky with full, green lights. The stars were always there to accompany a man's lonely footsteps. They had been with him on the night he first arrived in Botswana, and they were like sprays of flowers between the narrow, grim streets of the slums in which he had grown up. They would be there too after he passed away, and they were all the conviction he had that some quiet and good creator controlled and owned the earth.

Mma-Millipede was saying much the same thing to Paulina. They sat out in the yard, near a bonfire of logs which the men of the village had lit, as a sign of death in the house. He stood for a moment outside the range of the firelight and listened to the murmur of Mma-Millipede's voice. Not only Jesus Christ had observed this but Mma-Millipede too – that this earth was not the final abode of man. It was a place of sorrows, a wilderness in which his soul wandered in restless torment. The soul had to accept this. But the young woman whom she so wisely counselled drooped her head and arms forlornly to the ground.

No words, however wise, could explain the awfulness of death, not while the living were firmly attached to love, child-bearing, child-rearing, hunger, struggle, and the sunrise of tomorrow. Life had to flow all the time, for the living, like water in a stream. Makhaya held it in his hand. It was the little bundle of wood carvings. Yet he stood where he was until the two women slowly became aware of his presence.

'Makhaya!' Paulina exclaimed, jumping up and rushing towards the faint outline of his white shirt. 'Oh, why did you take so long to come?' she cried brokenly, and a torrent of hot tears spilled onto his shirt like a small waterfall. He slipped one free arm around her thin, bony waist.

'Aren't you glad I've come now? Don't cry. I've brought you something.'

But even when she had untied the bundle near the firelight, with trembling fingers, this small waterfall continued to drench her arms and blouse and skirt. Mma-Millipede had to join in too with long, slow teardrops and many 'Bathos' while they examined the carvings, one by one. After a time Makhaya could see that they were actually laughing in spite of those tears because they both knew the boy, with his oversized scarecrow coat and big smile. They saw how he had killed a snake in the bush, brought it back to his hut and carefully copied the patterns of its body onto the wooden handle of a porridge spoon. But the handiwork on the little crocodile was different from the small boy's rough strokes. It had the smooth, polished finish of an old professional hunter and woodcarver and such a man had passed by the small boy's cattle post one day and exchanged his own professional work for that of a cheerful little boy. And what other way was there to mourn the death of such a boy? Makhaya liked it this way, for he imagined the small boy the way he had been, standing quite close by and observing it. It made his heart feel very peaceful. It reminded Mma-Millipede that her back was aching and she was very tired. He stood up and accompanied Mma-Millipede all the way to her home, her tired feet shuffling quietly on the path beside him.

She sighed deeply to herself in an absent-minded way, but as they were about to part company she said, 'Well, I say, my son, this is a world full of sorrows.'

'Yes,' he said.

But in spite of agreeing with Mma-Millipede his heart continued to feel peaceful. Perhaps he would have the courage to make children in such a world. For in this kind of lull from the inner torture of his life, he could think clearly. He was just an ordinary man and he wanted to stay that way all his life. None of the tinsel and glitter of the world attracted him but just what there was to live on and make do with in a village like Golema Mmidi. They were going to start shooting up everyone one day, and George Appleby-Smith would come to him and say, 'I'm sorry, but the government wants you to leave because you're a security risk.'

And you wouldn't know what they meant by that because Africa was your country and there was no place else where a black man would come into his own and eventually lift up his head with dignity. Perhaps the whole world would still pretend not to understand your state of mind.

'We're morality,' they'll say. 'For God's sake stop the slaughter, we're on your side. We're morality and we're on your side.'

But in the meanwhile he walked back to a firelight in the Botswana bush with these unending tortures stilled for a bit. He hoped to find out something because there were too many riddles and ironies these days, even in the African bush. He understood a man like Gilbert perfectly, as though life never did anything haphazardly but prepared people for their friends and threw them together at the right moment for some more obscure purpose than building dams, tobacco co-operatives, and cattle-feeding grounds. Maybe he would not survive with his 'security risk' status, but the world would not rid itself of African men. He would always be there, but not any longer as the white man's joke, or his 'munt' or his 'kaffir' or his 'boy'.

CHAPTER TWELVE

A week after Paulina Sebeso's child had been found dead in the hut at the cattle post, the village of Golema Mmidi awoke to a day such as they would never forget. Looking back, the people even wondered aloud as to how it had all begun with such an ordinary event as the sunrise. Most of the women were up and about at dawn these days as they now had husbands to attend to, and from every yard a smoke haze arose as they all prepared the early morning tea and porridge.

Paulina found she had to wear two faces these days, one for when she was in a crowd and one for when she was alone. When she was alone, she smiled to herself because she was happy and could not reconcile this happiness to the loss of her boy and all her cattle. Mma-Millipede would have said that it was one rare occasion when the Lord took away with one hand and gave with another because it was seldom that the Lord ever gave a woman a man like Makhaya. Of course, Makhaya still observed some African customs like just coming and staying with a woman without first marrying her and then being indefinite about the date of marriage which might take place even after two or three children had been born. But which African man really loved a woman the way they could all see that Gilbert loved Maria? By love a man stuck to one woman, but African men liked the woman who stayed up the hill and the one in the valley and the one in the next village, all in the same nice indiscriminate way. In this way Makhaya differed from all African men, so Paulina reasoned. He had a lot of funny things to say for himself too, not all of which she understood, but she would have fought anyone with blows who questioned her loyalty to Makhaya. So she made the tea with a gay, light heart and then set a pot near the fire for bathing water.

I'll have to do this and that today, she said to herself, nodding her head as she ticked off the items and carefully poured the tea into the cups. Makhaya had told her not to slosh any of it onto the saucer. Even homes of mud huts must be run like a hotel, he said, with everything spick-and-span, and the small girl ought to be bathed from head to toe every night. Talk about a wonderful man who cared about all these small things. Not only that. The tobacco the women were to grow had been the talk of the village ever since the men had come back.

They had all been to the farm to stare in fascination at the tiny experimental plot of olive-green tobacco leaf. So, this was what their wives and sweethearts were up to now, they said to each other, flushed with pride, the same way the ancient hunters of history must have reacted when they came back from hunting trips and found their wives had cultivated the wheat and domesticated a few wild animals for their meat. Indeed, what else was this small venture into tobacco growing but to arouse an interest in the men in the production of cash crops? The men would eventually have to take on the task of producing those acres and acres of tobacco. But first they would have to stay home. Could a twenty-eight-mile fence be erected for a cattle-holding ground, Gilbert had asked? Of course, they said.

And the men were prepared to pool their labour for the big job, but just right now they were sorting out how to keep alive what cattle they had left. This was problem number one until help arrived, three weeks from now, in the form of emergency rations and a spare borehole.

Paulina saw Gilbert walking into the yard now to fetch Makhaya so that they could go to the ranch. And Makhaya was still asleep even though she had awakened him fifteen minutes ago. He seemed to like getting up in a commotion of hurry. Paulina rushed about flustered and breathless for five minutes until the two men walked out of the yard. Then she bent down, poured the remainder of the bath into a basin, picked it up, and was about to enter the hut to wash when, to her amazement, she saw a silent figure crouched down near the entrance of her yard. It was one of Matenge's servants.

'Good-day, friend,' she said apprehensively. 'What do you need?'

The servant looked up, a sly grin on her servile face. 'I am sent to bring you to court. The chief has a case.'

'I?' Paulina asked, stupefied. 'But what have I done?'

Again there was that sly grin. This wretched creature in smelly rags and tatters was the last contact with mankind that Matenge had. He had been muttering and fuming to the servants for some days now, and the grinning was the arrogant pride of someone who is always kicked around yet needed by the master.

'You ought to know what you've been up to,' the servant said. 'All I can say is that I am sent.'

'Agh, leave me alone,' Paulina said impatiently, and walked into the hut.

But when she came out the servant was still there, crouched down, and she began to be afraid, wondering what she had done to offend Matenge. And all she could think of was that she had forgotten to report the death of her son to the chief. It was a custom but surely a court case could not be made out of forgetfulness? She even pulled the little girl about roughly as she dressed her for school, so nervous and unsettled did she feel. Also, today was the day when she and a group of women were to harvest the first batch of tobacco. They would soon join her in the yard. She turned to the servant, wanting to wait for her friends.

'I suppose the chief is offended because I forgot to report the death of my son?' she asked tentatively.

'I really don't know,' the servant said, with that maddening grin.

Paulina decided that she would no longer speak to this dreadful person but she took her time, dishing up a plate of porridge for herself and her child, waiting for her friends. She liked company at all times, especially when there was trouble.

Just at this time too, the six old men who sat on the village council were receiving the message to attend court and, like Paulina, they were stunned and apprehensive. Matenge never called them unless it was to destroy an inhabitant of Golema Mmidi. He had never done one act of kindness towards the villagers, seeming to be placed there only for their torture. They gathered their tattered coats about them and shuffled towards the centre of the village.

Paulina's friends stepped into the yard at that moment and straight away decided to accompany Paulina to the court case. Along the way they picked up Maria, then Dinorego, and Mma-Millipede. The news travelled swiftly from hut to hut, and men and women immediately set down their chores for the day and made their way to the village centre. They were even excited in a silent way as though they had known this day would arrive when they would all face their persecutor of many years.

They had been straining together in one direction for years, and Matenge had been straining in the opposite direction, always pulling them down. Because of this they had politely avoided him, but today they wanted to see his face when their cattle were dying while his cattle were safe, way up on the northern border where a river flowed the year round and the grass was good and salty and green. They wanted to see this man who had all the privileges, who had never known a day of starvation in this country of two years of good rain and seven years of drought. They wanted to know what his mood was like after these years of silence and mute disagreement. They wanted him to know they were not after his Chevrolet or big house. They would even tell him this with gentle smiles and pleasant gestures and reassure him that it was only their lives they wanted to set right and he must not stand in their way. He was there through their tolerance. They would even be able to tolerate ten thousand Matenges, but the disagreement between him and them was that he said no, no, no to every-thing they wanted to do. But they were the people of Golema Mmidi to whom too many tyrants and unscrupulous men had said no, no, no, and people like the people of Golema Mmidi could not be hunted, hounded, banished, and persecuted for-ever and forever and forever. Were they to be driven to the vultures that now soared overhead in the blazing, dead-white sky? Very well then, the whole village, as one man, would go and die in the bush if that was all a tyrant wanted of them. If you said no, no, no, and kept your claws in a people's heart, what else did you want but that they should all die? You were so unreasonable.

These thoughts ran through the minds of all the villagers as they hurried towards the home of Matenge. It wasn't any longer Paulina Sebeso who was to be persecuted alone but the whole village of Golema Mmidi. Thus, when all the villagers suddenly found themselves meeting face to face at the village centre, they looked at each other and smiled and laughed with a load taken off their minds because they were at last of the same mind. Only three people were absent – Gilbert, Makhaya, and Pelotona, the permit man.

Matenge had not expected this. He stood in the shadow of his enclosed porch, watching the crowd. When they turned and walked towards the gate of his yard, he retreated indoors, in panic, running from window to window and door to door, barricading himself inside. The servants, observing his panic, crept like stricken shadows out of the back door and fled into the bush. He was left alone with his panic in a dark, locked house. He walked to one of the windows and looked down into the yard. The villagers had all seated themselves on the ground, with their faces turned expectantly towards the house, waiting for him to come out. And they would wait and wait and wait now because this was the end of the road for them and Matenge. Big, slow tears rolled down the rutted grooves of his cheeks as he stood there, watching them.

Why did he cry? The greatest moments of his life had been when he had inflicted suffering on his fellow men. People were not people to him but things he kicked about, pawns to be used by him, to break, banish and destroy for his entertainment. That was the tradition in which he had grown up, and maybe he could not be blamed for taking full advantage of it. Most chiefs were half Matenge and half the casual charm of his brother, and they lived on their own weird tightrope as fathers of the people. Half the time they turned on the charm, just in the nick of time to save themselves from damnation. But they were all an evil, cruel crowd. Only Matenge had not known how to turn on the charm to save himself.

Was he crying now because, for the first time in his life, he was feeling what it must be like to face a tomorrow without any future? That was what those upturned faces meant. He would have to go away. They weren't going to tolerate a man like him any longer because he would not give way nor understand that they needed co-operation from the man at the top to whom everyone had to go for permission to progress. The Matenges and Paramount Chief Sekotos did not have to lift up the spades and dig the earth. It cost them nothing to say yes, yes, yes, build your dam because we have no water in this country. But it gave them a deep and perverted joy to say no, no, no. The end of it was that Matenge had to barricade himself up, not because the villagers were about to rise up and tear him to shreds, but because he was an evil pervert and knew it. Only you could not understand why a man like that stood there crying like a forlorn and lonely child.

A flock of vultures gathered overhead, circling in the sky, eyeing the villagers with extreme interest and curiosity, so accustomed had they become to feasting on anything in sight, and it was the long, lazy, swooping flight of the vultures over the centre of the village that confirmed to the three men at the cattle ranch that something had gone seriously wrong in the village of Golema Mmidi. They had been waiting for the village men to come to the ranch. Cattle had to be trucked, rations distributed. But all that had faced them for a half an hour of waiting was this eerie silence. Then the flight of the vultures. Gilbert and Makhaya and the permit man looked at each other as much as to say: What now? Then they walked along the footpaths, passed the deserted huts with rising alarm. No Paulina. No Maria. And even the farm workers had left off their duties.

The three men got into the Land Rover and drove to the village centre and right up to the gate of Matenge's home. They climbed out a little uncertainly and stood near the gate. Everyone turned around but for a while no one spoke. And there was just this silent, shut-up house with the gleaming Chevrolet in the yard. Even Dinorego failed to explain the situation, and once more the villagers turned their heads towards the house.

'What's happening here, people?' Makhaya asked at last, in a loud, clear voice.

'We're waiting for the chief to come out, son,' Dinorego replied, without turning around.

How long had this strange game been going on, Makhaya wondered. Without further thought, he began walking calmly towards the house. He climbed the steep flight of stairs and disappeared from the gaze of the villagers on the dark, enclosed porch. A moment later they heard a tremendous crash as Makhaya broke down the door. Then a long silence. The villagers all arose and also climbed the steep stairway. Those in the forefront stood looking silently for a while into the big dining room, not at the luxurious couches, carpets and high-backed kingly chair, but at the dead, still body hanging from a rafter. Makhaya had the phone in his hand and was talking to George Appleby-Smith.

'I can't say for how long,' he was saying. 'Must I cut the rope?'

'Are you sure he's dead?' the inspector asked.

'I can't say,' Makhaya faltered. 'I'm not sure, except that he's quite still.'

Makhaya paused and a twisted spasm of pain swept across his face. Could the man hang like that with all the villagers staring in?

'There's been some trouble here today,' he continued on the phone. 'I don't know the details, but the whole village is here.'

'Okay, cut down the body. I'll be there in about ten minutes,' and Makhaya heard the man at the other end slam down the phone.

In his office George Appleby-Smith stared sightlessly at the wall. Things always went this way in this goddam country. Every village was a hornets' nest where someone had to be irrevocably got rid of. Someone had to go round the bend, die, or be driven out. Life was always extremes, harsh blacks and whites with no soft greys or in-betweens or compromises. He'd long seen Matenge was a crack but in this kind of goddam country where everyone was bullshitting around, the cracks and nuts and loose bolts had the upper hand. Even his good friend Paramount Chief Sekoto was a crack and nut and loose bolt. He smiled to himself. Today, after it was all over, he'd go and have a quiet beer in the railway pub – to a fellow whose guts he admired. He hadn't thought Gilbert would stick it out to the end. He'd long expected him to become a loose bolt too, with all the nonsense that was going on in Golema Mmidi.

He picked up the phone, still smiling to himself. A moment later he heard the gay, bubbling voice of the Paramount Chief, 'Hullo, hullo, George. How's things?'

'Have you got a coffin, pal?'

'Ha, ha. Gracious me, George. Don't tell me you want to die now. You're just a spring chicken.'

'It's not me,' said that familiar, casual drawl. 'It's your brother Matenge. He's gone and killed himself.'

There was an abrupt silence at the other end, and George could quite clearly see Chief Sekoto put on his funeral face. Chief Sekoto was a play-actor on all occasions. He lived life with his face while his heart remained calm, empty, and serene.

'I'm very sorry to hear this news, George,' he said.

'So am I,' George said dryly.

'I'm coming right over with the coffin,' Chief Sekoto said.

But he remained holding onto the phone in an absent-minded way. How many beasts would have to be slaughtered? How many relatives to insult by not sending a personal invitation to the funeral? How to squash the scandal of the suicide? Oh, oh, the mess and fuss and bother. The talk, talk, talk. He closed his eyes. Even in death his brother upset his digestion for the whole day. He put the phone down, dusted his hands, and waddled briskly out of the office, carefully adjusting his funeral face. Along the way to his home he met his secretary.

'Pule,' he said, in a sombre voice. 'Please order a coffin. Put it in the truck. I'll have to go to Golema Mmidi as brother has just died of a heart attack.'

He said this to several people, even the wife. Matenge had died of a heart attack. He wanted to create confusion. The people of Golema Mmidi would come up with their own story, but once there were two conflicting versions, people would doubt everything, even if they saw the rope around Matenge's neck. And they would soon become bored. But a suicide, in a chief's house? Oh, oh, oh. It would go down in history. Most of all, things had to go smoothly, quickly. Chief Sekoto had lots of practice too. He buried everyone – concubines, commoners, royal relatives, and foreigners. And he put his funeral face away one hour after the dust of the earth had enclosed the coffin. This time there was a heavy feeling in his heart. It wasn't easy to dismiss the intense, dramatic face of his brother. As though it was a question mark before life. As though his brother had suffered because he had wanted more things than a man should desire for one life and then life itself had frustrated all these desires. As though his brother had been the helpless victim of terrible, private hungers. What else made a man do all the things his brother had done? And a great shadow of gloom clouded Chief Sekoto's outlook that day. By the time he arrived in Golema Mmidi, he wasn't play-acting anymore but was genuinely upset.

He found the villagers seated quietly and patiently in the yard as he drove the big truck with the coffin through the gate. A few men moved to the truck to lift down the coffin and carry it into the house. Chief Sekoto got out and stood for a moment leaning against the truck, trying to take stock of the situation. There was that desperately earnest young man, Gilbert, also leaning against his Land Rover and looking up at the sky where the vultures circled and circled. Chief Sekoto could picture so clearly the day Gilbert had walked into his office and Chief Sekoto had thought him mad with all his talk about the poor. The poor were just the poor, and the commoner was just the commoner, and they were not very interesting people to Chief Sekoto. They lived such stupid lazy lives. They were so filthy in their habits that a mud hut was all they deserved.

How was Chief Sekoto to know that there was a quiet and desperate revolution going on throughout the whole wide world? People were being drawn closer and closer to each other as brothers, and once you looked on the other man as your brother, you could not bear that he should want for anything or live in darkness. Maybe he knew nothing about this because this revolution belonged to young people like Gilbert and Makhaya.

These young people only puzzled a man like Chief Sekoto. If he had had the good looks of the handsome refugee what a colourful drama his life would have been! One dramatic love affair after another. And here was the young man, wasting his life away in the bush. Someone told him they did this because they were communists – all this permission requested to build dams and register co-operatives. He had queried his friend George about this communist business, and his only reply had been: Bullshit. George had all the top-secret information too, and Chief Sekoto never doubted his word. Besides, there were mad people and mad people. He had never lost a night's sleep over the presence of the two young men in his tribal reserve, but he had lost plenty of sleep over his brother.

He straightened his short body and waddled briskly up the stairs. There was a crowd of people in the big dining room and the coffin was on the floor. He averted his gaze from the body of his brother, which was stretched out on a couch, and walked over to George, who stood by himself at the far end of the room.

'What happened?' he asked in a whisper.

George shrugged. 'People say they wanted to have a peaceful discussion with the chief,' he said, keeping his face expressionless.

'What was this peaceful discussion about?' Chief Sekoto asked.

'Their cattle are dying,' George said, then just kept silent.

Chief Sekoto looked at him, puzzled. 'I don't understand,' he said. 'Did my brother kill himself because people's cattle are dying?'

George gave his friend a long look before replying, then he shrugged again. 'Just a week ago,' he said softly, '. . . just a week ago we found a dead child of this village at the cattle post. He died a most horrible death from malnutrition. We held no one to blame for it because you can't prosecute droughts and famine. But today your brother wanted to prosecute the mother of this child for some unknown offence. The people of this village came to attend the trial. That's all they did.'

Chief Sekoto looked at the ground. He did not know what to think because if he did he might have felt too, and that would stifle and choke him. It was all a bad tragedy, his brother, the poor. But George Appleby-Smith stared at everything with peaceful eyes, even the way the village men gently lifted the body of Matenge into the coffin. He would never be able to close his eyes to all these people in rags and tatters and no shoes. They were all he really lived with in his daily work. They were so poor, yet it never occurred to them to steal. Because of this the prisons were nearly always empty. A murder case turned up once in a blue moon. Instead, you found yourself inspector of a police station where a lot of absent-minded people walked in to report that they had forgotten their blankets on the train. Could you please find their blankets? You got other curious things happening to you, too. Once, for a year, almost at the exact same hour each afternoon, a big white goat would step into his office and walk around sniffing the untidy jumble of papers. Then walk out again. He never found out to whom that goat belonged because he never directly involved himself with anyone, but both goats and people loved George Appleby-Smith. And he appreciated this deeply.

The men lifted the coffin and carried it out to the truck. A lot of the villagers, including Mma-Millipede and Dinorego, had decided to accompany Paramount Chief Sekoto and would stay over in his village for the funeral. The rest of the dazed and stunned villagers slowly began to make their way homeward, still unable to utter a word. You have to be loved a bit by the time you die. People can only say good things about the dead, and if you've left no treasures on this earth, what's there to hold onto except a terrible pity? Perhaps the people of Golema Mmidi were afraid, too, that they had really killed Matenge, in a strange gathering-together of all their wills. It was as if they did not want any evil to impose itself on them, and they had all silently decided to suppress it. They found it difficult now to break the cohesion and singleness of purpose that had drawn them together that day. Until late that night they kept on grouping and regrouping in each other's yards, drinking bowls of sour-milk porridge, discussing the weather and how hot it had been that day. But not once did they mention the name of Matenge, though he was in all their thoughts, hovering like a great, unseen shadow over the whole village.

This strange mental disassociation from the events of the day also took place in Gilbert, Makhaya, and Pelotona, the permit man, when they arrived back at the farm for a late lunch together. They held some half-hearted, distracted conversation about rationing water until the emergency borehole had been sunk. But they lapsed into unexpected intervals of silence. You couldn't ever forget Matenge, not once you had met him face to face and he had spat his venom out at you. Matenge made you doubt the basic goodness of mankind. He made you think of all the people who are only half like him, and this completely shattered the innocence and trust with which you might approach fairly harmless people who do a bit of evil now and then to entertain themselves.

Gilbert had been roughed up inside more than all of them. He had had to do a complete somersault of thought and feeling after his arrival in Golema Mmidi. No one had told him there was such a thing as an African oppressor, nor had he expected to find a Matenge exploiting his own people through the cattle-speculating business. Hundreds of white men did it and were continuing to do it with efficient ease in Botswana. But an African robbing Africans? And he had tortured himself through many sleepless nights at the ease with which he had destroyed Matenge's cattle-speculating business. There were other things too – the pathetic way in which Matenge always backed down when confronted by a superior.

But if a man like Gilbert had really kept his mind on the Matenges, who were an inverted whirlpool of seething intrigues, on the crazy semi-literate politicians like Joas Tsepe, he might have overlooked the kind of people almost everyone overlooked – the Dinoregos and Mma-Millipedes. At the most bitter times of Gilbert's stay in Golema Mmidi, Dinorego had always said: 'I think the Good God don't like it.' But he said it as though the 'Good God' was quite nearby, listening, observing, and Dinorego, his screwed-up face listening to the 'Good God', was what had made Gilbert stay and stay. And he mixed it all up with a thousand and one things: the way he smelled the summer rain on the far, flat horizon, four or five months before the first, fat globs of raindrops fell two by two, three by three on the parched earth. Enormous thunderstorms brewed and boiled on these far-off horizons, but it never rained and people never ploughed, until one unsuspecting day it rained in sheets and so hard that the roar of the rain drowned out the volcanic thunderclaps.

What was he looking for? What was he doing? Agriculture? The need for a poor country to catch up with the Joneses in the rich countries? Should super-highways and skyscrapers replace the dusty footpaths and thorn scrub? It might be what he said he had in mind; at least, he said this to excuse himself for the need to live in a hurricane of activity. But the real life he had lived for three years had been dominated by the expression on Dinorego's face, and God and agriculture were all mixed up together after these three years. Yet it was a real God this who stalked his footsteps along the dusty pathways, who listened with quiet interest to the discussions on agriculture. Gilbert had no clear explanation of how he had become certain of this, but there was a feeling of great goodness in this country.

But Mma-Millipede had the beginnings of an answer as to why everything was so mixed up. She had traced the course of man's whole destiny through her studies of the wandering tribes of Israel. Sometimes a man's God was like Solomon and he decked himself up in gold and he built a house that was a hundred cubits in length and fifty cubits in breadth and thirty cubits in height. Gold candlesticks, cherubims, and pomegranates adorned this house, which had forty bathrooms. And there were bowls and snuffers and spoons and censers and door hinges of pure gold. And all that the followers of Solomon could do was to gape and marvel and chronicle these wonders in minute detail. Even Solomon's wisdom took secondary place to his material possessions and dazzling raiment. Then came a God who was greater than Solomon, but he walked around with no shoes, in rough cloth, wandering up and down the dusty footpaths in the hot sun, with no bed on which to rest his head. And all that the followers of this God could do was to chronicle, in minute detail, the wonder and marvel of his wisdom.

There were two such destinies which faced Africa – that of the followers of Solomon and that of a man with no shoes. But the man with no shoes had been bypassed, scorned, and ridiculed while the Solomons stalked the land in their golden Chevrolets. Who would eat then if all the gold and pomegranates went into the house of Solomon? Who would bathe if all the water went into his forty bathrooms? Who would have time to plough if everyone had to join the parade to watch Solomon pass by in his Chevrolet of molten gold, his top hat and silk shirt, glittering in the African sun? For that's all that Solomon wants – a lot of gapers and marvellers. And things were mixed up because there were too many Solomons and too many men with no shoes, and no one could be certain who would win out in the end – except that the man with no shoes was often too hungry to stand in the parade these days.

And that was what it boiled down to in the end – a silent and fascinating battle between the Solomons, and aspiring Solomons like Joas Tsepe, and the God with no shoes. The Solomons made the most noise in the world, hopping from one international conference to another, bowing and scraping to the left and right. But the God with no shoes continued to live where he always had – in the small brown birds of the bush, in the dusty footpaths, and in the expressions of thin old men in tattered coats. He was just wondering what all the fuss and clamour was about, you know, these international brotherhoods, the sounding brass and tinkling cymbals, because he really owned the world and the fish in the ocean. It amused him to see all these fellows strutting about, with no humility, forever scheming and plotting to gain what would never be theirs.

The way this God with no shoes carried on might easily delude you into thinking he was a charming halfwit like Paramount Chief Sekoto or hesitant about truth like Mma-Millipede or tortured and tormented like Makhaya. He changed about from day to day contradicting and confusing himself by all he had to learn, never certain of anything the way the fortune-tellers were. He had upset Makhaya this day by stacking the cards one way and then toppling them another. He had packed all these cards up in a precarious pyramid and stood by while Matenge picked off the topmost card. It would have been different had Matenge really victimized Paulina for whatever he wanted to victimize her for. Maybe her association with Makhaya. But then a man like Makhaya would not have stood by with tied hands. He would have had blood on his hands by now and been in some cell, with George Appleby-Smith lecturing him on how he had let him down. But the God with no shoes, with his queer, inverted reasoning, had brought Makhaya, a real and potential murderer, face to face with the body of Matenge just hanging there and hanging there.

'Don't you see?' he had said softly. 'Murder is small-minded business.'

Did you really trust a God like that? He made you take a long and perilous journey along a road where everyone threw things at you. Then he said you were small-minded if you wanted to throw things back. Why didn't he do something about the throwers then? Because one Matenge died and another replaced him, and no matter which way you turned there was always a Matenge there to throw something at you. And Makhaya knew that that day was always ahead of him. He would come face to face with one of these grinning, ghoulish oppressors and have nowhere to run anymore. And he would just lift up his arm and knock him dead with a mighty blow, right between his grinning eyes. And he might turn round to this invisible God who tormented his life with question after question and knock him down too. Someone had to go into oblivion – either a Makhaya or the oppressor. And Makhaya did not mind if it was he. Because a man could not go on taking it, all the filth and lies and hypocrisy. He might like to step right out of it into a black, silent death, never to live again.

'What are you thinking about, Mack?' Gilbert asked, at last, in a tired, depressed voice.

Makhaya raised his hands with a helpless gesture. 'I don't know,' he said. 'I don't know if I'm thinking at all.'

It was this quiet, hollow feeling inside all of them that made them feel so low. It was as though they had strained so hard against a heavy, unyielding door, only to find it wasn't there anymore. They could not, all at once, total up the good things in this struggle, how it had made them true comrades, how they would not ever have clarified their ideas had they not lived under the shadow of blind opposition. These things would come with tomorrow, when all the hard work had to be done and even Makhaya would find, in spite of himself, that he had to live and give up his morbid speculations on oppressors and oppressed. Even this Good God whom Dinorego said was 'everywhere about' stood watching them that evening with an amused look in his eye. Why didn't Gilbert talk about how exciting irrigation farming would be in Golema Mmidi? Everyone would want to do it now. Just look at the way everyone was shocked out of their minds! Did this fellow Gilbert think progress was as easy as learning to drive a tractor? People had to be given shock after shock to wake them up good and thoroughly, and preparations for progress took place long before progress even started. As for the oppressors! Did you mean Joas Tsepe would win the election as councillor for Golema Mmidi? Maybe anywhere else but not in Golema Mmidi. They would much prefer Mma-Millipede, who mixed up spiritual counselling with practical advice and whom the Good God had long prepared for this position. In fact, there was not anything he would not do for a village like Golema Mmidi, which was a place he had especially set aside to bring all his favourite people together. He wanted them to show everyone else just how quickly things could really change, how ordinary people could get up and do things for themselves and produce enough for their needs and have some left over for sale. But why were they all so boring this evening? Ah, but he was a little bored too. His favourite mouthpiece, Dinorego, was away at the funeral.

Therefore the Good God cast one last look at Makhaya, whom he intended revenging almightily for his silent threat to knock him down. He would so much entangle this stupid young man with marriage and babies and children that he would always have to think, not twice but several hundred times, before he came to knocking anyone down.

He wandered along the footpath, in the direction of the sunset, and stopped for a while in the yard of Paulina Sebeso. She was busy at her smoke-haze fire, preparing supper, but she paused and looked up expectantly as she heard familiar footsteps. It was Makhaya coming home. His long dismal train of thought made him overlook the still, glorious ball of hot, red light which hung in the sky. He was about to start saying those impractical things to Paulina, you know, like this world is not a fit place to live in, but she came rushing towards him with her hands outstretched because she had been deeply frightened at the way he had walked up the steps of Matenge's house, as if he would just be swallowed up by a monster and would not mind. He was like the wind or a fluid substance you could not hold onto. She grasped hold of his hands with that half-laughing, half-puzzled expression, perhaps even shocked to feel that his hands were large, solid bone, slightly warm and damp. He was solid all over, strong and muscular, but the inside of him, the expression of his face was so strange and unreal. What did you say to such a man?

She asked, 'Will you have some food?'

He smiled. She was the best of all women he had known – no sulks, no dead eyes, no dead anything about her.

'So much has happened so quickly,' he said. 'I forgot to ask you if you'd like to marry me. Will you, Paulie?'

After all, he had said he wanted to marry someone. Didn't he? But even though Paulina said yes a bit too quickly, she hardly believed it. As though everything was uncertain, new and strange and beginning from scratch.

Maru

*For George Macpherson,
Leshelwa, Tsebe, and my son.*

PART ONE

The rains were so late that year. But throughout that hot, dry summer those black storm clouds clung in thick folds of brooding darkness along the low horizon. There seemed to be a secret in their activity, because each evening they broke the long, sullen silence of the day, and sent soft rumbles of thunder and flickering slicks of lightning across the empty sky. They were not promising rain. They were prisoners, pushed back, in trapped coils of boiling cloud.

Like one long accustomed to living in harmony with the earth, the man had continued to prepare his fields for the seasonal ploughing, and even two brand new water tanks had been fixed to the sides of his small new home to catch the storm water, when it rained. He wanted a flower garden of yellow daisies, because they were the only flowers which resembled the face of his wife and the sun of his love. If that were one of his preoccupations, there were a thousand others as well. Maybe life was too short. Maybe life had presented him with too many destinies, but he knew that he would accept them all and fulfil them. Who else had been born with such clear, sharp eyes that cut through all pretence and sham? Who else was a born leader of men, yet at the same time acted out his own, strange inner perceptions, independent of the praise or blame of men?

'I'll be going home now,' he said quietly, to a group of three men working on the construction of vegetable beds.

He had hesitated before speaking. The men were no ordinary farm workers, but close friends who had surrounded and protected him all his life. He added a word or two which made them shake their heads behind his back and mutter: 'Maru is always impossible!'

'Ranko,' he said sharply, pretending annoyance. 'Didn't I tell you not to break up the clods? They are for conserving moisture in the soil.'

Ranko looked up, raised one hand and rubbed the side of his nose. Sudden, sharp words and the mention of his name threw him into confusion. Ranko meant 'big nose' in Setswana, and when had people not had vegetable garden soil raked in a fancy way? Every new and unacceptable idea had to be put abruptly into practice, making no allowance for prejudice. It was painful, like his big nose, and who knew where life and destiny would take the three of them as long as their lives were attached to Maru? They began shaking their heads, and the gesture was very deep. The man who slowly walked away from them was a king in their society. A day had come when he had decided that he did not need any kingship other than the kind of wife everybody would loathe from the bottom of their hearts. He had planned for that loathing in secret; they had absorbed the shocks in secret. When everything was exposed, they had only one alternative: to keep their prejudice and pretend Maru had died. But did it end there? Was that not only a beginning?

Only Maru knew the answers. He paused awhile and looked towards the low horizon where the storm brooded. The thorn trees turned black in the darkening light and a sudden breeze stirred the parched, white grass. There was so little to disturb his heart in his immediate environment. It was here where he could communicate freely with all the magic and beauty inside him. There had never been a time in his life when he had not thought a thought and felt it immediately bound to the deep centre of the earth, then bound back to his heart again – with a reply. Previously, the stillness with which he held himself together to hear the reply had always been disrupted by people. People were horrible to him because they imagined that their thoughts and deeds were concealed when he could see and hear everything, even their bloodstreams and the beating of their hearts. If they knew all that he knew, would they not have torn him to shreds some time ago, to keep the world the way it was where secrets and evil bore the same names? It was a vision of a new world that slowly allowed one dream to dominate his life.

A little brown, dusty footpath turned away from the roaring busy highways of life. Yellow daisies grew alongside the dusty footpath and danced in the sun and wind, and together the footpath and the daisies would make his heart bound with joy. As soon as the first rains fell he would plant those yellow daisies along the footpath leading to his home – so simply and precisely did he translate his dreams into reality. At least, the present was simple. But there was a depth of secret activity in him like that long, low line of black, boiling cloud. There was a clear blue sky in his mind that calmly awaited the storm in his heart and when all had been said and done, this earth would be washed clean of all the things he hated. He slowly continued his walk home, his gaze turned towards the horizon. It was very beautiful.

So quietly did he enter the house that his wife looked up fearfully from her work of preparing the table for the evening meal. He sometimes had vicious, malicious moods when every word was a sharp knife intended to grind and re-grind the same raw wound. Most certainly, no memory remained in her heart and mind of previous suffering. Most often she felt quite drunk and mad with happiness and it was not unusual for her to walk around for the whole day with an ecstatic smile on her face, because the days of malice and unhappiness were few and far over-balanced by the days of torrential expressions of love. Maybe a dark shadow had been created to balance the situation. Maybe some blot of human wrong had to happen to force Maru to identify himself with the many wrongs of mankind. He moved too swiftly and surely. He never doubted the voices of the gods in his heart. It was only over the matter of Moleka that he was completely undone, not the way one would expect a wrong-doer to be undone. He was thrown off balance by the haunting fear that he would one day be forced to kill Moleka, one way or another.

There were two rooms. In one his wife totally loved him; in another, she totally loved Moleka. He watched over this other room, fearfully, in his dreams at night. It was always the same dream. Moleka would appear trailing a broken leg with blood streaming from a wound in his mouth and his heart. No one ever cried with such deep, heart-rending sobs as his wife did on these occasions. Often he would start awake to find those hot tears streaming onto his arm from her closed eyes.

'Why are you crying?' he'd ask, pretending not to know. But she would see the tears too, yet be unable to account for them on waking because she had no mental impression of her dreams, except those of the room in which she loved Maru. There was nothing he could invent to banish the other room. He seemed to be its helpless victim and it was not much to his liking, as jealousy was almost an insanity in him and the inspirer of it was nearly his equal. No one else was. To Moleka he had made so many concessions, he did not care to make others. He had ensured that Moleka had the next best woman in the world. The next best woman in the world had more intellectual attainments than his wife. She had style and class and immediately impressed people as someone worth noticing and listening to. All these things flattered Moleka, as he was also a man who impressed people. What did he want with a woman who meant nothing to the public? In fact, until the time he married her she had lived like the mad dog of the village, with tin cans tied to her tail. Moleka would never have lived down the ridicule and malice and would in the end have destroyed her from embarrassment.

There was always the public. A man with a public eye tried to please them. Once he had decided to act, he had based his calculations on what was good for Moleka and what was good for him. He brooded over this. Perhaps he had seriously miscalculated Moleka's power, that Moleka possessed some superior quality over which he had little control. Was it a superior kind of love? Or was it a superior kind of power? He'd trust the love but not the power because power could parade as anything. He'd weep too, if he really believed that Moleka had a greater love than his own. What his heart said was that Moleka had a greater power than he had, and he had felt no remorse at what he had done to the only person he loved as he loved his wife. This brooding and uncertainty made him malicious. Perhaps his heart was wrong and a day would come when he would truthfully surrender his wife to Moleka, because he had decided that Moleka's love was greater than his own. If this mood was upon him, he would walk in through the door and say: 'I only married you because you were the only woman in the world who did not want to be important. But you are not at all important to me, as I sometimes say you are.'

It could turn the world to ashes. All the fire and sun disappeared because his words were inwardly lived out in his deeds. That evening, he was happy. He thought about the yellow daisies. He walked in at the door and said, softly: 'My sweetheart.'

They were the most precious words, if you only knew the horror of what could pour out of the human heart; a horror that seemed most demented because the main perpetrators of it were children and you were a child yourself. Children learnt it from their parents. Their parents spat on the ground as a member of a filthy, low nation passed by. Children went a little further. They spat on you. They pinched you. They danced a wild jiggle, with the tin cans rattling: 'Bushman! Low Breed! Bastard!'

Before the white man became universally disliked for his mental outlook, it was there. The white man found only too many people who looked *different*. That was all that outraged the receivers of his discrimination, that he applied the technique of the wild jiggling dance and the rattling tin cans to anyone who was not a white man. And if the white man thought that Asians were a low, filthy nation, Asians could still smile with relief – at least they were not Africans. And if the white man thought Africans were a low, filthy nation, Africans in Southern Africa could still smile – at least they were not Bushmen. They all have their monsters. You just have to look different from them, the way the facial features of a Sudra or Tamil do not resemble the facial features of a high-caste Hindu, then seemingly anything can be said and done to you, as your outer appearance reduces you to the status of a non-human being.

In Botswana they say: Zebras, Lions, Buffalo and Bushmen live in the Kalahari Desert. If you can catch a Zebra, you can walk up to it, forcefully open its mouth and examine its teeth. The Zebra is not supposed to mind because it is an animal. Scientists do the same to Bushmen and they are not supposed to mind, because there is no one they can still turn round to and say, 'At least I am not a—'. Of all things that are said of oppressed people, the worst things are said and done to the Bushmen. Ask the scientists. Haven't they yet written a treatise on how Bushmen are an oddity of the human race, who are half the head of a man and half the body of a donkey? Because you don't go poking around into the organs of people unless they are animals or dead.

Some time ago it might have been believed that words like 'kaffir' and 'nigger' defined a tribe. Or else how can a tribe of people be called Bushmen or Masarwa? Masarwa is the equivalent of 'nigger', a term of contempt which means, obliquely, a low, filthy nation.

True enough, the woman who gave birth to a child on the outskirts of a remote village had the same thin, Masarwa stick legs and wore the same Masarwa ankle-length, loose shift dress which smelt strongly of urine and the smoke of outdoor fires. She had died during the night but the child was still alive and crying feebly when a passer-by noticed the corpse. When no one wanted to bury a dead body, they called the missionaries; not that the missionaries really liked to be involved with mankind, but they had been known to go into queer places because of their occupation. They would do that but they did not often like you to walk into their yard. They preferred to talk to you outside the fence. They had a church, a school and a hospital in the village, all founded by a series of missionaries. At that time the church and school were run by a man and his wife. There is little to say about the man because he was naturally dull and stupid, only people never noticed because he was a priest and mercifully remained silent for hours on end. He had a long, mournful face. His mouth was always wet with saliva and he frequently blinked his eyes, slowly like a cow. It was the wife who was to live forever in the memory of the child.

It is preferable to change the world on the basis of love of mankind. But if that quality be too rare, then common sense seems the next best thing. Margaret Cadmore, the wife of the missionary, had the latter virtue in over-abundance. It made her timeless, as though she could belong to any age or time, but always on the progressive side. It also made her abusive of the rest of mankind, because what is sensible is simpler than what is stupid. She had a temperament – high-strung, nervous, energetic – that made her live at the speed of a boat shooting over the rapids. Her plump cheeks were flushed by her self-imposed exertions. Continuous abuse of the rest of mankind, which moved at three quarters of her pace, had sometimes led her into situations where she was in danger of being assaulted. She had a lively sense of humour. She took revenge with a sketch pad and pencil. She gave orders and, while waiting for them to be carried out, she'd sketch the harassed face of her victim, with a note underneath for future reference, like: 'He's nice, but stupid.' It prevented her from hurling out a continuous stream of abuse.

To ensure that things happened at the speed she required, she was in the habit of getting as many people onto the job as possible. Thus, when the hospital supervisor rang up about who had died, and apologetically added that she was an untouchable to the local people, she had the coffin carried into the hospital while the grave was being dug in the churchyard. Later, when it was all over, she would conduct a one-sided, reflective monologue with her husband, George: 'I wonder where these people are buried? They don't seem to be at all a part of the life of this country.'

On this occasion her thoughts involved her. She kept her eyes screwed up reflectively as she absent-mindedly bottle-fed the baby of the dead woman. A number of things had happened all at once. Margaret Cadmore was not the kind of woman to speculate on how any artistic observation of human suffering arouses infinite compassion. She put the notes down on her sketch pad. One sketch captured the expressions of disgust on the faces of the Batswana nurses as they washed the dead woman's body for burial. She scrawled a note under the sketch: 'These are not decent people.'

Her dislike of the nurses flowed out of her observation of the dead woman. As she walked into the hospital, energetically demanding the body, two nurses conducted her to a small back room where the slop pails were kept. There on the stone floor lay the dead woman, still in the loose shift dress, more soiled than ever from the birth of the child. There was horror mingled with her hysterical shouting, only she no longer cared to lecture human prejudice directly.

'Why the damn, blasted hell haven't you washed the body for burial?' she shrieked.

She was plump. Her mouth was shaped as though she was permanently laughing but she wore tinted glasses and, combined with the shouting, appeared fierce. The nurses jumped in alarm and rushed for pails and soap and water. It was only when they washed the body that they exposed their prejudice, and the reason why the body was not on a stretcher but on the stone floor. From habit she whipped out her sketch pad, then paused. The sketch would not come so rapidly. It was a mixture of peace and astonishment in the expression of the dead woman, but so abrupt that she still had her faint eyebrows raised in query. What suffering had preceded death? And what had death offered to surprise her so? She had even started to laugh.

Quite unconscious of the oddness of her behaviour, Margaret Cadmore walked to several angles of the room, studying the dead woman's expression. The note she scrawled at last said: 'She looks like a goddess.'

She took in too much after that: the thin stick legs of malnutrition and the hard calloused feet that had never worn shoes. She took in also the hatred of the fortunate, and that if they so hated even a dead body how much more did they hate those of this woman's tribe who were still alive. Maybe she really saw human suffering, close up, for the first time, but it frightened her into adopting that part of the woman which was still alive – her child. She had no children, but she was an educator of children. She was also a scientist in her heart with a lot of fond, pet theories, one of her favourite, sweeping theories being: environment everything; heredity nothing.

As she put the child to bed that night in her own home, her face was aglow. She had a real, living object for her experiment. Who knew what wonder would be created?

There seemed to be a big hole in the child's mind between the time that she slowly became conscious of her life in the home of the missionaries and conscious of herself as a person. A big hole was there because, unlike other children, she was never able to say: 'I am this or that. My parents are this or that.' There was no one in later life who did not hesitate to tell her that she was a Bushman, mixed breed, half breed, low breed or bastard. Then they were thrown into confusion when she opened her mouth to speak. Her mind and heart were composed of a little bit of everything she had absorbed from Margaret Cadmore. It was hardly African or anything but something new and universal, a type of personality that would be unable to fit into a definition of something as narrow as tribe or race or nation. Her educator was like this. As she swore at everyone, regardless of their status, so did she tear to pieces any idea that even remotely had no grounding in good sense. And it was the simplicity of her approach and arguments that created the impression that she could open any door, make the contents within coherent, and that she stood for all that was the epitome of human freedom. Good sense and logical arguments would never be the sole solutions to the difficulties the child would later encounter, but they would create a dedicated scholar and enable the child to gain control over the only part of life that would be hers, her mind and soul. She would have to take them and apply them to the experiences gained in a hostile and cruel society. They would mean in the end that almost anything could be thrown into her mind and life and she would have the capacity, within herself, to survive both heaven and hell.

No doubt, she lived on the edge of something. The relationship between her and the woman was never that of a child and its mother. It was as though later she was a semi-servant in the house, yet at the same time treated as an equal, by being given things servants don't usually get: kisses on the cheeks and toes at bedtime, a bedtime story, long walks into the bush to observe the behaviour through binoculars of birds, and lots of reading material. Dancing through it all was a plump woman with twinkling eyes whose ideas and activities were like a permanently bubbling stream. The child used to watch it all with serious eyes. There was nothing she could ask for, only take what was given, aware that she was there for a special purpose because now and then the woman would say: 'One day, you will help your people.' It was never said as though it were a big issue, but at the same time it created a purpose and burden in the child's mind.

It was only when she started going to the mission school that she slowly became aware that something was wrong with the world in relation to her. She was the kind of child who was slyly pinched under the seat, and next to whom no one wanted to sit.

It was odd, because she had a vantage point from which she could observe the behaviour of a persecutor. What did it really mean when another child walked up to her and, looking so angry, said: 'You are just a Bushman'? In their minds it meant so much. Half of it was that they were angry that she had the protection of a white woman who was also their principal. What was the other half? What was a Bushman supposed to do? She had no weapons of words or personality, only a permanent silence and a face which revealed no emotion, except that now and then an abrupt tear would splash down out of one eye. If a glob of spit dropped onto her arm during the playtime hour, she quietly wiped it away. If they caught her in some remote part of the school buildings during the playtime hour, they would set up the wild, jiggling dance: 'Since when did a Bushy go to school? We take him to the bush where he eat mealie pap, pap, pap.'

One day they were dancing away in savage glee, when they were pounced on by Margaret Cadmore: 'What the damn, blasted hell is going on here?' she shrieked. 'I'll have you all expelled, do you hear? I want no more of this nonsense!'

But it was Margaret Cadmore who was upset the whole afternoon. Her sharp eye had seen the one small, abrupt tear and the ugly expressions on the faces of the torturers. She liked to experiment but she dreaded drains on her emotional resources. She most probably imagined she was crying. It was only her nerves, and she was heard to mutter irrelevantly to any teacher within earshot: 'I can't understand beastliness because it would never occur to me to be beastly.'

By evening she thought she had the situation under control. That is, emotion no longer interfered with her reasoning. The only difference was that there was no bedtime story that night, no twinkling eyes, only a few solemnly spoken words: 'They are wrong. You will have to live with your appearance for the rest of your life. There is nothing you can do to change it.'

It never stopped the tin cans rattling, but it kept the victim of the tin cans sane. No one by shouting, screaming or spitting could un-Bushman her. There was only one thing left, to find out how Bushmen were going to stay alive on the earth, because no one wanted them to, except perhaps as the slaves and down-trodden dogs of the Batswana. That half she would be left alone to solve. Margaret Cadmore succeeded in only half her experiment – that if an environment provided the stimulus and amenities of learning, any human mind could absorb knowledge, to the limit of its capacities. Allowance had to be made for all living beings. An allowance for life had always been made for really vicious people, who for too long had said the kind of things to helpless people which really applied to their own twisted, perverted hearts. Those who spat at what they thought was inferior were really the 'low, filthy people' of the earth, because decent people cannot behave that way.

From that eventful evening to a day seventeen years later some wonder had indeed been created. Margaret Cadmore had produced a brilliant student, whose name, identical to hers, was always at the top of the list of passes. That the brilliance was based entirely on social isolation and lack of communication with others, except through books, was too painful for the younger Margaret ever to mention.

The old white-haired lady was retiring to England. There was still one term left before her 'experiment' passed out as a fully trained primary school teacher. She came in a car with pretty floral dresses and a pair of white shoes and practical last-minute advice.

'Don't wear lipstick. It won't suit you, but here's some eye make-up because you have eyes as pretty as stars. Don't forget to shave regularly under your arms and apply this perfumed powder. Don't forget to write to me.' The old plump lady pretended to cry, dabbing at dry eyes with a dry handkerchief.

One abrupt tear shot out of the young girl's eyes. The years at the teacher training college had passed by with little torture. Because of the regular appearances of the white woman and the unashamed public kisses on the cheek, she had been mistaken by the students for another variant of the word 'Bushman'. It was also a name they gave to the children of marriage between white and African. Such children bore the complexion of members of the Bushman tribe.

'Is that your relative?' they asked curiously. And she had replied, 'Yes.' There was, maybe, a little more respect granted to a half-caste, but in her heart she had grown beyond any definition. She was a little bit of everything in the whole universe, because the woman who had educated her was the universe itself. There was nothing on earth that was not human, sensible and beautiful that had not been fearlessly thrown into the mind of the pupil, from Plato to W. B. Yeats. It was W. B. Yeats who had made the pupil cry. She could not grasp him.

'Damn it!' her educator had exclaimed, impatiently. 'You can't understand him because you can't hear and see the lake water lapping,' and she whipped out the sketch pad. Yeats had to be there too even though he spoke of a land other than her own arid surroundings.

It was everything between them that caused a tear to shoot out of the young girl's eye. She had been more than an educator. She had been humour, laughter, fun, unpredictableness, a whole life of vibrating happiness. It ended abruptly as she walked to the car. It was hard to imagine life without her. The future looked lonely.

A month later the young girl received a curious postcard from England. The ink was smudged in a number of places, as though the postcard had been posted during pouring rain, or the writer of the postcard had been crying profusely. It said, simply: 'I had to do it for the sake of your people. I did not want to leave you behind. Margaret Cadmore.'

Four months later she was appointed to her first teaching post in a remote inland village named Dilepe. It felt like being a millionaire for the first time. She had thirty pounds, in a new handbag from her adopted mother, to ensure that she lacked nothing while awaiting her first pay cheque. The three-hour journey by truck passed by in frantic, enjoyable mental shopping for all the things she would need to buy – a pot, a kettle, blankets, a plate, and other odds and ends – in the two days left free to her before the start of the first term of the school year.

It was the height of summer. There had been a little rain and the bush on either side of the road was slowly turning green. Insects had crept out of their long hibernation, and every now and then when the truck driver stopped the truck for a rest, their shrill, piercing, high-pitched wail stunned the ears. A little of that mood of summer happiness infected her heart, which was always so quiet and repressed. She had to struggle to control an urge to jump out of the truck and run away into the bush. The truck driver would surely have thought her mad. She was seated next to him in the front of the lorry and he was silent for most of the time, except to assure her that he would put her down at the school. She hesitated to tell him that it was still school holidays.

It was just past the lunch hour when they arrived at Dilepe. Fearful that the truck driver would put her down at an empty school building and she look a fool, she jumped off at his first stopping place. It was a post office where he had mail to deliver. Directly opposite was a shop which was a combination of butcher, restaurant and greengrocer. She looked at the shop longingly. She would have liked to walk in and buy food but she had never done anything as bold in her life. She stood where she was, becoming petrified. The truck driver touched her arm and picked up her suitcase.

'Come, we'll go eat,' he said, as though aware of her lostness. 'Then I'll put you down by the school.'

There was something hilarious in his insistence that the school was her proper stopping place, and her own lack of not knowing what to do next. She followed him blindly, because he seemed quite at home and at ease in his surroundings. He took her to a partitioned-off room where there were a few tables and chairs. He made a great fuss about ordering her food, insisting that the knife and fork be carefully wiped. It was the stricken, helpless look on her face that so touched his heart.

'You must not be so afraid of the world, Mistress,' he said kindly. 'People can't harm you.'

There it shot out again, one single abrupt tear from one eye.

Was that really true? Did many people behave like him, so spontaneous in their kindness? They ate in silence. Suddenly the truck driver pricked up his ears, his face alight with interest. The tap, tap, tap of high-heeled shoes approached their way. He swung around in his chair as one elegant leg swung through the partition.

'Mistress Dikeledi,' he called out loudly. 'Don't you teach at Leseding School?'

She was so startling and unexpected in her elegance that

anyone could draw any number of conclusions about her and still be puzzled. The clothes were too bold, the skirt too tight but the feel of her was like a cool, lonely breeze, the kind that calms the tense, stifled air of a summer afternoon. She had a way of looking at people with one quick, wide stare, then immediately looking away into a far-off distance as though she did not particularly want anything from life or people. She had a long, thin, delicate face, with a small mouth, and when she smiled she seemed very shy.

She walked over and sat down at their table, immediately lighting a cigarette with a quick, almost hidden movement of her hands.

'Hullo, Josh,' she said quietly.

She threw a quick look at the girl opposite her, then added: 'We were expecting her. Don't worry. I'll settle everything.'

The truck driver stood up and walked away. He still had many places to call. The young woman named Dikeledi looked away into the distance and spoke at the same time in that cool, assured voice: 'Would you like some tea?'

'Yes, please,' the other young woman said.

Dikeledi looked down. A slight frown flitted across her face. It was the first time the other had spoken and she could not quite place her in the scheme of things. The near perfect English accent and manners did not fit her looks. In fact, not one thing about her fitted another and she looked half like a Chinese and half like an African and half like God knows what.

'What's your name?' she asked at last.

'Margaret Cadmore,' the other said.

'Is your father a white man?' asked Dikeledi.

Since the atmosphere between them was so relaxed, the other young girl spoke without hesitation:

'No,' she said. 'Margaret Cadmore was the name of my

teacher. She was a white woman from England. I am a Masarwa.'

Dikeledi drew in her breath with a sharp, hissing sound. Dilepe village was the stronghold of some of the most powerful and wealthy chiefs in the country, all of whom owned innumerable Masarwa as slaves.

'Don't mention this to anyone else,' she said, shock making her utter strange words. 'If you keep silent about the matter, people will simply assume you are a Coloured. I mistook you for a Coloured until you brought up the other matter.' (By 'Coloured' Dikeledi meant children of mixed marriages who also could look half Chinese, etc.)

'But I am not ashamed of being a Masarwa,' the young girl said seriously. 'Let me show you something.'

She opened her handbag and took out a small, framed picture.

'My teacher made this sketch of my mother the day she died,' she said, and handed it to Dikeledi. Dikeledi took the picture, glanced at it with that strange, wide stare, then looked away into the distance, an almost smoky haze clouding her lovely eyes.

'Did a white woman write that?' she asked. 'And about a Masarwa? "She looks like a goddess"?'

Her face suddenly broke into a pretty, shy smile.

'I am not like you, Margaret,' she said. 'I am afraid to protest about anything because life easily overwhelms me, but you are right to tell anyone that you are a Masarwa.'

Dikeledi deliberately under-played her own achievements. She was quiet, no gongs sounded, but she was a drastic revolutionary. She was the daughter of a paramount chief and the first of that crowd to put a good education to useful purpose. They all had, and their relatives had, the best education but the best

238

was used as an adornment of their social status. Dikeledi had no need of employment but unlike others who made wealth synonymous with idleness, wealth gave her the freedom to specialize in what interested her most. In fact, barely half a year ago she had returned from England with a diploma in early childhood education. It wasn't for her own sake either that she drew in a sharp, hissing breath.

It was an instinctive, protective gesture towards the person sitting near her. Dikeledi had taken two slaves from her father's house and, without fuss or bother, paid them a regular monthly wage, and without fuss or bother, they dressed well, ate well and walked about the village with a quiet air of dignity. There was something Dikeledi called sham. It made people believe they were more important than the normal image of humankind. She had grown up surrounded by sham. Perhaps it was too embarrassing to see people make fools of themselves, because at one point she said: 'I'll have none of that.' She was not alone in that decision.

She looked at her watch. It was almost three o'clock. She pushed away her tea cup and smiled: 'You have no accommodation and here we are, idling the time away.'

They stood up together. Dikeledi raised her hand.

'Wait here,' she said. 'I'll find someone to carry the suitcase to the car.'

They both thoroughly surprised each other. Margaret was amazed by her certainty that someone would carry a suitcase simply because they were asked to, as though the elegant woman was accustomed to being waited on, hand and foot. Sure enough, Dikeledi returned in a minute with an eager, obsequious man who heaved the suitcase onto his shoulder. She had not said anything about personally owning a car. She had not really said anything about herself, Margaret realized, and the neat, small, highly polished car with a pile of mail in the back seat only heightened the mystery. There was the truck driver, too, who seemed to know her well, and to whom she had spoken with such courteous, informal respect.

'She can't be what I think she is, an ordinary person like myself,' Margaret thought uneasily.

Dikeledi drove as carefully as she talked. She turned the car onto a small, dusty road that ran along the bottom of a hill.

'I'm taking you to Moleka,' Dikeledi said. 'He usually attends to the accommodation of new teachers.'

As she mentioned the name, Moleka, a happy smile lit up Dikeledi's face. She had been in love with Moleka since doomsday. There had been one quarrel in particular, but many others as well. After their quarrels he seemed quite happy if he never saw her again, but she was always restless afterwards, until some excuse presented itself for her to throw herself in his path. It was said of Moleka that he had taken his heart out of his body and hidden it in some secret place while he made love to all the women in the village. Dikeledi was the only woman who knew that. The quarrels were about where he had hidden his heart.

At the end of the road, a notice board proclaimed 'DILEPE TRIBAL ADMINISTRATION.' There was a long row of office blocks, at the end of which was an imposing structure of modern design, painted in a contrasting range of brilliant colours. Dikeledi drove towards the brightly painted building and parked the car just outside the small gate. They kept pace, walked up a flight of stairs, then turned slightly to the left and into a long, beautifully furnished office.

A young man sat alone. Next to him was an unoccupied chair. The young man looked up and frowned as he saw Dikeledi. There was silence. He shifted his head. He did not look at Margaret but right through her head, to the wall. There was a heavy thunder-cloud around his eyes. He looked grim and vehement and gruesomely ugly. When he spoke his voice had such projection and power that the room vibrated slightly.

'Are you the new teacher we were expecting?' he asked.

'Yes,' she said faintly.

'You've come too late,' he said. 'All the accommodation for the year has been taken up.'

He shifted his head to Dikeledi with a look that said: 'All right. Go now.' Then he looked down and continued his paperwork.

There was nothing to do but go. As they walked down the stairs, Dikeledi said: 'I might have to accommodate you in my own home.' She bent her head to adjust herself to this idea. She had lived alone for some time, and liked it that way. She added: 'If Maru was here you would have found accommodation on the spot. He is almost a god in his kindness towards people, not like that swine.'

The words were hardly out of her mouth when 'the swine' appeared right behind them. He was smiling now. His teeth were enormous. He said: 'I know you like to praise me, Dikeledi.' That happy look again swept over Dikeledi's face. In her eyes there was the tenderness and devotion of a dog. She seemed to have no control over the dog love, even though the man obviously took it for granted and was flattered. He scratched his head: 'Oh, I just remembered that the old library was vacated last week and the books moved to the new library. This teacher can use it for accommodation. I'll take her right over.'

He moved quickly, took the suitcase out of the car and transferred it to a white van, then held open the door of the van. Dikeledi said: 'I'll come in a little while to see if you are settled,' and walked over to her car.

There was something not yet said. They liked each other.

Margaret had never seen anything like it in her life. The man slammed the door shut, turned on the ignition, then there was a cloud of dust. First one goat jumped out of the road. Then six, seven or eight more. People jumped. Both people and goats looked outraged. He kept on smiling. He was royalty, the son of a chief. He'd grown up making goats and people jump. It was nothing. By the time the van swooped up a hill towards a small building she was white around the mouth from shock. It was as though there was a long trail of death behind them. As she set her feet down and looked behind, the dust of their journey still rose in the air. He seemed not to notice, having his mind fixed on his own life. He picked up the suitcase, pushed open the door and walked inside, placing the suitcase just inside the door. She followed silently. The man frightened her deeply.

It was a long single room, fifteen feet in length, with four windows. It was in good condition except that it was covered in layers of dust and cobwebs. There was only one piece of furniture, a low trestle table. Perhaps the man was retrieving his breath. He slowly paced up and down, head bent, deep in thought. She had her back to him. A big black scorpion, disturbed by their entry, scuttled with angry speed across the room, its tail alertly poised to strike. Behind her, she could hear the man walk towards the table and raise it as though to fold its supports and remove it. The day was almost over. It was too late to purchase a bed from the shop. Perhaps scorpions could not climb up tables. She swung round and burst out nervously: 'Please don't remove the table.'

He kept quite still, his hands touching the table. He did not turn round. When he spoke she could hardly recognize his voice. It had deepened in a strange way. There was something sweet in it, like a note of music, yet he only uttered one word: 'Why?'

242

'I am afraid of the scorpions,' she said.

He turned round slowly.

'I knew you were going to say that,' he said, as though he were talking to an old friend, whose faults and failings were quite well known to him. But there was a trick to him, some shocking, unexpected magic. A moment ago he had been a hateful, arrogant man. Now, he had another face which made him seem the most beautiful man on earth. It was only his eyes, as though a stormy sky had cleared. What was behind was a rainbow of dazzling light. Though unaware of any feeling, something inside her chest went 'bang!' Her mouth silently shaped the word 'Oh,' and she raised her hand towards her heart.

He looked away, but when he turned his head again and looked at her there was pain and enquiry in his eyes as though he did not quite understand what had happened, as though he had been presented with something strange and unnatural which was beyond his control and he did not like it. He bent his head, trying to withdraw himself, walked slowly to the door. The scorpion crossed his path and he quietly crushed it with his foot. He paused by the door and rested one hand on the door post.

'I'll fetch you a bed,' he said, humbly.

How did life prepare one for the unusual? It only defined what work you ought to do, what you ought to eat and when you ought to eat. But no one ever said anything about your feelings. There was a strange feeling in her towards the man, as though she were ashamed of him. She heard the van move down the hill. She laughed a little, then spoke out loud: 'But I am not that important.' He had made her feel as though she were the most important person on earth, when no one had ever really cared whether she was dead or alive, and she had been so lonely. The loneliness had disappeared like the mist before the warmth of a rising sun.

243

It was more than that, too. There had been no backbone to her a short while ago. Now something had stabilized her.

He seemed to have said silently: 'You see, you don't have to be afraid anymore. First there was one of you. Now there are two of you.' It was that generous.

She walked to the door. Below her the village of Dilepe spread out and swept towards the horizon. It was a network of pathways and dusty roads weaving in and out between a tortured layout of mud huts, as though people whimsically said: 'we want to live here', and made all the little pathways and roads follow their whims. A thousand wisps of blue smoke arose silently into the air as a thousand women prepared the evening meal beside their outdoor fires. That peace and those darkening evening shadows were to be the rhythm of her life throughout that year, and Dilepe village was to seem the most beautiful village on earth.

She was really no longer lonely.

The moon was so bright that few stars appeared in the sky. Moleka walked along the footpath, his hands in his pockets, deep in thought. He had an appointment with one of his innumerable girlfriends, but being in an absent-minded mood he walked right past her hut. His thoughts so absorbed him that he even continued past the outskirts of the village and into the bush. A full yellow moon rose high into the sky. He paused at last and looked around him. Perhaps it was only this – the light in the sky and the quietly glittering beauty of the earth – which matched a portion of his body that felt like a living, pulsating sun.

Alone now, he slowly raised his hand to his heart. How was it? Something had gone 'bang!' inside his chest, and the woman had raised her hand to her heart at the same time. It was not like anything he had felt before. Dikeledi was the nearest he'd ever come to loving a woman and yet, even there, Dikeledi made his bloodstream boil by the way she wore her skirts, plainly revealing the movement of her thighs. With Dikeledi it was a matter of the bloodstream. And what was this? It was like finding inside himself a gold mine he'd not known was there before. Yet he could have sworn that he was totally unaware of the woman until she spoke. Something in the tone, those soft fluctuations of sound, the plaintive cry of one who is always faced with the hazards of life, had abruptly arrested his life. With Dikeledi it was always distractions. She was too beautiful, physically. With the woman there were no distractions at all. He had communicated directly with her heart. It was that which was a new experience and which had so unbalanced him.

He shook his head and sat on a rock.

'It's madness,' he thought. 'I hardly know her.' What were her legs like? He could not say. All the force of her life was directed to her eyes, as though that were the only living part of her. Something killed the old Moleka in a flash and out of one death arose, in a flash, a new Moleka. It was the first time he had spoken to a woman in humility, but not the first time he had felt humbled by some quality in another living being. He screwed up his eyes, puzzled. Some other person had prepared him for his encounter with the woman. There was something eluding him and he could not immediately remember the other person. There was someone like her, someone who walked into a room and made no impact but, when you turned around again, they owned your whole life.

'I have come to the end of one road,' he thought, 'and I am taking another.'

He'd lived like a spendthrift millionaire. There was something about him, or in him, that made people walk into a room and turn their heads: 'Ah, there's Moleka.' He took that physical fascination and traded it all on women. There was always enough and some to spare. Maybe he grew accustomed to having a shadow next to him.

'Moleka,' the shadow would say, shyly, 'I'd like you to introduce me to so-and-so.'

Moleka would have been just on the point of making a proposal to Miss so-and-so, but he would immediately hold out his hand.

'Of course, Maru,' he'd say. 'I shall arrange everything.'

They were the words of a millionaire. There were also ramifications and ramifications. When had he and Maru not lived in each other's arms and shared everything? People said: 'Oh, Moleka and Maru always fall in love with the same girl.' But they never knew that no experiences interrupted the river and permanent flow of their deep affection. It was Moleka, so involved in this river, who never had time to notice the strange and unpredictable evolution of his friend. He never knew about the gods in the heart and the gods in the earth but he could always see the light of their conversation in his friend's eyes. It was the light that Moleka was so devoted to. He never asked whether he might have a light of his own or that he might be a startling personality in his own right. His face was always turned to what he saw as the most beautiful person on earth. Thus it was that thousands of people noted the dramatic impact of Moleka, but he would always cast his eyes across the room to see if all was well with Maru.

It was only Maru who saw their relationship in its true light. They were kings of opposing kingdoms. It was Moleka's kingdom that was unfathomable, as though shut behind a heavy iron door. There had been no such door for Maru. He dwelt everywhere.

He'd mix the prosaic of everyday life with the sudden beauty of a shooting star. Now and then Maru would share a little of his kingdom with a Miss so-and-so he had acquired through Moleka. But it never went far because it always turned out that Miss so-and-so had no kingdom of her own. He used to complain to Moleka that people who had nothing were savagely greedy. It was like eating endlessly. Even if they ate all your food they were still starving. They never turned into the queens and goddesses Maru walked with all his days.

Throughout this time, Moleka was the only person who was his equal. They alone loved each other, but they were opposed because they were kings. The king who had insight into everything feared the king whose door was still closed. There was no knowing what was behind the closed door of Moleka's kingdom. Maru had no key to it, but he knew of its existence because if he touched Moleka's heart with some word or gesture a cloud would lift and he would see a rainbow of dazzling light.

The clue to Moleka and Maru lay in their relationships with women. They were notorious in Dilepe village for their love affairs, and the opposing nature of their temperaments was clearly revealed in the way they conducted these affairs. The result was the same: their victims exploded like bombs, for differing reasons. At the end of a love affair, Moleka would smile in the way he smiled when he made people and goats jump out of his path, outrage in their eyes. There was nothing Moleka did not know about the female anatomy. It made him arrogant and violent. There was no woman who could resist the impact of his permanently boiling bloodstream. But he outraged them, and horrible sensations were associated with the name of Moleka. Moleka and women were like a volcanic explosion in a dark tunnel. Moleka was the only one to emerge, on each occasion, unhurt, smiling.

It was different with Maru. At the end of a love affair, a deep sorrow would fill his eyes. He often took to his bed with some indefinable ailment. The victims, too, displayed alarming symptoms. The strongest fled as though they had seen a nameless terror. The weakest went insane, and walked about the village muttering to themselves. Maru always fell in love with his women. He'd choose them with great care and patience. There was always some outstanding quality; a special tenderness in the smile, a beautiful voice or something in the eyes which suggested mystery and hidden dreams. He associated these things with the beauty in his own heart, only to find that a tender smile and a scheming mind went hand in hand, a beautiful voice turned into a dominating viper who confused the inner Maru, who was a king of heaven, with the outer Maru and his earthly position of future paramount chief of a tribe. They only saw the social gains that would accrue to them and it made their behaviour despicable to his all-seeing eye. Someone always died but their deaths often turned him into an invalid. It was nothing for Maru to be laid up for three months on end over a love affair. Doctors said: 'Take those pills.' And Maru said: 'What for?' And doctors said: 'You have TB.'

None of the victims could ever explain the process of her destruction, nor its cause. Everyone took it for granted that there was something called social position and you had to scheme and fight for it, tooth and nail. That is the world, they said, as though all the evils in human nature were there by divine order and man need make no effort to become a god. Thus, the women whom Maru made love to were highly envied. People said: 'Oh, and when is the marriage to take place?' A month or so later the girl would flee the village or become insane. A terror slowly built up around the name of Maru because of these events. In their conversations at night they

248

discussed the impossible, that he was the reincarnation of Tladi, a monstrous ancestral African witch-doctor who had been a performer of horrific magic.

Moleka knew of all these things. They were the root cause of his violent, over-protective attitude towards Maru. It was a difficult situation. On the one hand, Maru had all the stuff that ancient kings and chiefs were made of. People had acclaimed those around on whom they could build all kinds of superstitious myths. Yet the fear and terror magicians inspired made them live with their lives in the balance. Who knew how many murder plots were constantly woven around the life of Maru? People looked to the day when he would be their chief. But a lot of people, and these included relatives, spent the days counting the nails in his coffin. He aided the counting by always taking to bed with those indefinable ailments. He had only five friends in a village of over fifty thousand people. They were Moleka, his sister Dikeledi, and three spies – Ranko, Moseka and Semana. Of the five, Moseka and Semana were shadows. From Ranko, Moleka and Dikeledi, Maru was inseparable. But it was only with Moleka that he shared all the secrets of his heart, because Moleka was a king with his own kingdom. Since no other came so close to the heart of Maru, they invented all kinds of rubbish and horrors. Moleka alone knew that all the visions and vivid imagery Maru was subjected to directed Maru's footsteps along a straight road – that of eternal, deathless, gentle goodness. Moleka walked blindly through life. He walked blindly through all kinds of sensational love affairs. The one great passion of his life was his friend, Maru.

These words were forever on the lips of Moleka as he and Maru sat together at the sunset hour, discussing the day's events:

'Nothing will ever separate us, my friend. We shall love each other, forever.'

Maru would smile quietly. One day he had a reply for Moleka. It was a message from the gods who talked to him in his heart. He said to Moleka: 'One day we will part, over a woman.'

'But that's impossible!' Moleka exclaimed.

He said that because he had never loved a woman. When he did, he wanted to kill Maru. Not even as he sat alone in the moonlit bush that night did he recall those words of Maru's. He screwed up his eyes, puzzled, as though something was eluding him. Then his mind took up the threads of his own life. He said: 'I have come to the end of one road, and I am taking another.'

He bent his head a while longer, lost in thought, then added: 'I kept my heart for her alone.'

It seemed the greatest achievement of his life. He felt reborn, a new man. No, he felt as young and innocent as a three-year-old child.

It was the first day of the new school term. All the teachers who had been at the school throughout the previous year stood at the doors of their classrooms. They had already received their allocations of new pupils before the school closed for the summer holidays. The only addition to the staff, Margaret, stood near the principal's office. She looked at a group of three teachers who stood to one side, among them Dikeledi. They taught the beginners' grades. It really felt as though she could walk across to the three women, who were still waiting to have their new pupils registered in the principal's office, and feel welcome. It was Dikeledi. In the course of two days they had fallen into a relationship of wonderful harmony. There was no tension, restraint, or false barriers people usually erect towards each other. It was mostly Dikeledi. It was mostly her temperament: 'I'm all right. I don't want anything from anybody.' It made you want to give her the whole world and your heart too.

The principal of the school belonged to that section of mankind which believed that a position demanded a number of exaggerated mannerisms. He kept his coat unbuttoned. He walked as if in a desperate hurry, which made his coat-tails fly out behind him. There might have been a time in his life when he had smiled naturally – say, when he was two years old. But he had a degree and a diploma and with it went an electric light smile. He switched it on and switched it off. It was painful when he was with important people, when it remained switched on. He also behaved as though life were a permanent intrigue. Nothing could be done in a straightforward way. He was a little like Uriah Heep, and a belly-crawler to anyone he considered more important than himself. He had to impress you with knowledge. This was as painful as his smile. His voice was heavy, determined and an authority on everything. When his face was in repose, his thick lower lip hung down on his chin.

Margaret's advance papers had aroused his curiosity considerably. Even the sight of her. He made the same error as Dikeledi, assuming she was a Coloured. That was unusual too. Such children always worked in the shops of their white fathers. He thought he'd have something to talk about, such as that she must be the first of *their* kind to teach in *their* schools. He'd also have to keep a sharp eye on racialism. Those types were well known for thinking too much about their white parent, not about their African side. He eventually approached Margaret with his electric-light smile.

'Ah, Miss Cadmore,' he said.

Off went the smile, down came the lower lip. He frowned.

'I have decided to form an additional class outside the beginners' grade. As you know, the beginners' grade is the foundation of a child's life. I have the best teachers there, like Mistress Dikeledi. I like to have a clear conscience on the matter. I have continuously pressed the authorities, at meetings and elsewhere, to limit the number of pupils each teacher can handle in the beginners' grades so that they give of their best. Er . . .'

He paused, and looked at her closely. There was interest, curiosity there.

'Excuse the question, but are you a Coloured?' he asked.

'No,' she replied. 'I am a Masarwa.'

The shock was so great that he almost jumped into the air. Why, he'd be the sensation of the high society circle for a week! He controlled himself. He looked down. He smiled a little. Then he said: 'I see.'

The whole day he fretted. School closed just past noon. The office of the education supervisor was a stone's throw from the school. Usually they sat chatting over three or four cups of tea. Today, the list of beginners seemed endless. He kept noting out of the corner of his eye that the Masarwa (she was no longer a human being) seemed to be extraordinarily friendly with Dikeledi, who, in his eyes, was royalty of royalty. Should he warn Dikeledi that she was talking to 'it'? 'It' surely had all the appearance of a Coloured.

'There's been some chicanery,' he muttered, over and over again.

As soon as the noon bell rang he could be seen walking at a desperate pace to the office of the education supervisor. He slowed down at the door and shuffled in. The education supervisor did not go to the extremes of the principal but he was a comic too. He was a phenomenon of the African localization circuit. He was an exact replica of a colonial officer, down to the Bermuda shorts. He looked up at the principal from under his eyes.

'Seth,' the principal said. 'There's been some chicanery.'

'How so?' the other queried.

'I have a Masarwa on my staff.'

The man Seth whistled softly.

'It's the Margaret Cadmore woman?' he said, looking serious. 'God, this is going to raise hell among the Totems here.'

He grabbed some files and ran his eyes down the application list. There was no requirement for a person to define his tribe or race. He looked very annoyed.

'They're going to blame me,' he said. 'I only look at qualifications. She was top of the class the whole way through. How the hell did she get *in*? God, Pete, this is a mess.'

Without seeing him, he stared at Pete, the principal. Again, he whistled softly through his teeth.

Pete grinned.

'She can be shoved out,' he drawled. 'It's easy. She's a woman.'

The man Seth held up his hand.

'Wait a bit,' he said. 'I'll sound out the opinion of the Totems. Her qualifications are good. She couldn't possibly have got there on her own brains. Someone was pushing her. We don't know who and they might be important. The Totems will soon dig out the truth. They know what shoes you wore last year.'

Pete looked at him slyly. Things were not the same in Dilepe village since the old paramount chief had died towards the end of the previous year. The Totems were all on hot bricks. A new man was to be installed some time during the year and he was an unpredictable quantity. The terror of him, too, was that he was practically unapproachable, unless he chose to make the first move. They all had to watch the pinnacle, then mouth everything the pinnacle said.

'You know they are all afraid of Maru,' Pete said. 'They want to be on his safe side. They don't know which his safe side is. They don't know what he is going to do but they fear him.

There's no such thing as Totems around here. There's only Maru.'

Seth just looked at him.

'Not everyone is that scared,' he said. 'I've heard from a good source that he won't make it to the day of installation. Did you hear about his latest ailment? It's diabetes.'

The conversation became side-tracked. The Totems or royalty of the village were their favourite conversation piece. Eventually one name stood out: Morafi, the younger brother of Maru.

Funny how birds of a feather flock together. Pete, Seth and Morafi were always in one another's company and indeed formed a social élite of their own. The things that amused them were the kind of things that caused suffering to others. Morafi was the chief producer of the entertainment. People were inclined to protest these days when suddenly deprived of their property. Like most Totems, Morafi was a cattle thief and he had had a heyday of thieving while his father was alive, his father being a thief as well.

Cattle thieving worked like this: it was known that the Totems owned the best bulls. Sometimes a handsome bull appeared amidst the herd of an ordinary man and he'd suddenly find himself surrounded by the vultures. Usually scouts did the dirty work. They'd say to the petrified man: 'I say, where did you get the money to buy such a bull? It can't possibly be yours. You must have stolen it from the chief.' And without further ado off they would go with the beast. How it was ever tolerated can only be explained by the terror the chiefs inspired in the hearts of the people. The terror grip was relaxing though. Too many people were becoming educated and questioning things. The men who were now in danger of losing their lives overnight were men like Morafi.

Morafi was revolting because his inborn stupidity was coupled with total insensitivity. First, he assumed that everything was all right with him because he was the son of a paramount chief. He had big, bulbous protruding eyes which were completely vacant of thought or feeling. His neck was covered in layers of fat. His stomach hung to his knees because he ate too much and drank too much. He was about seven foot tall and like Pete, the principal, he had an acquired laugh. It was staccato, squeaky – eh, eh, eh. His eyes never smiled. They were always on the alert for something to steal. He was such a shameful personality to anyone with the slightest sensitivity that perhaps the effect of him on the oversensitive Dikeledi and Maru clarified their own destinies. He thought his little intrigues had driven them out of their father's home but they preferred to live as far away from him as possible. Of late, since he had had his father's mansion and slaves to himself, he had taken to staring at everyone with intense, screwed-up eyes: 'Do you get the message? I am terribly important.' He had also found out from the doctors that only a miracle could save Maru's life this time. He was an assiduous counter of the nails in Maru's coffin.

Morafi took Seth and Pete as the height of the intellectual hemisphere. It was his habit to condescend to discuss the important issues of the day with them. It exhilarated and uplifted him. He listened seriously as Seth explained his side of the matter that evening:

'I really don't know how it happened,' said Seth. 'I've always said: If a person's qualifications are good, that's enough for me.'

Morafi looked thoughtful.

'I really wonder what Maru is going to do about the problem of the Masarwa,' he said. 'Things are moving ahead for this country, and they are the only millstone. I don't see what we can do with people who can't think for themselves but always need others to feed them. Mind you, they seem quite contented with their low, animal lives.'

Pete also looked thoughtful.

'There's a real mystery about that one at the school,' he said. 'They don't look you in the face and say, "I am a Masarwa." It was like a slap in the face. The statement was so final, as though she did not want to be anything else. I had given her a loophole. Coloureds are just trash, but at least she could pass as one. It would have saved us an awful lot of bother.'

Pete achieved his ambition. From that evening he was a sensation among the high society of the Totems. They all listened to him with bulging eyes. Who had ever said, 'I am a Masarwa'? It sent thrills of fear down their spines. They all owned slaves. Only two Totems were excluded from the buzz, buzz, buzz. But they heard because the whole village was alive with it by the week's end, and both Dikeledi and Moleka acted in their own ways and independently. The action of one crippled Pete, the action of the other caused a wave of shame to sweep through the hearts of ordinary people.

At that time the beginners' grade consisted of children of a varied age range. Most of the girls were six or seven, but the boys who worked as cow-herds started school from about the age of ten to fourteen. Pete coached a fourteen-year-old boy, and by early Monday morning the whole class of the Masarwa teacher was prepared for what was to take place. The only sign they gave of their preparedness was nervous giggles as they filed into the classroom. But as she closed the door and walked to the table to call the roll, a deathly silence fell upon the children. She looked up. A boy at the far end of the room had his hand raised. She knew there was something wrong. For the first week they had been restless, absent-minded. They had hardly noticed her, being involved in their adjustment to their new situation. Now they all stared at her with fascination and attention. A cold sweat broke out, down her back.

'Yes?' she asked, unsmiling.

The boy shook his head and laughed to himself. 'I am thinking about a certain matter,' he said.

Then he looked directly into her face with an insolent stare: 'Tell me,' he said. 'Since when is a Bushy a teacher?'

The room heaved a little and the whole classroom of children blanked out before her. Yet she still stood upright with wide open eyes. From a distance their voices sounded like a confused roar: 'You are a Bushman,' they chanted. 'You are a Bushman.'

It froze the whole school. There was not a teacher who did not know of the buzzing between the principal and the Totems over the weekend. They even knew what was to happen next. They waited for his drawl: 'But Miss Cadmore, why can't you control your class? You are disturbing the whole school.'

In fact, he was on cue, except that half-way across the quadrangle he saw Dikeledi streak ahead of him into the classroom of the Masarwa. He jerked himself back on one leg, looked to the left and right and started running back to his office. He still heard her voice. It was like murder, shrill and high like the shattering of thin glass against a wall: 'Stop it! Stop it! I'll smash you all to pieces! She is your teacher! She is your teacher!'

A few of the teachers in the senior classes smiled to themselves. Dikeledi had run the school for some time. She was the only person who did not understand backstabbing. They all had knives in their backs from Pete. They pulled them out that morning.

The principal sat in his office, struggling to gain a semblance of self-respect. His calculations had excluded Dikeledi. He had a pencil draft of a report on his desk: 'I find Margaret Cadmore an ineffective teacher. She is totally incapable of controlling her class . . .'

'The bossy little bitch has buggered up the works,' he muttered, over and over again.

He and his like thought only that way. They were only angry when their plans to inflict suffering went haywire. They never for one moment dreamt that their victims had passions too and that these passions were terrifying in their violence. Dikeledi was the only one among the privileged who got close enough to a traditional dog to find out the truth. She walked into Margaret's classroom during the lunch break. They had fallen into the habit of eating lunch together. She had a tin of fat cakes. Up until Margaret had brought sandwiches of Marmite, fat cakes had been her favourite food. Marmite was a new item to her, and she devoured it ravenously.

'Why did you keep quiet?' she asked pointedly.

The other young woman kept her head bent. It surprised her that they agreed about everything. She liked the fat cakes. They were made with eggs.

'I was surprised,' she replied, quietly. 'They used to do it to me when I was a child but I never felt angry. Before you came in, I thought I had a stick in my hands and was breaking their necks. I kept on thinking: How am I going to explain her death? I thought I had killed a little girl in the front desk who was laughing, because I clearly saw myself grab her and break her neck with a stick. It was only when you started shouting that I realized I was still standing behind the table. I kept saying, "Thank God, thank God! I haven't killed anyone".'

Dikeledi swung one leg onto the table.

'It's funny how we agree in feeling,' she said. 'I saw the little girl too. She put her hand to her throat when I shouted at them. I kept on looking at her because her mouth went dead white. I thought: Poor little swine. They have been taught to be brave about the wrong things and laugh about the wrong things. Someone will have to teach them decency, because their parents won't.'

The door was pushed open. It was Pete. He had a little speech for Dikeledi about how she ought not to be running around the school during school hours. She flung it back in his throat with her bold, careless stare. Even his electric-light smile looked sick.

'Er . . . is everything all right?' he croaked.

She kept silent. He backed out. He made another mistake, of looking into a room where the teachers of the senior classes were drinking tea together. One of them had seen him look to left and right, then dart back to his office. They now greeted him with rocking laughter. That was all. Something unhinged in him. He spent the rest of the morning talking to himself in his office. How had things backfired like this on a surefire case? What would the children say?

There was worse to come. By noon a greater sensation had swept through the village. The Totems cringed. It seemed as though the world was ending. Next to Maru, they instinctively took Moleka as the most powerful man in the village. A servant, not a Masarwa, who worked in Moleka's home spread the word that they no longer knew what was what. He said that all the Masarwa slaves in Moleka's home sat at table with him when he ate. The whole village was involved. There was no longer buzz, buzz, buzz. Something they as Africans liked to pretend themselves incapable of – being oppressive and prejudiced – was being exposed. They always knew it was there but no oppressor believes in his oppression. He always says he treats his slaves nicely. He never says that there ought not to be slaves. At this point, just past noon, when everybody was saying they no longer knew what was what, Maru returned. He had been away, visiting some remote villages, to make himself, so he said, familiar with his future work as paramount chief.

Ranko had the most stupid and uncomprehending face on earth. It was like rock in its total lack of expression. When people approached him or talked to him he said: 'Er? What's that?' as if he could not understand one word. So they said: 'Goodness, what a fool he is,' and left him alone. In his freedom he employed himself in the only occupation he liked. He was Maru's spy, not of any ordinary kind. Nothing ordinary was ever associated with Maru. Ranko had a camera inside his brain. It did not need to talk, only sit on the edge of any situation and take pictures, including the minutest detail. Who can explain the situation? Maru had too much intuition. He liked his inner intuitions verified. He employed Ranko to verify them. People said that Maru had second sight. He had. He could tell people what their secrets were, but he always had Ranko verify them. Ranko was like Moleka. They both wanted to protect a personality too original to survive in an unoriginal world. Their loves differed. Moleka's love was objective, ideal. As long as he held Maru up as his ideal, he loved him. Not so Ranko. The day Maru died, so would he. He had no other life.

Maru lived within the area of the offices of the Dilepe Tribal Administration. Barely three hundred yards away from his home was the home of Dikeledi. Both homes were constructed with slabs of orange sandstone, hewn from the surrounding hillside. They were built at the foot of the hill, on a slight incline, and long flights of highly polished staircases led to enclosed porches where they often sat and ate their meals. The wheels of their cars had made two diverging tracks to their homes.

He glanced towards the home of his sister as he stepped out of his car. She had not yet arrived from school. He turned and ascended the staircase. So very little disturbed the peaceful serenity of his life. He was a man who talked and walked slowly, with a languid grace, loosely swinging his long arms at his side. The people who surrounded him really merged into a background where there was little noise or upheaval. He'd say to a servant: 'I'd like this,' and it would be there, but what he liked or needed was reduced to the barest minimum. It was the same with people. The majority were greeted as though they were passers-by he would never get to know. Those he wanted or loved became the slaves of an intensely concentrated affection. His was not the kind of personality to rule the masses. They knew it and disliked him for never being there on show. And yet, at the same time, he was highly popular among ordinary people. His manner towards everyone was of courteous, informal respect. Disciples like Dikeledi copied him in everything. He set the tone, seemingly, for a new world.

Ranko was already seated at the dinner table when he entered the porch. They did not bother to greet one another because their bloodstreams were one. Maru washed his hands, wiped them on a towel, then sat sideways on a chair at the table and crossed his legs. Immediately a servant appeared and placed a tray of covered dishes on the table, then walked away. Ranko did not make any move to eat. He stared a little into the distance and quietly unrolled his camera:

'There is a little trouble in the village about a Masarwa who was appointed a teacher at Leseding School. Who knew about the Masarwa? Her certificate said: "Here is a teacher with Grade

A for every subject." This news was spread by the education supervisor. Accordingly, people examined the new teacher the day she arrived. They smiled: "Why, she is a Coloured," they said. "This is most unusual. Look at the light complexion."

'The next day people noticed that the new mistress had dignity and respect for everyone. People decided to change their minds about entering their children for Maroba School. They said Leseding School was so fortunate to have so many first-class teachers like Mistress Dikeledi and the new mistress with dignity. I thought to myself: "Why, there will be a commotion at Leseding School on opening day if the whole village enters its children there. Let me examine the new mistress for faults."

'I met her at the general dealer's where she was buying household goods. She picked up the parcel of household goods and walked away. Lesego, who served her, said: "Hmm, hmm, you have forgotten your change." She did not hear. She continued walking, her eyes searching the ground. I said to Lesego: "Give me the change, I want an introduction." The change was two pounds. I caught up with her and said: "You are rich to throw away money, hey?" She stood still, took the change, then began to feel the parcel in her arm. Then she said: "I have lost my handbag." So I said: "The handbag is hanging on the arm which is carrying the parcel. Better let me carry the parcel in case you lose the arm which is carrying the handbag and the parcel."

'I was surprised to see that she could not laugh, only cry quickly, with one eye. I thought the strange manner of crying meant "thank you", because now and then she looked at my face. Soon she became forgetful and started searching the ground with her eyes. Moleka had given her the old library room as a home but there she was, walking to Hong Kong. I said: "Where are you going?" She said: "I am going home." I said: "You are proceeding in the wrong direction." So she laughed a bit, then stopped. Then laughed again. This happened all the way up the hill to the house. I thought to myself: "She has a major fault. How can such a forgetful person teach children?"'

Ranko paused briefly. The car of Dikeledi took the track to her home. She stepped out, noted the presence of her brother, then quietly ascended her staircase. Ranko continued:

'Mistress Dikeledi was just as much head over heels in love as I was. When we came to the top of the hill she took a mat and chair from the car for the comfort of the house of the new mistress. She shouted at me: "Go away, Ranko. We have secret matters to discuss and you are a spy." Then she removed the parcel from my arm by force. Since I was head over heels in love I decided to keep silent about the major fault of the new mistress, and too many people took their children to Leseding School on the opening day.

'That very afternoon people were looking at each other with shock. They said: "Did you hear? The new mistress says she is a Masarwa." By evening they began to laugh: "The eye is a deceitful thing," they said. "If a Masarwa combs his hair and wears modern dress, he looks just like a Coloured. There is no difference." Those with children at Leseding School debated the matter. They were trying to accustom their hearts to their children being taught by a Masarwa. They said: "Prejudice is like the old skin of a snake. It has to be removed bit by bit."

'Moleka, who heard that the principal and the high-ups were planning trouble for the new mistress, could not make allowance for the slow removal of prejudice. He removed it all in one day. He told Seth, the education supervisor, that there was good food in his house on Sunday. When Seth arrived he found all the Masarwas in the yard of Moleka also seated at the table. Moleka took up his fork and placed a mouthful of food in the mouth of a Masarwa, then with the same fork fed himself.

'Seth removed himself from the house in great anger. He shouted for all to hear: "I shall have no further dealings with Moleka."

'Trouble broke out at Leseding School this morning. It was contained by Mistress Dikeledi. After the school closed I removed a piece of paper from the floor of the principal's office.'

He paused and handed a crumpled piece of paper to Maru. It was the partially drafted pencil report Pete had prepared. Then he continued: 'People are angered by the behaviour of Moleka. They say his action was too high-handed and has created confusion. There is no place for a Masarwa, whom everyone has seen behaving like a low animal in drink and filth, and he wants to force matters and stir up trouble. From the side of the high-ups and the principal of Leseding School, matters went like this . . .'

Then he carefully reported the words and behaviour of Seth, Morafi and Pete, who thought God was on their side and had opened their mouths too wide about their prejudice. After a while there was silence between the two men, then Maru asked:

'How did Moleka become involved with the new mistress?'

Ranko replied: 'You will see for yourself that Moleka is a changed man. The day the new mistress arrived she had no bed, so Moleka loaned her a bed of the tribal property. By accident, that same evening, I saw Moleka walk far out of the village. He was searching the ground with his eyes. I thought: "What can be the matter now? Moleka is always in trouble because of his bad behaviour. But this must be very serious. Look, he passes the home of Grace, yet he was mad for her yesterday. Let me follow." When we came to the boundary of the village I had to remove my shoes because there was too much moonlight and no place to hide. I didn't want to disturb his thoughts.

'He sat down with his head bowed for a long time. Then he spoke out aloud: "I have come to the end of one road and I am taking another." A little while later he said: "I kept my heart for her alone." A little while later he stood up, still searching the ground with his eyes. Again he passed the house of Grace and went to his own home. I thought: "What's this? Moleka has not missed sleeping with a woman since the age of twelve."

'The next day I passed by the office. Usually Moleka says: "Hey, Ranko, you damn fool, come here." That day he forgot to swear. He said: "Ranko, please fetch me a packet of cigarettes at the shop." While attending to other matters, my heart was worried about Moleka in case he should be losing his mind. His thoughts were too deep. I did not see into his heart but there are no Masarwa slaves in his house now. Today I thought: "Perhaps the new mistress has bewitched him, the way Mistress Dikeledi and I are bewitched."'

Maru laughed a little. The cinema screen was highly entertaining to him. It seemed as though Ranko had been specially born to teach him about the oddness in the human mind and heart.

'Has Moleka made any proposals to the new mistress yet?' he asked slyly.

'No, that's gold,' replied Ranko. 'He keeps his mind on the gold mine and does not care what people think of his behaviour.'

'You know, Ranko,' Maru said, unashamed of gossiping about his best friend, 'I can't stand a man like Moleka. He has so little emotion that when he finds a speck of it he thinks it's a mountain. That's why he's troubling everyone. Also, it's not good for a man, once he has found his heart, to wear it boldly on his sleeve. He also wipes his nose there. I shall have fixed him up by five o'clock when we leave the office. Please find Moseka and Semana and be here with them by that time. I am tired of those eye-sores, Morafi, Seth and Pete.'

He turned, rinsed his hands, wiped them and stood up. Outwardly he appeared calm, but something was violently agitating his heart. It was a nameless distress, of the kind when one has a premonition of bad news to come. He paused briefly at the top of the staircase and looked out on the sweeping spread of the land, sleeping in the shimmering heat of the midday summer sun. Unconsciously he spoke his thoughts out loud: 'I am lonely,' he said.

Slowly, he descended the staircase and walked to the home of his sister. She was still eating, on the porch. She looked up quietly as he seated himself. They did not greet one another. Their bloodstreams were one. He poured himself a cup of tea from the pot on the table. His sister's house had a direct view of the office where he and Moleka worked. For how long – was it years – had she sat and watched all the comings and goings of Moleka? And he had not cared.

'Ranko tells me that Moleka is trying to change the world by himself,' he said. 'Yesterday, all the Masarwa in his yard sat at table with him. He shared his plate of food and his fork with one.'

'He did?' Dikeledi said, astonished.

Suddenly Maru's heart felt light and gay. If Dikeledi did not know, who was there to tell the other woman how much Moleka loved her? His heart expanded with generous lies.

'Oh yes,' he said, smiling. 'Ranko was just explaining the matter to me. Apparently people don't like the idea of a

Masarwa teaching their children. Moleka decided to teach Seth a lesson, to show him that a Masarwa is also a human being. Seth was there at lunch and saw everything. One fork of food went into the mouth of the Masarwa and the same fork went into the mouth of Moleka. I told Ranko that Moleka is a scoundrel but he has a heart of gold.'

So many suns lit up the face of Dikeledi and her eyes melted with tenderness.

'I agree with you, brother,' she said, almost singing the words. 'Moleka has a heart of gold.'

She sat quite still, lost in a golden glow of love, forgetting all the quarrels, the evil associated with Moleka, his arrogance. It was as though he had always had God under his skin.

'Are you going anywhere this afternoon?' her brother asked quietly.

'Oh no,' she said. 'I am up to my ears in work. I have a whole year's preparation to do in two days.'

'All right,' he said. 'I'll see you again, after five o'clock,' and he stood up. Moleka had already approached and entered the office. He wanted Moleka to be there before him, and to be seated. Who knew what would happen next? His heart was too agitated. If he had time to be alone, he knew he would be able to sort out the cause with his gods, who talked to him in his heart. But something this time was forcing him to move blindly into something. He ascended the short flight of stairs to his office, turned to the left and paused at the door.

Moleka looked up. At first Maru blinked, thinking he saw almost a replica of himself before him. The savage, arrogant Moleka was no longer there, but some other person like himself – humbled and defeated before all the beauty of the living world. So is that what love is like, he thought. And you can't hide it? Arrested, he looked a little deeper, first into Moleka's eyes, which he saw as two yellow orbs of light, and then deeper, into his heart. The humility was superficial, perhaps in keeping with his changed view of himself, but what was in Moleka's heart, now that the barriers were broken, made Maru's heart cold with fear. It was another version of arrogance and dominance, but more terrible because it was of the spirit. Moleka was a sun around which spun a billion satellites. All the sun had to do was radiate force, energy, light. Maru had no equivalent of it in his own kingdom. He had no sun like that, only an eternal and gentle interplay of shadows and light and peace.

'He is greater than I in power,' he thought, at first stunned, taken aback by the sight. Then he thought: 'How was it that nothing sealed my doors? I always knew who I was. Moleka had to wait until his door was opened by another hand. Moleka is only half a statement of his kingdom. Someone else makes up the whole. It is the person he now loves.'

He knew from his own knowledge of himself that true purpose and direction are creative. Creative imagination he had in over-abundance. Moleka had none of that ferment, only an over-abundance of power. It was as though Moleka were split in two – he had the energy but someone else had the equivalent gifts of Maru's kingdom: creative imagination. Why, any wild horse was also powerful and where did wild horses go? They jumped over cliffs. Moleka and his stupid brain could send all those billion worlds colliding into each other. Did the sun have compassion and good sense? It had only the ego of the brightest light in the heavens. Maru preferred to be the moon. Not in any way did he desire Moleka's kingdom or its dizzy, revolving energy, but somehow a lifetime of loving between them was over in those few seconds. He averted his head in embarrassment and pain and quietly moved to his chair beside Moleka. There was a pile of neatly typed mail in the outgoing tray for him to sign. He had been away for three weeks and all that could be heard for some time was the scratch, scratch of his pen as he signed the letters. After a while his eye wandered to the tray marked 'Miscellaneous'. A roughly pencilled note, in Moleka's bold scrawl, lay carelessly flung on top of a pile of papers. As his hand moved towards it, he noted out of the corner of his eye that Moleka started violently.

'What a fool he is,' he thought. 'Behaving like a sixteen-year-old girl.'

He read the note: 'Property of Dilepe Tribal Administration. 1 bed, 1 mattress, out on loan to teacher, Margaret Cadmore, assistant teacher: Leseding School.'

He turned and stared directly at Moleka's profile. Moleka kept his face shut in to himself, seemingly preoccupied with his work.

'This Margaret Cadmore must be the Masarwa who is causing trouble in the village,' Maru said.

Moleka turned round and looked Maru in the face. There was no expression or comment in his eyes.

'I don't know of any Masarwa who is a teacher,' Moleka said flatly, crying out for a showdown. He knew of Maru's spies and spies.

A glint of something dangerous, threatening, shot into Maru's eyes.

'I'm not like you, Moleka,' he said, with heavy sarcasm. 'I still own the Masarwa as slaves. All my one hundred thousand cattle and fifty cattle posts are maintained by the Masarwa. They sleep on the ground, near outdoor fires. Their only blanket is the fire. When the fire warms them on one side, they turn round and warm themselves on the other side. I have seen this with my own eyes. What will they do when they hear that a certain Masarwa in my village is treated as an equal of the Batswana and given a bed from my office? Won't they want beds too, and where do I find all those beds, overnight? I want the bed you loaned to the Masarwa teacher returned, immediately.'

He pushed the pencilled note towards Moleka. Moleka took the note, seemed to re-read it, but he was struggling to clear his head of the roar inside it. How had he and Maru become strangers and enemies, so abruptly? He jerked his face back to the face of his friend, who now had his own face shut in, seemingly preoccupied with his work.

'I'll get the bed returned,' he said, but the undertone was so violent it meant: 'I'm going to murder you.'

Moleka stood up and walked out of the office. Maru raised one large hand and covered his face. He was laughing. He had a number of bombs to set off in the village of Dilepe. Some would explode soon, some a little later. This was the first time Moleka was out of it, and he was laughing because Moleka appeared just as much a fool as everyone else to his scheming and plotting. He stood up and watched from a window as Moleka gave orders to two clerks to take his white van and recover the bed. Moleka did not want to do the dirty work himself. Maru looked at his watch. The time was four o'clock.

Fifteen minutes later the white van stopped outside the solitary old library building on the small hill. Being absorbed in her notebook, Margaret did not immediately put down her pen at the van's approach. She was seated at a small table under a window and at first turned round with surprise when one of the men knocked at the open door. She stood up and walked across the almost empty room. There was little furniture. Apart from the small table and chair, there was a bed with a floor mat, a large wooden packing box, neatly covered with a clean white cloth on which was arranged a tea set, a plate, spoons, knife and fork. Next to this was a small paraffin tank stove with two plates, on one of which stood a kettle. A few books leaned against each other on the floor. Her clothes were still in the suitcase. There was an odour of freshly applied floor wax and an old wax oilcloth which covered the room from end to end sparkled in the late afternoon sun. Cheap, but very pretty floral curtains, handmade, hung at the windows. It seemed to her the most beautiful home on earth.

As she walked to the door her eye was attracted by the white van outside. For a second her heart stopped beating, then continued at an accelerated pace. She turned to the men, almost too eagerly. They just stared back at her. One of them seemed to strike her a blow in the face. He said: 'Moleka has sent us to recover the bed.'

She placed one hand on the door post to steady herself. The events of the morning rose like a wave. The abrupt demand for the bed made her mouth go dry with fear. She said: 'Oh!' It meant so much, all at once: I am going to lose my job. They are going to drive me out of the village. Why have I been thinking of him every spare moment of my life, since the day I first saw him?

'Why so suddenly?' she asked, struggling to regain her shattered equilibrium.

'He did not explain,' the older man said. 'He just told us to bring back the bed.'

Then he looked down, shame-faced, embarrassed. He was part of the village life and knew about the mutterings concerning the Masarwa teacher. Even so, she was a teacher of their children and deserved some respect. That was his opinion. She could feel it. It gave her the kind of courage she did not normally possess. She said: 'It's a little late for me to get another bed from the shop. Could I not have a day or two to order a new one? I am sorry but I forgot to ask the secretary how long I may borrow the bed. He told me they usually lend beds to teachers.'

The two men looked at each other. They had never done anything so dreadful in their lives. The older man spoke again:

'Moleka is a reasonable man,' he said sympathetically. 'If you present your case to him, he will surely let you keep the bed for a day or two. Come, we will take you to him.'

She quickly closed the door behind her and walked with the men to the van. Oh, what, what to do? There were the children. She had not yet recovered from the shaking up of the morning. And now this! Why loan her a bed only to humiliate her with its abrupt removal? Were they all saying, like the children: 'You are a Bushman?' Perhaps she did not care about the bed. She wanted to see him again. Perhaps she would be unable to stand alone against a whole village of people who did not want a Masarwa teacher. She'd see by his face and then make her own decisions. There was a limit to which a human being could be an experiment, especially if he or she were so unprepared for something new.

The driver stopped the van outside the office. She climbed out and walked up the short flight of stairs, then turned left. She paused at the door. Two men were in the office this time. Neither looked up from his work. She stood there, trapped. Perhaps they had secretaries whom one should approach first. Just as she was about to retreat, Moleka said: 'Come in,' but his face was like stone and he did not look up. There was nothing to uphold her. Should she even try to claim that she was human?

'The request for the return of the bed is so sudden,' she said nervously. 'Could I keep it for a day or two until I buy one from the shop?'

How her whole future depended on his reply, yet his face remained stone.

'It is I who want the bed returned today,' a voice said.

She jerked her face, startled, towards the speaker. He had been outside her visual range. A look of surprise and enquiry flitted over her face. He was a replica of Dikeledi, in the delicate construction of his face, with those same faraway eyes, except that his mouth was full and wide. He looked as though he was half smiling, friendly, gentle, but his words did not match his voice. That was final authority; no one could contradict.

Suddenly she felt as if her throat were being choked. The man was Dikeledi's brother. Dikeledi spoke of him with reverence. And how much had Dikeledi invaded her own life without giving her these awful details – that she, Dikeledi, was related to someone like this who had slaves as part of his hereditary privilege? Did you ever sort out one thing from another with people, especially when you were a no-people? Did you trust intuition, and if you did, how did you explain Moleka and his talking heart – first there was one of you, now there are two of you?

'I'll return the bed,' she said, and walked out as if she were facing her death. How was she to know the true size and nature of this sudden adversary? Almost everyone grovelled before him, because of his position. But she had looked down at him, indifferently, from a great height, where she was more than his equal. It had nothing to do with the little bit of education she had acquired from a missionary. He treated everyone as a single, separate entity, and measured the length and breadth and depth and height of their inner kingdoms with one alert glance. There was every kind of foolishness in the world. People who had nothing were as evil and malicious as Pete, and as false. People who had kingdoms were careful not to betray those gods who dwelt inside those kingdoms. How few they were. Almost everyone wrecked his nervous system like the screech of cheap music.

Some time passed and then Moleka silently left the office. It was nearing five o'clock, but Maru continued staring absent-mindedly at the wall. A picture slowly unfolded itself before him.

How often had it haunted his mind. There was a busy, roaring highway on one side, full of bustle and traffic. Leading away from it was a small, dusty footpath. It went on and on by itself into the distance.

'Take that path,' his heart said. 'You have no other choice.'

Each time he hesitated. It was too lonely. No other companion trod that road. Maybe the loneliness would drive him to the busy highway, where he would meet his doom. But as he faced the choice again that late afternoon, springing up on either side of the footpath were thousands and thousands of bright yellow daisies. They stirred in the sunlight and cool breeze and turned faces of faint, enquiring surprise in his direction. Then they danced all by themselves. The sight was so beautiful that his heart leapt with joy. He stood up in a fearful hurry, like one with many preparations ahead of him. He waited for a while at his home, where he met Ranko, Moseka and Semana as arranged. Then the three men went their own ways into the village, while in the swiftly gathering darkness he walked to the home of his sister, Dikeledi. She still had her head buried in her notebook, and was filling it in with neat, rapid handwriting.

'I'll make some tea,' she said, jumping up and putting it to one side, relieved to have a genuine excuse to stop work.

He sat down and absorbed himself in his own thoughts. Soon his sister returned with the tea tray. She still held it in her hands as she talked.

'I saw my colleague enter the office not so long ago,' she said. 'It made me curious.'

'Moleka loaned her a bed,' he said. 'I made her return it.'

She put the tray down on the table so roughly that a little of the milk in the jug splashed up into her face.

'Why?' she asked sharply.

'I did it to quieten the village,' he said. 'People expect a Masarwa revolution, because of Moleka's behaviour on Sunday.'

'There's no such thing as Masarwa,' she said, a sudden shrill edge in her voice. 'There are only people.'

'Oh,' he said sarcastically. 'You think you have found a bit of humanity and can lecture to me?'

'Have you ever tried sleeping on the hard floor?' she asked, also curling her lips in sarcasm.

He turned his head a little and smiled. She was so confused and angry, she averted her head and picked up the sugar bowl. Nothing had to be wrong with Maru. He was her god.

'I don't like anyone to be wiser than thou about my actions,' he said, in a quietly threatening voice. 'I don't care whether she sleeps on the hard floor for the rest of her life but I am not going to marry a pampered doll.'

Dikeledi rocked backwards on her high heels, and half the sugar in the bowl reeled onto the floor. There was something like hysteria in her laughter. She thought she had everything right but suddenly an abyss opened up in front of her. She had to jerk her mind away from the words: 'But you can't marry a Masarwa. Not in your position.' How could she say that, when not so long ago she had said there was no such thing as a Masarwa?

'Why are you laughing?' he asked, sounding very angry.

'I am shocked,' she said, truthfully.

'About what?'

'Between the lunch hour and now, people don't suddenly decide they are going to marry. I think you are joking.'

'I am not,' he said.

She kept quiet for a while to control the hysteria. She put the sugar into the tea and handed him a cup, but her hands trembled and the tea cup rattled. She could not drink her tea. She was upset and distressed and burst out: 'I don't like your jokes,' she said. 'They are about a human being. If people heard even a whisper of this they would instantly plot to kill her. You know how stupid and cruel prejudice is. It can't think beyond its nose. Besides, I am involved. We loved each other from the day we met. There was no difficulty about establishing the friendship. Even there I was surprised. I knew the love had to grow, gradually.'

He kept silent a while. He was almost tempted to expose Moleka and the real cause of his sudden suicide from Moleka the savage to Moleka the god. Who else made a god overnight but a goddess? If there was one thing that would kill Dikeledi, it would be to know who had found the heart of Moleka and that she had had no key to open the iron and steel doors of his kingdom. There was a world apart from petty human hatreds and petty human social codes and values where the human soul roamed free in all its splendour and glory. No barriers of race or creed or tribe hindered its activity. He had seen majestic kings of the soul, walking in the ragged clothes of filthy beggars. He could bring this home forcefully to her but the truth would destroy her and he needed her alive and stupid for his future plans. He hesitated, with pain in his eyes. Always, at a push, he told a half truth, or an outright lie. Perhaps Moleka would give her the kind of shaking up to make her rise beyond a narrow view of love.

'I hate you, Dikeledi,' he said, vehemently.

She looked surprised.

'When you think of me,' he said, 'you think of me as they all do, that I am their public property to be pushed around and directed by what they think is right and good for me. Has it not occurred to you that I might despise, even loathe them? Three quarters of the people on this continent are like Morafi, Seth and Pete – greedy, grasping, back-stabbing, a betrayal of all the good in mankind. I was not born to rule this mess. If I have a place it is to pull down the old structures and create the new. Not for me any sovereignty over my fellow men. I'd remove the blood money, the cruelty and crookery from the top, but that's all. There's a section of my life they will never claim or own.'

He could not see her face in the dim light but he saw her shake her head as though she was not following everything. In her mind he was irrevocably a paramount chief. Yes, he was good enough to be God but half the glitter and impact of him in her mind was his earthly position. Had she not time and again said to friends: 'Maru is a real chief. He is a little bit like the chiefs we had in the old days, before the white man arrived'?

How was it then that he had inherited so much blood money and so many slaves whose only blanket was an outdoor fire? Had they not all been a little like Morafi, with a few principles, and these principles had saved them from outright damnation? Maybe he concentrated on his immediate situation. It was African. It was horrible. But wherever mankind had gathered itself together in a social order, the same things were happening. There was a mass of people with no humanity to whom another mass referred: Why, they are naturally like that. They like to live in such filth. They have been doing it for centuries.

Should he bother to explain to her the language of the voices of the gods who spoke of tomorrow? That they were opening doors on all sides, for every living thing on earth, that there would be a day when everyone would be free and no one the slave of another? That people no longer needed chiefs and kings and figureheads who wore dazzling garments and ruled with the philosophy that there was never enough, so those who had had to put their foot down on those who had not? New kings were arising indeed. The stature and majesty would always be there, but the kings who arose now were those of the soul who could never betray their gods of goodness, compassion, justice and truth. The downtrodden were hearing the message of their humanity. Who could contain the fury of centuries of oppression and despising? Certainly not the Morafis of the world. But people like himself, to whom a little bit of goodness was incompatible with a little bit of greed. There had to be perfection. It had to be almost ready-made, for use.

Had he not struggled with this in all his relationships with people – that goodness between friend and friend was mutual, and goodness between lover and lover also? With all his insight, he had been unable to turn a sow's ear into a silk purse. On each occasion he had simply thrown away the sow's ear and behind him was wreckage and devastation, too terrifying in its explosive vehemence. No wound had healed. He had only to touch the scars for them to bleed all over again: 'I hated her because she thought too much of herself. I hated her because she was only flesh. No flowers grew out of the love, and when I said: All right, this is over, she still thought the flesh had captivated me forever, until I had to kill her. I killed them all because of their greed.'

Should he explain every secret to Dikeledi? Maybe she would not fall in so easily with his plans. He needed a puppet of goodness and perfection to achieve certain things he felt himself incapable of achieving. He could project the kind of creative ferment that could change a world, but he was not a living dynamo. She was. So was Moleka. All he wanted was the freedom to dream the true dreams, untainted by the clamour of the world. Moleka and Dikeledi were the future kings and queens of the African continent, those of stature in character and goodness. He, Maru, was the dreamer of this future greatness. A whimsical amusement filled his voice once he began to speak again.

He said: 'Drink your tea. It is getting cold.' Then he paused, while she raised the cup to her mouth.

'I'm sorry I shocked you,' he said. 'I never intended accepting the chieftaincy. I was only born in it to see its evils and its effects on society. Everything I have done has been an experience, an experiment. I just move on to more experience, more experiment. When she walked into the office this afternoon, I merely said: That's one more experience for me, but it shows all the signs of being a good one. A woman like that would ensure that I am never tempted to make a public spectacle of myself. We'd never make the right, conventional gestures. People would never get over it, the embarrassment: "Why, she's only a Masarwa." They'd not know where to look because they spend their lives judging each other by things of no consequence.'

He began to laugh quietly. Half of him was a demon. He was only afraid of Moleka, who had his eyes and his heart and saw everything his way. Dikeledi also began laughing. His words so truly evoked the image of her new friend and certain oddities in her behaviour. If anyone approached Margaret Cadmore, she slowly raised her hand as if to ward off a blow. Sometimes she winced, but the raised hand was always there as though she expected only blows from people. There was something else funny about her. She was a shadow behind which lived another personality of great vigour and vitality. She raised her hand to hide this second image from sight, but the two constantly tripped up each other.

Dikeledi had seen that morning also that she was very violent and dominant but seemingly unable to project that hidden power. You were never sure whether she was greater than you, or inferior, because of this constant flux and interchange between her two images. It was only Dikeledi who had a permanent platform and could bound from one thing to another with little change or ill effects. Half the fascination the other woman held for her was that her breaking point could so clearly be seen – as though one part of her broke down and was mended by another, and so on. Dikeledi's affection said: 'I must take care of her.'

Dikeledi recovered her fun and bounce. She said to Maru: 'Now tell me, when is this sudden marriage to take place?'

'Oh, in my own time,' Maru said. 'I have other things to arrange first.'

'Are you going to make a formal proposal? You know, like: "I'd like to marry you, Miss Cadmore. What do you think about it?" People usually do that first in case the other party is not agreeable.'

Maru felt a little anxious all of a sudden.

'Dikeledi,' he said, sharply. 'This is a secret between you and me. As for proposals, who else do you think would want to marry her, besides myself?'

'Of course one can't say with women,' Dikeledi said. 'She could never have as many admirers as I have but I was surprised to see Ranko carrying her parcels home the other day. I thought: Where did she pick up Ranko, and so soon? Ranko had a besotted look on his face. He could not stop smiling. I had to chase him away because his behaviour was so embarrassing.'

'You must report the progress of the Ranko affair to me,

Dikeledi,' he said seriously. 'Also, report the minute she mentions the name of anyone who has taken her fancy and I shall mess everything up.'

Dikeledi shook her head: 'It's a risk you are taking, brother. She might not like to marry you. We have a free world these days. People often say "no".'

'Dikeledi,' he said, deadly serious. 'If I came to you one day and said: "Look here, I have long controlled the affairs of your life. You can't even cry unless I will it. Now, if you don't agree to marry me, you will stare at the moon for the rest of your days," what would you do?'

Dikeledi tilted her head to one side. You went through the unbelievable with Maru. He really made people do everything he said they would, and could create such a tangle of events with his spies that it was simpler and less harassing to carry out his orders. She could not sum up the other woman. Obviously someone, perhaps the teacher she often referred to, had sheltered her from a lot of encounters with life. Dikeledi could make no secret of the fact that, in relation to men, she often suffered from high blood pressure, except that the trouble with the bloodstream had eventually boiled down to one, unattainable man.

'Women are not alike, brother,' she said. 'Of course, I'd choose you, not the moon. I'd say, "Maru is quite an ugly man but the moon is too cool for my liking." My friend is just the opposite. She is cool. You can't tell whether she can boil or not. If she can, she's not used to it because you can't see it on her face.'

He kept silent, smiling to himself. Things had always worked out that way. Moleka raised the blood pressure of even a stone, but he did other things, the way the rain made the grass and flowers bloom. When had they not worked hand in hand? They would do so again, except as enemies this time. The way he saw it, it could not be helped, but he intended coming out on top, as the winner. It was different if his motivation was entirely selfish, self-centred, but the motivation came from the gods who spoke to him in his heart. They had said: Take that road. Then they had said: Take that companion. He believed his heart and the things in it. They were his only criteria for goodness. In the end, nothing was personal to him. In the end, the subjection of his whole life to his inner gods was an intellectual process. Very little feeling was involved. His methods were cold, calculating and ruthless.

It could not be imagination. He had never been inclined that way. The real, the immediate, the practical – that was his heaven and he was to resolve his destiny in one night and find himself back where he had always been, the Moleka who found it too dangerous to allow his mind to soar off the ground. What happened afterwards was a jumble of a hidden depth of music that had briefly stirred his heart and given him a strong desire for revenge. But he acted then from a safe platform, each time balancing the real, profitable and attainable against the fantasy and each time choosing the bird in the hand. Who knows what dreams could have emerged from the music in his heart had he been allowed to obtain the inspirer of the music? Because that evening he was all at sea. He seemed to have opened up a pathway as yet unknown to him and just as he was about to set foot on it, with tender eyes, everything was lost. There were only doors again and what was behind them was to remain a mystery.

It must have been two weeks now, his mother calculated, that she had been afflicted with having Moleka at home. Life with Moleka was a series of high dramas, always ending in paternity cases. There were already eight motherless children living in her yard, their only justification for being there that they all looked like Moleka, with his distinctive, thundercloud brow. Her life was a continuous harassment of women, fighting over her son. It was good enough for the motherless children that she had had only one child and an enormous amount of maternal feeling. There was never any trouble with Moleka – apart from women. Yet there he was, titivating himself each evening and going out for more trouble. How long this had been going on she could not say, except that he was her son and she was used to him. There was no way in which she condemned him. She coddled and pampered him as if he were a three-year-old boy. After all, he was her only child.

Suddenly, he began behaving in an unnatural way. He was home each evening. He seemed uncertain of his next word or action and many hours passed in brooding silence. She watched with mounting anxiety, fearing, like Ranko, that he might be losing his mind. It happened that Sunday; he turned the whole house upside down by seating himself at table with the slaves of the yard. It was not that which upset his mother. Moleka had had no other companions. He had grown up with the slaves as playmates and was just as much coddled by them as he was by her. It was the talk and confusion in the village and her clear observation of his strange behaviour at home.

But there was no woman in sight. Over the years she had put a crease in her forehead to help her pretend anxiety for all the women who fell in love with her son. Over the two weeks the crease in her forehead became very real. Frequently, during the day, she burst into tears. Just as the situation became intolerable, Moleka went out again and the next morning, as usual, there was another woman. This time she was afraid. Sparks were flying in all directions. Who would have thought a long-standing friend and relative could have caused such upheaval in

283

the life of Moleka? She could clearly picture his face the previous evening. He'd sat for a while, on the edge of a couch in the dining room, and slowly wiped his hand across his brow, as if under great stress. When she had enquired, 'Are you not well, my child?' he had turned and looked at her with pain in his eyes. With Moleka emotion was heightened, dramatic. She could see the pain pass like continuous waves over his eyes. He kept silent. After a while he stood up and walked out of the house, forgetting to titivate himself.

That was what the sea was like. He was trying to grasp a depth of what he had lost and trying to grasp a depth of what he might gain. Why had he hesitated for two weeks? Was it because of his closeness to Maru and that they had always shared their experiences? Because he had not hidden anything until the last, fatal moments, when it was too late. Maru had surprised him by showing a side of his nature he'd never suspected was there. Look how he had spoken about owning slaves and thinking of his own comfort and pocket first. Something had fallen between them that afternoon like a deadly knife. It was incompatible with the tender, reflective mood which had enclosed his mind over the past two weeks. He had suffered under another, unfamiliar mood. He suddenly forgot everything about making approaches to a woman. He had not known what to do, what to say as a beginning and had walked round and round in circles at home. Always, something spoke to him in his heart, like deep, sweet music. He listened intently. It was a new experience for him. Previously he had only heard that such things existed, from Maru. They were stories he listened to with interest but could not comment on. They did not arouse his curiosity either. Maru always fell in love, but not he. He had sometimes seen a light like the sun shine on Maru's face. This time he felt the sun in his own heart. There was more to it as well, as though a voice moved there and spoke to him: 'But we are surely not strangers, Moleka?'

It changed too if the mover of the voice was distressed, like that evening: 'Help me. Ought I to go away? It might be that my appearance this time prevents you from recognizing me.'

That was what he struggled with. Half of him felt that he formulated those words because he was thrown off balance and at sea. He was no Maru who could ride the tides of all kinds of fancies. He doubted his heart, his mind. But distress eventually made him walk slowly out of the house.

'Perhaps I shall knock at the door and introduce myself formally: "I have just come to see if you are comfortable. If you have not enough money to purchase a bed, I can always arrange a loan." Then I shall walk away,' he thought.

But the thought of even talking to her created such a turmoil in his mind, such a roar in his heart that he stopped for a while and stared at the pitch dark night to regain his composure. As he walked along again, he analysed his feelings. His heart had grown into its own fullness, too suddenly, and he had no control over it. There was also a feeling that he constantly held his heart against hers, or his mouth against hers, and that all human language had now become superfluous and a sacrilege. With other women there was a stream of comfortable small talk, but how was he going to talk when the roar in his heart choked his throat?

'Perhaps I ought to return home and let this matter work itself out slowly,' he thought. 'I am not myself.'

In reality, he had lived many kinds of married lives. They consisted of giving orders: Do this! Don't do that! I'd like my back scrubbed this very minute. But a horror of shyness overcame him as he thought of these things in contrast with the woman who now lived in his heart. They seemed too far removed, too remote, in the same way that he had not yet had time to see if her legs pleased him or not. Then that seemed the problem to him. There was no barrier of the spirit. He had talked straight to her heart. The effect of this had been to raise almost insurmountable barriers over the physical. It was as though some other person had to find her limbs and say: All right, proceed. You may love this woman's body as well. He paused again. Again he thought: 'Perhaps I ought to return home. I am not myself.' But his feet slowly continued in the direction that led to the old library on the hill. At the foot of the hill, he paused once more and looked up. The light of a lamp shone through one of the windows. A peace settled on his heart as though the burning lamp made everything seem normal and the person within that room engaged in some activity such as eating or cooking or drinking tea. It fitted in with his idea of formality: 'I have just come to see if you are comfortable . . .'

Almost joyfully, he began to climb the hill. He had not got halfway when a voice called out: 'Moleka!'

It was Ranko. He stopped and spoke in a low, deadly voice: 'What are you doing here, Ranko?'

Without any hesitation Ranko replied: 'Maru said he expected you would come this way. He asked me to give you a message. He said: "Tell Moleka to remember that he enjoys life on this earth. This is not the end for him. He will have a long life."'

There was silence. Then Moleka ground his teeth in savage fury and made an angry exclamation that sounded half like the roar of a lion.

'I would not like to be killed by a low person like you, Ranko,' he said, furiously. 'Don't you know that spying is the lowest occupation on earth?'

Ranko kept silent. Two furies raced through Moleka's heart. The words of Maru, through his mouthpiece, Ranko, were a declaration of war. He could not accept it. It meant everything was over before it had begun. And he also knew that, although he had no Ranko, he had a control over the situation. Maru acknowledged what had awakened in his heart. The woman was just as unapproachable to Maru as she was to him. He turned violently on Ranko:

'Since Maru thinks he can send messages to me, through spies, you can also take a message to him. Tell him I say that the day he approaches her, I will burn his house down. He is lucky if I don't kill him too.'

It was only as he walked away that the shock of the abrupt encounter with Ranko gradually overcame his mind. What was this he'd seen? When had Maru had time to fall in love and move so swiftly? Look at that terrible message: 'This is not the end for him. He will have a long life.' How did a person in his right mind relate Maru's behaviour of the afternoon towards the woman with what Ranko had revealed this evening? Maru had fooled him. Again a wave of fury swept through his heart. Did it mean that a love since childhood was over in a few hours with such a betrayal?

Unconsciously his feet took him in the direction of the house of Maru. He knew his every habit, that he sometimes sat by a window for hours with his own thoughts, unless occupied with work or a guest. He was there this evening, clearly outlined by the lamplight, seated near the window, with his thoughts. Moleka stood outside, in the dark night, all kinds of murderous thoughts rushing through his mind. He did not know it but he was regaining his hold on the practical, the immediate. Here was something he could grasp at. He had been unable to grasp at his love. It had almost deranged him. For two hours he stood there but by the end of it he had brought himself fully under control. He was Moleka, but with something added.

No sooner had Maru risen to retire than he began to pity himself out there in the dark night: 'My whole life is upside down. I wander with no place to rest my head, yet he goes to bed peacefully.' It still seemed to him illogical, the vileness of Maru's behaviour and his own inability to bring swift retribution on Maru. Someone had to die that night because of the fury in his heart. Maybe he'd go and find Ranko and kill him. Just as he turned, his eye fell on the home of Dikeledi. Her laughter and mockery over the years – 'Don't you even dare touch my fingernail, Moleka' – and the way she contradicted her words by thrusting her thighs in his face, suddenly gave him an outlet for his pent-up rage. Let her start that nonsense again – 'Don't you dare touch my fingernail . . .' – and he would throttle her to death on the spot.

He had not noticed for how long her house had been in darkness, but as he tapped lightly on a door which led to her bedroom it was not a second before a match went scratch-scratch and the lamp was lit. She came padding to the door on bare feet.

'Who is it?' she asked.

Moleka kept silent. She flung open the door and peered out, then drew back, startled. Moleka walked straight in through the open door to the bedroom. He sat down on the bed, then turned and stared at Dikeledi from under his thundercloud brow. She stood at the end of the room near the door, too surprised to grasp how everything had happened so suddenly. At last she said, crossly:

'What are you up to, Moleka?'

'You think I don't know about your notebook,' he said, imp- ishly. 'Last night Moleka slept here. The other night Moleka slept there. Grace is now his latest. Well, I want to satisfy your curiosity. Tonight I'm going to sleep here.'

He bent and started to untie a shoelace.

'Moleka,' she said, frightened. 'You can't do that. Haven't we always treated each other with respect?'

'I haven't locked the door,' he said, coolly. 'Run to the home of your brother and report that I'm molesting you. He and I will settle the matter together with fists.'

She stared forlornly into the distance. It had always been like this. He said the wrong, crude things that jarred against the delicacy and beauty of her love for him. Why, she had even fallen into bed with her heart melting with love after what Maru had told her about Moleka and the slaves in his house. He was, to her, the greatest devil-may-care hero on earth. Not even Maru could compare to the dashing image of Moleka in her mind. Since she kept so silent, he paused in the act of undoing his other shoelace.

'What are you thinking about?' he asked.

'I was feeling so proud of you,' she said sadly. 'Maru told me about how you put Seth to shame on Sunday . . .'

She could not add that he rarely managed to live on the glittering peaks of his achievements. Her eyes filled with tears. He set his foot down and turned his head towards her, with glittering eyes. He could have taken his revenge that moment. There were ways of killing people without knives and guns and he had only to say: 'I did it for her, because I love her,' and Dikeledi would have been shot dead by an invisible but fatal bullet. She thought she was the queen of Moleka's heart. There was no other woman her equal in the village. She had ignored all his love affairs because she towered above every other woman of her kind, in her world, intellectually and morally. For a brief moment Moleka balanced things: 'I won't get her from Maru,' he thought. 'He's the devil.' Dikeledi might be his only salvation. She was, after he had glimpsed the heights of love, the next best woman on earth. He swung his whole life towards the bars of Dikeledi's prison.

'I did it for you,' he lied, slowly. 'I knew you were her friend.'

She never questioned anything. Moleka was even baffled and hurt by the one trembling hand she placed on his knee. He had hardly been aware of when and how she had moved across the floor to sit beside him. He averted his head in embarrassment. Where did a love like that come from when he had no equal to match it in his own heart? He had just begun to learn about other things, a pain of something which is earned and lost, and earned and lost again. There were things he'd do for others, never gaining any reward. There were glittering peaks of sacrifices and services given to others, but known only to him, in his own secret heart. A wry humour twitched at the corners of his mouth. He turned to Dikeledi and said in an almost conversational tone: 'I guess I've always loved you.'

She also fell in with his mood: 'I see that you are just going on undressing yourself but it is not to my liking.'

'I have no more women left, Dikeledi,' he said, comically. 'You are the last on the list.'

This did not displease her but she kept quiet, thinking about all those children born helter-skelter, here and there. So she said: 'As you know, I'm not narrow-minded about anything but I could not endure to have a fatherless child.'

Moleka gave a snort of laughter: 'Then why do you advertise your thighs?' he demanded. 'I'd like you to stop that. You think men don't know what you mean when you walk around swinging your thighs like that? They can't take their eyes off you and here you want to pretend all kinds of innocence before me. Women like you are the cause of all the trouble in the world.'

He was laughing with one side of his heart. He stood up a moment later and blew out the lamp. A wave of pain swamped him from head to toe. He had been given a blow such as he had never experienced before. He was not sure of his survival.

'Dikeledi!' he said intensely, with desperation in his voice. He meant: 'Help me! I have lost everything I ever loved.' He meant Maru. Later, although he never wanted to admit it, he had at last accidentally found a dwelling place for his restless heart. Dikeledi's kingdom was like that of the earth and its deep centre which absorbed the light and radiations of a billion suns and planets and kept on dreaming and brooding, recreating life in an eternal cycle. Moleka must have scratched his head and smiled to himself. At least he had stumbled onto something that was a true complement to his own kingdom of radiant energy. Still he felt cheated, baffled. How had one woman set his heart aflame and he had turned around and given all that fire into another woman's keeping? It was as though a pre-arranged trap had been set for him, as though the organizer of the trap was alertly one jump ahead of his every need. It was not at all to his liking.

Ranko, who watched over the surprising events of the night, was also rattled. He was already seated at the breakfast table, drinking his coffee, when Maru appeared. No sooner had Maru sat down than he burst out: 'Moleka is a damn nuisance! He has now taken Mistress Dikeledi as his concubine.'

Maru averted his head. He wanted to shout with laughter but that would have upset Ranko, who adored his sister. He looked at the opposite wall and said carefully: 'Don't worry about that, Ranko. Moleka will one day live down the scandal of how he made his own wife a concubine. You must pass by Moleka's home today and tell his mother that I don't approve of his treating my sister like a cheap concubine. Tell her, that when the time is ready, I shall expect her to counsel her son wisely because this is a very serious matter.'

These words relieved Ranko's troubled heart. Why, Mistress Dikeledi with her ways and education was real gold. He chuckled to himself, thinking of his encounter with Moleka on the hill, then he unrolled his camera, describing Moleka's every word and gesture in detail. Maru forgot his usual dignity and composure, threw back his head and laughed with his mouth wide open. After a while he calmed down and remarked philosophically to Ranko: 'Why must Moleka have everything? He's always touched gold and handled it carelessly. I've always touched straw. This time I'm stealing the gold because I've grown tired of the straw.'

Then he sat quietly drinking a number of cups of coffee. The sun had just begun to show its head above the hill and streaks of its early gold light splashed onto the open field in front of him. He loved this part of the day best when everything was being born anew and the air was cool and fresh on his face. His life was so rhythmical that everything seemed to happen in the same order each day, except that today his sister's car was still outside her house. She normally left before the sun could show its head above the hill, because school started early. She always walked coolly down the stairs in a neat, tight skirt with a billowing blouse, but this morning she was late and flustered and the skirt of her bright cotton frock flared out around her pretty legs as she ran down the stairs.

A lot of things had changed. He stood up a while later and walked to the office. Moleka was already in and seated. Neither greeted the other and for a while they worked in tense silence. Then Moleka said: 'You are making a mistake. She belongs to me and you won't get her.'

'That's what *you* say,' Maru said, sarcastically.

'I suppose your spies have already told you that I spent the night with your sister,' Moleka said, contemptuously.

Maru kept silent.

'I'm not going to marry Dikeledi,' Moleka said, pulling down his thundercloud brow.

Again Maru kept silent.

'I hate you!' Moleka said vehemently.

'You may,' said Maru coolly. 'But don't underestimate me. I am not afraid when fighting for what is my own.'

Moleka was so angry that he picked up a pile of papers and walked into the office of the typist and began pacing up and down, not saying a word to the astonished lady. After a time the lady noticed that things were very cool between Maru and Moleka, not like the old days of roaring laughter and jokes. The news flew around the village. Maru was angry with Moleka because Moleka had taken his sister as his latest concubine. It was the kind of tangle and confusion of events Maru revelled in. Half truths, outright lies, impossible rumours and sudden, explosive events were his stock-in-trade. He used them as a cover up for achieving his goals. People would thwart him otherwise and he never liked to be side-tracked. He never cared about the means towards the end and who got hurt.

Even Dikeledi fell in with his games. As usual she walked into the classroom of her friend with her tin of fat cakes. At first she was too distressed and uneasy to note the dark smudges of a sleepless night under her friend's eyes. Her own inner mood was one of riotous, tumultuous happiness. She put it to one side, briefly, looked very thoughtful and then said: 'I know about the bed. I don't know what got into my brother. He does not usually behave that way. In any case, we live our separate lives and don't always agree. I don't want you to be angry with me.'

Margaret kept silent and looked down.

'I have a spare bed at my home,' Dikeledi persisted. 'I can get it delivered to your home while we are still at school. You would be small-minded if you did not accept my gift.'

Margaret looked up, startled. Their friendship was too unfathomable to her, as though she could not make an effort to analyse her feelings towards Dikeledi and it would drift on and on like this, continually getting into deep water.

'I'm not small-minded,' she said, smiling.

Dikeledi immediately dived into the packet of Marmite sandwiches, sat on a desk, tilted back her head and quietly threw her thoughts into her own heart. She was thinking: 'Moleka's kisses taste like Marmite sandwiches. Moleka's kisses taste like roast beef with spicy gravy. Moleka's kisses . . .' And while she dwelt on these earthly things, a very spiritual look of divine happiness appeared on her face. Her companion, sitting opposite her, watched this pretty communication in silence. She had an unexplored gift. Half consciously, her hand moved to a sheet of paper and a pencil and, without any faltering, concentrated on capturing that lovely expression. Fifteen minutes later she put down the pencil and covered the paper with one hand. Dikeledi awoke to reality on the tail end of that secretive gesture. She sprang off the desk: 'Hey, what's that?' she said eagerly. 'Let me see it.'

She snatched up the paper. There was Dikeledi, her face uptilted, exploring heaven. She was a vain woman and highly flattered. First she said: 'I'm keeping this.' After a moment she said: 'Please take out the picture of your mother.'

She compared the two. The styles of both artists were almost identical, almost near that of a comic-strip artist in their simplicity, except that the younger disciple appeared greater than the master. It was a difference of temperament. The older Margaret Cadmore had been essentially a cold and unemotional woman, insensitive to the depths and heights of life, and the young girl highlighted these latter qualities, at the same time emulating her skill for rapid reproduction of life, on the spot.

'Did you learn this from your teacher as well?' Dikeledi asked, shyly.

'Yes,' Margaret said.

'I like your work better,' Dikeledi said, much put out, as though her friend had suddenly jumped up a notch or two in her estimation. She wanted to say something like: 'But your people were naturally gifted this way. There are all those rock paintings,' and the words choked in her throat. Nothing tallied with Margaret Cadmore, whether Bushman or what, so she said: 'Your teacher must have been a good woman to share everything with you.'

'No,' Margaret said, surprised. 'She was not good. She was rich. She kept on throwing things away. I used to feel myself catching them, and that is how I learned.'

Pete, the principal, was in trouble of a strange nature. Something dreadful had happened to him the previous evening to turn him overnight into a hollow-eyed, nervous wreck. The previous day had been bad enough for him. He had lost face and the teachers of the senior classes had straightened their backs. He had been unable to stop muttering to himself, even during the afternoon, and the people with whom he lodged had several times looked with appalled faces towards the closed door of his room, from which his muttering could be plainly heard. The women began whispering among themselves, doubting if they had a normal person in the house.

At sunset, he emerged dressed for an evening out. He was his own, quiet reserved self again as he shuffled out of the house. The women sighed with relief. He was a good boarder, who paid well and on time for all services. Money was not his bad point and that was all they were worried about.

Then, from about ten-thirty onwards that evening, such a terror filled their lives as they had not known in all their born days. They heard hard running footsteps, and the door was almost bashed down. They sat up in bed, frozen with terror, listening to the heavy, laboured breathing of the principal in his room. Then his muttering began again and continued throughout the long night. The man looked at his wife and his wife looked at him. The man's old mother crept into the bedroom. Their silent looks said: 'He has lost his mind.' They started shivering. He was not just anyone: he had a position. His position stifled their eagerness to shout for help.

The events leading up to this happened thus: By sunset Pete had recovered his nerve. He had formed an ultimatum which he intended presenting to Seth: 'Either the Masarwa teacher goes or I go.' That was fair enough. He could not have a repetition of the morning's events with Dikeledi getting out of control and the senior teachers laughing in his face. To his amazement, on his arrival at Seth's he found both Seth and Morafi in high spirits. He could hardly sit down before Morafi drawled: 'Well, what da ya know? Maru has shown his true colours. He walks around like a saint but touch him on his soft spot and he's just like everyone else, only worse. I'm no angel but I would not dream of taking a bed away from a woman. What da ya say, Pete?'

Pete was clearly baffled, but when he heard the full explanation his spirits soared so high that he hardly recognized himself. He was the most sensitive of the three demons and more aware than they were of a distinction between good and evil. His own actions hovered in a haze between those extremes. He could be stricken with conscience but he enjoyed double-dealing greatly. African life in a remote village afforded no other entertainment.

There was only one man he had set apart from all the double-dealing: Maru. He was precious because he was socially unobtainable. The few who had stepped inside his door talked about it for weeks, then it was reduced to scandal. They only went to pry out secrets he kept hidden away. Suddenly, the god who dwelt on those lofty heights seemed very real and easily approachable to a man like Pete. In fact, he seemed another Pete. They were both reserved, with delicate mannerisms.

'I never thought Maru would do a thing like that,' he said, a mixture of joy and calculation spreading over his face.

Morafi and Seth nodded their heads wisely. They did not like to say the obvious. Maru also kept slaves and was behaving like all slave owners. But somehow the matter was now beyond their concern. There was a moment when all they could think of was the Masarwa teacher. Now she would be got rid of by Maru. They felt cleansed and uplifted, drawn together in warm fellowship for the first time. Seth was always back-biting about Pete to Morafi and Pete was always back-biting about Seth to Morafi; and Morafi jiggled the threads between the two. He often felt himself the saint because both Seth and Pete feared to back-bite about Morafi as he was a Totem. To think that they had spent even a moment's worry over the Masarwa teacher, and only to have Maru outshine them in shameful behaviour! She would not last a day longer. The whole village was behind Maru because he was already, in name, their paramount chief. They felt like saints. The devil would rule. Morafi even managed a few words of pity for the oppressed.

Just after ten o'clock, Pete left on foot for home. He walked with his hands in his pockets, a smile on his face, from the warm, glowing comradeship of the evening. A long stretch of field separated the exclusive area where the top-class civil servants like Seth lived, and the rambling village arrangement of mud huts where Pete lived. The night was pitch dark and he kept his face down to see the faint outline of the footpath. He had been unaware of any other person nearby. Few people moved out after sundown. Suddenly a voice quite near his ear said:

'Tladi is going to get you for your evil deeds.'

And that was all. He froze to the ground. Fright made him query: 'Who?'

'Tladi,' said the clear whisper behind his ears.

He shot his eyes this way and that. There was nothing to see. It was too dark. Besides, he had heard no footsteps. It was different if you said God and conscience. God the abstract had never lived, but every African demon had once been a man with a reign of terror. Many things had distinguished Tladi from every other demon or god. He was indiscriminate about who was good and who was evil. He terrorized all. Children grew up on those tales, old people still had Tladi as a living memory. A blind horror overcame Pete. It was only the people he lodged with who heard his clamour and alarm. He heard nothing. Even in the safety of his room his alarm did not subside. It needed only such a suggestion for the whole horror of his inner nature to be exposed to him. The night was a nightmare. Every single person he had back-stabbed passed in parade before him.

By dawn he was haggard from anguish and a totally inefficient human being. As though he knew this, he did not attend school but shuffled straight to Seth's office. Unfortunately, Tladi had been busy there too. What he saw was another Pete, haggard and reduced to inefficiency like himself. They said nothing, but stared at each other with the horror of people exposed to all the torture of the demons who parade the African continent. They were intelligent. They knew it had a real, living source. Even then they could not bring themselves to utter the name: Maru. They only knew, as others before them had known, that somehow they were on his bad side and that life was not worth living if you were on the bad side of Maru. He'd terrorize you into the grave.

Three bombs went off in Dilepe village, one after the other. First, Pete the principal fled. Then Seth the education supervisor fled. Then Morafi kept looking over his shoulder for two days and he also fled. No coherent explanations were ever given, except that the people who lived with them all thought they had suddenly lost their minds. Only two men slept soundly at the end of that week. They were Moseka and Semana, who had been working overtime. Dikeledi was promoted to be the principal of Leseding School.

PART TWO

The rhythm of sunrise, the rhythm of sunset, filled her life. In the distance, a village proceeded with its own life but she knew not what it was – who married, who died, who gave birth to children – nor the reason why two women on her pathway, back and forth to school, continually insulted each other in vile language for stealing each other's husbands. She was not a part of it and belonged nowhere. In fact, so quiet and insignificant were her movements that the people of Dilepe village almost forgot that there was such a thing as a Masarwa teacher. Now and then she caught their eye on her way to the shops or to school. They would laugh a bit, turn to each other and say: 'There goes the friend of Mistress Dikeledi.' She had no life outside those words.

Yet there were half suns glowing on the horizons of her heart. It was Moleka. Now and then she would pass him in the village. She could quite clearly see that he made a secret of the matter but his eyes glowed like the early morning sunrise when he glanced at her briefly. The strange thing was that the love aroused no violent emotions but blended in with the flow and rhythm of life in Dilepe. It was something to be accepted, painlessly, because there was no question of who loved whom. She thought: 'He will never approach me, because I am a Masarwa.' And it was something her whole way of life had prepared her for. Love and happiness had always been a little bit far away from life as other people lived it. There could have been no better training ground than that of Margaret Cadmore senior, whose own heart continually muddled her and who had been a woman who lived without love, without her equal in soul stature. She had missed something and was often irritable and impatient, like an unmarried woman, but the effect of it had made her draw on her own inner resources, in order to survive the ordeal of being married to a dead and stupid man.

The young girl had no confusion of heart, only the experience of being permanently unwanted by society in general. There was an inverse cycle in this. It had created in her an attraction for the unpredictable, for the types of personality most people could not abide or get along with, and for all forms of vigour and growth outside the normal patterns. Maybe she had loved a man like Moleka a thousand times, in the same odd, secret way. It did not disrupt her stability but it made the village of Dilepe hallowed ground. He fell in somewhere with those sunrises and sunsets, and the huge, spreading beauty of an old *mokoba* tree, just outside her window. There was a public water tap under the *mokoba* tree and all day barefoot women trailed up the hill to fill their water buckets and carry them home on their heads. They too fell in with the sunrise and the sunset, and her quiet dreams at night. It was like living in the shade where everything was quiet and peaceful, and she might have fallen asleep inside herself had not three companions created a hurricane of activity out of her non-working hours. One companion was Dikeledi, about whom much has already been said. The other two were a mother goat and her baby.

The encounter with the mother goat was very dramatic. She had been sitting on a rock at the foot of the hill, absent-mindedly chewing the cud in a queenly way, when their eyes met accidentally. Taking this as a suitable introduction, the goat quickly arose from the stone and followed her up the hill, the baby panting behind. She was big and snow white, the baby pitch black, with shiny, curly hair. He was barely a foot tall and about one week old. Thinking that people of the surroundings might accuse her of goat stealing, she turned round anxiously and said: 'Prr, prr, go away!' But the goat only stared back astonished, slightly insolent: 'I know my way around here. Are you so sassy as not to want visitors?'

She led the way up the slope with animated footsteps. The child cried: 'Mme, mme, don't walk so fast. I can't keep up with you.' His mother paid no heed. She was intent on making a breakthrough. It wasn't every day that there was an opportunity to collect gossip. She was old as goats go and age brought wisdom and boldness. She quivered from head to tail as Margaret put the key in the door, then, not awaiting an invitation, she stepped high and mighty into the house. She threw her revolving, ancient, hooded yellow eyes around the room and said: 'Ah! So that's what it's like inside?' Then she shot a wicked look at Margaret and added: 'My curiosity will get me killed one of these days, but I can't control it.'

The child had by this time caught up with his active mother. He dived for the udder. The journey up the hill in the broiling midday heat had made him so thirsty that he made loud, snuffling noises as he gulped down his drink. His little back part stuck up in the air and he frisked his tail like a windscreen-wiper. Goats, like people, know whom they can take advantage of and, as far as the mother goat and her child were concerned, they had arrived, to stay. The ageing queen slowly made her way to a position near the door. A touch of arthritis had set in. She creaked down carefully, placing a portion of her head and nose in the sunlight, which streamed in through the door, and immediately started to doze.

Not so the little one. He performed a few delicate acrobatics and waltzes all by himself across the floor. A moment later he stopped and made a puddle, and onto it added a few neat pills. Then he was off again, then puddling. Life was too good to him. He radiated joy. The owner of the room watched in fascination as she sat down to a lunch of tea and bread with some stew left over from the previous evening. So intrigued was she by the antics of the glowing little goat that she still had her plate in her hand an hour later when Dikeledi's car stopped outside. Dikeledi burst in in a flurry of excitement, then stopped, appalled. The puddles and pills were all over the floor and the acrobatics were going on and on.

'Get these beasts out of here!' she shouted. 'Come on! Prr! Prr! Outside, you damn nuisance! Outside, you damn pests!'

This was just what the old queen wanted. She rose quickly, on stiff forelegs, raised the hair on the back of her neck and, lowering her head, charged at Dikeledi. Dikeledi fled screaming across the room: 'God, help me! The beast is not normal.'

Alarmed at the sudden roar of laughter inside her, Margaret slid off the bed and half pushed her head under it. She stuffed a portion of her skirt into her mouth, to stifle her laughter. Dignity and Dikeledi were the same names and only a day or so ago she had become principal of a school, too.

'Margaret!' Dikeledi screamed, trapped in a corner. 'What are you doing? Help me. The beast is going to kill me. It's got rabies.'

'I'm looking for a shoe to hit the goat,' a stifled voice said, but it only moved deeper under the bed.

Seeing that she had the situation under control to her satisfaction, the queen slowly moved back to her position at the door. The child had watched all, with wonder in his eyes. He hopped, leapt and skipped over the floor for another drink. Margaret crept out from under the bed. She carefully avoided looking at Dikeledi.

'I wonder what's going on here,' Dikeledi said, regaining her composure.

'She did the same to me,' Margaret said. 'I can't chase her.'

'I suppose she thinks she's the Queen of Sheba,' Dikeledi said, looking scornfully at the goat.

A roar of laughter came from Margaret. Dikeledi, who thought her name for the goat highly inventive, laughed too. She stepped daintily around the puddles and pills and seated herself on the chair near the bed.

'I came to ask you something,' she said smiling. 'Please make another picture of me. I lost the one you made the other day.'

It was a lie. She had taken the sketch home and shown it to Maru. He had taken it and put it in his pocket as if it were his rightful possession. Not any amount of pleading would make him give it back. All he said was: 'She will make lots more for you.'

Why, she had not thought of that. A gold mine was a gold mine. Its production ought not to stop with one dig. She thought she ought to set her face in a pretty pose and be patient while Margaret set her plate down and looked around for paper and pencil. But her own heart was laden with sorrow. She was not confiding by nature. She kept her affairs to herself. They were the more terrible to endure because of this. Moleka had gone on his rounds again, most probably with that cheap girl, Grace. She had no way of undoing her love for Moleka. It seemed a burden she would carry for the rest of her life because her heart remained stubbornly fixed on him as though no other man in the world existed. A mournful expression filled her face and she slumped a little in the chair, depressed. Sometimes, she smiled through the tears which dripped onto her lap.

The other, uninvolved person watched this alertly and captured that mingling of smiles and tears. The little puddles and pills on the floor dried up. The Queen of Sheba and the Windscreen-wiper dozed in the slanting rays of the afternoon sunlight. In the silence it seemed an hour had passed. At last Dikeledi arose. She hardly glanced at the sketch in her hand. She did not say goodbye. She walked thoughtfully to the car and drove away. Not long after that the Queen of Sheba and the Windscreen-wiper took their way down the hill. Margaret stood at the door of the old library and watched their homeward journey until they were lost in the maze and tangle of pathways and mud huts. As always, a thousand wisps of smoke arose from a thousand outdoor fires as a thousand women began to prepare a thousand evening meals. The peaked caps of the mud huts stood out in sharp, black relief against the darkening sky.

'Why did she cry?' Margaret wondered, uneasily.

Her own heart was so peaceful. She stood where she was, empty-handed, but something down there belonged to her in a way that triumphed over all barriers. Maybe it was not even love as people usually think of it. Maybe it was everything else; necessity, recognition, courage, friendship and strength. There was nothing to grasp then, or cry out for. It was continuous, like the endless stretch of earth and sky, and if she never knew anything other than his name, the feeling was greater and more generous than life, as though her heart said: 'Wait and that will grow in its own time. Wait and you will grow in your own time, but slowly, like eternity.' It freed her to work and live with vigour.

She turned indoors and slowly swept up the pills of the Windscreen-wiper. Then she closed the door, lit the lamp, set the kettle on the stove, sat down and stared deep into her own, peaceful heart.

The schools had closed for the holidays that morning at the end of the first term. Fifteen days of leisure were ahead, except for Dikeledi who had to depart that afternoon for a conference of principals of primary schools in a village two hundred miles away from Dilepe. Knowing this, Margaret was surprised when her car stopped outside the old library. She had been busy waxing the old oilcloth but she quickly arose to her feet and walked to the door. Dikeledi had an enormous parcel in her arms and was smiling mysteriously. She walked straight in and placed it on the bed. The outer wrapping had already been removed and its contents examined.

'Hurry up and have a look,' she said impatiently. 'I have to go.'

Margaret lifted the lid, then abruptly sat down on the bed to steady herself. Inside was an assortment of every kind of material an artist could need – oils, water colours, charcoal blocks, drawing ink, paper and brushes.

'Did you buy these?' she asked, stunned.

Dikeledi averted her head. They had been ordered by Maru. 'Yes,' she lied.

'They're very expensive,' Margaret faltered.

'Don't worry about that,' Dikeledi said. 'I want the pictures.'

She looked sharply at Margaret. She had a message to deliver: 'You must experiment with everything in that box, see,' she said, like one talking to a little child. Margaret looked up quickly, with the gesture and sudden turn of the head of a very young child with its first toy. That was the last link she had with coherent, human communication. How did Dikeledi leave the room and when did she leave? She could not say. Life was totally disrupted and another rhythm replaced it which made day and night merge into a restless fever. It had a beginning like the slow build-up of a powerful machine but once it had started the pitch and tautness of its energy allowed for no relaxation; the images and forms, the flow and movement of their life imposed themselves with such demanding ruthlessness that there was no escape from the tremendous pressure. It was as though, subconsciously, everything had been arranged especially for that time and for those days when it did not matter if she could not eat for two or three days, or if she ate at four o'clock in the morning. There was a part of her mind that had saturated itself with things of such startling beauty and they pressed, in determined panorama, to take on living form.

Somewhere, in the blur, the little Windscreen-wiper kept on dancing and snuffling down his milk and the Queen of Sheba walked the earth with majestic calm. At some stage her hands trembled uncontrollably and she stood up to make tea or wash with a fierceness quite out of proportion to those simple, ordinary activities. It was like all those other agonies of life which she had endured in silence, only those agonies had been linked with everyday things. Now she had lost the link completely, like a non-swimmer suddenly thrown into deep water. She could not discipline and control the power machine of production.

Dikeledi did not see those two days of total collapse and breakdown because by the time she came back it was all over. She only picked up, joyfully, the end product, those sheets and sheets of paper which exploded with vigour and movement. Everything else looked the same, the old oilcloth glittered in the afternoon sun and the kettle boiled on the stove. Her friend still moved around in her quiet, insignificant way. The big, dark patches under her eyes from all those sleepless nights and foodless days were rapidly receding. But Sheba and the Windscreen-wiper had taken the full blast of it. They had been stared at with savage intensity. They had been subjected to sudden, blinding blows if they thought a certain object on paper was edible and had been astonished, when a plateful of food that was not shrubs or husks, had been thrust under their noses, yet they would not give up their regular, routine, daily visits, not for anything in the world.

'How did you do all this work?' Dikeledi gasped, carefully piling the thirty sheets of seemingly neat, detached activity on top of one another.

Margaret turned round and smiled. There was no word to explain the torture of those days, but out of it she had learned. Something inside her was more powerful than her body could endure. It had to be brought under control, put on a leash and then be allowed to live in a manageable form. She would never do work like that again. Everything else would be at a slower, studied pace.

'I had a holiday,' she said simply.

Dikeledi shook her head.

'I am ashamed to steal all these pictures,' she said. 'But I have to. They are so beautiful.'

'You may take them all,' Margaret said, knowing she was a millionaire.

As Dikeledi gathered the sheets together, she separated three of them. They were not of Dilepe village, the Queen of Sheba, or of herself. A theme ran through them. There was a pulsating glow of yellow light dominating pitch black objects.

'What's this?' she asked.

Margaret put down the teapot and walked over to where Dikeledi was seated on the bed. She hesitated when she noticed

309

which three pictures Dikeledi had set to one side. And yet, Dikeledi accepted anything; there was no blockage in their communication.

'I had a strange experience,' she said slowly. 'Each time I closed my eyes those pictures used to fill all the space inside my head. One picture was of a house. Everything around it and the house itself was black, but out of the windows shone a queer light. It did not look like lamplight and it revolved gently. While I concentrated on this picture, it slowly faded and another took its place. There was a wide open sky and field. I saw the pitch black clouds envelop the sky, but when I looked at my feet the whole field was filled with yellow daisies. They stirred a little as though they were dancing. Their movement also created this effect of gently revolving light. The next moment I was surprised to find myself walking along a footpath between the lovely daisies. I looked up again and a little way ahead I saw two people embrace each other. I stared quite hard because they were difficult to see. Their forms were black like the house and the sky but, again, they were surrounded by this yellow light. I felt so ashamed, thinking I had come upon a secret which ought not to be disclosed, that I turned and tried to run away. Just then a strong wind arose and began to blow me in the direction of the embracing couple. I was terrified. They did not want anyone near them and I could feel it. I dropped to the ground and tried to grab hold of the daisies to save myself from the strong wind. At that moment I opened my eyes. The funny thing was, this happened again and again until I put the pictures down on paper.'

She had separated the scenes into three. The house stood alone with its glowing windows; the field of daisies and the lowering sky made their own statement; and, on their own, two dark forms embraced in a blaze of light. Dikeledi picked up the last picture. The outline was very clear, even though the faces and arms and bodies were blacked out. She followed the silhouette of the taller person with her eye, then raised her hand to her mouth to stifle an exclamation of surprise. It was unmistakably that of her brother, Maru. She turned an uneasy glance on Margaret, who stared back at her quietly with no change of expression.

'You frighten me,' she said, her eyes wide and startled.

'Why?' Margaret asked, surprised.

'Do you always see things like that?' Dikeledi asked.

'Yes,' she said. 'I drew all the pictures from pictures from my mind. I first see something as it looks but it looks better when it reappears again as a picture in my mind. The only difference with those three pictures was that they were new. I had not seen them before.'

Dikeledi picked up the pictures in her arms. She was feeling agitated. Margaret raised her hand a little: 'Wait,' she said. 'I am pouring the tea.'

'Hmmm?' Dikeledi said, absent-mindedly.

'Have some tea,' Margaret said.

'No,' Dikeledi said. 'Not now.'

She looked into her own heart and walked out, deep in thought. Life appeared to be a mystery, a deep interwoven tangle. She had had a glimpse of something new and altogether outside her usual speculations. How had he done it? How had he projected his dreams on someone so far removed from him? That sort of thing was meat and drink to Maru but it changed the picture when some other living being was on the receiving end of his dreams, especially such a true and sensitive recorder as Margaret. There were many things she doubted about Maru. He was too rich in speculation and mystery. But Margaret? Everything about her was direct, purposeful and straightforward.

311

'Why,' Dikeledi thought, 'She has changed my life. I am becoming a more sincere person.'

She stopped the car outside her brother's house, picked up the paintings and walked up the long flight of stairs. He was sitting on the porch, drinking tea. She placed the pile on his knee.

'Here is your payment, you rogue and thief,' she said. 'How do you think I feel, always stealing for you?'

Without a word, he straightaway separated from the rest the three pictures.

'What did she say about these?' he asked.

'Oh, those are only dreams,' Dikeledi said, in a deliberately careless voice.

'I was waiting for them,' he said quietly.

He raised his head a little and stared into the future, with great joy in his eyes. Dikeledi, in turn, stared at him, enraptured. At times he could look a very beautiful man. His eyes seemed to say: 'Oh! . . . I am going to be so happy.'

'I want my pictures,' she said softly.

'You will get them when I have no more need of them,' he said.

He had the pictures neatly mounted on a long board and placed against the wall of the room where he sat alone with his thoughts. They were a companionship between the present and the time when he was ready to live a different life. On the surface, he lived much the same life, that of a pampered person who had never lacked anything, but in an undercover way he made feverish preparations for a freedom and life wherein everything he owned would be his, not other people's blood money and stolen goods.

'We suppose you will accept the chieftaincy quite soon?' the elders of the tribe questioned him.

'Not yet,' he said. 'My health is not so good.'

And they went away, shaking their heads sympathetically. Nothing could change the fact that he was born their king, even if he was a strange one who delayed accepting the crown. Moleka, who watched his every move with suspicion, could betray him to no one. Before Dikeledi he kept silent about his heart, his thought being that she was the bird in the hand, while birds in the bush were too difficult to obtain. Besides, Dikeledi's house was a good look-out point on the actions of his one-time friend. It was his intention to expose Maru to the whole village should he ever dare to take as his concubine that silent, isolated person on the old library hill. Moleka was sure he was after something like that, and it gave him a savage pleasure to note that Maru could find no opening anywhere. He also kept the fire boiling between them with many subtle threats. Dikeledi, who could have enlightened him on her brother's secrets, was now totally absorbed in her own painful love affair with Moleka. She had questioned Maru on the fact that he and Moleka appeared enemies. Maru said it was over Moleka taking her as just another one of his string of concubines.

'Surely that's my affair,' she had replied, haughtily.

'Not entirely,' he said sorrowfully, because he was stricken with guilt at having made Dikeledi the pivot of his plans. In another way, he was in the same position as she was, waiting to acquire a love that he, like Dikeledi, felt ought to be his.

It was more painful for him because he had to make bold moves on very intangible substance. He'd stare wistfully at those three beautiful pictures of the house, the field of daisies, and the dream of a great love, and question himself: 'If we have the same dreams, perhaps that means something.' In the end, he sent Moseka and Semana to a place many miles from Dilepe to prepare that house, and to Ranko he would confide this and confide that when they sat in the room where he kept the pictures.

'She's a great woman, don't you think, Ranko?' he'd say eagerly. 'Who can paint pictures like that?'

'Oh yes,' Ranko would say and slap his hand on his knee and roar with laughter. He had never seen anything like the actions and acrobatics of the little Windscreen-wiper. Sometimes he seemed about to walk right out of the paper, licking his tiny pink tongue, he was so alive and busy.

Maru took in the whole range and depth of the pictures. It was as though he had fallen upon a kind of music that would never grow stale on the ear but would add continually to the awakening perfection in his own heart. She chose her themes from ordinary, common happenings in the village as though those themes were the best expression of her own vitality. The women carried water buckets up and down the hill but the eye was thrown, almost by force, towards the powerful curve of a leg muscle, resilience in the back and neck, and the animated expressions and gestures of the water-carriers as they stopped to gossip. They carried a message to his own heart: 'Look! Don't you see! We are the people who have the strength to build a new world!' And his heart agreed. Dikeledi, with her delicate expressions and coddled life, was given the same treatment, until she too belonged amidst the vigour of the goats and water-carriers. What she was trying to give birth to had carved wounds around her mouth and eyes. Even the happy pictures – Moleka was here last night – had a guarded, cautious, reserved look in the eyes and out of them a third Dikeledi was emerging, who sat alone and aloof and stared with deep, penetrating eyes on the value of her own kingdom. It was as though, once she knew everything and had uncovered her own worth, she would awaken and share her gifts with those who needed them. The portraits and sketches traced this unfolding of the soul.

He wished he could leave the matter with the remark he had made to Ranko, that the creator of all this vitality was simply a great woman in herself, with no other attachments or identification. Being so highly individualistic himself, he dreaded working out any conclusions along those of tribe or race. But the conditions which surrounded him at the time forced him to think of her as a symbol of her tribe and through her he sought to gain an understanding of the eventual liberation of an oppressed people. There was this striking vitality and vigour in her work and yet, for who knew how long, people like her had lived faceless, voiceless, almost nameless in the country. That they even had a life or soul to project had never been considered. At first they had been a conquered tribe, but the conquered were often absorbed through marriage. Who could absorb the Masarwa, who hardly looked African, but Chinese?

How universal was the language of oppression! They had said of the Masarwa what every white man had said of every black man: 'They can't think for themselves. They don't know anything.' The matter never rested there. The stronger man caught hold of the weaker man and made a circus animal out of him, reducing him to the state of misery and subjection and non-humanity. The combinations were the same, first conquest, then abhorrence at the looks of the conquered and, from there onwards, all forms of horror and evil practices. The Batswana thought they were safer than the white man. He had already awoken to the fact that mistreated people are also furious people who could tear him to shreds. They were still laughing with such horror in their midst, finding it more inconceivable than the white man to consider the Masarwa a human being. Thus the message of the pictures went even deeper to his heart: 'You see, it is I and my tribe who possess the true vitality of this country. You lost it when you sat down and let us clean your floors and rear your children and cattle. Now we want to be free of you and be busy with our own affairs.'

At this point in his thinking a great agony would fill his heart and he would walk over to Dikeledi.

'Ask your friend if she would like to marry a Masarwa,' he'd say.

Dikeledi would bring back the reply: 'She says she does not know.'

That was why he dreaded any tribal or racial identification. You could not marry a tribe or race; at least he could not. Such things interfered with the activities of his gods who bade him do things outside any narrow enclosure or social order.

He liked his own dreams and visions. They created an atmosphere where not only he but all humanity could evolve. They stretched across every barrier and taboo and lovingly embraced the impossible. There was no such thing as a slave or any man as an object of pity. But while he looked ahead to such a world, he was no fool. The vicious, the selfish, the cruel – those too he saw, and their capacity for creating misery. Where he could, he nailed them to the ground, but always alertly with no intention of becoming their victim. And he intended following his own heart without in any way becoming the victim of the stupid, senseless, cruel society into which he had been born. Hence his lies and evasions.

The battle between Moleka and him was one of visionaries, but he had trained Moleka to look at life with a visionary eye. Why then should Moleka assume superiority over the master? They kept their horns locked like that: 'You won't get her.' 'And you won't get her.' But Moleka was at a dead end, powerless to make a move either way, powerless to make his love evolve beyond a glance. He, Maru, had his spies running up and down, smoothing the way for his future. He did not rest either, but began secretly and quietly to undo the ties of his birth. As for his love, it could grow and grow beyond the skies or the universe. It knew no barriers. Now and then, he could do with a little confirmation of his dreams, as when Dikeledi had brought him the pictures.

All these dreams and thoughts took place in moments of optimism which alternated with periods of great despair. Arrogance was a show with him, to frighten people. He was very humble.

At such times he would think: 'What will I do if she does not love me as much as I love her?' A terrible reply came from his heart: 'Kill her.'

Dikeledi supplied the easel and board; also the huge square of off-white canvas cloth, which together they stretched tightly and pinned to the edges at the back of the board. There were other tender little gestures. She had collected a number of lids of old tins and, afternoon after afternoon, she sat on the floor patiently blending different shades of oil paint into a texture which resembled the natural colouring of the earth of Dilepe at the sunset hour.

The Queen of Sheba and the Windscreen-wiper had started having trouble with their diet. The summer was over and every shred of grass had disappeared from the ground. From a miller in the village, Dikeledi had purchased a bag of husks for Sheba and her baby and they continued to swell with fat and happiness while the other village goats were reduced to lean skeletons, eating bits of dried, wind-blown paper in their desperation. The funny thing was that the owners of Sheba and the Windscreen-wiper never seemed to bother about their comings or goings or how they spent their days or what they ate. They lived somewhere in the maze of huts and dutifully returned home each evening. They were a source of many jokes between the two friends.

'I have a funny feeling about Sheba,' Dikeledi would often observe. 'I think she is a human being in disguise. Have you heard about the witches in this country? They can turn themselves into lions and buffalo. Sheba was once a witch who was starving and turned herself into a goat. She behaves just like a beggar who is also a blackmailer.'

Of course Sheba would pretend great indifference to these remarks but her child would listen very alertly, then in goat language say: 'It's true. It's true. My mother is a witch. Look at how black I am,' and he would take a great leap through the legs of the easel. They were indeed becoming very superior goats. The Windscreen-wiper had learned the ways of civilized human behaviour and now made his puddles and dropped his pills outside.

The days were so happy they seemed to speed by on wings. The same things were done each afternoon and the picture of Dilepe, at the sunset hour, slowly unfolded on the canvas. Dikeledi only became more pensive and silent towards the latter part of the year, while her friend Margaret grew in strength of purpose and personality. Perhaps constant communication and affection assisted the subconscious change in the way Dikeledi became more like Margaret and Margaret more like Dikeledi, or perhaps it was Dikeledi's love which brought to the forefront the hidden and more powerful woman who dwelt behind the insignificant shadow. The slowly unfolding landscape was very much part of this emerging personality who had lived with and loved someone in silence for a long while.

'I am composing this for Moleka,' she told herself, well knowing that the day would never arrive when she would be able to approach him with a gift or thank him for removing the loneliness from her heart. It was never only the sun which went down over Dilepe but his shadow behind the sun and the memory of her first evening in the village when she had stood alone in the dusty room and laughed a bit and felt the most important person on earth. Then she had denied it: 'But I am not that important,' and those spontaneous words had echoed through the events and solitude of the subsequent months. Each day, at sunset, she walked to the door and looked out at the whimsical arrangement of huts and pathways, the darkening shadows and the whispers of blue smoke in the still air. They made her heart say other, spontaneous things; that this peace and flow and continuity was only a brief resting place, that one day she would have to say goodbye to him, that there was an accident in the whole arrangement and he had only been a kind passer-by who had given a helping hand to a lost soul. It was as though she had put out her hand and said: 'No, no, don't go so soon. I can't manage without you. I need someone to lean on.' Because he still stood there, at the door, in that arrested, humble pose and she stood, the days through, quietly leaning on his shoulder.

In the end, she began to compose that scene. Its contours began from the slope of her hillside, encircled the village and swept towards the horizon where a half-sun gazed with a glowing eye into her heart. Only the two people who stood at the doorway with their still, unchanging love remained forever anonymous.

Dikeledi caught the mood of her purpose and the depth of peace and eternity which built up in the work. It was at odds with her own painful, restless heart which had love one day and lost it the next. She would intrude now and then with her anguish.

'I wish I was like you, Margaret,' she said, wistfully. 'You look as though you could live like this forever. You look as though you don't want anyone or anything except this library, the painting you are doing now and your school work. I feel so restless. Sometimes I could just rush out of this village, forever.'

Margaret turned around and looked at her, quietly. They did not know how near they were to killing each other. One of them was the top dog, just then, silently and secretly drawing on all the resources of the sun. The other knew she lacked something. It was there one day, gone the next. They had only to mention his name and one of them would die. Margaret, who was in the more powerful position at that time, compressed her lips. Any other woman would have said: 'I am peaceful because Moleka loves me.' But then she was not any other woman. She was a Masarwa. She thought Dikeledi would reply: 'Don't be silly. Moleka can't possibly love you. You are a Masarwa and he's . . .'

So she said what she thought Dikeledi would like to hear: 'I am peaceful because I have nothing and I want nothing.'

It was reasonable, even if not truthful. Dikeledi had several times asked her if she would like to marry a Masarwa, as though a Masarwa was a special freak in Dikeledi's mind. Dikeledi's mysterious smiles quite escaped her.

'You might say so,' Dikeledi replied, smiling as though she were hiding something behind her back. 'You might think you have nothing, but to my way of seeing things you are quite a beautiful woman. You will be surprised at whom you will marry one day.'

She was to remember those words one day when certain events occurred to throw her from the quiet, static niche she had found for herself. That peace was only for one year. It was to depart forever after that. She was to become another Dikeledi who alternated happiness with misery, finding herself tossed about this way and that on permanently restless seas. She would have preferred that static, endless hour which moved neither forward nor backward. Fate carried out another destiny through which, by force, she had to move onward and onward, uncertain, ill at ease. There must have been a premonition. She recorded the hour of peace.

The events, when they occurred, went off, one after the other, like bombs. They were well-timed, too. There were two more days left before the close of the school year and the beginning of the long summer holidays. On the second-to-last day, Margaret put the last touches on the canvas of Dilepe at the sunset hour. The tip of the tail of the Windscreen-wiper had not yet dried when Dikeledi burst excitedly into the room. In fact, she had been in an up-and-down state for the past week, distracted, absent-minded, wistful and sometimes hysterical. Once she said abruptly to Margaret: 'I'm going to get married,' but did not stand still long enough to explain whom she was to marry. The whole village knew and was still buzzing over the commotion. They were openly saying that the marriage was a forced one, and eyeing Dikeledi's thickening waistline. There had been whispers from Moleka's mother about how she had been terrorized into forcing the issue and everyone was going buzz, buzz, buzz, especially as Dikeledi was getting fat in the wrong places. Dikeledi picked up the snickering and giggles behind her back and spent a great deal of her time crying in her house. Since Margaret was the only one outside the village gossip whose attitude and affection remained unchanged, Dikeledi couldn't bear to mention the whole sorry affair until the last possible moment.

Even on that day she only remained long enough to remove the canvas, hardly glancing at Margaret's forlorn face, which clearly said: 'I want it for myself. It is the only record I have of something which profoundly affected my life.'

She stood alone in the room, feeling drained and exhausted. For a whole year her life had been this room and the paintings. It had been a most terrible discipline but the reward had been the production of that canvas. And then again, it felt as if a cycle had completed itself and that what was behind was done with, was finished.

'Maybe she was right to take it away,' she thought. 'I only seem to say goodbye to everything.'

How was she to know that Moleka would receive her gift after all, in an unexpected way, and that the message of its stillness and peace would reach his heart and that he would know he was as powerful and continuous as the earth and the sky? It would set him free and give him the space and time to attend first to affairs at hand. In this strange tangle of secret events, secretly they all assisted each other. When Dikeledi tentatively offered the canvas to Maru, he stared at it coldly for some time and said: 'No, you keep it. I don't like it.'

'But it's very beautiful,' Dikeledi protested. 'It's her best work.'

'It's not for me,' he said.

His expressionless face told her nothing, but as time went by she was to be surprised at the adoration and attention Moleka lavished on the picture. It was to seem as though he came home each night specially to look at it, then wash and eat. It was to become an immovable part of their life together.

Of all this, Margaret knew nothing. Only, that evening as she walked to the door the magic of the sunset hour was gone. Maybe it was because the rains were so late that year and the

322

hot earth was baked to powder by the sun. The shimmering dust of the day became mingled with the irritated wisps of smoke from the fires, as though the women who cooked outdoors were harassed and bothered by the heat and dryness and kept on disturbing the fire. Something was over and lost. A great unease filled her heart. She looked for a prop, for anything to help her recapture those lovely hours. But not even the Queen of Sheba and the Windscreen-wiper were there to walk down the hill in the late sunlight. They had not appeared as usual that day. The unease turned to foreboding. She closed the door, walked to the stove and put on the kettle. Even those usual gestures were of no avail. The peace in her heart had flown away.

By morning, after a restless night, she had made up her mind to leave Dilepe for a short while, if only to take a short train journey to another village or area. It was the last day of school. There was nothing to do. Even the promotions of the children had been completed on the previous day. From many classrooms came singing as the children grouped themselves together to entertain one another with concerts. Dikeledi came and joined Margaret's class with that of another teacher for a concert. Then she rejoined Margaret in her classroom. Her eyes were red with weeping.

'I wanted to talk to you,' she said.

Then there was a long silence, before she said: 'You will come to the wedding tomorrow afternoon?'

'Yes,' Margaret said, surprised, not knowing that the marriage was to take place so soon.

'Tell me,' Dikeledi said. 'Would you marry someone only because you were going to have a child?'

Margaret hesitated and shifted uncomfortably. They had never had personal discussions before and she knew nothing about Dikeledi's private life, except that now and then she attended parties where she made rude and hilarious comments about the high society of Dilepe.

'It would depend on the man,' Margaret said tentatively.

'That's the trouble,' Dikeledi said, nodding her head. 'All I know is that I love him. He tells me he loves me but you don't know where you are with Moleka . . .'

She saw Dikeledi's mouth move a while longer, but no sound reached her. A few vital threads of her life had snapped behind her neck and it felt as though she were shrivelling to death, from head to toe. The pain was so intense that she had to bite on her mouth to prevent herself from crying out loud. Oh, what did all the reasoning help now? There was a point at which she was no longer a Masarwa but the equal in quality and stature of the woman who sat opposite her. It was their equality which had given Dikeledi the unconscious power to knock her down with a sledge-hammer blow. No other woman could have killed her, but she knew Dikeledi through and through and her soul was a towering giant. She tried to raise her half-broken neck, to say some word that would be a remembrance or even a coherent recollection of the affection they had lived with for a year, but her throat was a tightly constricted knot of pain. She pathetically balanced the still unbroken part of her neck in the palm of her hand.

All this passed unnoticed by Dikeledi. She was swamped by her own sea of troubles, but still alive, still swimming. She had no idea that a near corpse sat opposite her. After a while she looked at her watch. It was ten-thirty. She stood up restlessly and said: 'I'm going to dismiss the children.'

Somewhere, vaguely in the distance, the bell rang. Then a roar rose from over two thousand voices as the children fled in all directions for the beginning of their holidays. There were a few scattered murmurs of voices. Dikeledi walked to her car, and departed. Then silence.

Margaret got up carefully, on shaking legs. Everything was unbalanced and broken. She slowly reeled homewards but it was no longer the earth and sky; only a still, cold, dead world with no sun. By the time she reached the bottom of the hill, she drew in her breath with painful gasps. There was at least some place to hide, and she crawled determinedly forward. Halfway up the hill, a woman carrying a water bucket on her head turned to her anxiously and asked: 'What is it? What is the matter?' She tottered past, breathing painfully, without replying. The woman stared after her, open-mouthed.

Outside the door, in a blinding daze of pain, she saw the little Windscreen-wiper, alone. He was trembling from head to toe in an agony all his own. The previous day he had seen his mother slaughtered before his eyes. It had almost deranged his mind. His owners had tied him to a tree and that morning he had broken free of the string and run away. He darted into the safety of the room. She pushed the door shut. The remaining threads went snap, snap, snap behind her neck and she half stumbled, half reeled to the bed and fell on it in a dead faint.

The water-carrier spread the news among her friends: 'The mistress who lives on the hill is so sick, she is dying.' This was soon picked up by Ranko, who ran in alarm to Maru.

'Is she sick, Ranko?' he said smiling. 'Is she dying? Don't worry about that. Let her suffer a bit. It will teach her to appreciate other things.'

In spite of their gossip, the whole village turned up at the wedding party. The invited guests were inside Dikeledi's home. The uninvited spread themselves out in the field and revelled in a continuous flow of home-brewed beer and slices of meat roasted on the coals of an outdoor fire. Indoors the invited guests behaved no better and as late afternoon wore on they became very drunk until little discrimination was left between who was invited and who was uninvited. Everyone mingled happily. It only mattered that the beer did not end.

Three people alone remained sober. Dikeledi anxiously watched over the hostility of the two men. She knew well enough that Maru had forcefully engineered the marriage and Moleka's eyes said all kinds of things of a highly dangerous nature to him across the room. She noted that if Maru moved here, Moleka would soon follow. He never took his eyes off Maru. Frequently, Dikeledi ran into the bathroom and burst into floods of tears. A murder was surely going to take place between Moleka and her brother. She could not know that Maru was silently enjoying himself. He had his own programme well-timed. He had also arranged that the beer should flow like an unending river and, hearing this, it was not long before every inhabitant of Dilepe was drawn to the area. It was a wedding to end all weddings.

At about seven o'clock it was pitch dark, and Maru approached Dikeledi and said he was going home as he was tired. Moleka saw him moving towards the door and roughly caught Dikeledi by the arm: 'Where is he going?' he asked suspiciously.

'He is going home,' she said, bursting uncontrollably into tears.

Moleka walked onto the porch. By the torches of firelight in the field, he saw Maru ascend the stairs. Shortly after, he lit the lamp in the front room, moved about a little, and seated himself, as a dim shadow, behind the thick curtains. Moleka went indoors. He began to relax; he was fond of beer. He drank two pints, went onto the porch and noted that Maru still sat at the window. He stopped long enough to pass a curse on Maru: 'You will sit like that for the rest of your days but you will never approach her,' and went indoors for more beer.

Just as Moleka uttered the curse, Ranko slowly turned the van up the slope of the hill which led to the old library building. Inside were Maru, Moseka and Semana. The van stopped. Maru flicked on the torch and walked to the door, followed by his comrades. The whole village was still, the roar of its life being concentrated at the home of Dikeledi far in the distance. Not even the flickering torches of firelight could be discerned. The door was unlocked. Maru pushed it open and walked straight to the bed. She still wore her clothes of the previous day and had not moved her position. Her eyes were wide open. They did not flicker as he flashed the torchlight into her face. It frightened Ranko out of his mind and he burst out: 'I told you she would be dead by today.'

'She's not dead, Ranko,' Maru said gently. 'It's only her neck that's broken.'

A flicker of surprise moved over the still face on the bed. It was true. How did he know? Who was he? She frowned, struggling to assemble her shattered mind. Maru watched intently, then turned to Ranko: 'You see? Get busy and put these things into the van. See you leave nothing behind. I'll fix her up.'

Of course, Ranko made a great show of minding his own business but he pricked up his ears and listened to everything as he helped Moseka and Semana remove the small pieces of furniture to the van. As he listened to the persuasive voice – now gentle and understanding, next moment impatient – his heart expanded with devotion. Maru could talk a donkey into growing horns.

'You think my neck was not broken a thousand times over like that because you did not love me,' he said softly. 'It's not an ailment you die of. Sometimes you recover in a moment, especially when the cause of it is a worthless man like Moleka. You think I don't know everything? Moleka did not want to approach you because he is such a tribalist. I watched everything, thinking you might see that I loved you too. Dikeledi gave me all your pictures, except the last one.'

He could quite clearly see the movement of her eyes in the dark and that she had begun listening intently, with surprise.

'I can show you the house you painted some time ago,' he said. 'Would you like to see it?'

Since she kept silent, he became impatient: 'Self-pity is something I don't like. Other people have suffered more than you. You must stop this self-pity. There's nothing hurting you anymore.'

His words were true. She had been so cut off, so choked, so throttled that quietly the smell of the earth began to seep into her nostrils again and even the saliva started to flow in her dry mouth. She moved her limbs and they tingled painfully from idleness but the blood in them began to flow. What kept her silent was this stunning event. She could make nothing of it. Perhaps she was dreaming. She struggled to an upright posture, but even to regain her life and movement again was a joy in itself. She had been incapable of movement or thought or feeling for hours and hours and hours and a portion of her mind which was still alive felt it keenly as the past year had been the most vital and vivid of her life. She was to question that sudden breakdown, that sudden death later, but what filled her now was this slow inpouring of life again.

'Where are you taking my things?' she asked, and the tight knot of pain no longer constricted her throat.

Before he could reply, Ranko, at the far end of the room, dropped the torch on the ground with a loud crash. He had been making a last-minute check to see if any item, other than the bed, had been left behind. His flash-light had disturbed the sleeping Windscreen-wiper, who made a loud grunt. Ranko, his nerves stretched to breaking point over Maru's affairs, sped across the room.

'There's a strange animal here, Maru,' he said.

'Ranko, you are a fine spy. Go back and kill that lion,' said Maru, enjoying himself.

He could feel the bed shaking, as though she was trying to suppress her laughter. She said: 'It's the goat.'

The Windscreen-wiper padded softly across the floor. He was captured by Ranko and began to yell about murder. Once Ranko had solved that, he stood by the side of the van scratching his head. There was a great deal of silence from the inside of the room. He feared to enquire because he did not like to disturb Maru when he was concentrating. Perhaps he was arranging his marriage. If so, it took quite some time and the three men watched the constellations shift their positions in the sky.

'All right. We can go now,' he said, startling them out of their reflections.

Then Maru too turned and looked at the sky, while his friends collected the last object in the house. What would the future be like? He couldn't tell, but at that moment he felt as if he had inherited the universe. He turned to the woman standing silently beside him, and said: 'We used to dream the same dreams. That was how I knew you would love me in the end.'

What could she say, except that at that moment she would have chosen anything as an alternative to the living death into which she had so unexpectedly fallen? He was not just anything but some kind of strange, sweet music you could hear over and over again. She was beginning to listen. It was not strange. She had heard it before.

As she climbed into the van, the Windscreen-wiper was on the front seat making stifled noises from his trussed-up mouth.

She debated with herself a moment. He was not her goat, but she kept silent and decided to steal him. Ranko turned the van slowly down the hill, wound it through the maze of pathways and onto the highroad that led out of Dilepe. They were heading straight for a home, a thousand miles away where the sun rose, new and new and new each day.

It was just after midnight when Dikeledi gave him the note. It was from Maru, who had instructed her to give the note to Moleka at that hour. It said: 'Moleka, by the time you read this I shall be many miles away from Dilepe. I am marrying too, almost at the same time. Remember that people quarrel but they should always make it up again. Maru.'

Moleka walked out onto the porch and looked across at the house where a lamp still burned in the front room and a dummy sat by the window. He began to laugh and thought: 'So he has fooled me once again. I knew I'd never get her from him. He's the devil!' And he laughed and laughed.

Everything else went smoothly for Dikeledi after that. She found she had a real husband who had begun to tire of people making a noise in his house. She watched in admiration as he began to give orders left and right. As he closed the door he turned to Dikeledi and said:

'Did you know that Maru had planned to run off with the Masarwa school teacher?'

'Oh no,' she said innocently.

'I was very surprised to read about it in the note,' he said.

When people of Dilepe village heard about the marriage of Maru, they began to talk about him as if he had died. A Dilepe diseased prostitute explained their attitude: 'Fancy,' she said. 'He has married a Masarwa. They have no standards.'

By standards, she meant that Maru would have been better off had he married her. She knew how to serve rich clients their tea, on a snowy-white tablecloth, and she knew how to dress in the height of fashion. A lot of people were like her. They knew nothing about the standards of the soul, and since Maru only lived by those standards they had never been able to make a place for him in their society. They thought he was dead and would trouble them no more. How were they to know that many people shared Maru's overall ideals, that this was not the end of him, but a beginning?

When people of the Masarwa tribe heard about Maru's marriage to one of their own, a door silently opened on the small, dark airless room in which their souls had been shut for a long time. The wind of freedom, which was blowing throughout the world for all people, turned and flowed into the room. As they breathed in the fresh, clear air their humanity awakened. They examined their condition. There was the foetid air, the excreta and the horror of being an oddity of the human race, with half the head of a man and half the body of a donkey. They laughed in an embarrassed way, scratching their heads. How had they fallen into this condition when, indeed, they were as human as everyone else? They started to run out into the sunlight, then they turned and looked at the dark, small room. They said: 'We are not going back there.'

People like the Batswana, who did not know that the wind of freedom had also reached people of the Masarwa tribe, were in for an unpleasant surprise because it would be no longer possible to treat Masarwa people in an inhuman way without getting killed yourself.

NOTE

This Virago edition of Bessie Head's two novels *When Rain Clouds Gather* and *Maru* has been restored from various authoritative sources. Our aim was to provide an edition that approximates Bessie Head's intentions as closely as can be determined and to intervene as little as possible.

The corrections we have made to *When Rain Clouds Gather* are therefore fairly minor – restoring some short passages that somehow went missing, reinserting paragraph breaks, and correcting errors that had crept into the text over the years.

However, in *Maru* there were a number of imprecise and sometimes misleading expressions that were carried from the typescript through the various editions, and these we have attempted to clear up.

A *Motswana* is a member of the ethnic *Tswana* group; *Batswana* is the plural. *Motswana/Batswana* can also refer to political status, as in citizen/citizens of the country, *Botswana* (place of the Tswana). *Setswana* is the language of the Batswana, and Tswana, without any prefix, is often used as an adjective, although *Botswana* is sometimes also used. Similarly, a *Morolong* is a member of an ethnic Tswana sub-group living in southern Botswana and northern South Africa; the plural is *Barolong*.

Masarwa is considered a derogatory term for people of *San* ancestry (the singular is *Lesarwa*). Currently the people of Botswana use San or *Mosarwa* (plural *Basarwa*). Bessie Head almost certainly knew that *Masarwa* was a derogatory term. *Bushman* is usually derogatory (as is evident in *Maru*), but it is sometimes used for its recognition value overseas. In *When Rain Clouds Gather*, 'inferior tribes' and 'minority tribes' and, in *Maru*, 'slaves' probably refer to San/Basarwa. We have left Head's use of Masarwa/Masarwas as is, because to change it would undermine her challenge to Botswana attitudes about the San. The most correct approach of course would be to refer to the people by the names they call themselves, such as !Kung, Naro, Bugakhwe, Dx/ana, and so on.

The prefixes *Mma* and *Rra* (sometimes *Ma* and *Ra*) mean literally 'mother of' and 'father of', respectively, but are also used as terms of respect for older people who are not necessarily relatives. Mama and Papa serve the same function in speech; to address someone as 'Mama' or 'Mother' is a form of respect.

Bessie Head was a very keen listener with respect to the variety of English spoken in Botswana. She reproduced, most obviously, the repetition that is common in many African languages, including southern African languages. So, for example, 'Pelotona, the permit man' is repeated throughout *When Rain Clouds Gather*. Repetition is used not only to emphasize but more often to intensify the meaning of a word or expression.

In addition, she brought other forms of Setswana English into her work. In *When Rain Clouds Gather*, for example, Dinorego on two occasions uses 'can/can't' in a way that is typical of Setswana speakers of English, and is a direct translation of a Setswana verb construction indicating intention. In *Maru*,

334

perhaps the most obvious example is the description of the 'Dilepe diseased prostitute' at the end of the book. Correct English would be 'diseased Dilepe prostitute', but the former construction is very common.

Words explained in the texts themselves have not been glossed. Unless otherwise noted, all words are from Setswana.

For generous access to materials, we would like to thank Mr Adam Dixon of the Howard Gottlieb Archival Research Center at Boston University, USA (typescripts of both novels), and Ms Gasenone Kediseng of the Khama III Memorial Museum in Serowe, Botswana (galleys of the Simon & Schuster edition of *When Rain Clouds Gather*).

Mary Lederer and Craig MacKenzie, Editors
Leloba Molema and Tiro Sebina, Glossary

2010

GLOSSARY

Batho!	the full expression to which this word refers is *Batho tlang lo boneng!*, meaning 'Oh, people come and see!'
Bodibeng	the place of deep water
Dikeledi	tears
Dilepe	axes, suggesting conflict, acrimony, or fighting
Leseding	place of light or brightness
Lesego	luck, blessing
Lorato	love
Maroba	heifer or young woman of marriageable age (singular *moroba*). Also plural of *leroba* (hole)
Maru	dark thunderclouds
Maseko	Zulu word referring to a tripod on which one places a pot when cooking over an open fire
Matenge	from the Ndebele root *-tenga* meaning to buy
mealie pap	corn or maizemeal porridge
Mma-Millipede	millipede in Setswana is *sebokolodi*; it is common practice for people to use the English equivalent of their Setswana name (so Mma-Millipede might be Mma-Sebokolodi); millipedes are very common in Botswana after rain

mokoba	an acacia tree
Moleka	one who tries. Also from *molekane* (close friend)
Morafi/morafe	ethnic group. Also from *rafa* 'to remove something in small portions' (for example, grain out of a storage basket)
Moseka	the one who litigates or sues
munt	person, from Zulu *umuntu*. A derogatory term used against black South Africans
Pelotona	big heart (i.e. generous)
Pule	rain (from *pula*)
Ramogodi	father of one who earns lots of money, father of one who is growing up
Rankoane	father of the little nose
Sebeso	sacrifice, burnt offering
Sebina	champion dancer, one who carefully observes custom
Sekoto	short and round, plump
Tladi	lightning, a thunderbolt
Totem	a member of a chiefly family